•BALDWIN'S LEGACY BOOK ONE•
CONFRONTATION

NATHAN HYSTAD

Copyright © 2019 Nathan Hystad

All rights reserved.

No part of this publication may be reproduced, distributed, or transmitted in any form or by any means, including photocopying, recording, or other electronic or mechanical methods, without the prior written permission of the publisher, except in the case of brief quotations embodied in critical reviews and certain other non-commercial uses permitted by copyright law.

This is a work of fiction. All of the characters, names, incidents, organizations, and dialogue in this novel are either products of the author's imagination or are used fictitiously.

Cover art: Tom Edwards Design

Edited by: Scarlett R Algee

Proofed and Formatted by: BZ Hercules

ISBN-13: 9781674910802

Also By Nathan Hystad

<u>The Survivors Series</u>
The Event
New Threat
New World
The Ancients
The Theos
Old Enemy
New Alliance
The Gatekeepers
New Horizon
The Academy
Old World
New Discovery

<u>The Resistance</u>
Rift
Return
Revenge

<u>Baldwin's Legacy</u>
Confrontation
Unification
Culmination

Red Creek
Return to Red Creek
Lights Over Cloud Lake

PROLOGUE

Tarlen ran along the outer edges of the crowded stage, hoping to catch a glimpse of the Regent as his personal carriage hovered toward the wide-open platform. He wondered how many of his people were gathered. It had to be close to the entire city, perhaps more, as dozens of vessels had arrived each day for the last week in preparation for the festivities.

His father had spoken to him about the possibility of their humble world joining the ranks of the Concord, but Tarlen couldn't let himself believe such rumors. The Concord was a collective of the universe's most powerful planets, and he doubted there was anything Greblok could offer that they didn't already have.

"Hold on, Tar," his sister Belna called from behind him. She could never keep up with him, even though she was older by two stars.

"Fine, but you better not make me miss seeing the Regent," Tarlen said, impatiently tapping his foot on the dusty ground.

The floating carriage settled at the rear of the dais, and Tarlen hung at the far side of the platform, recognizing that this would be his best bet at seeing their ruler in person. The Regent didn't emerge often, and the last time he'd visited, Tarlen had been stuck working for his father. He wasn't going to let that happen again. He glanced toward the massive crowd, searching for his parents among the horde. His mother would have forced her husband to stand at the back, safely away from the dense crowd, far from the press of bodies.

"I don't see what the big deal is," Belna said with a huff. She was out of breath, and Tarlen laughed as she craned her neck to see over the edge of the stage. "It's only the Regent."

A guard watched them from his standing position a few yards away, and Tarlen hoped the man hadn't heard his sister's foolish words. "Shhh. Keep it down, Bel. They can detain you for less." He didn't imagine that was true, but better to err on the side of caution.

The crowd erupted in a cheer, and they began to chant the word "Concord" from somewhere in the middle. Within a minute, the entire promenade was shouting the name over and over; a harmonious and captivating sound. Tarlen felt compelled to join them, and he peered out the corner of his eye to see Belna uttering it quietly, mouthing the word. Her dark brown eyes were wide and round, the joy not even lost on his sister, who was always so pessimistic.

A massive screen floated beyond the stage, and the crowd grew silent as the Regent appeared on center stage. He was old, older than Tarlen remembered. Gray hair covered his thin head, and his spine had a stoop to it. He raised a gnarled hand, and you could have heard a pin drop among the thousands of onlookers.

"Greetings, citizens of Greblok. Thank you for coming to hear me on this wonderous day. It's not only the biggest day of my ninety-star life, but of this world's million-star span. We've accomplished a lot, and because of our newly discovered mines under the deepest seas, our people have gained entry into…" He paused, and Tarlen leaned forward. His breath was held, waiting for the words to emerge from the elderly Regent's lips.

Tarlen peered around the few heads blocking his view to see the real man, not the version on the gigantic screen. Even from here, Tarlen noticed the Regent grinning, a glimmer of youth in his aged eyes. He continued: "Entry into the Concord!" He shouted the last bit, and the crowd erupted in cheers. Tarlen had never heard anything so loud, and he glanced at his sister with a huge smile across his face. She was crying happy tears, as was everyone around them.

Being part of the Concord meant so much. Tarlen could leave this world; he could join a Concord cruise ship. He could be anything he wanted to be. Dreams of new opportunities fluttered through his mind as the chants and catcalls of joy echoed around the city center. It felt like his blood was alive, and he didn't even notice the wet streaks pouring down his own cheeks.

"We herald a new era for Greblok, for you all!" The Regent raised his arms high into the sky. On the screen where the live video feeds were playing, the man looked immense. His back was straighter than it had been a moment ago, and even his hair appeared less gray.

Things were going to change, and Tarlen was filled with enthusiasm. "Can you believe it?" his sister asked from beside him.

He thought about what the Regent had said about underwater mines. It was the first he'd heard of them, and he wondered what exactly they held. It didn't matter. It was exciting enough for the Concord to take them into their fold, almost unbelievable.

The sky was crystal blue today, and Tarlen's gaze drifted from the outstretched arms of the Regent to a tiny dot growing larger with each passing breath. He watched it, expecting to find it was only an envoy from a neighboring city late to the party.

It kept expanding in size.

The Regent was speaking again, but Tarlen's heart was beating faster now, the thrumming of his pulse blocking the sounds of the crowd from his ears.

His sister tapped his shoulder, and he turned to her wonderful smiling face. Tarlen pointed to the incoming object, and Belna followed his finger, her mouth opening wide as she saw it. Dozens more of the dots emerged from the sky, each coming incessantly, filling Tarlen with dread.

He shouted for the guard's attention, but the man was watching the Regent with fascination. The entire crowd was captivated by the speech, and Tarlen didn't think anyone else had spotted the invasion.

He ran, grabbing Bel's wrist, pulling her along. They were already on the edge of the crowd, and he moved to the rear, searching for their parents. A ripple of cries carried from the mass of his people. Shouts of joy turned to fear in the snap of a finger, and soon everyone was running, pushing each other, trying to reach safety as the cylindrical pods lowered and commenced firing.

One dropped directly above Tarlen, and he moved faster, trying to avoid the destruction. The ship was terrifying, matte black and tube-shaped. Red blasts fired from below it, striking his people with impunity.

Tarlen was knocked to the hard-packed dirt, his hands striking the ground. Rocks cut into his palms, and he pulled his fingers away from the press of boots all around him. Then the panicked people were gone. A red beam hit directly beside him, and Tarlen saw the group vanish as they were vaporized. He found the strength to stand. Miraculously, Belna remained there, gaping toward one of the ships as it moved farther into the promenade, wreaking havoc.

"Belna, we have to go!" he shouted, grabbing her arm. His hand left a streak of blood on her as he tugged her into action.

The ground shook as they ran farther from the crowd. Tarlen's eyes scanned frantically, but he couldn't find his parents anywhere among the devastation. There were fewer people moving at this point, and the sound of blasts mixed with screams filled the entire city square. It smelled sickly, like blood and terror blended together.

There had to be over a dozen of the ships, each ten times greater than the Regent's carriage. His sister stopped, looking up, and Tarlen tried to pull her along. "Bel, we have to go!" he shouted, losing hold of his sister's arm.

He glanced to the sky, where one of the cylinders lowered a few steps from them.

"Tarlen!" Belna cried, but Tarlen was pushed aside, knocked to the ground. He scrambled to his feet to avoid being crushed by the running people. Loud, angry pulses tore through the skies, tearing apart the stage. The Regent was visible on the huge screen, and Tarlen peered over in time to see the man running as a beam cut through the stage, gashing the Regent to pieces.

He tried to fight the overwhelming press of bodies, but he was outnumbered, and the only way to escape was to leave his sister behind. "Bel!" Tarlen shouted again, but he couldn't find her. She was smart. She'd find a way out.

His decision made, he ran as fast as he could, drifting away from the crowd as the newly-arrived enemy ships continued their assault. Tarlen noticed at least five Greblok Defenders rising in the sky, emerging from the Regent's palace, and he realized how ill-equipped they were compared to the attackers.

The dogfights didn't last long. Pieces of the Defenders

crashed to the ground in a fiery mess, and Tarlen jumped out of the way as a burning body plummeted a few yards in front of him. He screamed in fury as he moved, his thin legs pumping, forcing him away from the streets and into the countryside.

He bent over, panting and coughing, under the canopy of a tree, fighting to not be sick. The ground shook even at the river's edge, explosions detonating all around. There were no more Defenders. The city was annihilated in the span of a few minutes.

Tarlen and his sister had a muster point, a cave in the hillsides where they'd meet each other to avoid chores or long workdays at their father's shop. He was sure she'd come there when she made it out.

He headed for the hills, running along the riverbank until he found the rock bridge someone had built years ago, creating a place to cross the roaring water. Tarlen's feet moved through the motions, and he was soon on the far side, the cityscape shrinking in the distance as he raced from it.

Tarlen wiped tears with his forearm as he stopped, his legs unable to keep moving. He searched the horizon, where more of the cylinders ruthlessly attacked other cities and nearby villages. They were under heavy assault, and Greblok had no real defense.

Were his parents alive? Was anyone going to come help them? A million questions coursed through his fearful thoughts as he plodded along, hidden from prying eyes by the dense tree cover. He ended up at the hillside; the same cave he and Belna had been visiting since they were children sat hidden in the rocks, and he sought the safety of the haven.

Night came, and the barrage of noises halted so suddenly, Tarlen thought he might have gone deaf.

There was no way to determine how long he'd been hiding in the cave entrance, watching the terrible light show. It was dark, and Tarlen's legs burned as he propped himself up, unable to stop staring at the destruction. The world looked to be on fire. It was so foreign, Tarlen struggled to comprehend what he was seeing.

Within minutes, the cylinders were gone, but evidence of their arrival was all around him as the entire skyline burned with a hot orange glow.

Tarlen slumped to the ground and waited for his sister.

ONE

Thomas Baldwin walked through the corridors one last time before it was spoiled forever. He could grow used to this: the solitude, the silence. In less than five hours, there would be over three hundred crew members filling the ship, but now, for a few more minutes, he was the sole inhabitant of *Constantine*.

He bristled at the name and wished the Concord would have heeded his suggestions before going public with the official title. Once the media and the Concord worlds grabbed hold of the story, there was no turning back.

"You old codger, you would have loved the attention, wouldn't you?" Tom grinned despite himself. It could be worse; he could still be the commander on the *Cecilia*, one of the Concord's longest-running vessels. After spending eight years aboard the ship, he was going to miss parts of it; very few selective parts, but... it was easy to grow attached to something, even an old vessel.

Cecilia was one of a kind, apparently both in life and in her AI form on the ship. Tom had grown up hearing stories about her from his grandfather, and according to him, the admiral that became Baldwin's previous ship's namesake was a legend.

Constantine hadn't been activated yet, and Tom was both dreading and anticipating the AI modeled after his grandfather. He tried to clear his head, but there were dozens of lingering concerns floating around inside his mind, bumping into one another as he prepared to launch the brand-new starship.

"Captain Baldwin." He tested out the title. "Captain Thomas Baldwin."

"Are you talking to yourself?" a voice asked from behind him. His heart raced as he spun to see Executive Lieutenant Reeve Daak leaning against the wall, as if she was casually hanging out at a lounge.

"I thought I was alone." That was his explanation, and she didn't press him on it.

"What do you think?" she asked, waving an arm in the air, indicating the ship as a whole.

"It's a masterpiece. The Concord have really outdone themselves this time," he told her.

"Have you been to the boiler room yet?" she asked.

Tom paused, unsure what she was talking about. "The boiler room?"

"Engineering. That's what my previous captain called the guts of the ship." Reeve grinned, and Tom felt his walls lower slightly. He had only met select members of the crew, and most of those occasions had been fairly formal. One of the downsides of becoming a new captain: the Concord chose your crew for you.

On paper, Tom was pleased, and he knew the list of applicants for *Constantine* had been lengthy. The Concord used a mixture of statistics and personal interviews to find the most skilled and compatible crews; at least, that was what the admiral had told him. Tom thought there was more to it. There always was when politics became involved.

"Engineering. Of course. Lead the way," Tom said.

Reeve wasn't in uniform, and he found the sight abnormal. He was used to spending every waking moment in the black pants and long-sleeved slate-gray shirt, with the Concord's logo of their first vessel hovering over a full moon etched on the breast. His own uniform sported a red collar, the captain's color. It still felt odd, after so many years wearing orange as commander.

"Have you found your quarters yet?" he asked, trying to sound conversational.

"Not yet. I wasn't supposed to be on board for three hours, but I just got the call from the top. The engines were sending out some abnormal readings, so they asked me to run some diagnostics," Reeve told him.

"That can't be good. We haven't even left dock," Tom said, wondering if he should worry yet.

"Better to find out any issues now. Believe me, we've been over this ship a million times. *Constantine* is regularly running scans, internally and externally. If there's an issue, we'll find it and deal with it." Reeve led him through the well-lit corridor in the ship's center.

They stepped onto the pedway, the glass rails allowing them to see the greenery below.

"Can you imagine?" Reeve asked, not elaborating, and Tom only nodded.

"It's all quite elaborate," he told her, and she stopped in the center of the pedway to lean her elbows on the railing. Thick strands of her hair hung over her face, and she brushed them away, revealing the brightest red eyes he'd ever seen. Even for a Tekol, her eye color was unique.

"Gardens on a Concord cruise ship, with water and greenhouses. This is next-level stuff, Captain." Her eyes danced before she looked away from Tom, staring at the misting water spraying from under the pedway. The entire room was comfortable, the perfect balance of temperature and humidity.

He'd spent so much time aboard starships that the only

green space he saw was when he headed to other Class Zero-Nine planets. Only then, the trees were usually bizarre, the wildlife different from Earth's in some innocuous way. Since *Constantine* was the flagship of a new era, the Concord hadn't held back on their long-awaited additions. It was a far cry from his previous posting, where you were more likely to see a patched-up wall or loose wires dangling in the bathrooms.

From the pedway, he glanced above, seeing each of *Constantine*'s ten levels opening into the center of the ship. The main officers' residences would overlook the topiary: another benefit of being stationed on the flagship.

Reeve appeared deep in thought, but a second later, she readjusted her stance and kept walking.

"Reeve, you were on *Vox* last, right?" he asked the chief engineer. He was unfamiliar with a lot of the crew, but he had attempted to study as many of the executive crew's files as possible. On paper, Reeve Daak was the smartest person assigned to *Constantine*, himself included.

"That's right. I spent the last ten years tinkering on that rust-bucket," she told him.

"This must be a big change," Tom told her.

She shrugged as they moved through the halls. "It's a big change for all of us. Three hundred crew; half of them are newly graduated from the Academy, and the other half were spread across twenty vessels in the Concord Fleet."

Tom had to laugh. "You know more about it than I do."

Reeve stopped, the lightness to her voice lingering as she briefly set a hand on his forearm. "Captain, I promise to keep the ship running smoothly on a functional level. It's your job to make sure the crew does the same."

A younger Tom might have resented the comment, but he was working on his attitude. The Concord had chosen him out of nearly one hundred thousand officers around their network, and he wasn't going to mess this up.

"You have a deal," Tom assured her.

"Are you nervous?" she asked.

"I'd be lying if I said otherwise," he admitted.

"Good. I'd be worried if you weren't. I've followed your career," Reeve told him, and Tom raised an eyebrow.

"Is that so?"

"Sure. I mean, the grandson of the famed Constantine Baldwin. Who wouldn't be interested?" she asked.

Tom sighed. It always came to this, and he'd tried to mentally prepare himself for it again. The luster had worn off quickly on his last posting, but here, with all the attention the ship was garnering, he'd be in the spotlight again: not for his own accolades, but for those of his grandfather.

"I'm sorry. I'm sure you get that all the time. I can't imagine. If it helps, my grandfather never did anything but pick rocks from fields in the wastelands of Nolix," Reeve said jokingly.

He was going to like this one. "I'm don't think that helps, but I'm glad you found your way out."

"Me too."

"I see another Daak on the crew manifest. Relative?" Tom asked.

"My brother," she said. "He's a bit of a stick in the mud, but he's loyal as a guard dog."

"That's a good thing in a chief of security," Tom said, smiling at her.

They arrived at the main elevator, of which there were five side-by-side, and Reeve chose the center one.

"Engineering," she told the computer, and the lift lowered to the bowels of the ship. Tom had never worried about the ship's drive much on his previous charge, mostly because it was always damp and musty in the room. When the elevators opened, he was half-expecting the same conditions.

Tom couldn't hold back his impressed whistle, and Reeve glanced at him, smiling wide to reveal a mouth full of sharp teeth. "I told you this was next level. You should have seen my last ship. It was like a bathroom in a bar on Reepa."

Tom knew exactly what she meant, having frequented enough of the dives himself. "I've seen the schematics so many times, but this…" He ran a hand along the beige composite walls, and noticed the lights flashing brighter as they walked through the open room toward the glowing sphere. Blue energy crackled and flickered as they neared it, and Tom searched for the center, where the black ball of Bentom floated weightlessly.

"It's so… beautiful," Reeve said, and Tom didn't argue with her. While it was aesthetically appealing and was the basis for the ship's star drive, the black mass of energy always made Tom feel slightly uneasy. The chief engineer remained smiling as she crossed the room to the wall, which was lined with countless screens. They projected out holograms, and her fingers moved deftly across them. Even from here, Tom could tell she was running duplicate and triplicate scans on the system's drive, seeking out the anomaly with depth they couldn't achieve remotely.

"Is Constantine activated?" Tom asked nervously, wondering if he should get the introduction out of the way before he was surrounded by hundreds of other crew members and Concord officials.

Reeve shook her head. "Not yet. He's ready, but they want to make an impression at the soft launch."

The soft launch. Tom almost laughed at the title. Essentially, *Constantine*'s maiden voyage was a cushy diplomatic assignment that would only take a week or so. It was as good a test run as one could hope for, but Tom would rather be out there along the Border, ensuring the Concord's safety.

"What could be so different with this ship's AI?" he asked, not sure he was ready for the answer yet.

She wiggled her pencil-thin eyebrows and grinned again. "We'll have to wait to find that out." The computer screens went dark, and Reeve wiped the holograms away with a flick of her wrist. "Everything checks out from here. Must have been a glitch."

Reeve showed Tom her office, and he noticed there was a bed in the corner. "Planning on some late nights?" he asked.

"This job can be strenuous, especially when there's an issue. I was stranded on the *Pliatese* for a week with no engines, and life support dipping every hour. We slept on the floor, two hours at a time, until we figured it out," she said.

Tom had read a similar account in her records. "You mean when *you* figured it out."

"We were a team," Reeve admitted, and Tom liked her more for it. She was smart, but her ego was in check. He couldn't say the same for the rest of the crew.

They walked away from the Star Drive's core, and Tom glanced at it as the lights flicked off.

———————

*B*rax waited in line to step foot on the already-famous *Constantine*. He peered at his shirt, smoothing an invisible crease. *You're going to be fine. You deserve this.* His sister had pinged him earlier, informing him that she was already on board. Leave it to Reeve to arrive before everyone else. Apparently, she'd taken a tour with Captain Thomas

Baldwin. *What a brown-noser.*

They were twins, but that was where their similarities ended. Brax touched the Concord symbol on his breast with pride as he stepped through the glass corridor leading from the Lunar Station to his new home for the next few years – hopefully. He refused to glance up, excruciatingly aware that the millions of stars gleaming down at him would send him swaying.

Brax wondered if there had ever been a chief of security on a cruise ship that was afraid of space. Surely there must have been, but the assumption granted him little comfort.

Someone stopped in front of him, and he bumped into the stranger as they gawked at the immense size of the ship's hangar. Brax was larger than the man, and they stumbled forward together.

"Sorry about that," Brax said, reaching out to tap the man on the shoulder.

The uniformed man spun, grinning wide at Brax. "Lieutenant Commander Brax Daak!" He was nearly six feet tall, his Concord uniform pure white. His hands were gloved, and Brax saw the tight collar around the doctor's neck.

"You must be Doctor Nee?" Brax tried his luck. He'd read the files, but to him, it was hard to tell the Kwants apart, if only because he hadn't spent any real time with them, for good reasons.

The doctor must have noticed Brax backing away a step, because he nodded. "Don't be alarmed. We Kwants are only deadly if you're exposed to prolonged skin contact," Nee said with a smile, and Brax could only nod along, pretending not to be terrified. "Plus, I wear gloves and carry the antidote. Nothing to be concerned about."

"If you say so," Brax told the man, and cleared his

throat. "I'm sorry. Nice to meet you, Doctor."

"Likewise." The doctor's skin was a light shade of green, his hair white-blond, making his slotted yellow eyes appear even brighter.

The hangar was filling up as newly-arriving shuttles let the crew members out. Brax stood out of the way, the doctor coming to lean on the wall beside him. "Quite the sight, isn't it? Brand new ship, captain with a famous lineage. This is the stuff legends are made of."

Brax bit his tongue. He was only here because of his sister, Reeve. He wanted nothing to do with making history. His job was to keep the crew safe, to protect his twin from harm.

A familiar elderly man at the end of the hangar climbed up a few steps and raised a hand in the air. "If I could have your attention. The entire crew is now aboard, and many are milling about, taking a brief tour of the ship. You will be split into groups of fifty, and a special guide will walk you through the levels, showcasing your new station, the *Constantine*, in its splendor. We'll reconvene in the courtyard at twenty-one hundred." Admiral Hudson stepped down and the doctor turned to Brax, his yellow eyes staring hard at the security officer.

"Buddy up?" Doctor Nee asked, and Brax ran a hand over his bald scalp.

"Sure. Have you seen your medical bay?" Brax asked, wondering if he was the only one who hadn't been on the ship yet.

The doctor shook his head. "No, I haven't been on board before now. You?"

"No, but I've been through the simulators a dozen times. I was supposed to have a walkthrough before anyone else came aboard. I'm the chief of security, and I wanted the lay of the land without crowded halls," Brax told his new friend.

Nee threw him a wink. "Expecting trouble?"

Brax leaned closer, his voice low. "Should I be?"

"I'm only kidding around with you. Are security officers always so stiff?" Nee asked.

Brax's tense shoulders loosened. "It's kind of a required disposition for the trade. That, and we all drink too much coffee."

"I find it comforting that our muscle won't fall asleep on duty," Nee said with a laugh.

The doctor was growing on Brax. "Shall we?"

They were separated into groups, and Brax and Nee were pushed to the front, being the senior ranking officers in their group of fifty. "Shouldn't we wait for our tour guide?"

A hologram flickered on near the hangar's entrance to the ship, and a young face stared into Brax's eyes. "It would appear that your tour guide is already here, Lieutenant Commander Daak," the hologram said.

Brax stepped away in shock and reached a hand out to the lifelike apparition. His hand passed through it, the man's chest glowing a light blue.

"Please refrain from touching me," the man said, turning to their group. "I am Constantine Baldwin, this vessel's AI."

"But you're... young," a uniformed woman said quietly from beside Nee.

"Yes. Constantine was young once, just as you will eventually be old. The Concord elected to personify me with a young avatar, a version of Constantine before he saved the Concord at the Yollox Incursion fifty years ago. Does anyone recall that from their studies?" the AI asked.

Everyone raised their hands, including Brax. They'd heard the stories about this man; he was a legend in the

Fleet. Hell, he was a legend outside the Fleet. Every last living person in the known galaxy knew who Constantine Baldwin was.

Brax wasn't sure how much of the real man was in this AI, but if it had an ounce of Baldwin, they were in for a treat. All of their ships had an AI, mostly the hero their vessel was named after. But this… Constantine Baldwin looked so real, like he was a living man talking to them. Brax shuddered, the hair raising on his forearms.

"If we're done gawking at me, let me show you around your new home," Constantine said, motioning Brax and Nee forward. They took the lead and entered the ship. The halls were immaculate, and everything smelled… so *new*. There was no other way to explain it. Brax found his hands shaking in anticipation as they advanced through the corridors, the AI telling them about the ship along the way.

"The ship took three years to manufacture, the longest of any standing Fleet starship. Construction was done twenty-four hours a day and utilized over ten thousand drones and separate robotic units to assemble the parts. Once the frame was complete, pressurized, and sealed, humans and other Concord allies worked together to bring different cultural elements to the technology and aesthetics," Constantine told them.

Brax had taken some ribbing from humans back in his Academy days, but for the most part, the Concord had changed over the years. Other than his dark green eyes and pointed teeth, he was basically the same as a human. *Only… stronger and smarter.*

Nee watched everything with interest and tugged at Brax's uniform sleeve when he wanted to show his new friend something. Brax soaked it all in, anxious to find his sister and meet his new captain. He hadn't heard who the first officer was, but he'd met most of the crew briefly during a training exercise a few weeks prior. The commander hadn't been in attendance because of a scheduling conflict, and Brax had been waiting to find out who was Captain Thomas Baldwin's second-in-command.

They continued the tour, and a lot of the crew nodded to him or approached him upon seeing his violet collar, denoting his high rank. On this starship, there were only three Executive Lieutenants, and he was one of them. His sister was the chief engineer. He was chief of security, and from what Brax had read, a Zilph'i man named Ven finished off the leadership roles, unofficially the crew chief.

"Glorified babysitter, if you ask me," Nee said, as if reading Brax's mind.

Brax glanced at the doctor, wondering why he'd suddenly spoken about the other executive, and then he spotted the man across the corridor. The two groups were being funneled into a surprise area, and Brax could already feel a difference in the air as they walked slowly toward the doorways.

"Is that… Ven?" he whispered to the doctor.

"The one and only. Can you believe they succeeded in finding an Ugna?" the doctor asked him, but Brax hardly heard the question. He'd never seen one up close, and he was learning how important this posting was to the Concord: from the high-tech AI of the Concord's most decorated captain, to that man's grandson leading the new flagship, to somehow finding a fabled Ugna as a crew member. All the pieces were coming together, and Brax wondered why he'd been included in this all-star cast.

People were filing in through the double doors at the end of the corridor, and Brax noted the gasps coming from each of them as they walked inside the courtyard. He could only stare at his new counterpart, Ven.

The doctor walked past the gaping Tekol officer and

stuck his hand out toward the albino alien. "Pleasure to meet you, Executive Lieutenant Ven. I'm *Constantine*'s doctor. You can call me Nee."

Ven blinked bloodshot eyes and stared at the gloved hand before shaking it. "What an archaic form of greeting. Is that commonplace among the Concord Fleet crew?"

This seemed to startle Doctor Nee, and Brax stepped in, joining the conversation. "It's a little out of date. An old human greeting," Brax assured the pale man. Ven was bald, tall and thin, and Brax stood before the man, the polar opposite of him. Brax was dark-skinned, broad where the other was narrow, and they appraised one another.

"Then let us refrain from utilizing it, seeing how none of us are human. You must be the chief of security, Brax Daak." It wasn't a question.

"That's correct," Brax said, almost forgetting that his collar's color denoted his position.

"Well met."

Brax had a lot of questions, but the demeanor of the Zilph'i telekinetic convinced him to let them rest for the time being. He pointed toward the room everyone had settled in. "Shall we see what all the fuss is about?"

Ven turned on a heel and stalked away, leaving Doctor Nee shaking his head after the strange encounter. "This should be fun. After you."

TWO

Commander Treena Starling paced her quarters. By now, everyone was on board the ship, and they'd be walking through the corridors, gawking at the fancy gym, the five-star chef's mess hall, and the state-of-the-art entertainment sector, but Treena was hiding out in her room.

"You need to face them eventually," she told herself.

Treena lifted her arm and squinted as she held it in front of her eyes. It looked like skin. It felt like skin. She let the arm hang at her side and sighed. An unnecessary action, but she was still far too human inside to forget commonplace reactions.

She walked over to the bathroom, for which she had no need any longer, and wished she'd asked them to dismantle it. The setting reminded her too much of what she wasn't. She appeared as Treena Starling: her eyes were the exact same color; her hair, parted with a slight cowlick, exactly as it had been since she was a little girl. But... she was really across the room.

Treena closed her eyes, took a breath, and turned the light off, crossing the open living space toward the bedroom. The lights remained deactivated, as she'd programmed them, and she beheld the unmoving human body lying there, gentle cloth straps lifting her off the bed surface as it did for a few hours a day. Her muscles would be massaged, ensuring there was no atrophy or bed sores. She forced herself to stare at the husk of a woman her human form had become.

This Treena had no hair, and a glowing wire plugged into her brain from behind her skull. The electrodes passed through, sending signals to the artificial body she was currently moving around in. She was a woman in two places at once. Part of her was paralyzed on that bed; the other inside this machine, controlling it. It had been two years, and she still woke up in her new body every day with a scream of terror.

Treena didn't think she'd ever grow used to it, to blinking her eyes open in a robotic form. She hadn't disconnected from this vessel since the early days. Then, the pain and confusion had been unbearable. It was too real being left alone in her real skin, unable to move, unable to even think clearly through the agony.

As hard as this was, she had to become accustomed to it, because it was *her* now. She glanced at her reflection again, seeing the orange collar denoting her rank as *Constantine*'s commander, and she allowed herself a brief grin. Would she ever have assumed this rank without her circumstances? Treena tried not to consider it. She should be dead, by all accounts, so she wasn't going to dwell on what-ifs.

Treena set an artificial hand on her real body's arm, and gently squeezed it. "We're going to be fine," she told herself, and saw a finger twitch. Her real face was unmoving, her eyes closed, but Treena spotted a tear escaping between her eyelids to roll down her cheek. She wiped it away as gently as a mother would, and told herself it was all right.

Treena stood tall, brushed a hand over her uniform's creases, and crossed the room. It was time. There was no more hiding behind closed doors. "Ship. Windows half dark," she commanded the computer, and her windows showcasing the topiary below brightened, allowing her to see through them. Beneath her view were hundreds of officers, crew members, and ship staff of various races. Not all of them would be making the trek with *Constantine*, but most were.

"Here goes nothing," she told herself. The door sprang open as she tapped the console beside it, and she emerged from her quarters for the first time since being secreted to the ship a few days ago. She'd spent the time studying the ship's manifest and newly-created attributes. This was the six hundred and tenth Concord cruise ship ever manufactured in an official capacity.

It was the finest vessel ever made. She was honored to be part of this crew, even if she was here because some bureaucrat wanted to make a statement. She was determined to do her job, and do it damned well.

Treena walked through the corridors, white-walled and bright. Each step took her farther from her body lying on that bed inside her quarters, and initially, she had thought she might be hesitant to leave her own side. Now, as she strode with purpose to the gathering in the ship's center, she felt free, and she pushed the guilt away.

The elevator took her to the main floor, Deck Four. She had the schematics almost memorized at this point. Decks Five to Ten overlooked this section of the ship; Decks One to Three held Engineering and any subsystems a massive vessel like this needed. Plumbing, Electrical, Maintenance, Environmental Services... all of it was located on the lower section of the ship.

"Deck Four," the computer advised her as the elevator stopped. She was the sole occupant, and she stepped out, emerging into the cramped open-air space.

Treena froze in her footsteps, nearly turning around at the press of bodies around her. There were too many people here, too many wandering eyes, too many faces staring at her.

She thought she heard someone whisper her name. "Is that Treena Starling?" someone asked.

"It can't be. She died," another replied.

Treena forced a slight smile and kept moving, heading through the ship's gathered crew and toward the edge of the huge room, where Captain Thomas Baldwin stood with Admiral Hudson and the others. She noted the albino, Executive Lieutenant Ven, the Zilph'i trained with the Ugna. She'd never met one before and was actually excited by the prospect.

Brax Daak stood there, eyes wide as he saw her ascending the stairs, and the room was filling with commentary, all of it seeming to be about Treena. She let it wash over her. *You have to let them get used to the idea.* She heard her mother's words to her before she'd left home last week. *If you're standoffish, they'll turn on you.*

Brax was imposing, powerful but lean. The light reflected from his bald head, and his dark green eyes bored into her as she nodded to the chief of security. He appeared to loosen up enough to smile at her.

Chief Engineer Reeve Daak stepped away from the group and walked right up to her, wrapping Treena in an unexpected hug. "It's so good to meet you, Treena. I'm Reeve."

Treena laughed, caught off guard by the sudden act of kindness. She hugged the Tekol woman in return. "Likewise," she said quietly, and Reeve apparently remembered where she was, stepping in line with a bow of her head.

Ven didn't move to say anything, and that only left the captain. "Treena. Glad you made it," he said, letting a little sarcasm out. He was the only one Treena personally knew. Baldwin had been the commander of her first posting, when she'd been a lowly junior officer in training for the Concord Academy.

Baldwin didn't hug her, nor did she attempt to embrace him. But she noted the compassion in his face, and she liked him even more for it. "I wouldn't miss it for the world. Any of them."

Admiral Hudson smiled wide, motioning Treena to stand on the other side of him. "Now that we're all here, we can begin." His words amplified across the courtyard. Huge screens around the room revealed zoomed-in images of the legendary admiral, and the entire gathered crew cheered for a moment, until he slowly raised an arm to stop them.

Treena studied the courtyard. It was strange to see greenspace onboard a vessel like this, but it created something special for the crew. There were small ponds, flowing water along the edges of the room, and mist sprayed on a timer, giving the plants much-needed humidity. Treena's sensors could feel the heat, but she noticed how others were sweating in the cramped area. She didn't think it would always be so warm, but with over three hundred people packed in, things were bound to be muggy.

"Today marks a new era for the Concord as a whole. We have forty-three partners spanning hundreds of thousands of light years, and the Founders couldn't be more pleased," the older man said.

Treena noted how, out of the major four Founder races, there was no Callalay member on the executive crew. That would raise a lot of questions. There was always one of each four. This crew had two Tekol, one Zilph'i, and two humans, if she could call herself a human any longer. The Zilph'i were a prestigious race, the original Founders, but for *Constantine* to have one of their Ugna aboard was a special marking of their partnership.

The admiral was talking, and Treena forced herself to stop all the introspection and listen to his speech.

"We're working toward a bigger and better future for everyone in the Concord, and the first step is adding Greblok to our list of partners. They will be joining the Concord, and you, the crew of our new flagship *Constantine*, will be ushering them through the process," Admiral Hudson said emphatically.

This garnered more cheers, and Hudson only smiled, his eyes crinkling up at the corners. "With that being said, let's have a word from this ship's namesake."

Treena noticed Captain Baldwin motion to step forward, when a figure appeared from midair to stand at the front of the stage. Tom stopped in his tracks, and his jaw dropped enough for Treena to notice, before clamping shut again. So Tom hadn't met his grandfather's avatar yet. This should be interesting.

"Greetings, crew. Many of you have met me during your tours of the ship. I am Constantine. I'm a projection of the great Constantine Baldwin, but I'm not him. I have some of his memories and thoughts embedded into me, but due to Concord restrictions, those are limited to functional and tactical sections only. If you met me during my life, I won't remember you." The AI image laughed, and many joined him. Treena saw that Tom didn't.

Tom's jaw appeared clenched; he squinted as if he was pressing away some pain. Treena understood only too well.

"I'll be here, should anyone need me. I can be projected in up to twenty locations at once, and have expertise in many areas of the ship. If you're looking to become a better Oolet player, I can help you out," Constantine said, garnering more laughs.

Constantine was young, thin, and wearing a black uniform: none of the gray of their modern outfits. He had no rank colors, separating him from the others. He was the spitting image of the legendary man as he'd captained his very first vessel over fifty years ago. Treena recalled how every young girl had thought he was the most handsome man ever, with those piercing blue eyes and a strong profile. There were always images of the man everywhere on the colonies: Concord propaganda, assuring the masses that the Concord was always there, protecting them.

"Without further ado, I give you your captain. The real Constantine Baldwin's grandson: Captain Thomas Baldwin." The AI waved toward Tom, who gave the visage a grim smile before taking the stage. The AI flickered and vanished as Tom began to speak. He looked exactly like his grandfather at forty.

"This has been a great honor. When I first heard the Concord was developing a brand new state-of-the-art vessel, I was excited. I never expected to get that call from the admiral, asking if I'd like to captain her. Constantine Baldwin was my grandfather, and the man was a hero of mine. I take great pride in my name, and my lineage, and I can only hope to do him proud aboard this vessel. I have faith that with your assistance and dedication, we can bring the Concord's dreams to fruition," Tom said, pausing to let the crowd cheer and clap. A few people sent shrieking whistles through the room, and the noise levels lowered as a full minute passed.

"We leave in a week, so please, take this time to adapt to your regular schedules. Meet your team and get acclimated to the ship, because in a few days, we head to Greblok to welcome them into our great Concord," Tom said with finality.

More cheering. Treena watched Tom closely and knew the speech had been well-rehearsed. He was a man of few words at times, and he hated the attention his name carried

Nathan Hystad

with it. He'd forever been trying to avoid the shadow being a Baldwin brought with it, and here he was, wearing it like a cape for all to see. It had to be hard on him.

"With that, have a fun night, and your shifts commence in the morning," the admiral said.

Treena Starling found herself caught up in the thrill of the new ship. It was the first time since her entire previous crew had died that she'd felt anything but sorrow.

"Bridge," Baldwin said in the elevator. He was finally alone, broken free from the constant shaking of hands and introductions. He'd had a couple of drinks, which left his head swimming uneasily. He wasn't much of a drinker, and now he remembered why. He rested a hand along the elevator wall, steadying himself as the elevator lifted. The bridge was beyond Deck Ten. It jutted out from the top of the ship, a smaller vessel raised above it, made to evacuate the executive bridge crew at a moment's notice, should the need arise.

He couldn't imagine a captain abandoning his crew like that, but it was written in the Concord's handbook. The captain was an asset. The Concord spent a lot of resources training and developing their talent, and to them, losing an asset was a liability.

"Bridge," the neutral voice of the computer said, and the doors to the elevator opened.

Tom stepped inside, taking a deep breath as he closed his eyes. It was so new, so sterile. _Cecilia_'s bridge had decades of life in it. It had smelled like a mixture of the crew, the stress and fear of battle, the joy and exhilaration of exploration. This was something different, a clean slate.

And it was Tom's for the taking.

The bridge was bright, almost too bright at the moment. The top was domed, the floor light gray and hard. The viewer was expansive, almost twice as big as his last ship's. Two helm seats sat on the floor at the front of the space. One would be occupied by a lieutenant, who would pilot the ship. Most of this was done by the computer, but it still needed orders. The other seat would be filled by one of their executive officers.

Reeve would spend most of her time in Engineering, but she'd also trade off up here. Tom wanted them all used to bridge shifts. Her brother would work with their fighter team and Lieutenant Basker, which at the moment was a skeleton crew. Once they were sent off on a more dangerous or longer mission, that would change.

Tom walked to the center of the bridge, where two other seats remained empty. The captain's chair was beautiful, dark brown and plush. He'd never sat in one, even when he'd had the bridge on *Cecilia*. Now he took his time, settling into the chair. It felt right.

He pictured the bridge full of life, stars swimming through the viewer, and he waved a finger, pretending to make an order.

"Do I need to call for a medic, sir?" a voice asked from behind him, and Tom jumped from his seat, finding the AI standing there, cross-armed.

"I was…"

"It's okay. You haven't been to the bridge yet. Are you settling in?" Constantine asked him.

Tom returned to the chair, and the AI came to take Starling's seat beside him. "This is too weird."

"What is?" Constantine asked.

"This. You. Having a young version of my grandfather beside me on the bridge," Tom told him.

"I understand," Constantine said. "If it helps, it's strange for me too."

"How so?" Tom asked. The AIs weren't supposed to have feelings or emotions. They were tactical representations only, but none had ever looked so lifelike. Tom couldn't help himself. He stretched his hand out, his fingers passing through the projection.

"I'm a new type of AI, never seen before. I... I am more Constantine Baldwin than anything else," he told Tom.

"Do you remember... them?" Tom asked.

The man turned to stare at him. "Them?"

"My parents. Your daughter," Tom said.

The AI shook his head. "When Constantine was this age, his daughter was five years old. I don't have his personal memories in place."

Tom found himself unsure how to feel about that. He almost wanted the connection to them, but knew it was for the best. "Good. I'm glad to have your expertise aboard. We'll make a good team."

"Yes. I agree, Captain," Constantine said. His eyes went wide, the pupils flashing red. "I'm getting a message. The admiral is coming to the bridge and has alerted the rest of the executive crew."

Tom's blood froze. "What is it?"

The doors opened and the admiral stepped through, tailed by Treena Starling, Ven, and the two Daaks.

Tom stood, waiting for the news. "What's going on, Admiral?"

"I received word from Nolix," the admiral said, referencing the Concord's home base planet. It was where the Tekols hailed from, and both of them glanced nervously at one another. Tom wondered if the rumors of Tekol twins occasionally sharing emotions were accurate.

"And?" Treena urged the older man impatiently.

"We've lost communication with Greblok." Admiral Hudson appeared exhausted, as if the day's festivities, mixed with the urgent news, had deflated him.

"What do you mean, lost communication? What do we know?" Tom asked.

"Nothing. We were in touch with them about the coming week and the steps moving forward after the inauguration, and suddenly, nothing. The messages appear to go unheard. No replies," Hudson told their secure group.

Ven, the tall man, stood at least ten meters from the nearest computer console, yet it sprang to life. Tom saw buttons being pressed as if by a ghost, and images appeared on the previously dark viewer for all of them to see. Tom had never seen an Ugna in action before, and the telekinesis display alarmed him slightly.

"This doesn't bode well for our mutual forthcoming relationship, Admiral," Ven said stoically. The picture was of Greblock; Tom knew from the distinct dusty orange landscape below thin clouds. Beyond was a rough-shaped moon, which was a tenth the size of the world below. "Do you think they're hesitating due to the negotiation agreements?"

"What negotiations?" Tom asked, suddenly feeling foolish. He was trained in so many aspects of the Concord, but most of it was exploration and defense. He didn't have much experience with the government side of the Concord, but he was quickly learning that was going to change.

"How do you think planets gain access into the great Concord, Baldwin?" the admiral asked.

"I… They have something the Concord needs," he said, the answer becoming clear.

"Exactly. Greblok recently discovered an ore deep below their oceans. It's the most conductive material the

Concord has ever seen. It can be used to replace an element in the cables we use on our ships and, more importantly, in our cities. This is a huge win for the Concord, Baldwin. We need this agreement to happen," Hudson said, desperation evident in his voice.

"Then we'll make it happen. When we go in a week…"

Tom was cut off by Hudson. "No. You don't have a week. You leave tomorrow," he said.

Tom's heart beat faster, and he saw the look of uncertainty spreading across the others' faces. "Sir, no disrespect meant, but there's no way in hell we're ready to launch by tomorrow. The crew only arrived today. *I* only got here today. This is the first trip any of us have had to the bridge," he said, perhaps a little too aggressively.

The admiral glared over at Tom, his eyes puffy and red. "Baldwin, there are at least ten other captains within a day of here that would jump at this chance. Don't make me put a call in."

The threat was palpable, and Tom stood rigid, not trusting himself to speak.

"We'll leave tomorrow, sir. Don't worry about that," Treena Starling answered for him, giving Tom a tiny nod of her chin.

The admiral looked between the two of them and sighed. "Good. Find out what's going on. If they're trying to play hardball, we can work with it. If something's happened to them, the Concord needs to act. These are peaceful times. Let's ensure no one has crossed the line here. Understood?"

"Fully," Tom said, and the admiral stalked off, leaving their group alone on the bridge.

THREE

*T*arlen woke with a shout, his hands coming over his head protectively. His eyes jumped open, scanning the dark space around him. There were no bombs going off, no red lasers tearing the land up, just him alone in a cave.

Images flooded his mind from yesterday. "Belna! Are you here?" he called hesitantly. No one answered. He'd been so sure his sister would have escaped the carnage and made it to their safe zone, but his hopes died with the silence. From inside the cave, all he could hear was the rush of the wind echoing through the stones along the hillside.

Tarlen stretched, his back popping as he did so. He wiped his eyes with dirty hands and crossed the dusty ground, heading for the cave entrance. It was dull outside, the sky cloud-covered and bleak. Visibility was poor, and the smell of smolder filled his nostrils as he stepped to the rocky pathway.

"Belna…" he whispered to no one. Wisps of smoke lifted from the cityscape in the distance, most of the deep orange glows of fire all but out now. He couldn't tell what time of the day it was, the star's position hidden behind the smoke-cloud mixture.

A shrieking noise emanated from the west, and Tarlen's head snapped in that direction. It sounded like a monster come to life. Was it far away? He couldn't tell. The sound came again and again, a constant pulse of terror.

That was the direction of the ocean.

He recalled something about the new underwater mines. Was that what the invaders had been after? If it was important enough for Greblok to receive attention from the Concord, who knows who else might have been interested in the commodity. Tarlen's father was a bookkeeper, and he'd exclaimed how much business he was expecting after the mining operation was in full swing.

There was no sign of the invaders in the sky, at least not below the clouds, and Tarlen moved into the open, suddenly extremely thirsty. The river was close. He stumbled over the dusty path, eventually finding the flowing water. It was clear here, and even though his parents had warned him not to drink from unfiltered streams, he drank deeply, not having any other options.

His stomach grumbled, reminding him he hadn't eaten anything in a day. It could be worse. He could have been vaporized in the attack. The walk usually only took around a half hour, but Tarlen bided his time, trying to stay out of plain sight. There were a few treed copses along the way, and he took to the cover, his legs getting scratched by the wild brush. By the time he entered the city boundaries, he was covered in sweat, his face sticky with dust.

Tarlen swept his dark hair from his eyes and found the edge of the sidewalk. He blended in well enough with the beige stone buildings, his clothing being much the same muted tone. Most of the structures were now piles of rubble, destroyed by the invaders. Smoke filled the city air, and he blinked quickly as he walked, his eyes becoming red and tender.

His father's shop was nearby, and Tarlen clung to a hope that he'd arrive to find his parents with Belna, safe and united, awaiting his triumphant return. There were bodies strewn about, pieces of his neighbors in the streets, and Tarlen held off a scream as he saw his teacher on her back, her legs missing. He stumbled away, tripping on something. It was another body, this one headless. He cried out, unable to stop himself.

Tarlen ran. Away from the destruction, away from the death, but he couldn't escape it. Once he spotted the first body, he saw them everywhere. Pieces of his people were spread all over the city, at least the parts not vaporized in the assault.

His skinny legs pumped as fast as they could, and he wasn't certain where he was going. Tarlen heard the angry pulses in the distance again, coming from over the ocean, and he turned to look. Before he could spin his head around, he hit something that felt like a wall.

"Calm yourself," a voice said as Tarlen fell to the ground. A plume of dust shot up around him, and Tarlen coughed. A big hand reached toward him, extending its assistance.

Tarlen peered at the huge man with bloodshot eyes. "Who are you?" He saw the man had a gun strapped to his hip, and his uniform was familiar. He was one of the Regent's guards.

"I'm Penter." He pulled Tarlen up easily. "Where did you come from, son?"

Tarlen cringed at the man's choice of words. He needed to find his father. "I saw them coming. I tried to get my sister away, but we were separated. I hid in the caves," he said, feeling a wash of shame envelop him.

"Good idea. There have to be more," Penter said.

"More?" Tarlen asked.

The big man pointed to a building that remained, and Tarlen saw a handful of faces peering out an open window. He didn't wait. Tarlen raced to the people, searching for his family. "Mom, Dad, Belna?" There were only seven inside, and none of them were his family. Tears found him now, and he slumped to the floor, crying as an older woman crouched beside him, attempting to console him. "I have to find them. I have to try."

"We must stay hidden. You tell me where you live, and I'll take a look," Penter told him.

A small child waddled over and passed Tarlen a mug with water in it. He took it and drank it greedily. "Thank you."

"Have something to eat. Rest. Let Penter take a look," the woman said. Her eyes were kind, her arm bandaged. She had a hard bun and gave it to Tarlen. He bit into it, the rough edges scratching the inside of his cheeks.

"I'll go with you. I have to find them," he said, no longer allowing himself to cry. He was too old for that, and they needed him to be strong.

The pulsing screeches grew louder, and the little girl clutched Tarlen's arm in fear. "What's that noise?" Tarlen asked the guard.

"That's the Statu," Penter said quietly.

"The Statu," Tarlen repeated softly. They were things from children's stories, meant to frighten you to do chores. They were hideous monsters, dropped from space to snatch misbehaving children from their beds as they slept soundly.

"How can you be sure?" a man asked from the corner of the room. The walls were bereft of art, shelving knocked to the floor in the attack. Tarlen realized that this had been someone's home only yesterday. Now that person was likely dead, along with everyone else.

"The ships. Someone in my family saw them attack during the old Wars," the guard said.

The old man's face scrunched up in a ball. "Why are they here? I thought they were defeated, all destroyed?"

Penter shrugged with exaggerated movements. "How should I know? That was fifty years ago. I'm sure not all of them were at the last battle. My uncle used to drink too much ale and mutter how they'd eventually return to be a thorn in the Concord's ass."

Tarlen couldn't believe what he was hearing. Penter really thought the Statu had returned. It couldn't be. Everybody knew they'd attempted a takeover along the Border, destroying anything that could help the Concord, and then, more bravely, inside Concord space. He shuddered thinking about it.

If the Statu really were here, was there any hope for Greblok at all? All he had to do was picture the utter devastation outside, and he knew there wasn't. His world was over, his people slaughtered. When Penter finally waved for Tarlen's attention, telling him they were ready to go search for his parents, Tarlen found he barely had the strength to nod along.

―――――――

"Lost in thought?" Reeve's voice carried across the bridge. It was early, but Brax was usually up a couple of hours before his shifts each day. It gave him time to work out, eat, shower, and start the day with a clear mind and strong body.

He was staring out the viewer, watching the planet below. It was a beautiful Class Zero-Nine world: lush, abundant. The locals were still excited by their inclusion into the Concord a decade later, to the point of being irritating with their pleasantness.

Brax had spent the last couple of days soaking up the sun and relaxing with his sister before taking this posting.

It had given them some much-needed time to catch up, since he'd been stationed on a different ship than her for the previous five years.

"Not lost, per se. Just taking in the sights." He glanced to the right, where a pale moon orbited Kevis VII.

Reeve came to stand next to him, and he saw her glance around before leaning her head on his arm. She was a head shorter than him, and she only came to his chin in height. It was a rare moment of familiarity on the bridge, one that wouldn't happen again once their mission was underway.

"How have we not spoken about Treena Starling?" Reeve asked softly.

The commander had yet to report to the bridge for the day, but Brax still peered around to make sure no one was listening before he responded. "It's a shock. I thought she died."

"I'd only heard she'd survived, but no one spoke about it again, and I just assumed… you know, the worst," Reeve said. Her red eyes shone brightly as they watched the world below together.

"Apparently, she healed up nicely," Brax said, and Reeve raised an eyebrow.

"Do I sense an attraction from my brother?" she asked playfully. She always knew how to press his buttons.

"Stop that." He straightened, hoping no one heard her. "We're on the bridge."

"Settle down. You're always so by the book. Maybe you should loosen up once in a while," Reeve told him. He was sure that was, at bare minimum, the thousandth time in their lives she'd said those exact words.

"I'm only here because of you, Reeve. I have to play by the book. Not everyone gets by on their extreme intellect, joking their way through the ranks," he said through sharp teeth.

She rolled her eyes at him. "Sure. And you just happen to be here on this ship because of me. Did I mention that I never once suggested you for the position?"

He hadn't known that. "Should I be offended?"

"No. From what I hear, the Concord hand-selected each and every member of the executive team. Baldwin didn't even have a say," Reeve told him.

This was news to Brax. "Seriously?"

"Again, I didn't hear that firsthand. Not that I think the captain would straight-out tell us he didn't choose us, but don't you think it's a little strange?" she asked.

"It is. Has this precedent ever been set before?" he asked. Reeve understood the Concord's history better than anyone else he'd ever come across.

"Don't think so. This stuff isn't available in public records, but I think every captain has always at least been given options to choose from," she said in hushed tones.

"And what about the obvious missing Callalay member?" he asked his sister.

"That's beyond me. I'm going to ask around, but I don't want to be nosy. Our people will be happy to see two Tekol on the bridge, though. How amazing is that? There have never been two Tekol siblings in the same executive ranks, let alone twins. We're…"

"Famous?" He finally let himself laugh, letting her infectious attitude fill him.

"I wouldn't go that far… but we're on our way." Reeve turned around, staring at the door as the rest of the crew began filing in. "Looks like it's time to work. I'd better return to the boiler room. See you soon, brother."

"Yes, sister," he said, drawing out the title and smiling at her.

Reeve stopped and greeted the commander and captain before walking by Ven without so much as a glance.

The strange albino didn't seem to notice.

Thomas Baldwin looked every inch of his role. He stood straight-backed, hands at his sides as he stepped in front of his captain's chair. His hair was short and brown, gray speckling the edges as if he'd dyed it to be perfectly symmetrical. Baldwin even had a cleft chin. It was as if the man was sculpted to be in a leadership role, and Brax appreciated the fact that the man seemed unsure of his own abilities yet. He thought it was going to be a good challenge working together and figuring out their new positions as a team.

"All systems are a go, Captain." Ven sat at one of the two front helms positions, and a Zilph'i woman wearing a white collar, denoting her rank as Junior Officer, took the primary pilot's seat. She was tall and thin, like the telekinetic man beside her, but she was dark-skinned, her hair long and brown instead. It was hard to believe the two were of the same race. Brax hadn't studied much about the Ugna, but knew there'd only been one in Fleet history to work on a Concord cruise ship, which made this a momentous win for them.

"Very good, Executive Lieutenant Ven." Captain Thomas Baldwin took his seat, and Commander Treena Starling sat in her position beside him, her face impassive as the viewer showcased Kevis VII below. Their ship had been finished out here, away from the throngs of attention.

Brax found his seat at the edge of the room, checked the weapons systems twice, and confirmed with the computer that they were functional. He really hoped he could operate them on the real ship. He'd learned the new technology inside and out in the simulators, but he found there were usually some drastic variances between theory and reality.

"Nothing to report from the inside, Captain,"

Constantine's AI said, suddenly appearing in the center of the bridge.

Baldwin jumped back, startled, and it had surprised Brax too.

"Can you please either announce yourself or appear at the edge of the room?" Baldwin asked the AI.

"If that satisfies you, then yes, sir," Constantine said, a slight smile on his lips.

Brax had never seen an AI quite like this before, and wondered how much of the old hero was really in there. From what he'd heard, the real man had been a bit of a joker when he had to be, and a stubborn hardass when necessary.

"We were supposed to have a procession, camera feeds, and a visit from the Concord Prime Minister, but since Greblok has gone dark, we go alone, which I prefer," Baldwin said.

"Orders, sir?" the Zilph'i woman asked.

"Take us out. Set course for the Oanush sector," Baldwin said. "Thank you, Junior Officer Zare."

"Course is set," Zare told the bridge. "Four point two standard cycles before arrival."

Baldwin nodded. "Move us out," he said, and the ship began to detach from the massive station it had been linked to during the final stages of construction. Ven switched the camera feeds showing on the viewer, and they watched from the vantage point of the station as the ship emerged into space, free of its shackles.

Brax thought the ship looked magnificent. A truly epic vessel, and he was filled with pride at being chosen by the Concord for this prestigious assignment.

FOUR

*T*reena Starling sat in the private bathroom stall, feeling the very human urge to throw up, but she wasn't able to. This form didn't have a stomach and didn't ingest food or liquid. It had taken all her composure to sit on the bridge and watch as their ship moved from the station to space. From there, the engines had activated, switching from impulse to hyperlight, sending the stars scattering into streaks as they powered through the expanse at immense speeds.

She'd been on a few ships since her accident, mostly tucked away in a room with no way to see out a viewer. The last time she'd watched space through a screen like this, her ship and crew had been destroyed at the Border.

"You're fine, Treena," she told herself over and over. No one else even seemed to be aware she wasn't a human. They stared at her like she was a ghost, and she half expected someone to try to wave a hand through her as though she was an AI like Constantine. Close enough.

Treena sat up, ready to put this foolish behavior behind her. She was the commander of the Concord's flagship, not a new recruit. It was time to start acting like it. She emerged from the bathroom, returning to her seat beside the captain.

He was reading something on his console, and she noticed him scanning through the ship's personnel manifest, mouthing names as he stared at images. He was still trying

42

to learn the crew's names. He saw her catch him, and he gave her a slight shrug. "I didn't have a lot of time to prepare. They sprang this on me a month ago, and I only made it to Nolix last week," he told her.

Did Baldwin know about her? She wanted to ask him but couldn't bring herself to. He had to. He was the captain.

They'd been traveling for a day now, and this was her second shift on the bridge. Treena wondered how long it would be before someone noticed she didn't eat in the mess hall with everyone, or drink any liquids.

The shift was coming to a close, and the door opened, the chief engineer walking through. She caught Treena's eye and waved her over.

"Go ahead. Things are running smoothly here," Baldwin said without ever looking up.

"Thank you, sir. See you tomorrow," she told the man, and crossed the bridge to join Reeve at the exit.

"I haven't seen half of the ship yet, and I thought you might like the stretch," Reeve said.

As much as Treena wanted to return to her dark room and hide from the others while off duty, there was something comforting about Reeve's inclusion. "Sounds like a good idea."

They stepped into the elevator, and Reeve asked the computer to bring them to Deck Four.

"What's here?" Treena asked her companion. She knew this was the deck where Medical was, along with the training facility, complete with a lap pool.

"I haven't formally met the doctor yet and thought we could do that together. See if he wants to grab a tea or something with us," Reeve said, flashing a smile.

Treena suppressed the panic she felt at the idea of beverages. She could drink if necessary. There was a way to drain the liquid later, but she'd only tested it in the early months after the accident.

Signs along the walls pointed them to the medical bay, and Reeve didn't buzz before entering. She walked assuredly through the doors, which sprang open on her arrival. It was quiet, and Treena stepped inside the bay, taking a look around. It was so clean, sterile like the rest of the ship, only amplified here. Everything was bright, and there were three solid exam beds in the open room; she saw at least five private rooms along the far wall.

The doctor emerged from one of these rooms, a short, stocky man behind him. "The injection will help with your issue, and if it persists, come and see me in two days' time. And, Mr. Clayton, can I suggest cutting back on the sugar?"

The man rubbed his own shoulder and gave a sheepish nod to the alien doctor before glancing up and seeing there was an audience. "Commander," he mumbled as he walked past them.

Doctor Nee's eyes sparkled as he saw visitors, and he instantly came over to greet them. "Well, I was beginning to wonder when I'd finally meet you two. I'm Doctor Nee." He stuck a hand out, and Treena shook it without a second thought.

Reeve gasped, and the doctor sighed at her reaction. "I have a glove on. Why does everyone have to be so afraid of touching a Kwant?"

Reeve answered quickly. "Because you're poisonous to us."

"There is that, but I'll say it's overrated. As I told your brother Brax, I have the antidote on me at all times," he said.

Reeve appeared to warm up to him at the mention of her brother. Treena took the doctor in. His yellow eyes were animated, his white-blond hair nicely styled. He carried himself well, more classy than some of the Kwants she'd been stationed with before.

"I'm Treena Starling," she said, fully aware he knew who she was.

"Pleasure to meet you," the doctor said. "Has Reeve been briefed?"

"About what?" Reeve asked, but Treena stayed silent, unsure what he meant.

"That Treena is an android," Nee said matter-of-factly.

Treena sighed, another human motion from habit, relieved of her secret burden. Of course the doctor was aware. He'd be checking on her human body in the room.

Reeve stepped back, seemingly unaware of her action. "What do you mean?"

"I… I'm still Treena Starling. My body barely survived the attack. I was the last remaining crew member alive when they found us, and they kept me breathing. My brain worked, but I was trapped inside the husk of my withering vessel." Treena cringed at her casual dismissal of her real body. *Vessel.* Was that all she was?

"That's… amazing," Reeve said, coming closer. She moved a hand toward Treena's arm. "May I?"

"…Sure."

The woman felt the skin on her hand and tapped it slightly. "You feel human."

"They did a good job," Treena admitted.

"No wonder we hadn't heard anything about you for so long. This must be some top secret stuff. You know, with all the ethical ramifications involved with android avatars out there," Reeve said.

Treena had heard it all and didn't care. "I'm still alive. This is the only way for me to be a contributing member of the Concord, and I'm doing my job in whatever form possible."

Reeve raised her arms in the air, a sign of supplication. "I'm on your side. I'm glad you're here. We need a Treena Starling on board. You're a legend already. Can you imagine? A Baldwin, and Treena Starling controlling an android. The Concord sure went all out. Not to mention a telekinetic Zilph'i and a poisonous doctor," she added with a laugh.

Doctor Nee laughed with her, though Treena didn't quite see the humor of the situation. "I suppose word will get out now. Can I count on you two to support me?"

"Of course you can," Doctor Nee said. "I think you're a true inspiration, and I'm honored to be your doctor."

"Good. When you visit me, just be sure to wear gloves, okay?" Treena asked, her face impassive for a moment before succumbing to a smile.

This made Nee laugh again, and it seemed like they were old friends. "I have to be honest, it feels great to have this off my chest. It's been a trying couple of years."

"Has Baldwin been informed?" Reeve asked, her red eyes squinting.

"I'm not sure," Treena admitted.

The doctor appeared about to say something on the subject, when the lights flashed white, then red. The computer's neutral voice carried over the ship's speakers. "This is an alert. All scheduled officers to your stations."

"I supposed that means us," Reeve said. "Nice to meet you, Nee. Maybe we can have dinner this week."

He smiled at them. "You know where to find me."

Treena separated from Reeve as she moved for Engineering. The *Constantine* commander raced through the corridors, heading for the elevator to the bridge.

———

Yur Shen peered up at the blinking red lights and shuddered. Was the alarm because of him? Had he been found out?

As crew members ran through the hallways, not giving him a second glance, he relaxed. Why would anyone care about a maintenance crew member being added to the roster at the last minute? If he was going to last the long haul on *Constantine,* he needed to be calmer.

He tried to recall the orders he'd been given, and the main thing that stuck out in his mind was the command: *stay in the shadows.*

Yur did just that as more officers walked past with purpose, holding tablets and discussing the anomaly their ship's sensors had uncovered. His ears perked up, and he ran a hand over his ridged brow. No one ever noticed the man in the gray jumpsuit, walking around with an I-7902 maintenance cart. Standard procedure, standard work duty, standard uniform. Nothing about Yur was out of place, and he preferred it that way.

His orders appeared on his cart's screen, and he tapped at it, finding a map to the room that held the Star Drive. There had been a contained fire in one of the ancillary power cases, and his work detail was to wipe the blackened cabinets and repaint. Didn't they have robo-servers for this purpose? It didn't matter. He was used to doing menial tasks, but the fact that he'd one day be elevated to a new position, one far more powerful than a spy on board the flagship, kept him going.

The alarms continued to chime softly as he headed to the lower level, pressing his cart into the maintenance elevators. He was alone in the lift, and smiled as it settled to the bottom floor. His benefactor would be proud of how well he was doing.

He fought the urge to send a message to her, knowing it might be intercepted here. He needed to be careful, she'd told him. This ship had an AI unlike no other, and Yur had felt how much that scared her, even if her messages hadn't said so.

He moved through the halls, his pace even and slow, and eventually, he stopped at the main engineering wing.

Yur composed himself. A guard stood there, armed and bored. "ID," she said without interest.

He moved his hand toward her scanner, and it beeped. She stepped aside without another word. No one wanted to talk to Yur, the gray-uniformed maintenance man. He was invisible.

The room was amazing, even to his untrained eyes. This was his first visit here, and his gaze settled across the space at the crackling lines of energy around a miniature black ball. It floated there in the center of the container, drawing his attention. He wanted to touch the glass, feel the power. Instead he moved to the cabinet with scorch marks and began to wipe it with the special spray.

His benefactor had been clear in his mission. Yur glanced around, seeing a dozen or so screens showing various components within the bowels of the ship, each more complicated and elaborate than the last. He didn't understand what most of them did, but he recognized the device on the third screen. That was it.

Yur finished his task, painting the gray cabinet, and he stood back, admiring his work. He'd done a good job. He moved the cart forward, slowly walking behind it. No one paid him any mind, an older Callalay man with paint on his sleeves.

There were six people in the main engineering room by the time Yur reached the third screen, and he glanced across the space to where everyone had gathered, pointing at something on the main viewer. He covered his face as he spotted the Tekol chief engineer. He'd been warned to stay away from her. Something about a photographic memory.

"It's a ship."

"Why would there be a ship out here?"

"It looks dead."

"I've never seen anything like that."

"Everyone stop fussing about, and make sure we're ready for anything," the Tekol woman said, hands on hips.

Yur tried to ignore their nattering, finding that this was the opportune time. The image he was focused on showed glowing tubes, five of them intertwined and funneling into one output. He saw the location of the video feed's source, and he keyed it into his maintenance cart's computer. ER-1.96514. He shut the screen off, smiling as he secured the location of his target.

He knelt on the ground, fiddling with his pants leg, and he made sure the device he'd hidden under his cart was intact. It was concealed among various other devices, not that anyone would ever care to check his supplies. They'd have to see him to stop him.

Yur moved across the room, watching the viewer from afar, seeing the long, unmoving ship. He didn't know what it was, but it didn't concern him, so he left Engineering with one last glance at the heavy black ball that powered the entire Star Drive.

That something so small, seemingly insignificant, could affect so much gave him hope for himself. He smiled as he pushed his cart through the corridor, the guard not bothering to look up as he left.

He had the location. Now he just needed to bide his time until he was called to Deck Two.

---

*T*om Baldwin flipped the console screen off as the stars slowed around them. "Are you sure it's a vessel this far out?"

"That's what the sensors are saying," Brax told him from the edge of the bridge.

"Impulse speed, Ven," Tom ordered, and watched as they came toward a halt over a few minutes. "Where is it?"

The viewer zoomed from the image of empty space to a tiny speck that grew with each degree of magnitude. "What class ship is that?" Baldwin asked, not recognizing it.

"Scanning now," Ven said. "Sir, it's not on record in our files."

This startled Baldwin. "Excuse me? What do you mean, it's not on record?"

Ven turned in his seat to stare at his captain. Tom forced himself to meet the strange telekinetic's gaze. "I mean it's of unfamiliar stature. The shape and energy readouts aren't in our database."

Tom stood, stalking toward the viewer. The ship was long and thin, reminding him of a Kwants skimmer, but there were subtle differences. There were no visible markings he could see from this angle, and it was rougher than the skimmers. Perhaps an older model?

"Run it against a skimmer to compare, then show them to me side by side," Tom ordered, and Brax did this, pushing the results on the viewer.

"The skimmer is half the size, sir. This is most definitely alien," Brax said.

Alien. They'd left the docking bay less than two days ago, and already they'd encountered a mysterious vessel along their path to Greblok. There was so much riding on them arriving to their destination world, and Tom understood the ramifications of failure. He'd lose his new station, and if he was lucky, they'd probably demote him and stick him on some hundred-year-old freighter, making supply runs between Nolix and some backwater world famous for the galaxy's best animal fertilizer.

"What are we looking at?" his commander's voice asked, and she came to stand shoulder to shoulder with him in front of the massive viewer.

"Unidentified ship," Tom told her.

"Unidentified…?" she started.

"Perhaps if you were on the bridge, we wouldn't have to go over this a second time, Commander," Ven suggested plainly.

Treena frowned, but she stayed silent. Tom knew it was an honor to have an Ugna on board, but he'd speak to the man privately about rank when the two were alone.

"Have you attempted communication?" she asked, rather than playing into his games.

"Not yet. Junior Officer Zare, reach out to them with our standard Concord communication. Inform them we're here to assist should they need it," Tom said, and he returned to his seat. He silently hoped they returned communications stating they were fine and not in need of assistance. Then *Constantine* could continue on its planned journey to Greblok.

"I've sent the package, sir." Zare snapped her head back to her console, as if waiting for a reply.

"Keep repeating it. If there's anyone aboard, they'll eventually reply," Tom said.

"Sir, if I may?" Brax asked from his seat at the edge of the bridge.

"Go ahead," Tom said. He didn't know the man well

but was looking forward to working with him. He liked the deference he gave, and from early impressions, Brax was diligent and hard-working.

"*Constantine* has some new features, and I've already run a scan of the exterior using drones I released as soon as we arrived," Brax said.

"Go on," Tom urged.

"Their hatch... it's different than our standard four-prong attachment." Brax showed him on the viewer, using a corner of the screen to demonstrate his results. "If we wanted to board them, we'd have to use a force generator."

"Captain, this supports our findings," Ven said. "Every ship within this galaxy uses the same hatch attachment and has for over five standard centuries."

"That's right. Either this ship is from another galaxy or... it was manufactured before the Concord established guidelines on manufacturing space vessels," Tom said. This was growing stranger by the minute.

"I have a hard time imagining this ship has sat here for a long duration with no one stumbling over it," Brax suggested.

"You could be right, but how often did we have envoys traveling between Greblok and Kevis VII? There's almost no recorded data to suggest the two races have ever interacted," Treena said.

Tom nodded along. "She's accurate. There's a chance it *has* sat here. We won't know until we hear from them."

Zare turned, her long dark ponytail waving behind her as she shook her head, indicating there was no reply.

Tom had to make a decision. There were too many uncertainties, and he couldn't rightly leave the ship there without learning something about it. It would only take a few hours. They could make the time up. Reeve Daak had claimed this ship had the fastest engines ever created. He'd have her prove the theory.

"Lieutenant Commander Daak, you'll lead the team to investigate. Take the doc with you, in case they need medical attention," Tom said.

Brax appeared shocked at his orders, and Tom almost repeated them when the big man stood, nodding his acceptance. "Yes, sir."

His chief of security left the bridge, and Tom glanced at Treena.

"I'd like to go as well, Captain," she offered.

"Very well."

———————

*B*rax closed his eyes as their shuttle released from *Constantine*'s belly. He was in the front seat, piloting the vessel and trying to forget the vacuum of space beyond the five-inch-thick viewer, showcasing distant stars and nothing else.

"Everything okay, Brax?" Treena asked him.

"Sure. Fine."

"I have to say, I wasn't expecting to be sent off on an expedition so soon," Doctor Nee said. He sat beside Brax, and his slotted yellow eyes darted around in excitement.

"You don't have to seem so thrilled to be advancing on an alien ship, Nee," Brax said with a grin.

"*What joy and luxury will we find at the edges of the Universe? Only the Concord knows.*" Nee was quoting an old Academy textbook, one Brax had studied with for his entrance exam.

"Well, this must not be joyous or luxurious, because it's not in the Concord's files," Treena said.

"Aren't we pragmatic, Starling," Nee said.

Brax had the feeling the two of them had met. Nee had a habit of teasing those around him, and Brax felt comfortable with the man already. It was good to have a friend on board, one that wasn't his sister.

"Nothing wrong with being realistic. I'm not much of a dreamer," Treena said as Brax led them away from their massive vessel. *Constantine* had twelve shuttles like this, each stuck behind a sliding wall and mounted to the exterior of the ship. They didn't need any energy barriers, because they were each attached via their hatches, which, as Brax had told Baldwin, used the four-prong method. It wasn't only a cheaper option, according to the Concord, but a safer one. Too many ships had lost their energy field stabilizers in battles against the Statu in Constantine Baldwin's time as a captain. He was the one who'd suggested the change.

Brax wondered if the legend's grandson, Tom, was aware of this. Brax only knew himself because Reeve was obsessed with those kinds of details and was forever droning on about them. He wished she'd get another hobby.

"Ten minutes until arrival," he told them.

"What's our protocol if there are enemies on the other side?" the doctor asked.

"Wait, have you never been on an expedition before, Nee?" Treena asked, finally taking the upper hand. Brax laughed at their interactions.

The white-haired man stuttered. "Well… I… I've been on something resembling an expedition, once or twice."

"We have our military standard XRC-14 weapons and the smaller PL-30, as well as nerve gas, concussion grenades, and" – Brax patted his thigh – "a twenty-five-centimeter blade capable of cutting through steel. You do have weapons training, right?"

Doctor Nee sat up straighter in his seat. "I have the mandatory number of hours required to be positioned on a Concord cruise ship," he said, the joking tone lost from his voice.

"Then you'll be fine," Treena said. "If this ship is hundreds of years old, I doubt we'll have anything but bones to wrestle on the other side of the hatch."

Brax nodded his agreement and began his flyby of the long, narrow vessel. "Gathering energy readouts, but they're minimal. It appears their life support is functional," he said. He'd released the tiny drones earlier, and they were sending the shuttle detailed information as they received it from the target's computer system.

"I don't need this blasted helmet, then?" Brax asked, knocking on it with his knuckles.

"You may have your advanced weapons training, but did you take any courses on viruses, airborne or otherwise? Alien contagions?" Treena asked.

"Not that you have to worry about that," Nee said, and Brax felt lost at the comment.

"You all keep your suits sealed up tightly. No compromises there," Brax said, bringing the shuttle in closer to the black ship. It was at least fifty times the length of their compact vessel, the outer construction patchy from this close. It almost appeared like square sheets of metal had been welded into a hull, then painted over. The entry point was at the rear of the vessel, and Brax moved the shuttle in that direction, carefully adjusting the thrusters before spinning them to slow their arrival.

Once in position, he flipped the viewer's camera to show the reverse angle and backed the shuttle toward the hatch, which wasn't universal with theirs. This was where things grew tricky.

His sister had helped design the most current iteration of the force generator. The shuttle jerked lightly as he bumped into the alien vessel, coming to a stop. Brax deployed the magnetic field and stood from the pilot's seat.

The trip had been better than his last time flying himself in space. The company had helped distract him from the nothingness surrounding them. "Commander, can you assist me?"

Treena joined him at the rear of their shuttle, and she gave him a nod. He tapped the airlock separator, and a wall fell with a thud, adding a solid barrier between them and Nee at the front half of the ship.

When the computer console advised him that the front section was sealed properly, Brax strapped Treena to the wall using hefty cables, then strapped himself down. Treena smiled at him from behind her helmet, and he talked her through it.

"Have you done this before?" Brax asked.

"No. I've never had to board an unsanctioned vessel," she admitted. He'd guessed as much. He'd only done it once.

"I have to open our hatch. There will be a sharp tug on you, hence the thick lanyard attaching us to the wall. I'll activate the force generator, which will seal us from space long enough to cross through into their ship," he said.

"After you open their hatch," she said.

"Yes. But that's why I brought *him*." Brax pointed to the corner, where Constantine's AI image appeared.

"I'm glad to be of assistance. I thought I'd never be allowed any fun," the computer program said. "I'll pass through, accessing the computer system."

"This'll work?" Treena asked.

Brax hoped so. It was either that or painstakingly prying the thick metal hatch from the hull of the old ship they were attached to.

"We'll find out," he said. "Constantine, are you ready?"

"Ready," the AI said, flickering lightly. Brax had brought the portable AI device with them on the shuttle, and it was currently under the seat Doctor Nee occupied.

Brax tested his communicator with the doc. "Nee, can you hear me?"

"I can hear you, Brax. Don't forget to retrieve me before the fun parts," Nee said.

"We wouldn't dare," Brax said, and he reached for the console, preparing to board the alien vessel.

FIVE

Getting on board the mysterious stranded ship proved simple enough, and Treena was impressed with Brax Daak's abilities. He'd already proven himself a worthy crew member, which was more than could be said about herself.

They emerged onto the ship, Brax taking the lead, holding his huge XRC-14 easily. Treena left hers strapped to her back, and opted for the much lighter and compact PL-30. Doctor Nee emulated her, taking his handheld weapon as well. Beside her, Constantine walked noiselessly.

Her own boots clanged against the floor, making far too much racket. It was hard to move silently with suits on, but they were there for safety, not stealth. The corridor was dark, and they'd all flipped on their nightfeatures, rather than use lights like a beacon.

"I've told you, the ship is vacant. The computer system hadn't been activated in over six hundred standard years," Constantine told them.

"We don't take chances," Brax said.

They walked slowly, but eventually, their small expedition group found a doorway. Brax fumbled with it, attempting to open the slab. He found a manual handle after a minute, and Treena followed closely through it, her gun raised and aimed at the right corners of the new room, while Brax found the left.

"Empty," Treena said. The doctor bumped into her from behind and muttered an apology.

There was another console now, dimly lit across the room, and Constantine, the AI, turned to Treena. "I think I may be able to activate the ship's lighting system. Would you like me to attempt it?"

Brax was about to answer, when he must have recalled Treena was in charge, even though the captain had given him the responsibility of the mission. She wanted to play nice and didn't care one way or the other as long as they were on the same team.

"Brax, what do you think?" she asked, looking for guidance. It worked.

"I think it would be much easier to search the ship if we weren't bumping into walls. Go for it, Constantine," he said.

They stood in the center of the room, attempting to get the lay of the land as the AI flickered, then appeared near the console before entering the wall.

"I'm not sure I'll ever be used to that," the doctor said.

"None of us will," Treena concurred.

They waited with bated breath, Treena breathing hard beneath her helmet. It was an automatic function, one she was grateful for. If her artificial body didn't breathe, she wasn't sure she could handle the entire process.

Brax lowered his weapon after another minute, and Treena clipped hers onto the hip of her suit. The lights flashed on, sending long shadows across the grated floor. She flipped off her night sight and blinked, another impulse she really didn't need to do. The list was adding up.

"That's better," the doctor said.

Treena agreed, and attempted to make sense of the room they were inside. It was at the rear of the unfamiliar vessel, and was a cargo hold of some sort. The far wall held rows of lockers, blending so seamlessly into the surface it was impossible to tell without the real light shining on it.

Brax moved first, stepping across the floor to reach them first. Treena was right behind him. She felt for a handle, and when she didn't find one, she pressed on it, the locker door clicking and releasing. It opened with a squeak, and she wasn't surprised by the contents it revealed.

Weapons. She'd never seen guns quite like them, but their function was obvious.

Brax hefted one in his grip, lining up a shot while keeping his fingers far from the alien trigger. "We know one thing about them."

"What's that?" Nee asked.

"They weren't a trusting sort." He opened more lockers, and soon they counted at least twenty of the assault weapons. There was an assortment of armor – massive, Treena thought, even for someone Brax's size. She held a helmet in her hand and noted how angled it was, jutting wider near the mouth.

"Not quite humanoid?" she asked, shoving it toward the doctor.

Nee eyed it with interest. "This space could be for a multitude of reasons. Breathing apparatus or... mandibles."

Treena couldn't help but picture a terrifying insectoid army, and she cleared her throat out of habit. "Let's move," she said, suddenly wanting to be anywhere but the weapons room.

Brax took the lead, his gun rising again. It was much easier now that the lights were on, and she slowed, waiting for the trailing AI figure of Constantine to catch up. "Why is the life support on if the lights aren't?"

"I imagine the life support is powered at the most basic level of the ship's back-up system," Constantine said.

"Meaning?" she asked.

"Meaning they needed to keep it on for some purpose," the AI said.

"Was there anything in there that told you who they were?" she asked. She really wasn't too sure how the AI had even opened their system. She'd have to ask Reeve about it later.

"It's quite foreign to me. I used a binary program to access the lighting, but that's about the extent of my abilities," he said.

Brax opened the door by turning the manual lever, and he tugged it wide. They were in a corridor now, and it appeared much the same. Metal grate flooring. Basic walls with the odd blank screen embedded and a row of lighting above.

"Don't tell me this is the part where we split up and you send me with the immaterial computer program Constantine, please," Doctor Nee said, a smirk on his handsome face.

"Not yet. We wait until there's real danger before doing that to you," Treena told him, and his smile vanished in a flash.

Brax started the search by clearing five rooms on the left. They found each functional for a ship's purpose, but empty. Treena had expected some casualties, maybe. She almost wanted to find evidence of the race inside, but so far, she thought it likely they'd visited a kitchen, a washroom, and a meeting room.

"They have to have crew quarters somewhere," Brax said, crossing the hall to the other side.

Treena grabbed the handle of a door and attempted to turn it. Nothing. She checked to see if Brax was paying attention, and when she noticed him looking down the corridor, she snapped it open, using the added strength of her artificial body.

"You wanted quarters, you have them," she told Brax. There were four cut-outs in the walls here, which had to be beds. They were black and rounded. She walked over to one and ran a glove over it, feeling the rubber-like material bend to the touch.

"Bridge to Commander Starling. Update, please." It was Ven's gratingly calm voice carrying through her helmet.

"We've activated the lighting and are halfway through the ship. We've found no evidence of survivors, but also no deceased. We're recording all and will continue with the search. It's clearly unknown to us," she advised.

"Finish the tour and return to *Constantine*. We'll mark it, notify the Concord of its whereabouts, and continue our pressing mission," Captain Baldwin told her.

"Very well. We'll return within the hour, sir," she assured him. "Starling out."

They went faster. Treena sure there was nothing on the ship that meant them harm. She opened a closet, flipping through rows of clothing. They were all muted tones, long and flowing robes. It was difficult to tell what kind of creature would wear such a thing, or how they were utilized.

Doctor Nee held one out over his suit and moved it around as if attempting to make sense of it. "Does this go with my helmet?" he asked.

Brax shouldered past him, and Treena laughed at them both.

"The bridge has to be here," Brax said. They'd walked the length of the long, skinny ship, and there was only one place they hadn't seen on the single-level vessel.

He opened the door, and Treena raised her gun in a hurry. There were faces staring at them. At least a hundred.

"My stars," Doctor Nee said, walking forward.

"Stand down, Doctor," Brax ordered, but the man kept moving.

"They're in some sort of cryogenic pods. What harm will they do to me?" Nee asked.

Treena took the scene in, amazed at the find. There were numerous rows of the pods, stacking above one another up to the twenty-meter ceiling. Dim yellow lights pulsed from each pod; each of the inhabitants had closed eyes, and the pods beeped softly like a heartbeat.

They were gray, with ridged scale-like skin and thin mandibles around slotted mouths. She'd never seen anything quite like it.

Doctor Nee turned to Treena with a huge smile spread across his face. "I think we just met our new friends."

———————

*T*arlen paced by the doorway. "Come on. What are you waiting for?"

Penter rolled his eyes, angering the boy even more. "Patience is a valuable asset, son."

"Stop calling me that. I only agreed to hold off my search because you had food and water, and..." Tarlen's gaze drifted to the gun at Penter's hip. He left it unsaid.

"We're going now. We'll return this afternoon, everyone," Penter assured the residents of the house. The old man nodded like he didn't believe it and returned to heating up water for loose tea.

The action was so out of the norm to Tarlen. How could they be so calm when their whole world had just been attacked? Everyone they knew, gone. He didn't understand.

Penter seemed to feel his energy and set a meaty hand

over Tarlen's shoulder. "We all grieve in our own ways, and in our own time. Come. Lead me to your father's shop."

The light was dimming outside. Penter had made them wait until the daylight was waning, so they wouldn't be as visible to watching eyes. Tarlen didn't think the Statu really cared about a few living Bacals. They'd done all the damage they'd come for.

The terrible sounds continued to emanate from the direction of the ocean, and Tarlen craned his neck to see if there was any sign of ships through the smoke and clouds. The sky was clearer by this time, the smoke thinner. He almost thought he saw lights far in the distance.

"They came for our resources; that much is obvious. What I don't understand is why they had to destroy us all. They could have bargained," Penter said.

"If they're Statu, do you believe they would negotiate?" Tarlen asked.

"You're wiser than your youth generally permits."

"I'm sixteen stars old. I'm no child."

"You look younger. My apologies, sir," Penter said with a laugh.

Tarlen bristled. He was wiry, but his father had told him to be patient. There was that word again. "This way," he said, almost missing the turn. The city felt like a strange land: an unfamiliar terrain full of rubble and stones, not the home he'd been in his entire life.

Then, as the star crested behind the horizon, making their trip all the more difficult, Tarlen beheld the shop his father had run for the last twenty years. It was intact, and he almost cried out for them but bit his tongue, aware the enemy could be lingering.

He ran, his feet unable to stop from carrying him through the doorway. It was a stone building like the others, beige and ancient. Dust billowed as he stopped, finding the place empty.

"Mother, Father!" he shouted desperately. Penter arrived and didn't stop him. "Belna! Where are you?"

No response. Tarlen searched through the room but found nothing but heartache in each corner. He found the steps that led to their home above, and his bare feet plodded over the carved stone stairs. Penter didn't follow him, leaving him to explore his home alone.

Tarlen was glad for it, because he didn't want the big guard to witness his tears. He sat on his bed, head in hands, and wept, finally letting himself accept they were likely gone. Everyone was dead.

"They're all gone," he whispered. He wiped away the tears, found a shoulder pack in his closet, and filled it with some of his belongings. He took two pairs of pants, a light jacket, three shirts, and sandals. He moved to his parents' room but refused to enter. It felt wrong.

Belna's room was next, and he walked in slowly, clinging to memories with each object he found. He loved his sister dearly. What was he going to do without them?

A gold box sat on a stone desk, and he fidgeted with it, opening the hinged door. There sat the ring their mother had given to her when she turned twelve stars. She was meant to give it to her partner one day. Tarlen felt the weight of it in his palm, clasping a shaking hand over it. He found a leather string inside the box and ran the length of it through the ring, tying the band together at one end. He slipped it over his head, letting the ring settle to his thin chest.

"I'll never forget you, sister," he said, placing it below his shirt.

"Come on, son. Time to go," Penter shouted from the basement.

Tarlen followed him from the only life he'd ever

understood, and didn't look back as they turned the corner down the street.

SIX

"This puts us into a little bit of a dilemma, Captain," Treena Starling said.

Tom leaned away from the meeting room table, spinning slowly in his chair to look out the window. Their ship was idle, halted as they awaited his decision.

"I agree, Commander. We have an obligation to assist the inhabitants of this newly discovered vessel. We need to learn where they hail from, and why we've never seen their kind before. But we're under extremely strict orders to move to Greblok and decipher what's transpired there." Tom steepled his fingers as he spoke.

"May I suggest an alternative, Captain?" Ven asked. He towered over everyone from his seat beside Brax. He motioned to the table with a finger, and a water jug lifted. He pointed another finger, and the much smaller glass rose beside it. "We can attach their vessel to ours using an energy tether, and they'll essentially come along for the ride as we travel to our destination in hyperlight." The glass clinked against the jug, and they both moved across the table through the air.

He settled them down at the far end, not a drop of water spilled. Tom tried to not appear impressed.

"This is against regulations, Ven," Reeve Daak told the Ugna. "Taking the vessel may impede our primary objective. It's there in the Code. Subsection four, point one."

Tom was familiar with the Code, though perhaps not as well as Reeve, who'd seemed to memorize every minor detail of her life. "We use and abide by the Code, but there are times when other measures may be necessary."

"Sir, with all due respect, I'm not sure our first mission should be compromised in any way," his commander said.

Tom soaked it all in. They could bring the alien ship with them, but this was unprecedented. "We could leave it. Re-examine it on our return."

Doctor Nee interjected. "Sir, I'd like to have a look at one of them."

"Say that again?" Tom asked, not sure what the doctor really meant by that.

"I'd like to take one of them from the cryogenic pod. Find out what we can. Who they are, where they're from," Nee said, his expression serious.

"Hold it right there, Doctor. We're two days away from Greblok. We don't have time to be cracking open alien pods and hoping the being on the other end is even alive and can tell us a story. We do this by the book," Tom said, crossing his arms as if ending the conversation.

"Lieutenant Daak," Ven said, and Tom saw both Daaks perk up. Brax had been silent so far this meeting, and Tom appreciated the Tekol security officer not adding unnecessary opinions. Ven continued, looking at Reeve. "There is nothing against regulations, if I recall. We're merely offering aid to a stranded vessel."

"Semantics. The Concord states that you can, in an emergency, offer aid to a vessel if it belongs to a Concord ship," Reeve stated.

Tom watched the interaction between the two officers. The Zilph'i albino stood his ground, sitting straight and not breaking eye contact with the chief engineer. "We have no idea who these people are. They might well be members of the Concord. Perhaps they're in an unmarked ship. Perhaps they're members who were kidnapped aboard an enemy vessel, awaiting someone to rescue them."

Tom considered this, completely aware they had to stop waiting around. Greblok was calling, and he needed to maintain peace here. *Constantine* was his chance to stop hiding in the shadows, and to have his own command. He was the captain of a Concord cruise ship, and the most high-tech one ever created. This wasn't a time for him to grow indecisive.

"Ven, Reeve, everyone, thank you for the counsel. We bring them with us. I don't know who these cryogenically frozen people are, but I intend to find out. Now, how about we travel to Greblok, welcome them into the Concord, and bring our travelers to Nolix for scrutiny?" Tom told the assembled.

"Yes, sir," they all echoed, waiting for him to stand before they followed suit. He was starting to like the esteem they were giving him. He wanted everyone to get along, but there was rank for a reason. This ship needed a leader, not a follower.

"Reeve," he said, catching the woman's attention as she started away from the meeting room. "I'd like you to head the team. Bring that ship under our wing, so to speak. Ensure it arrives at Greblok with us, will you?"

Reeve grinned. "Yes, sir. Consider it done."

"Good. You have an hour." Tom left her standing there and headed to his office off the bridge. It was more prestigious than his former captain's office. *Cecilia* had been an older ship, although one of the Fleet's finest, in his opinion. Captain Yin Shu was Callalay, and anal to the point of obsessive compulsive when it came to order. Some of her habits had rubbed off on him, but Tom didn't mind.

He hadn't been given an opportunity to ask the admiral about the selection of his crew. Most notable was the absence of a Callalay in the executive crew. They were an ancient race, the first of the Founders to find space travel. It was the Callalay that had discovered Nolix, the home of the Tekol. Tom had often wondered why the Concord ran from Nolix rather than the original Founder's world, but no one had a straight answer. It had simply always been that way. Why question it?

Tom moved to the viewer on his wall, tapping at the console to zoom in on the alien vessel. Already, ships were moving toward it, ready to drag it toward *Constantine*.

"Constantine," Tom said, and the AI avatar of his grandfather appeared.

"Hello, Captain," Constantine said.

"What can you tell me about Greblok?" Tom asked. He'd read the briefing, but it was short, to the point, with little attention to the people, and a focus on their economy.

"Greblok is a Class Zero-Nine world. It is thirty-seven percent land, with two major oceans and three minor. The weather varies, as on most worlds, but nearly the entire population resides on a single continent. The land is desertlike: rolling dunes and sand everywhere. The capital is a city named after Malin, who's said to be a prophet from their early years. He led wandering groups of nomads together from all corners of the world and started the first city. Close proximity to fresh water and near the ocean for food." Constantine paused, and Tom smiled at the youthful face of his grandfather.

"That's more like it. Keep going," Tom said, taking a seat behind his desk.

"There are nearly half a million people in Malin, many living in original structures. The city is over three thousand years old. Population has been controlled by a few factors over the centuries. They've had no fewer than four major epidemics, plagues, killing a quarter of their people in the most recent outbreak. This was two centuries ago.

"The people do procreate, but there's also a genetic defect in twenty percent of the males, and they are unable to reproduce," Constantine said.

Those were all good reasons why the population had never exploded on Greblok. Tom had seen the pictures and was surprised they had space travel at all. "It sounds a little archaic."

"It's rudimentary by our standards," Constantine said.

"And they received space travel by trade?" Tom asked. That had been in the report, but spelled out in half a sentence.

"The Lothe visited them over a century ago. They mentored the Bacals," the AI told him.

"To what end?" Tom asked. There were rules in place about breaching contact with lifeforms not yet in space. Before the Concord was able to enforce such terms, rogue space travelers would head to unsuspecting planets and enslave them. It was unregulated, and a dangerous time before the Founders grew to power.

"The Lothe crash-landed in the ocean, or so the story goes," Constantine said.

"And they had no other option. Is that what they told the Concord?" Tom stifled a laugh. There was always a way around the rules. People had been bending and breaking them since the start of the Code.

"Correct."

"What of their mines? The admiral makes it sound like this conductive ore will be revolutionary. Do the Bacals even fathom what they have on their hands?" Tom asked.

"I wouldn't know that, Captain. I suspect they do not. Either way, Greblok entering the Concord is a huge honor, and they would trade anything to join us. Would you not?" Constantine asked.

Tom considered this. If he was living on a planet with limited space travel, and in an ancient city, would he want more for his people? Likely. But there was something romantic about the notion of staying on a planet: working a job, having a family… if you weren't one of the unlucky twenty percent of males.

"I'd want safety for my people, and the Concord would offer that. They'll also have no more disease as they have, and that in itself is a huge win. I supposed I'd trade the conductive ore. This Regent must not realize how much they could sell it for. Couldn't they buy protection and health care then?" Tom asked the AI.

"I suppose they could, though it would be unsanctioned, and could potentially pit them against the Concord," Constantine said.

Tom loved the Concord. He was part of an intricate network of worlds, with rules and consistency, but there were times he wondered what it was like to be on the outside looking in. That was why it didn't add up, Greblok going dark.

If they were so hellbent on trading their ore away, why stop communication right before the ceremony? A deep part of Tom's mind already had the answer, but he didn't want to let it out. Something dire had transpired on Greblok, and they were about to fly into a warzone.

It could be something else. Perhaps an asteroid had hit them? Maybe a radiation flare had disrupted their communication. There could be countless events that might have caused the outage, but Tom hated speculation, so he pressed it from his thoughts. He had one priority, and that entailed attaching the strange alien ship full of cryogenically frozen beings to his vessel, then continuing their trip to

Greblok.

"Will there be anything else, Captain?" Constantine asked softly.

"No. That'll be all."

The AI vanished, leaving Tom alone in his office with his thoughts.

———————

"*T*his was a good idea, Reeve," Treena told the woman to her left. Reeve raised her glass, filled with a thick dark brown liquid, some of it sloshing over the sides and splatting on the dinner table.

"To *Constantine*," Reeve said, and the others raised glasses along with her. Some, like Treena's, were filled with water. The captain, she noted, was one of them.

Brax was the other. He was an enigma, so different than his twin sister. His bald head made him appear more imposing. Most Tekol had long, thick hair, but his scalp was as smooth as an egg. Brax tapped glasses with Treena and gave her a forced smile.

"Yes, good call, Reeve," Tom said.

The dinner was great, according to everyone else. Treena had made an excuse to be late, so she'd missed the dining part of the meal. She told them she'd eaten as she'd worked, but she couldn't go on like this forever. She'd have to come clean with the crew.

She'd actually been in her room, sitting at the bedside of her real human body, machines moving it around, the cold metal prods stuck into her brain from behind her head. Treena had spent the first year unable to look at herself, then the next few months feeling so guilty, she didn't leave her own side. Now she wanted to find a balance. It was her lying there on that bed, and she couldn't forget that. No matter what happened, the lifelike vessel that was carrying her thoughts was *not* Treena Starling.

The feeling was unexplainable to others, not that she'd tried. Her mother had attempted to convince her that this was normal, but even the pushy well-meaning woman didn't have a leg to stand on. Being inside a robotic body, controlling it with her mind, was never going to be normal.

"Treena? Are you all right?" Brax asked her, and she nodded.

"Sorry, lost in thought," she told him.

"Worried about tomorrow?" the big man asked her.

"Not worried so much as excited," she said. "I haven't been on a mission in a long time. I'm trying to get used to it again."

"You're doing a great job. You were on point during our expedition," Brax told her. He sipped his water.

Tom was talking with the doctor, who was animatedly speaking of the aliens they'd discovered. "I think their exoskeletons are softer than they look. Almost like they have some give to them. I've never seen anything like it."

"But you haven't opened one of the pods, correct?" Tom asked.

"I haven't, but I very much want to. What stories they could tell! We have so much to learn," Doctor Nee said. His cheeks were red, his reptilian eyes bright in the dining room.

Constantine offered an amazing dining experience for the crew. You could eat at the mess hall daily, where a staff of twelve prepared meals around the clock. Once a week, each crew member could book a dining experience at a facility beside the mess hall. It was meant to hold meetings when visiting with dignitaries or potential allies. Tom appeared comfortable in the setting, and Treena suspected the man had grown up eating at a lot of fine establishments such as this. With the last name Baldwin, he sure wouldn't have wanted for anything.

Ven was noticeably silent, and Treena hadn't seen him using his mind to control anything during the course of the evening. "It has been a pleasant dinner, but I fear I need to return to my quarters." Ven stood, and everyone bid him goodnight.

Tom pressed his empty plate away. "I'd better get some sleep as well. Tomorrow, we arrive at Greblok. Thank you for setting this up, Reeve."

"Goodnight, Captain," Treena said, and they all watched as the man walked away, stopping briefly at the kitchen to thank the chef.

Doctor Nee and Brax each moved a seat closer, and then there were four of them.

"Since you're the military mind here, brother, what do you expect tomorrow?" Reeve asked him. She was slurring slightly, but no one else seemed to care.

Brax crossed his arms, sighing out a stale breath. "It's hard to determine. I worry someone with a vendetta might have done something."

"Who would have a vendetta?" Nee asked. His white hair fell from its perfect styling, and he swiped the longer hair away from his eyes.

"Could be a few races. There are many that petition the Concord each year for entrance. Then, out of the blue, the Concord invites a backwater world like Greblok? They would be upset," Brax told them.

Treena hadn't quite interpreted it along those lines. "I assumed someone found out how valuable the ore they were mining underwater was, and they came to take it before the Concord could."

"That's another likely possibility. We'll learn more

tomorrow," Brax told them. "Reeve, I think it's time we all go to bed."

Treena sensed a tricky relationship between the twins. Reeve was the super-intelligent one who was more prone to cutting loose, probably because she'd been able to coast to her position. Brax was her opposite, who'd arrived to his role by sheer force of will.

"Fine." Reeve didn't put up a fight, and the four of them left the dining room, Treena's glass untouched.

Tomorrow couldn't come soon enough. She longed to discover what they were facing on Greblok.

"Zoom, please, Zare," Tom said as they left hyperlight.

Greblok appeared on the screen. The skies were mostly cloudless on the visible section, and Tom noted how muted the land appeared. It was a true desert over on this continent.

"Their capital is halfway around the world, Captain, so we cannot check on it quite yet," Zare told them.

Tom glanced to Brax's position along the left edge of the bridge, and he nodded at the man, a silent *keep-an-eye-out* motion that the Tekol man appeared to comprehend. A couple of crew members worked at their stations behind and to the right, and Tom found he didn't know their names yet.

"Any starships in the vicinity?" he asked.

Ven replied from his common helm position. "None, sir."

"Good. Bring us in on impulse, and keep an eye out." Tom sat back in his seat and saw Treena gripping the arm of her chair. This had to be hard on her. He'd been in some sticky altercations, unsure if he or the crew were going to survive the day. He couldn't imagine what it had been like to nearly die along with the other two hundred crew members.

He was sure the survivor guilt alone would have done him in after a traumatic event like that. Without thinking about the protocol, he reached over and squeezed her hand in a supportive gesture. She turned to him but didn't say a word. He let go, feeling self-conscious, and cleared his throat. "Are any communications being reciprocated?" he asked.

"No, sir. Our messages are going unheeded," Junior Officer Zare told him.

"Where are you?" he asked quietly as he stood, stretching his back from the hours in the captain's chair. His seat was comfortable, but sitting that long always gave him aches.

Greblok arrived quickly as they moved for it. They passed a heavily-cratered moon, and the planet really came to life before their eyes. Tom had seen the images, but nothing did a world from space justice like seeing it with your own two eyes.

"Set course for orbit over Malin," Tom ordered, and in a quiet half hour, they arrived.

"Send this message, please." Tom spoke as clearly and concisely as he could. "Greetings from the *Constantine*. I'm Captain Thomas Baldwin, and we come on behalf of the Concord to welcome you into our ranks. This message is for the Regent. Please respond straight away. We've been unable to communicate with you for six days now."

They waited for a response, and when none came five minutes later, Tom felt a growing headache begin to press against his temples. "We have to go to the surface," he said. "Is everything prepped?"

"Yes, sir," Brax said. "Captain, I once again recommend you stay on board the *Constantine* while the commander and I bring a team on the expedition."

"Noted. I'll be going. Commander, you have the bridge and the ship in my absence," Tom said, and Treena stood in a hurry.

"Yes, sir." She took his seat as Tom followed Brax to the rear of the bridge to the sole elevator. Ven stood from his helm position and joined them, a Junior Officer coming to his seat to replace the Zilph'i man.

The elevator led to one place only: the awaiting ship above the bridge. *Constantine* had been constructed with some new features, and this was one of Tom's favorites. He could access his own private expedition vessel without leaving the bridge. It was meant to be a safety feature to extricate the executive crew in a crisis.

The elevator was smooth, shiny, and silver in color, and it was compact with the tall Ven and the wide-shouldered Brax beside him. The ride was quick, and seconds later, they emerged in the space between the bridge and its attached cruiser.

There were two armed guards flanking the ramp to the cruiser, and they stepped apart, making way for the executive crew to board.

"This is quite the ship," Brax said.

"Typically, we would have toured our cruise ship and seen this already, but dire circumstances and all," Tom told the Tekol chief of security, and the man nodded along.

The vessel was state-of-the-art. Everything was neat and exemplary inside. The seats were comfortable, and Brax took the pilot's chair while Tom sat beside him. Ven was relegated to the rear bench, and the two guards remained posted outside.

Tom ran a hand across the polished console. He

needed to be on the cruiser's maiden voyage.

"Setting course for Malin," Brax told him, and the ship detached, pressure hissing beneath them.

The viewer covered the entire front of the ship, and space appeared all around them. Tom felt the rumble of the thrusters, and it hearkened back to his days as a fighter pilot, as short-lived as they were. There were a lot of days he missed the thrill of the fight, but that was a younger man's game.

"Bridge to *Cleo*," Treena said, and Thomas felt a jolt of electricity course through him at the name. It was his mother's name. His grandfather's only daughter. He hadn't even been told about that, and he clenched his jaw, pretending not to be surprised once again.

"Go ahead, bridge," he said.

"We're picking up some strange anomalies below. There's something sending waves of energy from above the ocean near Malin," Treena told them.

"What kind of energy? What is it?" he asked.

"Sir, we're unable to verify."

Ven was using the side console to pass the information to the left side of their viewer. It was a graph showing a flowing energy movement. Tom couldn't make sense of it.

"Take us out," he told Brax, and the man nodded. "Bridge, we're going to investigate. Stand by."

SEVEN

Tarlen slept fitfully. He'd heard Penter arguing with the elderly man about staying there another day, but the guard had other ideas. Light had only begun to seep through the room's windows when the voices came once more.

"You can't stay here, old man," Penter said. None of them seemed to know his name.

"We will stay. There are children. Once the abomination is gone, we'll regroup and rebuild," the man said.

"Then what? We wait until they come again?" Penter asked, his voice a deep growl.

Tarlen sat up, rubbing the sleep from his eyes.

"Help will come," the man said.

"Then we need something to give them." The sound of Penter's heavy footsteps carried through the arched doorway.

"If you haven't noticed, all electronics have failed. They did something… fried the entire system," the old man said.

"You're right," Penter said, a frustrated sigh pushed from his cheeks. Tarlen watched them from the doorway, and he pressed into the shadow of the early morning light.

"Where did they take them?" the white-haired fellow asked.

"Take who?"

"I saw them attacking. At first I thought they'd

vaporized everyone, at least those they didn't bombard with pulse cannons and laser fire," the man said, his voice growing louder.

"Quietly. We don't want to wake the others," Penter said, and Tarlen glanced behind him to see the inactive forms around the room. "Say that again. You think they *took* some of our people?"

Tarlen saw the old man nod, white wispy hair in disarray. "That's what I'm telling you. I think they blasted them somewhere. I saw one woman plucked from the street. One moment she was there, the next vanished. No blood, no guts, no nothing."

Tarlen's heart raced. Maybe his family was alive. Maybe they'd been abducted by the invaders, not killed. Hope filled his chest, and he stumbled through the doorway. Both sets of eyes fell on him.

"We have to find them, Penter," Tarlen said.

"What are we going to do?" Penter asked, and Tarlen's anticipation dwindled.

Tarlen realized he knew nothing about the man, other than the fact he was one of the Regent's guards. He was confident the Regent was dead. He'd witnessed it up close.

"Do you have a family?" Tarlen asked the question softly, and the change of expression on the guard's face answered for him.

"Wife and a girl," he said.

"Then they might be alive!" Tarlen shouted, waking someone in the other room.

Penter shook his head. "No, son. They aren't. I found them. Parts of them, near the concourse. There's no happy ending for me, I'm afraid, and likely not for you either. Even if your sister or parents were taken, we can't save them."

"We have to try," Tarlen said, hearing the futility

behind his own words.

Penter surprised him by nodding. "Have something to eat. I'll pack some things. We'll head to the ocean."

Tarlen's enthusiasm flipped to dread as he thought about walking toward the terrible noise above the body of water. Even now, he heard it in the distance, a pulsing sound of fright. It was amazing how quickly something so scary could become background noise.

The cranky man passed a clay bowl with oats in it, and Tarlen ate it with a queasy stomach.

The journey took all day, and Tarlen's legs were aching, his sandal-covered feet blistering from the incessant walking. The star was low, shining brightly in his eyes. Most of the smoke had dispersed, the remnants of the attack all but gone from the air.

Hours ago, Tarlen had first seen the machine in the distance, hanging overtop the ocean like a hovering insect. It was massive, far greater than anything he'd ever seen, and he had no reference with which to compare it.

It was dark, gray, or maybe black. He couldn't quite tell then, but as they neared the water, he was sure it was slate gray. It was tall, with appendages jutting out at all angles, mostly from the top. Below, a crackling red power surged toward the water, creating a huge gaping maw in the liquid.

They were above sea level here, stopped finally by Penter.

"What is it?" Tarlen asked, not for the first time. Most of the journey had been quiet, filled with the occasional tidbit of each other's lives. Tarlen learned he hadn't lived much in his sheltered existence.

"Again, I don't know."

"Do you think it's emptying the ocean?" he asked the guard.

"Unlikely. It's something else. It's mining the ore below," Penter said, pointing at the red beam. "See how there are really two sides to the energy pulse?" He had to speak loudly over the screaming of the machine. It flashed every three or so seconds, blasting a piercing cry through the air.

Tarlen followed the man's finger, trying to see what he was explaining.

"The left side is lighter, the right darker. I think the ore is being carried on the right into the ship," Penter said.

Ship. "That's a ship? It's so huge," Tarlen said. The books he'd read always had starships that were long and lean, shiny and sleek, nothing like the atrocity here.

"That it is, son," Penter said.

"What do we do?" Tarlen asked.

"Wait. Build a camp. See what transpires. Stay out of their sight and see if we can find any Bacals working nearby," Penter said.

"Slaves?" The word felt dirty off his tongue.

"Slaves," Penter agreed.

Tarlen closed his eyes for a moment as the heat of the star vanished with its glow. A gentle breeze carried the salty scent of the ocean to his nose, and waves lapped against the rocky shoreline. If it wasn't for the screeching sound, Tarlen wouldn't have discovered that their world had been taken from them.

When he opened them, he thought he saw a tiny light flickering in close proximity to Malin. "Didn't you say all our power sources were fried?"

———

Yur Shen limped as he walked the corridors of Deck
Two. He'd been waiting for some time to receive the work
order on this deck, but from all the records he'd interpreted, the ship's crew was quite particular about who they
let in here.

Yur's supervisor, Olu, a cranky four-armed Desli
whose muscle had gone to flab years ago, had ended up
sick, giving Yur the opportunity to accept the task. He
grinned as he recalled sprinkling the powder into Olu's na-
tive beverage a day earlier. It turned out his benefactor was
right; Desli were extremely allergic to that spice.

As he thought about her, his communicator buzzed
lightly in his uniform pocket. This was most unusual. She
wasn't supposed to be contacting him for a few more days.

He glanced around the halls, seeing no one else nearby.
Deck Two had tall ceilings and sparse doors, as each room
containing the guts of the ship was isolated and removed
from the common crew. Everyone wanted a huge, well-
oiled cruise ship, but no one wanted to peek behind the
curtains to see how it all operated.

Yur slipped the device out carefully and held it in his
palm. A message spelled out in code, and he deciphered it
slowly.

Is the job done?

He shook his head and keyed in his response, using the
archaic symbols. The good news was, if anyone but him
tried to read a message, it wouldn't operate. It was linked
to his biometrics only. He sent the reply.

About to do the task now.

A few minutes went by, and he continued toward his
target. He was supposed to replace an air vent, but he
stopped at room ER-1.96514.

Be prepared. When I give the word, you kill it.

Yur thought about this. He knew he wasn't the brightest person in the universe, but logic prevailed. She wanted him to destroy this section of the engines, which he understood would wreak havoc on the Star Drive.

Where is my rendezvous? He sent the message, wishing he'd been smart enough to ask the question before.

You will be rewarded. Don't fret.

Yur stared at it, contemplating his options. What if this caused more damage than leaving *Constantine* stranded? It could set off a chain reaction, destroying the ball of Bentom, which in turn would kill him.

He didn't think she'd do that to him. He was too valuable an asset. She'd told him that before. Yur shook his head, angry at his own lack of faith in his boss. He typed a message and sent it.

It will be done.

Yur pressed a hand to the door of ER-1.96514 and, surprisingly, it was unlocked. With a quick glance toward the elevators, he entered the dark room. Soft yellow lights flicked on at his movement, and the thin hairs on the back of his hands stood up as the energy in the room hit him.

The space was massive: intricate wired panels lined the walls, each beeping and chiming as their red lights blinked continuously. He found what he was searching for in the far right corner of the room, and recognized the tubes. His cart was beside him, and he plucked the device he'd stowed inside, waiting for the right moment to use it, and activated it.

It beeped once, syncing with its pairing partner in his palm, and he crawled to the tubes, placing the device at the output tube where the other five coalesced. He double-checked to ensure the detonator was linked properly and rushed from the room, his leg aching.

Task complete. He sent the message and realized

something. The messages had been coming quickly. This meant his benefactor was close; otherwise, there would have been a longer delay.

As Yur walked toward the missing vent at the end of the corridors, it came clear. She was on this ship. This whole time, his boss had been on the *Constantine* with him.

He'd have no means of recognition, because he'd never seen her face. He wondered if he'd passed her in the corridors or perhaps seen her in the dining halls. A shiver of thrill coursed through Yur. He hoped she was pleased with his work.

———————

*I*t had been at least three years since Tom had lowered through the atmosphere of a new planet, one he'd never visited before. On the *Cecilia*, they'd been running along the Border, maintaining peace with Concord trading partners, ensuring pirate attacks were mitigated and everyone was safe. It was dutiful work, but it lacked the thrill of adventure and exploration that had drawn Tom to the Concord Academy in the first place.

The rush of seeing the landscape expand as they passed into the stratosphere filled his senses, pushing a delight through that made him feel like a new recruit again. This was why he'd joined, not because of who his grandfather was. Hell, even his parents hadn't enlisted, much to old Constantine Baldwin's chagrin.

His grandfather had dreamt that Cleo would join when she was a teenager. She ended up marrying an artist instead. Tom didn't remember much of his mom, just her blonde hair, always draping loose over her shoulders. She was warm to the touch, though her fingers were always chilled.

Tom could almost smell her, the most comforting scent of his existence.

His father he recalled even less. Short dark hair, stubble always on his chin. Crinkling eyes as he smiled at Tom, tousling his mop on his head. His fingers always had paint on them. Then his parents were gone, and Constantine took over raising him.

Tom wondered why he was being pulled into such a deep memory hole, and then it came back. The ship he was currently in was named after his mother. *Cleo*. The Concord had really done a number on him.

"Captain, we've arrived at Malin," Brax said, breaking the silence in the expedition ship.

"It's bad," Tom said, seeing the destruction all around. Over half the city appeared to be in ruins, various sections billowing smoke.

"It's recent," Brax said calmly.

"Send the drones, see if there are people around," Tom said, and instantly, their viewer showed images from four released cameras. They were tiny, sending details like temperature, air measurements, and barometric pressure through the ship's database for extrapolation.

"There," Brax said, nodding to the top left square on the viewer. It appeared to be a group of locals scrambling away from the city, heading the opposite direction from the ocean.

"Land," Tom said. "We need to learn what occurred. Those are… Greblokites, right?"

Ven chimed in from the bench behind them. "Bacals, sir."

"Fine. That is them?" Tom asked, squinting as he looked. It had to be. Everything they wore was a shade of beige, as if their entire wardrobe was made from the dust and sand they were surrounded by. Even from this high angle, Tom felt pity for the sad people. A little girl clutched something in her hand, and he used the camera's zoom feature, seeing her fall to her knees as the group climbed through a field of amber stone. A man leaned over, plucking the child into his arms, and he carried her as they traveled farther from the city.

"It's them. The Bacals," Ven said, now stating the obvious.

"They might think we're hostile." Brax flew in their direction, the drone moving to continue its search of the region. Their information was being processed inside *Cleo*'s software as they raced over the olden metropolis. As Constantine had told him, the city of Malin was ancient, and it was terrible to see such an old, established place destroyed.

"Then we'll have to be cautious," Tom said.

Brax landed the ship behind the group, who didn't appear to see them coming. The chief of security took the lead, the captain and Ven trailing behind.

It was evening, and the light was waning as they arrived at the locals. Tom had a gun at his hip but didn't expect to need it. His boots and pants were quickly covered in dust, each step kicking up more of the dirt. He couldn't imagine living among the desert like this. Where were the plants? He scanned the region, finding a few types of resilient plants, spikes sticking from their brown blotchy leaves.

The air burned slightly to breathe, but it was compatible with them and their physiology. A pulsing sound emanated from far away, traversing the distance until it was almost imperceptible from their position. It was coming from the direction of the ocean. That was where they had to go next. Tom expected they might encounter a battle when they did.

A gunshot rang out, an archaic system of propulsion and gunpowder, startling Tom with the loud noise.

"Stay down!" Brax shouted from the front of their group. He raised his hands in the sky, his huge gun set to the ground. "We're with the Concord. We're here to assist you!" he shouted this, his voice echoing across the rocks.

Tom glanced up to see the massive bald man walking closer to the source of the gunshot. He stood, confident the locals didn't mean them harm. "Let's go," he told the others, and they all cautiously stepped over the field of stones, careful not to catch a foot and twist an ankle.

The Bacals were very much human in appearance; oddly so. The Concord was full of many races, most bipedal and familiar, but other than the dark hair and thick eyebrows, these people could be from the same city as Tom.

A woman fell over crying, and a man helped her to her feet as they approached. Tom surveyed the hillside they'd stopped at and counted over twenty people.

"You came," a man said, his accent thick.

"You speak the language of the Concord," Tom said, and the man nodded.

"We learn from a young age. Our Regent, hail his eternal star, has always dreamed of joining your ranks. I suppose he died before it happened," the man said.

Brax and the guards were beside a group of locals, who were catering to a fallen child. Tom noticed the bloody torn bandage on the child's arm where part of their appendage was missing.

"I'm Captain Thomas Baldwin of the Concord cruise ship *Constantine*. We were meant to come as your welcoming party into the Concord, but communications ceased. Now we see why. What's your name?" Tom asked the man.

He was old, his back slightly bent, but his hair was unusually thick; his eyebrows danced as he spoke, gray speckled through them. He gave a bow of his head. "I'm Unif."

"And these people? Family?" Tom asked.

Unif's face grew sallow. "No. We are all mostly strangers. We found each other in the days after."

"What happened here?" Tom's voice was grave. "How long has it been?"

"We had our celebration four days ago," the man said. "The Regent announced we were joining, even though most of us already had an inkling. The word spread quickly."

"Then what?" Ven asked from directly beside Tom.

"They came from the sky," the man said before coughing roughly. One of the guards took water from his pack and passed it to the old man, who shared it with those around him before accepting a tiny serving.

"Who was it?" Tom asked him.

"We don't know. The ships… they were cylinders. They unleashed hell on our city," he said. "All our systems crashed instantly. Tell me, what of our other nations?"

Tom shrugged, inwardly cringing at the shape of the vessels. "We came here. There's no communication anywhere. I…" He glanced around at the expectant gazes of the kids and other people huddled at the hillside. "It's too soon to tell."

Cylinder-shaped ships. There hadn't been anything like that for a long time. It had been fifty years since the Statu War had ended, but the Concord had first seen the Tubers raiding a distant non-Concord world almost six decades earlier. The planet had hopes of joining their ranks, but an envoy had yet to travel there. He couldn't recall the name of the world.

"It couldn't be," Tom muttered to himself, and turned his attention to Unif once again. "And they laid waste? What of your…" He tried to remember their vessels' names, and it came to him. "Your Defenders?"

"Destroyed almost instantly. We never stood a chance," Unif said.

Brax was done replacing the wounded boy's bandage with a fresh one, and he'd given the kid a shot, which would quickly heal the harmed area. It was too late to help the loss of his hand.

"Unif, we're going to help you." Tom motioned for Brax to join him and Ven to the side, away from listening ears. "Ven, what do you think?" he asked the Zilph'i.

"I think they are speaking their truth, and we are facing an admirable adversary."

"How so?" Tom asked, not particularly liking the man's choice of words for the enemy.

"They managed to destroy all electrical components. We fabricated defenses against that a long time ago," Ven said.

Tom understood. "They likely didn't have such safeguards in place out here. Until they found out there was this superconductive ore beneath their oceans, this planet was destined for mediocrity forever. What they thought was the best thing that could possibly happen ended up being the opposite. It drew unwanted eyes to their planet. Damn it. If only we were a week earlier."

Ven crossed his long arms. "Captain, do you think we would have made a difference?"

"I would hope so," Tom said.

"If it's the Statu…" Ven started, and Tom cut him off.

"It can't be. They're destroyed, Ven."

"Captain, don't be so close-minded. The likelihood the Statu were actually destroyed is slim," Ven said, and Tom's head began to throb again.

"Look, my grandfather…" Tom's wrist vibrated, and he tapped it. "Go ahead, bridge."

"Sir, something is moving away from the ocean. It's…

big," Treena's voice told him.

Tom peered toward the water, which was at least thirty kilometers away. Even in the dusky skyline, he could see the outline of the ugly, gargantuan vessel.

"Sir, I think we've found the Statu again," Brax said, his voice surprisingly unwavering.

EIGHT

The sound of the pulsing ship stopped so suddenly, Tarlen nearly fell over.

"What's it doing?" he asked Penter, who was sitting along the edge of the cliff, observing the red beams pulling the ore from far below the surface. Waves were huge here, coming to splash all the way up the massive crag.

Penter moved away from the ledge, seeming to come out of a trance. His eyes were wide, his thick brow knotted and furled. "They're leaving." His voice was quiet against the lapping water, and both of them stood on the hard-packed cliff, watching as the red light flickered off, the pulsing sound no longer there.

Tarlen expected it to kick in again, to be bombarded by the noise and sights, but it didn't. The terrible vessel began to move from its hovering position near the water, and it kept moving higher and higher until he could no longer see it in the new night sky.

Were some of his people trapped on that ship? Was his family alive and enslaved? Tarlen felt so helpless as he slumped to the ground, unsure what he could possibly do.

Treena Starling ordered a full alert. The bridge erupted

into a bustle of activity as the immense vessel rose from far below.

"This is bad," Junior Officer Zane whispered from her helm position.

"Identify the vessel, please," Treena said to Chief Engineer Reeve Daak, whom she'd called from the "boiler room" when the others had departed to the surface.

"It's not on file, but judging by the appearance… it's Statu," Reeve said.

"That's what I thought," Treena said. "Weapons ready. Shields at full capacity."

"Done," Reeve said from her brother's usual station.

Treena considered firing everything they had on the ship, but there were too many unknowns. Doing so might spark an all-out war with a race they thought had been dealt with. In this case, she deemed it prudent to wait to see if they drew first blood.

"Shouldn't we hit them with the big guns?" Reeve asked.

The woman wouldn't have voiced her opinion so freely if it was Captain Baldwin leading the charge. "If we fire at them, the consequences could be dire for all of the Concord. Stand by." Treena watched as the vessel rose through the atmosphere and away from Greblok. A dozen or so ships released from its underbelly.

"They've sent a contingency of fighters," Zane advised.

"Zoom," Treena ordered, coming to stand directly behind the junior officer. The ships were cylindrical, clearly Statu Tubers. "Damn," she muttered.

She tapped the console in front of Zane. "Captain, come in."

"Go ahead, bridge." Tom's voice was oddly calm.

"Tubers. There's a dozen heading for us. I'd like to take them down, if it's all right with you," Treena said. She had the authority, but with Baldwin's connection to the Concord's most vindictive enemy of the last few centuries, she thought it best to get his approval first.

"Tubers. Damn it. Destroy them, Starling, and quickly. Don't let them get near my ship," Tom said.

"Yes, sir," Treena said. "You heard the man; hit them with everything this prize ship has to offer."

Treena wished Brax Daak was there. He was the most trained on the new weaponry, but his sister had obviously gone over the notes. Treena took control at the empty helm position and watched as the Tubers were targeted by the ship's tracking.

"If I may be of help, let me know." Constantine's AI appeared behind Treena, his arms crossed.

Three of the cylindrical vessels were destroyed in the first volley, and the rest were being picked off one by one as the cruise ship's defenses took over. Soon there was only one left, and it jumped from view.

"Where did it go?" Treena asked, trying to see it on the localized sensor map.

Reeve glanced over. The viewer changed camera angles, displaying the long alien ship attached to them. "It jumped into us, hitting our guests," she said quickly. The fire was quickly suppressed, as it found no oxygen to consume. *Constantine*'s passenger ship remained intact, but it was damaged at the tail end, near the cryopods.

"We have to save them," Nee said, coming to his feet.

"Go. Suit up. See what you can salvage," Treena said, wishing their expedition team would return.

The huge alien enemy vessel continued to move away, but no more Tubers came at the *Constantine*.

"Do we engage?" Reeve asked Treena, and she tapped her finger on the console, trying to decide if she would risk their crew on the departing Statu warship.

"Take us lower," Tom told Brax. "There." He pointed toward the cliffside, where two figures stood staring out at the dark ocean. The moon reflected off the deep water's volatile surface. Tom wouldn't have believed the sight if he hadn't witnessed the vessel leaving with his own two eyes.

"Captain, I think it wise we evacuate and return to our ship. The Concord is going to…" Ven began.

"The Concord needs to uncover exactly what happened, and these two would have seen it. Starling can take care of our people for another few minutes," Tom barked.

Brax set them to the rocky crag, aiming a headlight toward the figures. Tom exited the expedition ship, raising a hand in a universal sign of greeting. "We're here to help!" he shouted over the sound of their engines and the constant barrage of water against the cliff wall.

"Thank the Regent," a burly man said, shuffling over to Tom. Beside him stood a thin boy, dark hair and eyes on both of them telling Tom they were definitely locals.

"What happened?" Tom asked, nodding toward the water.

"They mined something. We saw it rising from under the waves, through a red beam and into the ship," the boy told him. His Standard was well spoken, with a hint of an accent.

"Captain, we need to leave!" Brax shouted as he ran from the ship. Ven was behind him, pointing at the dim skyline.

"Is that…?" Tom recognized the silhouette of the Tuber even from this distance.

"They're the ones that attacked us. They killed our

families. They're all gone," the boy said.

Tom saw a flash of pain over the older Bacal's face, his thick brow bunched in anger. He pulled a gun from his holster and ran toward the edge of the cliff as the Tuber neared them.

"Come on, we have to evacuate," Tom said, tugging on the boy's sleeve. The kid fought his efforts, shouting at the departed man.

"Penter, get over here!" the kid yelled.

Penter fired his small pistol toward the incoming ship, and Brax moaned, racing across the stone ground toward the local. He fired his own much larger XRC-14 at the Tuber as he called to the Bacal man.

Tom was already at their ship, Ven hopping in first, then dragging the kid inside. The Tuber was growing closer, and Tom wished Brax would either destroy the thing or come to his senses and run. When he realized neither of those options was being taken, Tom made a decision. "We have to fight the Tuber."

Ven nodded, lifting *Cleo* from the ground. It was too late. Even from here, their raised position above the cliff, he saw the constant pulse of Brax's weapon as it fired at the Tuber, the red blasts hitting a shield on the cylindrical ship.

"Ven, take them down!" Tom yelled, but a moment too late.

A beam cut out from the bottom of the Statu fighter, hitting Penter and Brax. One minute they were there; the next they were gone.

"Damn it! Ven, attack!" Tom ordered, but the Zilph'i didn't obey.

"Sir, the Statu initiated a molecular Mover, not a weapon. If we destroy them, we cannot retrieve Lieutenant Commander Daak," Ven said with little emotion.

Tom had almost forgotten about the Movers. "Bring us to *Constantine*." In a short hour, they'd learned what happened to their new Concord partners, found out their old enemy hadn't been wiped from existence as they'd thought, and Tom had managed to lose one of his executive lieutenants. It wasn't a great start to his first week as a captain.

———————

"Where's Brax?" Reeve asked the second the captain stepped onto the bridge.

Treena saw the pain in the woman's eyes.

"They took him." Tom didn't explain further. "Did you see the last Tuber come from the surface?"

The chief engineer nodded, her red eyes brimming with tears. "Yes, Captain."

"They used a Mover," Tom said, and the kid stepped around him, startling Treena.

"They took my friend Penter too. They might have my sister. They might have a ship full of my people still alive. They're going to make slaves out of them," the boy said, his words almost too quick to discern.

"Slow down," Treena told the kid. "Captain, this is huge. The Statu are back. We have to engage."

Baldwin shook his head. "We can't. Not when they have a ship full of Bacals." He glanced at the boy from the corner of his eye. "Not to mention the main reason the Concord wanted them to join in the first place."

"The ore?" Treena was fuming. "You're going to let them escape because they're carrying a load of conductive metal?"

Tom clenched his jaw in an already familiar gesture. He was telling Treena to stop testing his patience. She didn't care. Too many people had died at the Statu's hands. Her own lineage had more than their share of horror stories surrounding the bastards.

"You know it's more than that!" Tom shouted. Treena followed his gaze toward the zoomed-in image of the Statu ship. It smoothly glided farther away, in the direction of the moon, as a blue glow began beneath the vessel. The entire long ship shifted directions, making room for the massive thrusters on its underside. They pulsed: once, then twice, and the Statu vessel vanished.

Treena felt helpless as the ship escaped them. "We should have attacked. We shouldn't have let them leave." *Constantine* had them outgunned. That was the entire point of such a flagship. It was designed so they never had to worry about being overpowered again. It was supposed to be a new era, one of peace, but the Concord had been prepared for the worst.

"Then it's a good thing all our crew members are tagged, isn't it?" Tom wagged his eyebrows, and Treena jolted upright. He was right! This was new, and some races had objected – primarily the Callalay – but at this moment, Treena could understand the value.

Ven was already at the helm, using the computer to locate their chief of security. The map zoomed out, then farther. The path moved in a straight and definitive line.

"They're moving beyond the Border," Treena said, her hands clenching the top of Ven's headrest.

"Then that's where we go," Tom said. "Starling, come with me. We need to contact Admiral Hudson. Where's the doctor?" The captain looked around, and Treena realized she'd almost forgotten the attack on the alien vessel in all the excitement.

"Captain, our passenger ship was damaged by a suicidal Tuber. Doctor Nee went to see what they could salvage in regard to the cryopods," she told him.

"Of course he did. Ven, you have the bridge. Starling, let's see what we're dealing with." Tom started for the door when the kid's voice called out.

"Can I come with you?" the boy asked.

NINE

"What's your name, kid?" Tom asked the Bacal.

"I'm Tarlen, sir," he said, standing tall.

"Hurry along," Tom said, rushing through the corridors, the kid on his tail.

"Shouldn't we send him home?" Treena asked as they raced toward the cargo hold on Deck Five.

Tom shook his head. "There's not much left for Tarlen there any longer, is there?"

"No, sir. I want to help find your friend, and mine. Don't worry, Penter is a guard. He'll take care of your man," Tarlen said.

"That's good, because the moment he wakes up from the Mover's effects, Brax is going to be one angry Tekol. I wouldn't want to be on his wrong side when that happens," Tom told Tarlen.

The elevator stopped, letting them out on Deck Five, and the three of them entered the cargo hold to see Doctor Nee shouting orders. There were twenty or so crew members moving back and forth from the hatches, dragging cryogenic pods from transport ships.

"Report, Doctor," Tom said loudly enough for Nee to hear even among the clamor.

Doctor Nee turned. His usually perfectly-styled white hair was messy, his cheeks ruddy. "Captain, we managed to salvage over half of the pods. I hate to say it, but the others were destroyed in the attack. The ship is sealed off again, using a patch, but the damage was already done."

Tom flinched. They'd found an alien race and had managed to allow harm to befall them while the aliens were under their protection. It was going from bad to worse. He tried to think of a way to explain all of this to Admiral Hudson but failed at the moment. It was going to be a hard conversation.

The cargo hold was huge, thirty meters high, and twice as long and wide. There were nearly fifty cryogenic pods spread out in neat lines along the floor, their power sources stacked behind them. Tom didn't want to ask how painstaking of a process it had been to move them all here. The crew seemed exhausted from the endeavor.

"Doctor, this one is looking at me!" someone yelled from the center of the floor.

"What do you mean, looking at you?" Nee asked, his boots clanging against the floor as he rushed to the pod. Tom jogged over, Starling and the kid right behind.

Tom leaned over the pod, seeing the startled black eyes staring at him. "Is he awake?"

Nee was shoving the captain to the side, trying to open the pod. "We need to move it to my medical bay!" The pod's computer system was beeping, red lights flashing warnings Tom couldn't read.

"Then let's carry it there," Starling said, reaching for under the being's armpit.

Tarlen proved resourceful as he brought a four-wheeled platform cart over, and Tom and his commander settled the being on the cart while Doctor Nee fussed about the gaping alien. Its eyes were wide, fearful, and it gasped for breath. Nee pulled tubes free of its nose, which were little more than slits at the front of its face, slightly above its twitching mandibles.

It appeared to calm as it took deep breaths, its chest rising and falling beneath a dark brown jumpsuit.

"That's better. I'm Doctor Nee, and you are aboard a Concord cruise ship, the *Constantine*. We're going to make sure you and your friends are all right," Nee said with practiced expertise. Tom appreciated his candor.

The alien glanced around and attempted to lift its arm.

"Do you speak Standard?" Tom asked as its eyes settled on him.

It clicked an unfamiliar language. It tried to sit up, but the doctor was there, holding it down. Tom had no way to discern if it was male or female, or either. It glanced behind Tom to see the sprawling cryopods, and it clicked angrily. A hand flew up, grabbing Tom by the wrist, the grip tight enough to hurt.

"Calm down. We're helping!" Nee said, but it wasn't doing any good. Treena Starling placed two fingers on the alien, prying Tom away with unexpected strength.

Nee didn't wait for it to try again. He pressed a Medispray sedative against the creature's neck, and it instantly dropped hard against the cart. "So much for a breezy first contact," he said with a casual grin. "Let's get him to med bay where I can run some tests. See what we're working with."

Tom rubbed his wrist and saw Tarlen standing aside, staring at the alien with interest. "Come on, kid. Let's help the good doctor and find you somewhere to stay."

A few hours later, Tom waited for Treena Starling in his office. He was exhausted but didn't dare attempt to sleep before touching base with Admiral Hudson. Apparently, the man was recently indisposed, and Tom hated being blown off by the Concord at a time like this. What could possibly be bigger than the Statu's return?

A bell chimed, and Tom tapped a button on his desk,

sending the doors open. "Come in, Treena." He pointed to the chair opposite him. "How are you holding up? Not quite what we signed up for, is it?" he asked, attempting to make conversation.

"It kind of is… I mean, when we signed up for the Concord Academy. This trip, on the other hand, has been unexpected. Do you really believe it's them?" she asked. She looked so young, her hair pure blonde, her face unblemished. He ran a hand over his chin, feeling the stubble coming in. He almost thought about leaving to freshen up before the call came in from the admiral, but shoved the thought to the side.

"It has to be. I saw the Tuber with my own eyes. It used a Mover to take Brax and the Bacal. It's them," Tom said, wishing it wasn't true.

"How did this happen?" she asked.

"How did what happen?" Admiral Hudson's image appeared on the screen on the wall. He looked tired, matching Tom's mood.

"The Statu have returned, sir," Tom told him.

"I was hoping we'd heard wrong. Someone's in the room with me, Tom." The image zoomed out, revealing an old Callalay woman.

"It's an honor, Prime Pha'n," Tom said.

"This is Captain Thomas Baldwin, and his Commander Treena Starling," the admiral said, and the leader of the Concord nodded her greeting.

"Tell us what you saw," she said in Standard, her voice hard and weathered.

Tom advised them what had happened to Greblok. About the abduction of Lieutenant Commander Brax Daak, and the old ship full of unidentified beings in cryotubes. They listened without a word as he reported, and their lack of reaction said more than words could have.

"Good, very good work. Do you think they cleaned Greblok out of the ore?" the Prime asked.

"What…? I don't know. The ship was massive enough to hold an extensive amount," Tom said.

"Then Greblok is no longer needed," the admiral said softly, just loud enough for Tom to hear the words. His eyes crinkled as he leaned away. "Return to Nolix at once."

"Sir, is that all you have to say? We might have been at ground zero of a new war or the continuation of an existing one," Tom said, feeling his temperature rising.

"Baldwin, do you think we gave you that ship to be foolish? You return to Nolix and don't question me again," Hudson said. The Prime shook her head slowly, as if silently chiding Tom's disobedience.

He'd heard enough. "Yes, sir," he said, ending the call.

"What the hell was that?" Starling asked.

"That was the Concord giving us direct orders," Tom said.

"We can't leave. What about Brax? He's out there. We can track them. Use the expedition ship to rescue him," she said, standing up and resting her palms on his desk.

Tom didn't reply as he silently assessed the information. The admiral hadn't even appeared surprised by the news. His words stung Tom's ego. He knew there was a reason he'd been chosen as captain of their new flagship, and it had everything to do with his name, and nothing to do with his personality.

"We're far closer to them, sir. If we head to Nolix and wait for the Concord to send anyone after the bastards, it'll be a month before they reach him, if they even bother," Treena said.

"We don't really know each other, Treena." Tom wished they'd had longer together as a crew. "What will the crew think if we obey our orders and leave?"

Treena didn't answer right away. She hesitated, waiting a good thirty seconds before saying anything. Tom waited for her to speak, not wanting to rush her. "They'll accept the orders."

It wasn't what he'd been expecting. "But will they accept me as their captain?"

"They already have, sir. From my experience, you're bound to upset more of our crew by disobeying direct orders, especially ones from Admiral Hudson," she told him.

Tom leaned away. "He *is* only one of ten admirals," he said softly, as if that changed anything.

"But he's the oldest, the most battle-hardened. He was there…" Treena said, not having to remind him that Hudson was his grandfather's second-in-command during the War.

"That's what I don't understand. If he was there and saw the destructive capabilities of the Statu firsthand, why didn't he react differently? Why wouldn't the Prime want us to investigate further?"

"Because they spent a lot of resources on this ship and likely don't want it gallivanting off, never to be seen again," Treena said.

"What do you think we should do?" Tom asked, trying to read her. She was different, her expressions often hard to make sense of.

"I… can I speak candidly, sir?" she asked.

"Go for it."

"I think something strange is going on here, and frankly, I'm angry that we aren't in the know. They gathered us together to be a show crew, having Ven included, and the twins. Baldwin's grandson, and…" Treena stopped.

"And you. What makes you so special, Treena?" Tom asked, not trying to offend her, but wanting to understand the scenario.

She stared blankly at him before standing up. "There's something you'd better look at."

"Do we really have time for this, Commander?" Tom was losing patience. He needed to decide whether to belay the admiral's orders or set course for Nolix. Then there were the cryopod passengers to consider.

"You're going to want to see this," she said, and he joined her as she left his office. They didn't talk as they moved through the ship, heading to the executive suites. His was at the other end from hers, separated by a meeting room, giving him added privacy.

Treena's was on the opposite corner of the deck, tucked away past Brax's room, which for now was empty. She stopped at her door, staring him in the eyes. "I can't believe they didn't tell you about... my circumstance," she said, using the console outside her room to open the door.

It was dark inside, but Tom instantly heard the subtle sound of machines at work. A hum of energy cascaded across the floor, settling in his ears. "What is this?" he asked, looking around blindly while his eyes acclimated.

"This is my room. And that..." She stepped through the living space and through another door, waiting for him. "Is me."

He saw the body on the bed and audibly gasped in shock. The woman wore a medical gown. Her face was thin, her hair half-burned off. Her eyes were closed as her face tilted toward the ceiling. Behind her head, a cable plugged into her spine. "I don't understand."

"Captain Thomas Baldwin, meet the real Treena Starling," she said, her voice cracking at the introduction.

He didn't reply as his heart thrummed loudly in his ears. "You almost died. I always knew that. Why didn't I question how you looked... so perfect." He reached out, touching the withered body's hand on the bed. "I've heard of this sort of transferred cognitive function, but never so flawlessly. I thought they were years, decades from this."

"I guess not," Treena said, casting her gaze aside.

"Why didn't they tell me?" Tom asked her.

She shrugged. "No one informed me whether you were aware or not. I assumed that by now you would have mentioned it or stared at me more inquisitively. The doctor is the only one that has knowledge of this. And Reeve, since he couldn't keep it to himself."

"May I?" he asked, stepping closer to her android body.

She didn't move aside, and Tom felt strange as she stuck an arm out. He touched the skin, pressed his finger into her forearm, and sighed. "What does this change?" he asked, wondering why now was the time to show him.

"You wanted to understand why they chose me for the crew. I'm something new. Something shiny, just like you and this ship. We can't start off as a crew by letting one of our team be abducted. We need to go after Brax Daak, sir," she told him.

Suddenly, the room felt too small, too stuffy, and the constant beeping of the machines was overwhelming. "And when we arrive? How do we extract him out of there?"

Treena smiled. "Leave that to me."

Tom nodded, not only hoping that this decision wasn't going to get them killed, but that it wouldn't start a war that the Concord couldn't afford to lose.

Brax woke with a start. He was blind. His hands flew

before his face, jamming against something hard and damp. He groaned and turned his head away, seeing a blinking light some distance away. He wasn't blind after all. That was a good sign. Slowly, his eyes grew accustomed to the dim light, and he listened to the sounds around him, before he could see them.

Breathing. There was the constant sound of other people's lungs. In and out. In and out. That would explain the moisture on the walls. The lumpy floor he was able to see began to make sense. They were bodies.

He was beside a wall and had woken facing it. He made as little noise as possible as he sat up, not wanting to alert his captors to the fact he was awake. *What is this?* He tried to recall what had occurred, but struggled to.

Brax saw Tom's face, and remembered being on Greblok. The big local man had run to the cliff's edge, and Brax had followed him, trying to destroy the Tuber with his XRC-14. It had been a dumb move. Sure, during the War they'd managed to take a few of the enemy vessels down from ground support, but it wasn't common. And most of those Tubers hadn't been equipped with Movers.

Movers. He'd read the reports, witnessed the testimonials of what it felt like to be transported molecule by molecule by one of them, and he patted his body for reassurance. There were stories of people being moved and missing limbs afterwards. Some even lost organs. He assumed he'd know if he was lacking one of those. He'd likely be a pile on the ground, unmoving.

Someone called out from beside him. "Keep it down," Brax said through his teeth.

"Who… where are we?" the woman's voice asked, and he reached for her, placing his big palm over her face.

"Sister, you need to be quiet. What's the last thing you remember?" he asked, still trying to shake the fuzz from his own brain.

"I… we were watching the Regent. They came from the skies." She was crying now, a soft sobbing sound. "They killed so many. My husband."

"But they took you?" he asked quietly.

"I guess so."

Brax could see more clearly, and tried to assess the situation. They were in a cargo hold of some sort; the ceiling was around ten meters high. Cool air blew from vents above, and Brax assumed the same vents could press through a toxic gas if the group was deemed dangerous.

The room appeared to be rectangular, approximately forty meters long and thirty wide. People were scattered around the floor, most in uncomfortable positions, like they'd been dropped from a ways up while unconscious. He thought of the rag doll Reeve had had when she was a little girl. He used to torment it just to make her angry.

Another groan from nearby, and Brax saw the thick-browed guard from Greblok rise, rubbing his eyes with dirty hands. His eyelids went wide as he spotted Brax, who gave him a wave. "Your sight will improve," Brax told him, and he nodded wordlessly.

Brax felt for his gun on the floor, but it was gone. "Gun?" he asked the other man, and he saw the guy check his belt and shake his head.

"Gone."

"They must have walked through, picking us clean." Brax wasn't surprised. The Statu were a devious bunch. He'd heard rumors of them testing the Movers on larger scales during the War, but then no one had heard of the technology again for the next five decades. He was sure the Concord wanted the ability to transport matter, and was honestly surprised they hadn't found a way to steal the concept and utilize it.

Reeve had always been going on about it a decade ago, while she was finishing her engineering dissertation. Brax had been forced to hear all about future Concord technology concepts for a good two weeks, until she'd grown distracted with something else.

Now he wished he'd listened closer, and part of him wished his genius sister was with him to help navigate his current scenario. He did have a tracker in him, so the ship would be aware of his location. Were the Statu aware the Concord added the nanodevice to each Academy graduate? Brax doubted it.

Anything to have the upper hand. That's what his old professor would say. *When faced with impossible odds, choose to play a different game.* It was an old Code saying from years ago, but it still rang true. He needed to figure out their game, and flip it on its head.

Other people were coming to. They must have dosed the first batch harder than him and the guard. "What's your name again, friend?" Brax asked the man.

"Penter," he said.

"I'm Brax. We're going to try to keep everyone calm. I think there are around two hundred of your people in this hold at the moment. We have to be in a room on their main ship, the huge beast we saw lifting from the ocean. There will be other rooms like this, filled with more people," he told the man, who nodded along.

"What do they want with us?" Penter asked.

"Good question. If I were to guess, they wanted your ore, and they beat the Concord to it. They likely figured they may as well take some spoils of war with them," Brax said.

"Meaning?" Penter was frowning, scanning the room uneasily.

"Slaves. They wanted slaves." Brax hated the sound of

it, and it took a moment for him to even place himself into the same category as the rest of the captured Bacals. He was in the same boat as them, hurling through space on a terrible vessel, destined for a faraway world, likely well past the Border.

When it all dawned on him, he noticed his hand begin to shake, his heart threatening to burst from his chest. He closed his eyes, taking deep breaths. Four counts through his nose. Pause for two. Breathe out the mouth for six beats. He repeated the process and felt control return.

He had to be calm, for the sake of the rest of them. They were in this together. "Penter, we need to recruit some people to help the others. Let's find anyone with medical experience."

Brax and Penter began the slow process of moving through the captives as they were awakening, scared and in shock. He could only hope the *Constantine* knew he'd been captured, and not vaporized on that cliffside.

TEN

Tarlen lay in his soft bed, staring up at the manufactured ceiling. It was smooth and white; lights were built into it, recessed and giving off a soft yellow ambiance. He couldn't keep his eyes shut.

It was the first time he'd slept anywhere but inside a stone and mud building, always either his old home or at a friend's place. Now he was in a brand-new starship... in space. It was both exhilarating and scary at the same time, and he didn't know whether to laugh or cry at his scenario.

"Could be worse, Tarlen," he told himself, thinking about the people he'd witnessed being torn apart by the brutal red beams of the cylinder ship's gunfire. He wondered if there was a chance his family had been abducted rather than killed in the slaughter of his people.

The concept had been so foreign to Tarlen before. Greblok was an old world, instilled on value, ethics, and care for one another. The Statu had stolen that from them, destroyed his people, and for what? Metal? He hated them, and as he lay in bed, staring at this odd rounded ceiling in a bed that was too soft, in a spaceship that frightened and thrilled him, Tarlen vowed revenge.

But what could he do? He was a boy, hardly past his sixteenth star, with no way to fight them. He sat up, gazing around the room, and wondered why he, of all his people, had managed to gain entrance to a great Concord vessel.

There had to be a reason for his stroke of luck.

He was meant to help them, to become something greater than he'd ever imagined. Or maybe it was sheer happenstance that he was alive, with his very own room aboard the *Constantine*.

Tarlen wondered what time it was on the surface of his planet. In all the excitement of the last two days, his internal clock was turned upside down, but he was tired. He still couldn't sleep.

His quarters were almost half the size of his entire house back in Malin. There was a couch, a small kitchenette, and its own bathroom. He'd never had his own anything before. Tarlen threw the lush covers aside, the air cooling his skin. He saw a pile of clothing near the door, and reached for them, finding a Concord uniform in roughly his size. The black pants were slim, but a little loose around his thighs. He slipped into the shirt, a green color denoting rank, though he wasn't familiar with the colored system.

Tarlen stared in the mirror, seeing the Concord crest on his chest. Yes, he wanted this. It felt so right. He didn't know the meaning behind the ship over a moon, but he intended to find out. He felt the urge to learn everything about the great Concord his people were about to enter into a treaty with.

Tarlen attempted to fix his unruly hair, running a hand through the thick black tresses. Soon it was passable, though not in style with anyone he'd seen on board so far. Many of the crew were bald, being from various alien races he wasn't familiar with. Many were hard to differentiate, and others were quite obvious, like the albino man he'd met with Captain Baldwin.

He walked to the door and stood there, wondering how it opened. He felt like a fool, unsure how to operate something so simple and mundane. Eventually he remembered seeing the officer touch something – or did she speak to it?

"Door, open," he said, and he jumped away as the panel slid into the wall. He tried not to think about how much Belna would love being able to boss inanimate objects around.

The corridor was quiet. It appeared that people were either sleeping or on duty, and he turned his head from side to side, trying to decide in which direction to walk. He felt like he was doing something wrong as he started away from his room, even though he'd been told he had free access to the ship, as long as he stayed out of the way. The captain had winked at him when he'd given the order, and it made Tarlen like him even more.

Tarlen walked past the last of the crew quarters wing, and entered a foyer that ended with three elevators. He pressed a button like he'd seen the captain do, and waited until the door on one of the lifts opened. The elevator was empty, and Tarlen stepped into the bright box.

"What deck?" a woman's voice asked.

"Uhm…" Tarlen stammered, wondering where it was he was going. Then he recalled the affable doctor, and pondered what was happening with the alien from the cryopod. "Where's the doctor?"

"Deck Four," the computer replied.

"Then take me to Deck Four, please," Tarlen said politely.

The elevator moved, and stopped seconds later. "Thank you," he told the computer, and a man with a blue collar eyed him suspiciously as he entered the elevator afterward, as if wondering who Tarlen had been speaking with.

He kept his head down and saw it was busier here at

this time. The mess hall was to his right, and he went there, smelling food. A nice Callalay woman had brought him here hours ago, and his stomach was already grumbling again. There were a few officers in uniform inside, sitting at long tables, chatting amongst each other.

There was a tension in the air noticeable even to Tarlen's naïve eyes. These people were worried about the Statu, and from what Tarlen had witnessed, they had every right to be.

Tarlen stuck his head in the door, and when he smelled roasting meat, his stomach led him the rest of the way. He listened as he found the line, grabbing a plate before piling food on it with tongs.

"We can't go after them," one man said at a table behind Tarlen. "We'll be killed."

A woman responded, "Have you seen this ship? Do you think their primitive technology is any match for *Constantine*?"

"Are you forgetting that our chief of security isn't even on board any longer?" the man countered.

Tarlen knew they were speaking about Brax Daak, the man who had disappeared while attempting to help Penter fight the cylinder ship. What had they called it? A Tuber?

"What does that change? Then we go track them down, end what we thought Constantine Baldwin did fifty years ago, and return home heroes," the woman said, and Tarlen saw the happiness in her eyes as he sneaked a peek.

"You going to gawk, or move along, JOT?" someone said behind Tarlen. He turned to see a Zilph'i man, twice his own height and thin as a reed. His bald head was oblong, like it was stretched and pulled.

"JOT?" Tarlen asked, feeling like he was being insulted.

"Who are you? JOT. You know, junior officer in

training. Aren't you a little young for that uniform?" the Zilph'i asked.

It finally clicked. "Oh, this…" He tugged on the green collar. "I'm Tarlen."

The tall man nodded. "Vor."

Tarlen finally moved along, placing more food on his plate.

"Care to breakfast with me?" The Zilph'i was adding foods Tarlen wasn't accustomed to. It appeared the mess hall was a place where all crew members could find food from their home worlds. While there were no Greblok delicacies, he found the basic vegetable dishes easy on his stomach and eyes.

"That would be appreciated," Tarlen said, following the lanky man from the buffet-style serving section to an empty table. There were only about twenty crew members in on this off hour, and Tarlen was glad for it. He could still hear the conversation at the other table.

"I heard we were ordered to return," the man who'd been talking earlier said, hardly loud enough for Tarlen to hear.

"Nonsense. The captain wouldn't belay orders from Nolix," the woman said.

"You're right. I can't believe this is our first mission. I should have stayed on *Nevilon*," the man said.

Vor glanced at the two officers having the conversation, and peered at Tarlen as he poked a long bean with his utensil. "Do not heed their concern. We'll be fine. We're aboard the greatest cruise ship ever constructed. There's a reason we were sent here, I imagine."

"How do you mean?" Tarlen asked.

"Do you know much of my people, the Zilph'i?" the man asked, picking up a wriggling worm-like morsel with his fingers.

Tarlen tried to keep the revulsion from his face. "No. I'm from Greblok. We don't have much access to other worlds."

"Greblok? That explains many things, young Tarlen. Then this is far more prudent of a conversation for you to hear. It is oft said, in my culture, that the Vastness has more intricate plans for our race, and specifically, the Concord. We are but tiny specks of dust in the ever-expanding expanse." Vor spread his hands out, long fingers stretching over the neighboring chairs beside him.

"That doesn't make me feel any better," Tarlen told him.

"It wasn't intended to ease your mind. Rather, the prospect is meant to remind us that there are bigger things at play than our lives. The War was devastating. We lost billions around the Concord and over one hundred cruise ships, each with full crews. It was a time of death and destruction, but also of learning. We were resilient against the efforts of the Statu.

"Sometimes people feel as though the War happened so long ago, when in reality, it was but a moment in the grand scheme of our Vastness. It was a mere blink of the eye for Time, and they weren't wiped out as we were told," Vor said softly.

Tarlen found himself at ease with the odd man. "But there was only one ship."

Vor raised his hand, tilting it to the side so Tarlen could only see his smallest finger from the edge. "What appears as one is often more." Vor began to wiggle the other five digits, and Tarlen had to count twice to see the man had five fingers and a thumb on each hand.

"You're saying there will be more than the single ship that not only destroyed my people, took slaves, and stripped Greblok of its greatest mineral asset?" Talen asked.

"I am afraid to admit that I think so."

"If there are more of those…" Tarlen tried to imagine a dozen of the immense ugly ships arriving at a planet, fifty ships just like *Constantine* defending the world below.

Vor nodded. "We are immersed in the War, it appears. It never ended, but only paused. *Time goes on in the Vastness. Nothing ever starts or finishes, only continues.*"

"Is that from your books?" Tarlen asked.

"Yes. It's an ancient Zilph'i saying, taken by the Concord for their Code," Vor said with a hint of distaste.

"What of the man I met? Ven?" he asked, curious of the pale-skinned man.

"Ven? You have met Ven?" This Zilphi's eyes grew wide, his pupils dilated.

"Sure," Tarlen said.

"Then you truly lack knowledge of our people."

"That's what I said." Tarlen ate some of the meat, cutting it before testing the tender square. It was delicious.

"The Ugna is a rare genetic deformity among the Zilph'i," Vor told him.

"He's sick?"

"Nothing like that. He is elevated. The Ugna are born one in forty million on our world. They have abilities beyond our comprehension. They're raised in a secreted-away school for three decades while they harness their abilities. I have never met one of the Ugna, but I should much like to."

"What kind of abilities do they have?" Tarlen was curious. It sounded like something out of one of his books.

"They can move objects with their minds. The Ugna can read people and situations differently than most," he said.

"How?" Tarlen asked, and he saw from the look in

Vor's eyes that the man didn't have the answer.

"That is not for us to comprehend. Tell me of your people, young Tarlen," Vor said.

Tarlen ate the rest of his meal as most of the remaining people in the mess hall left, some starting and others ending their shifts on the great starship. He told Vor about his people, then his family, and it felt good to remember what he was going to be fighting for.

———

"*C*an we do that?" Reeve asked the captain.

Treena studied the man from his seated position at the end of the table.

"Yes, Lieutenant Reeve, we can," he said with conviction.

"This is unprecedented, is it not?" Ven asked.

Of all their executive officers, Treena had expected the strange telekinetic man to object the loudest. To her and the others' surprise, he seemed open to the idea of disobeying the Concord's leading politician and eldest admiral.

"Actually, there have been three cases of direct insubordination on file," Reeve said, making Treena stifle a laugh. There really was no end to the information in the woman's memory banks. She countered the intelligence with a playful nature that drew people to her. Treena was starting to enjoy her company.

"Three cases," Captain Baldwin said. "That's… fewer than I imagined." He rubbed his temples. "It's already been decided. We go after them. I apologize for the delay, but with the recent development with the strangers on board, and the postponement in communicating with the Concord, we're twelve hours behind the Statu vessel."

"Good. It gives us time to plan instead of reacting," Reeve said. She spun in her chair, making a full circle.

Ven watched the Tekol engineer. "Please inform us about these three cases of insubordination."

Reeve stopped fidgeting and stared at the Ugna man. "The *Nexi* ignored orders to guide an envoy of Oslio across the Border, and the diplomats were boarded, killed, then robbed."

Treena remembered that story from her training. The captain of the *Nexi* had a personal relationship with the Oslio leader that ended bitterly, causing him to refuse the mission. He'd not only been relieved of his duty, but he was also charged in the destruction of the Oslio ship, and to her understanding, continued to live out his days as an old man in one of their prisons.

"Yes, I recall that," Captain Baldwin said. "What were the others?"

"I don't think reliving prior insubordinates is going to help in any way, Captain," Reeve said. "My brother is with those bastards, and we're missing the fact that the Statu have returned after all this time. Perhaps we should be asking someone about them, someone who was there."

Treena glanced at the Tekol engineer; her red eyes were darker than normal today. "We don't have anyone on board that was around during the War."

Thomas Baldwin smacked a palm on the table. "We do." He came close to a smile, but Treena knew the situation was too dire for any sort of amusement. "Constantine!"

The AI appeared in the corner of the room. He looked so lifelike, and Treena felt a strange connection to the artificial man.

"Yes, Captain?" Constantine asked.

"Please, have a seat with us." Baldwin motioned to an

empty chair around the table opposite himself.

Constantine flickered and appeared in the seat. Treena hadn't seen him sit before, but if she didn't know better, he was just another human at the table with them.

"How much of my grandfather is in there?" the captain asked.

"As I told you before, all the strategic and…"

"So you remember fighting the Statu?" Reeve cut in.

"I do. Like it was yesterday, Chief Engineer Daak." His voice was as smooth as his skin.

"They're back. As you are aware," Thomas told the AI, who didn't react to the news. He was part of the ship, and would have heard this already. "We need to know everything you can tell us about them."

Constantine Baldwin's AI form sat straight-backed and began talking. "The Statu are an ancient race from a distant galaxy. We never did find their home system, not even after dismantling the countless vessels we salvaged during the War. There were no active starmaps indicating where they came from. It was as if they appeared out of thin air, attacked Cidas Twelve, and enslaved the race of Yu'ov."

"That was the first reordered invasion, correct?" Treena asked.

"That's correct. The Yu'ov weren't part of the Concord, and no one was aware of the disruption for a decade, amazingly enough," Constantine said.

"They used the slaves to build Tubers?" Baldwin asked.

Treena drummed her fingers on the table. They knew all this. It was ingrained in their minds from training at the Academy. With the Concord, history was important. A specific phrase from the Code stood out at that moment to her: *Without the past, there is no determining the outcome of the future.* This was one of those times. They needed to understand the Statu's motivations in order to stop them.

"Constantine, you had more experience fighting them than any Concord captain. You defeated them in the epic battle at the Yollox Incursion. What were they after? Why did they wreak havoc on the Concord?" Treena asked, and the room went silent, everyone awaiting the AI's reply.

"The Concord will say it wasn't personal with the Statu, that they were doing it because their race demanded expansion," he replied.

"And you? What would you say it was?" the captain asked.

"They were malicious. They didn't bend, ever. They threw their people and ships against us with reckless abandon, as if they didn't care if they survived," Constantine said, making Treena think of the Tuber that had flown directly into the alien vessel they were harboring, destroying itself in the process.

"Why have we never seen them?" the captain asked.

Treena thought back to her studies on the War. The Statu were always in gray armor, and any captured vessel was only inhabited by suits filled with unidentifiable liquid organic matter. It was sickening. The first time Treena had seen the pictures of the ooze pouring from an opened suit, she'd almost thrown up.

Constantine squinted and stared hard at the captain. "This may be overstepping protocol, sir, but…"

"Get on with it," Baldwin said impatiently.

"We've seen them, sir," Constantine said.

"What do you mean?" Reeve leaned forward.

Ven hadn't said anything in a long time, and Treena noticed his black eyes flick between the AI and the captain with interest.

"We've seen one of the bodies."

Tom stood up, his fists clenched at his sides. "Constantine, can you stop being so dramatic and tell us what the hell you know?"

"Yes, sir. It was during the Yollox Incursion, near the end. I led an attack against the lead ship over Yollox, and we disarmed it after taking a barrage of fire. Our fighters were depleted, and so were their Tubers. We were evenly matched that day, but we won out, getting a lucky shot on their shield generator. Once we took that down, we fired our pulses, shutting their energy power source off," Constantine said.

"And you boarded them? Why?" Treena asked.

Constantine's AI stared back with pale blue eyes, his face slack. "I was ordered to destroy every last ship they sent against us, but my gut was telling me there was an answer on one of their warships. We filed aboard, sending our entire security team there with the intent of taking one of them alive. I joined them."

"That hadn't been done before, correct?" Reeve asked.

"That's correct."

"And you found one?" It was Thomas' turn to ask.

The AI nodded. "We'd come to realize their suits were loaded with an injector. Should danger befall them, the suit would press the needle into their chest, essentially melting them, making their DNA unreadable. It was the strangest measure we'd ever seen. Drastic, to keep their identities hidden, and we never understood why."

Thomas remained standing, and he leaned over the table, hands on the hard surface. "And one of the needles failed?"

The AI nodded again. "We found one of the Statu. I had my executive lieutenant remove the helmet." Constantine stared across the room at the screen showing space and Greblok in the distance. If Treena didn't know better, he was far more than an AI representation of the man; he *was* Constantine Baldwin. If they could make Treena alive with a machine, what could they do with Thomas' real grandfather's memories?

They waited, Treena subconsciously holding her breath.

"It was a human. There was a human inside the Statu suit," Constantine said.

ELEVEN

"Where are they bringing us?" Abbil asked. The woman had come a long way in the short hours since she'd awakened in a panic beside Brax.

"I have no idea," Brax admitted.

So far, no one had entered the room they were all waiting in. Brax had done a head count, and there were two hundred and eleven of them filling the space. Twelve were dead, and Brax and Penter had helped separate the bodies from the others.

He glanced at the corner of the room where the lifeless lay, the others giving the dead wide berth. Three people were missing pieces of their bodies. One man, a foot; a hand on a child; and an ear on an older woman. The wounds were cauterized, but it was only something to worsen their already tragic tales.

"I'm going to search for a door again," Penter said, walking the perimeter of the room. Brax had nothing better to do, so he started in the opposite direction, slowly and painstakingly combing the wall for signs of an opening. The walls had sharp edges, the entire surface bonded together with a strong compound. He was careful to avoid cutting himself, and by the time he met Penter on the other side, they were both exhausted and angry.

"If they don't give us water, I suspect there will be more deaths soon," Penter said, and it was as if they were listening.

The ceiling spread apart directly in the center of the room, and Brax urged the resting Bacals away from the incoming gray-armored suits. No wonder they hadn't found any doors. They were below the ceilings. A platform lowered, with the Statu standing around it. There were four of them, thin guns in the outer two's hands. They didn't speak as the second pair rolled a cask of liquid forward, setting it down with a ladle on top.

"Where are we going?" Brax dared ask, standing tall. He was taller than any of the Statu, almost by a head, but they were armed, and he was in no position to make demands. But they ignored him and returned to the platform.

"You bastards! You killed my family!" a Bacal man shouted, running at the Statu. He was dead instantly as a beam struck his chest. The left Statu only fired once, directly at the man's head, and waved the gun around after the body hit the floor, as if to challenge anyone else. When the entire crowd remained still, they lifted away, leaving their captives alone once again.

"Damn it!" Penter said, rushing to the body. The man was obviously dead, and the people nearby were eager to move away from the corpse. "Such a shame. What did he expect to do?"

Brax felt for the victim. He'd been filled with such a rage that all logical actions were pressed aside. The dead man had only thought of his family, and now he would join them in the Vastness, if one were to believe in the Zilph'i ways.

"Help me move him," Brax said, not wanting to trouble the other Greblok folks with the burden. Penter grunted as they heaved the body to the edge of the room. That made thirteen.

They returned to find the cask already opened, people

drinking from the barrel, shoving at one another.

"Everyone back!" Brax shouted, taking charge. "You're acting like animals."

The people ceased shoving one another and stared hard into his eyes.

Penter stood beside Brax, helping him out. "What's happened to you all? Is this how a Bacal deals with adversity? No! We'll get through this. If you haven't met him, this is Lieutenant Commander Brax Daak of the new Concord flagship, the *Constantine*. Yes, the very same name as the great Captain Constantine Baldwin. We've all heard the stories of the Concord's victory over the Statu, and his own grandson is now in charge of the ship. He *will* come for us. Greblok was to be ushered into the Concord, and they won't turn their backs on us."

Brax was surprised by how much information Penter had absorbed in their brief discussions over the last few hours, but he had a way with words, for a guard. Brax saw hope flash across some of the faces nearby, and he hoped that the captain was going to help them. He wasn't holding his breath, but in the meantime, these people needed him.

"That's right." He stood in front of the water and tried to smile. "Everyone, please form a line. There's enough water for all. If you can't stand in line, raise your hand and we'll bring it to you."

Brax wondered how many of them were on this ship, and where they were being taken.

———

*T*arlen had managed a few hours of sleep and returned to his investigation of the ship. He'd been on Decks Seven and Eight, observed the training facilities, had been banned from entering the fancy restaurant in its off hours, and discovered a study hall and library where one could research anything in peace.

He was now on Deck Three – under the courtyard, he thought – at the edge of the starship, and he stopped a man he understood to be a Callalay walking by, a tablet in his hand.

"Excuse me," he said.

"What can I do for you?" the man asked.

"What's in there?" Tarlen pointed at the wall. There were huge doors leading to it, but he couldn't seem to access them.

"That's the hangar where we keep the fighters. Are you a JOT?" the Callalay man asked with a smile.

"In a way," Tarlen said, indicating his green collar. If it could get him into the hangar, he'd have said anything.

"How about I show you?" The man folded the tablet and clipped it to his belt, moving to the doors. He leaned over, staring at a computer screen. "Clearance 9651332."

"Welcome, Lieutenant Basker," the computer said, and the doors hissed wide.

Tarlen stepped inside, and his jaw dropped. This was the biggest room he'd ever seen. Five amazing ships were parked inside, and the room was dimly lit.

"This is the hangar," the man told him. "We have five fighters. Normally, there would be around twenty or so on a cruise ship."

"Why are there so few?" Tarlen asked.

"This was an unexpected mission, rushed out, and it was only supposed to be a diplomatic visit, welcoming Greblok into the Concord," the man said. "Go ahead. I can see you're interested."

Tarlen didn't wait. He rushed to the edge of the huge hangar and stood beside one of the fighters. It was black, the Concord logo etched on the side in white stencil. His head didn't even come up to the rear thrusters. The ship was sleek, long, and lean.

"There are wings for suborbital control," Lieutenant Basker informed him. "They don't get any better than this."

"Have you flown one?" Tarlen asked.

"I should hope so." Basker set a hand on the ship they were looking at. "This one is mine. Flown in over fifty missions, mostly Border runs. I wasn't expecting to even be here."

"Whose are these?" Tarlen asked, indicating the other four.

"These three are my team's. The last one is more ceremonial than the others," he said proudly.

Tarlen walked over to it, seeing it was a slightly different model, maybe an older iteration. "Whose is this one?"

"That is our esteemed captain's. He used to be one hell of a pilot," Lieutenant Basker said.

Tarlen hadn't known that. "Used to be?"

"Well, that was over a decade ago. He's been promoted a few times since then," the man added.

Tarlen wanted nothing more than to step inside the cockpit, to feel the ship around him as he raced through space, fending off Tubers.

"How do you become a pilot?" he asked the man.

"Are you really a JOT?" Lieutenant Basker asked.

Tarlen shook his head, coming clean with the man. He told him all about the attack, and how he wanted to find his sister. The man listened with grace, and Tarlen was grateful for it.

"Well, son, there's no way to tell if we'll find your sister, but I've been given the orders. We move out in the next hour. *Constantine* is heading past the Border," he said.

"What does that mean?" Tarlen asked.

"It means we're heading past the Concord's reach. It's dark space out there. Anything goes, and even more concerning are the unknowns we might face in the process," Basker said. "But the Code states that 'without the thrill of exploration, we are but lowly bottom dwellers in the sea of space'."

Tarlen thought hard about the words and nodded, accepting them.

He didn't want to be a bottom dweller. He wanted so much more.

———————

"*T*ake us out, Junior Officer Zare," Baldwin ordered. He watched the world through the viewer, doubting he'd ever return to Greblok again.

He was about to disobey direct orders to return to Nolix, meaning there would be consequences. Something felt wrong about his conversation with the admiral, and finding out there was a human inside a Statu suit in the War set off so many alarm bells in his head, it was still ringing.

"Constantine, please shut down all transponders on the ship," he told the AI waiting at the edge of the bridge.

The man flickered, vanishing one instant and appearing the next. "I have deactivated the transponders, sir. We will have gone dark to the Concord."

"And no one can send messages out, correct?" Tom asked.

"That is correct."

Tom was concerned that a troubled crew member might give them away to the Concord. The general population of the ship wasn't supposed to be aware of their actual orders, so he wasn't sure there would be an issue, but he couldn't be too careful. If anyone asked, he'd have their superior advise them it was a glitch in the new ship's untested software.

"Zare, set target and hit hyperlight," he told the officer, who nodded and did as instructed.

The ship didn't so much as lurch as the camera showed stars stretching before them. "Ven, what do we know about the systems we're heading through?"

Ven was in his standard seat at the second helm position, beside Zare, and he turned to talk with Tom. "We're first moving past the local system and will be out in under an hour. The Concord does have a partner along our trajectory, and we will be near their world in…" He tapped the console at his fingertips and continued, "Six hours and twelve standard minutes, sir."

"Who are they?" Tom asked. He'd never been out this direction. It was far removed from their most active and central hub.

"The Emial from Ipran, sir," Ven answered.

Tom had heard of them. He even thought he'd seen one or two of the Emial on board his ship, working in the kitchens. "We stay the path. If we stop, the Concord will learn we're off course," he ordered.

"Yes, sir."

The Border was huge, spanning millions of light years, and encompassing more systems and planets than he could comprehend. The majority of their Border Wars took place far away, almost the distance of the known universe. But that was the key word: known. There was so much past the Border, including deadly nebulas, asteroid belts, and exploding stars, not to mention the hundreds or thousands of undiscovered races of beings.

The few the Concord had encountered had been less

than thrilled to find there was a powerful group running such a massive sector of space. Still, the battles at the Border were rarely dangerous. He glanced at Treena Starling beside him, assuming she'd tell a different tale.

In her case, two hundred crew mates had been killed at the Border by a newcomer hellbent on making a name for themselves by attacking the Concord. In the end, they'd been hunted down, and Tom saw that the Prime Minister had ordered two vessels to attack their home planet. The files on the mission were classified above Tom's rank. He didn't need to read them to know the Concord would have destroyed the world and all its inhabitants. One didn't attack and extinguish a cruise ship without retribution.

Tom was using that same logic as his excuse for disobeying his orders. He needed to find out where the Statu were headed, and how to stop them. Even if the Prime didn't think that Greblok continued to be valuable to the Concord, word like this spread quickly across their partner worlds. Tom could already smell the uprising, and he was going to do what it took to prevent that from happening. The Concord couldn't afford to have infighting, especially with the Statu returning so suddenly.

"Captain?" Ven asked.

"Sorry, Ven. Say again?" Tom blinked hard. He hadn't slept in the last day, and it was beginning to wear on him.

"Shall I send probes ahead?" Ven asked.

"Of course." Tom watched through the viewer as tiny blue thrusters shot probes away. They flared brightly as their attached singularity pulses sent them through folds in space.

"I'll advise any useful readouts as the information returns," Ven said.

"Captain, I wish we had those jumpers on this ship," Reeve Daak called from her position at the edge of the bridge.

"Don't we all," Tom said. The technology was too far away. They could use the black matter to blast something minor into another system, like a melon-sized probe, but the power necessary to move an entire ship would rip a hole in space, creating chaos. Reeve would understand that much better than he did, but the concept wasn't lost on him. He was happy enough with the hyperlight their Star Drive allowed them.

"Captain, we're on the way, and I can tell you haven't slept in a long time. Go and rest. I'll stay on the bridge," Treena Starling told him.

He was about to ask when she'd slept last until he remembered that she wasn't really there, that she was a brain in another room, controlling a lifelike body that sat beside him in the commander's seat.

Tom nodded. "You're right." He stood up and ran a hand over his stomach. "I'm going to rest. Keep me posted on any developments."

Tom walked off, turning for a moment to stare at the viewer. Stars danced in the distance as they raced through open space, heading toward the blinking, moving target of a Statu warship.

TWELVE

Tarlen wandered the corridors and finally made it to the medical bay. He'd forgotten about it in the excitement of the last day and was glad when the doors opened. He spotted Doctor Nee across the room, talking to a woman lying on one of the patient beds.

Back home, there were doctors, and Tarlen always hated going to see them, mostly because it meant something was wrong. His practitioners didn't have a setup like this. Theirs were stone slabs with vials along the wall. Have a sore throat? Drink this, Tarlen.

Here everything was stark white, as clean and vivid as Doctor Nee's smiling teeth or his hair. "Young Tarlen, what a pleasure it is to see you again," he said so genuinely, it made Tarlen flush with pride.

"Hi, Doctor. I wanted to come by earlier, but I've been so distracted by the ship. It's amazing," he said, lacking the vocabulary to truly express his feelings.

"You're accurate there. What can I do for you?" Doctor Nee asked.

The woman remained on the exam bed, and Tarlen glanced at her. "You can finish. I'll stay out of the way."

"Why don't you take a seat, and I'll be with you in a moment," the doctor suggested, and Tarlen moved to the other end of the medical bay, finding four chairs in a row. There were some closed doors at the rear of the room, and one had a dim light underneath it, drawing Tarlen like a night insect to a flickering flame.

The doctor was still with his patient, so Tarlen stepped lightly across the hard floor and set his hand on the door's control panel. Finally understanding how they worked, he opened it to see the alien from the cryo chamber sleeping inside. There were machines all around, and Tarlen noticed the being was bound around the wrists and ankles with a glowing orange beam of light.

Tarlen was fascinated by the sleeping person across the private room, and stepped inside. A hand gripped his shoulder, holding him back, and he jerked his chin lower to see the doctor's glove.

"What are you doing in here, Tarlen?" Doctor Nee asked, his voice calm, even though Tarlen could tell he was angry.

"I'm sorry. I saw the light on and wanted to see how it was doing," Tarlen said.

"He," Doctor Nee corrected. "I've established it's a male, though the organs are slightly different than those of most races."

"Is he going to be okay?" Tarlen asked, and the doctor released his grip.

"It would appear so. I haven't brought him out of sedation yet, but I'm going to begin the process soon," the doctor told him.

"Can I stay?" Tarlen asked.

"I'm not sure that's a wise idea, son," Doctor Nee said, setting a gloved hand on Tarlen's shoulder.

"Why not?"

"You'll only be in the way, and we have no idea what to expect. He was agitated before, and I assume he won't be much more cooperative now." The doctor walked to the bedside, leaning over the mysterious sedated being.

"What about translating?" Tarlen asked him, remembering the clicking speech the man had used in the cargo hold.

"We need a baseline to work with. Once we have him awake and calm, we can begin the process," Nee told him. The doctor tapped a console on the wall and spoke into it. "Kelli, please join me in our guest's suite."

A minute later, a short human woman entered, smiling mirthlessly at Tarlen before moving to the other side of the patient's bed. She wore her hair short and sported a different uniform than the ship's other crew, hers white with no collar color.

"Tarlen, this is Kelli, the head nurse. Kelli, Tarlen is from Greblok," Nee advised them, and her eyes sprang wide.

"I'm sorry..." She didn't elaborate, and Tarlen only nodded his understanding.

"Kelli, please begin the process," Nee said, and Tarlen took a seat, not wanting to be in the way. The two moved with practiced care, and a few minutes later, the figure on the bed began to move, slowly at first, then a little more panicked.

"Let's give him something to calm him," Nee said, and Kelli pressed a few keys, the man settling quickly.

Nee raised the bed up and shone a light into the man's dark eyes. His mandibles clicked together, his nasal slits opening and closing as he searched the room.

Tarlen didn't feel scared by the man, only intrigued, and he stood, moving to the end of the bed. He raised a hand in greeting, and the man attempted to copy him. His hand only lifted halfway, the glowing binds around his arm stopping him short. He clicked more when he realized he was confined to the bed but didn't panic like Tarlen might have expected. They locked gazes, and the man leaned into his pillow, starting to click more.

"Doctor Nee to the bridge," Nee said into the console.

"Starling here. Go ahead, Medical," the commander's voice said.

"He's awake and talkative," Nee told the bridge.

"Ask Constantine Baldwin to join you. I understand he has translation programming," Starling said.

"Good call. We'll begin the process and update you when we learn anything," Nee said. "Constan…"

Tarlen jumped as the AI appeared, flickering at first, then remaining solid.

"You have need of me, Doctor?" Constantine asked.

Tarlen had never seen anything like it before, but had heard about Constantine from Vor. It was amazing. It looked like a real man, younger than the captain, even though the computer software held the memories of the captain's grandfather. It was all a little confusing to Tarlen, but he assumed he'd encounter a lot of that after leaving the surface of his home planet.

He'd never considered what was out there beyond his own world with any more than a passing thought. He was meant to work for his father one day, keeping books for businesses. That was his life mapped out, and now that had been flipped upside down. The possibilities of his existence had exploded, but only on the deaths of so many.

As excited as he was about these new things he was witnessing, he wished he could trade it all to be home with his family, eating at the dinner table and sharing their days with each other. That would never happen again.

More sharp clicks emerged from the patient, startled at seeing Constantine appear, and Tarlen snapped out of his daydream.

Kelli walked over to Tarlen, standing between him and the patient's bed. "Come on, Tarlen. I'll show you around.

Let's let them work."

"I'm going to show him a series of images…" the AI was saying as the door shut behind Kelli and Tarlen.

Tarlen couldn't wait to learn where the man and his people hailed from.

---

*T*reena was never tired. It was both a blessing and a curse. There was something therapeutic about growing weary and preparing for bed. She used to have a routine of cleaning her teeth, taking a steam shower, and drying her hair before brushing it. Part of the reason she'd kept her hair short was from the memories of her mother always nagging her about brushing it religiously.

There was technology for this, but her mother claimed it wasn't the same thing. She recalled crying while her hair was aggressively brushed as a child, and the moment she was old enough to choose for herself, she'd cut her hair short with her own scissors. Her mother was so angry, but her father had calmed her, saying it suited her round face.

Treena stared in the mirror, running a hand over her vessel's hair, and even though her fingers were lined with sensors, nothing felt right. She'd never feel wind against her face like she once had. Never taste a cup of coffee with the same effect. She'd never be in a relationship again – which suited her just fine, since he'd died while she'd been spared, for some reason.

There was no room for love in her heart any longer. Not without Felix.

"Bridge to Starling," the voice carried through her room speakers. The signal for the Statu vessel had vanished seven hours ago. That might have meant that Brax Daak had been killed, but his tracker was imbedded deep within his humerus bone. They would have had to vaporize him to destroy it, which wasn't fully impossible.

She sighed, shutting the lights off in the bathroom, and tapped the console. "Go ahead, bridge."

It was Ven speaking. "The captain has requested you join us. We've encountered… an anomaly."

"I'll be right there," she told the bridge, and grabbed her uniform, staring at the orange collar. Something was off about this mission. The ship had taken three years to build, and that had been rushed, but to throw together a crew so unfamiliar with one another, and end up at a site attacked by the Statu, was incredible.

If she hadn't been there with Thomas on the call with the Concord's Prime and Admiral Hudson, she wouldn't have believed they could be so cold and callous about the entire thing. Treena hated disobeying rules, but she smelled something afoot, and knew they were doing the right thing. This needed to be explored.

Perhaps if they'd been given more information on the call, she would have understood the reasoning for the orders, but they were disregarded without so much as a brief explanation. It rattled her cage, and she was glad Tom had felt the same way.

She donned her uniform, glancing briefly at her real body before leaving for the bridge. She arrived a few minutes later to find the captain huddled over a helm console with Ven and Reeve Daak.

"What did I miss?" she asked. It was one of those times she was glad she didn't need sleep. She'd been on the go for the last twenty-seven hours and had been about to take her first break. Reeve looked at her like she expected Treena to have purple bags under her eyes but didn't say anything when she saw a fresh-faced commander in front of her.

"Take a look for yourself," Thomas Baldwin said, pointing to the viewer. The viewer was zoomed in a hundred times, the image ever-so-slightly out of focus, but the picture was still clear enough to decipher.

"It's a wormhole," Treena whispered.

Ven peered up at her. "We've been following their trajectory, and this is where the signal vanished." He nodded to the viewer. "Actually, *that* is where it disappeared, to be more factual."

"They traveled into the wormhole," Treena said.

"Can that be done?" Thomas asked Reeve, who was sitting in Zare's second helm position while the Zilph'i woman was relegated to the edge of the bridge.

Reeve was typing away at the console, muttering inaudible words as her fingers flew over the screen. "I don't know, Captain. I mean, we've seen wormholes before, but none have ever been deemed stable enough to travel through."

"But the theory is sound," Treena said. She'd heard a lot of stories of distant races using wormholes as trade routes, but no real empirical proof had ever been recorded and stored within the Concord.

"The few we've found inside the Border were small and short-lived. There have been records of twenty-three active wormholes outside the Border, and the one the Concord investigated turned out to be a dangerous quasar," Reeve said.

"That's not entirely true," Ven said.

"What do you mean?" Tom asked, arms crossed over his chest. He was frowning, and Treena almost saw the options rattling around his brain as they stood side by side.

"The Zilph'i have attempted to travel through a wormhole," Ven said.

This was news to Treena, and evidently to the rest of the crew too, judging by the surprised looks on their faces.

"Impossible. Why wouldn't the Concord know of this?" Reeve asked.

"Because it was an Ugna vessel, and we don't fall under the umbrella of the Concord," Ven said, almost with a hint of distaste. Treena initially thought the man might be offended that he was forced to work aboard a Concord vessel, but working with him over the last few days had squashed the assumption. He seemed as dedicated as the rest of the crew, only a little more withdrawn and mysterious.

So much of the Ugna was unfamiliar to the Concord, and Ven wasn't forthcoming so far on details. Perhaps time would help him grow comfortable enough to share the real him. Maybe Treena would share her reality with them as well... eventually.

No one spoke, waiting for Ven to continue. He clued in and kept talking. "We have our own vessels, mostly for exploration. There's a lot to see out there, and the Ugna don't appreciate having others dictate the mission mandates. We create our own. You see, if I hadn't been selected to join *Constantine,* I'd be heading my own ship in our compact fleet," he advised them.

"If that's the case, why have we never heard of this fleet?" Reeve asked, her red eyes shining brightly as she stared at the albino man at the helm beside hers.

"Because I chose to keep this information to myself. Even now, I'm breaking trust by telling you," Ven said.

"But you're on our crew, part of the Concord," Tom said.

"Yes. One of many gray areas, sir," Ven said.

"What about the wormhole?" Treena asked, wanting to arrive at the crux of the story. One thing she knew about the rifts in space was that they were often unstable. If the Statu had taken their captives through this one, she didn't want to hesitate long before following after them.

"It appeared forty thousand light years from the Border, possible millions of Standard years ago. We found references to it in ancient texts from a long-dead race. The Ugna often study extinct cultures, in an effort to learn how to sustain the Zilph'i forever. It was a century ago that the rumors of the wormhole grew to more than that. We found the exact coordinates," Ven said, and Treena leaned in. She glanced over at Tom, and he was doing the same thing.

"What did you do?" Tom asked quietly.

"We sent a vessel to explore. Their mission was to traverse it, and head home from the new location, should they be unable to return through the wormhole," Ven told them.

"What was on the other side?" Treena asked, feeling like she knew the coming answer.

"That's undetermined." Ven averted his gaze and stared toward the rift in the viewer. "The vessel never returned."

"Great." Reeve slapped a palm on the console in anger. "What are we going to do? We have no idea what will happen if we attempt to fly *Constantine* through this thing. Are we certain the Statu even took this route? There are other explanations."

"There's another possible account," Tom said. "The Statu knew this wormhole was here, and they led us to it, destroyed our tracker right near it, and kept moving through normal space, figuring we'd assume they'd traversed the wormhole."

Reeve's face went pale, and Treena set a hand on the woman's shoulder as she stood behind Reeve's station.

"I don't buy it," Reeve said. "I think they took the

opening."

Treena watched the image, noting the strange distortion in the center of it: a perfect circle beckoning their vessel toward it. She was stepping across the bridge, moving for the center of the viewer without even thinking about it.

Treena thought the chief engineer was right, and she turned to tell the captain her opinion when the doctor's voice carried onto Ven's console.

"Bridge, you're going to want to hear this," Nee said. Treena could tell something was wrong, because the normally upbeat man's voice was strained and tense.

"Go ahead, Doctor," Tom said.

"We've managed to get our friend talking," the doctor told them.

Tom tapped the console hard with his pointer finger. "Damn it, Nee. We don't have time for games. Spit it out!"

Silence.

"Doctor, I'm not…" Tom started, but was interrupted.

"He claims to be Statu, sir. He says they're Statu."

THIRTEEN

*A*nother two days passed aboard their new hell. Two more of the Bacals had died overnight, and even though they had someone who professed to be a healer in their group, without supplies, there was nothing that could be done to prevent the deaths.

Brax was exhausted, having slept only a matter of hours. He was being foolish by pushing himself to the edge, and he finally lay down, closing his eyes to sleep. The room was filled with groans and hushed conversations.

At any given moment, there was a child crying, a soothing female voice, and a shouting man, almost without fail. Brax had stopped three fights from escalating, and Penter another two. The entire group was under a lot of duress, and Brax didn't blame them for being scared and frustrated. They'd witnessed the destruction of their homes and were now crammed into a terrible space with nothing but a barrel of water to sustain them.

No one knew where they were headed or who their captors were. Brax did, but he didn't tell the Bacals; not that it would do any good. They hadn't been involved in the War and might not even know who the Statu were.

Brax attempted to push all thoughts from his mind and concentrated on an image of a flame. He watched the orange ambiance flicker as if a light breeze was rustling inside his head. He could smell the wick burning, feel the heat from the tiny piece of fire. All that existed was the flame. *The Flame is life.* The words from the Code echoed as he repeated the mantra, concentrating on the image.

His body relaxed, and the noise around the room dissipated into nothingness. He was the only thing in existence, along with his flame. Sleep took him after a few more deep breaths.

Brax awoke to being shaken, and he reached out, clutching his attacker around the collar, cocking his other fist back to strike hard and quickly.

"It's me! Penter!" the man hissed, and pressed his finger to chapped lips. "Something's happening. You'd better get up."

Brax sat up, hearing none of the familiar cacophony of the passengers. It was nearly silent. "What is it?"

"I think we've landed," Penter said.

Landed? Already? That was too soon. Brax had expected the ship to carry them for weeks, at least. If they were only a few days out, they had to be within range of the Concord. That could be good news.

"None of the bastards have lowered from the ceiling yet?" Brax asked, standing and stretching his spine. It cracked in two spots, and he swung his arms around, easing the tension in his shoulders.

"Not yet," Penter said.

"What are they going to do with us?" It was Abbil, the woman Brax had first encountered. Since then, she'd taken a special interest in helping Penter and Brax with the other passengers.

"Only time will tell, but I suspect they won't be welcoming us like long-lost friends," Brax told her. She pulled her long dark hair back, using a piece torn from a sleeve to tie it away from her face. Abbil appeared ready to fight, but Brax didn't think it was a battle any of them would survive.

"Be cautious, Abbil," he warned her, and she nodded.

"Thank you," she told him.

Brax ran a hand over his head; dark hair was poking from his pate. "For what?"

"Everything," she told him quietly.

Penter was already moving through the throngs of his people, and Brax followed the guard, Abbil trailing behind him until they reached the water barrel. If they'd landed, it was likely their captors would be joining them very soon.

People were beginning to talk amongst themselves, and Brax thought he heard a loud sound through the noise. He raised his hand. "Can everyone be quiet for a moment?" he asked loudly, and the talking ceased instantly.

Bang! There it was again: a loud concussive sound. The ground shook slightly, and he was fully aware they were feeling the aftereffects of a pulse frag being deployed. It might have been from the room beside them.

"Everyone, listen to me. They are about to return to this room. No one dare attack them. If I'm right, they'll kill us upon any provocation," Brax said. The Statu had abducted a lot of people, and if they were on the huge warship, which he was sure they were, they might have thousands, even tens of thousands of Bacals on board. Killing one or two rogue groups would be effortless on their part, especially if you took their own muddled history into consideration.

Brax had studied the War more thoroughly than most cadets, and he was aware how eager the Statu were to send their own people to their deaths in battle. That meant life, especially that of their enemies, was of little consequence to the destructive race.

"What makes you say that?" Penter asked.

"That noise. I think that was the room over, and it didn't sound like a friendly arrival," Brax said as the ceiling began to spread wide. The lift lowered again, and he urged the nearby people to step away. The platform held twenty or so armed guards this time. They each wore the familiar armored suits from the War.

They'd learned those details at the Academy. They even had samples of the uniforms for the cadets to play with. Brax could recall the day he'd learned each suit had a mechanized device the Callalay had dubbed a Scrambler. If the Statu inside the suit lost vitals, it depressed into their skin, scrambling their innards into a gooey mess. It disgusted him then, and staring at the faceless suits, it still made his own skin crawl.

They were varying heights, none much taller than Brax would be inside a matching suit. With the helmets and boots, a couple were pushing over two meters in height. He stood nearest the armed soldiers, standing his ground, but not appearing threatening either.

"Where are we?" he asked the lead guard, not expecting an answer. There was no successful communication with the race on record. None of the pleas to barter or make peace had been accepted during the ten-year duration of the War. Not once.

The guards approached, each holding a crude gun up, aiming at the helpless people of Greblok. The weapons may not have been pretty, but Brax didn't doubt they would kill just the same.

"Everyone follow their orders," Penter said before Brax could. Brax was really starting to like the bushy-eyebrowed man. If there was any chance of escape, he was going to need Penter's help.

They were brought twenty at a time onto the platform and lifted away, with two armed guards accompanying each group of prisoners. Brax and Penter were left, even though they stood at the front of the line.

Numerous sets of people walked past them, settling on the platform: children with eyes full of tears, men with frowns and clenched fists. The entire process took about thirty minutes, and soon there was only one group left, and two guards remained.

Brax took them in. They were shorter, less imposing than some of the Statu, and one of their guns lowered as the guard motioned to a few people to step onto the platform. Brax considered attacking the guard, taking the weapon, and attempting to blast his way out of here, but he stopped short. He had no clue where they were or what was on the other side of the ship.

No, attacking them now would only end poorly, so he bided his time.

"Come on, friend. After you," Penter told him.

Brax stood on the platform, seeing that Abbil had waited for them. Her jaw was clenched tight, the muscles below her cheeks pronounced as the platform raised. Only the dead bodies remained in the dank room where they'd been held captive, and Brax said a silent prayer to the Vastness as they passed through the open ceiling.

———

The call had come at the beginning of Yur's shift. The cargo hold had been off limits to everyone since their ship had been attacked by the Tuber outside of Greblok. Yur wasn't supposed to hear what was on the ship, but he'd been nosy enough to learn it was stacked with cryo chambers from some mysterious alien race.

The entire bay was cordoned off from all maintenance and custodial crews, but there was an issue with the air ducts, and it was sweltering inside. When Olu hadn't been able to fix it himself, he notified Yur he needed assistance.

"You're good with this kind of thing, right, Shen?" Olu's voice was heavy, garbled, like he had too many teeth.

"Sure. I can fix anything," Yur said, meaning it.

The night before, his benefactor had sent a message saying he was to record everything in the bay. At the time, he hadn't understood, and she'd refused to reply to his follow-up queries. When he'd heard about the job, it was clear.

He had the tiny clip-on recorder stuck to his chest beside his flashlight. Side by side, they looked like one unit, which meant they were fully inconspicuous.

"Good, because I can't figure out for the life of me why in the Vastness this duct is blocked," Olu said, stopping at the pair of guards outside the hangar.

"IDs," the man said, eyeing Yur up suspiciously. They were both scanned in.

"Orders from Chief Engineer Reeve Daak, sir," Olu said, his tone lighter and more amiable.

"Good, because it's sweltering in there. Not a great place for the alien popsicles, if you ask me," the guard said with a grin.

He let them through the wide double doors, and Yur instantly began to sweat. To say it was hot was an understatement. Yur made sure he was recording and limped along the cryo chambers, moving slowly and methodically in order to capture as much detail as possible. He saw the beings inside, and cringed at the dark eyes staring back, the insect-like mandibles appearing dangerous.

"Get away from those, Shen. The duct is over here." Olu stepped onto a hover-lift, and Yur followed him on. From here, he got a good look at *Constantine*'s guests and hoped this was what his boss was after.

He'd been waiting for her to instruct him to detonate

the tubes, but so far, she hadn't seemed interested. He knew it would be soon. It had to be.

Yur turned his attention to the task at hand, not wanting to give Olu any reason to grow distrustful.

———

"Sir, I don't think he's ready for this," Nee said, pacing the main medical bay floor. The man had walked by so many times, Tom was starting to grow dizzy.

"Can you stop that, please?" Tom ordered.

The doctor halted instantly. "I mean it. He's been through some serious trauma, and I'm worried he might be confused. I suggest we allow him to sleep, unaided by drugs this time, and when he comes to, we can question him."

Tom appreciated Nee's concern for his patient, but now wasn't the time for tiptoeing around the issue. "Nee, we're past the Border, waiting at the edge of a wormhole, and our passenger is claiming to be a Statu. I'd say we have every right to badger the man until we learn the truth. Don't you agree, Commander?" Tom glanced at Treena Starling, who'd been eerily quiet this entire time.

"This doesn't add up, Captain," Treena said. She was at the edge of the room, staring at the distant wormhole through a viewer on the wall.

"No kidding. Which part are you referring to in particular?" Tom asked her.

"Constantine said the Statu were human," she said. "The being on the other side of the patient room door is far from human, wouldn't you say?"

"I have to agree with you there," Nee said, a grim, sardonic smile on his face.

"Well, aren't we lucky to have you as our ship's doctor." Tom couldn't help but ooze with sarcasm.

"Could Constantine be wrong?" Treena asked.

Tom glanced around, suddenly expecting the AI to appear, but he didn't. Was he always listening? It was a little off-putting. "He could be, but that would mean my grandfather had actually seen a human behind a suit. That could mean two things," he said.

Treena nodded. "The Statu were using our own people to attack us."

It clicked, and Tom couldn't believe no one had ever seen it before. He stood up, knocking over his cup of coffee. The cup clattered to the ground, not breaking, but spilling everywhere. A CleanBot rolled from the wall, sucking the liquid up, and gathered the cup, dragging it away into a cubby before vanishing itself.

"No wonder they were so willing to throw everything at us with reckless abandon. They weren't using their own kind. They were using humans!" Tom's hand flew through his hair at the idea. If the Concord knew this, why had they kept it a secret all these years? "Constantine!"

The AI appeared, blinking to life before their eyes. "Yes, sir. How may I assist you?"

Tom crossed the room to stand directly in front of the AI. It was eerie how much he looked like his grandfather, but a much younger version than Tom remembered. This Constantine had none of the crows' feet, the frown lines, or the gray beard he'd worn as he passed sixty years old, but Tom did feel a connection to the AI nonetheless.

"Constantine, you told us the captured Statu was identified as a human inside the suit. Why was this never revealed to the public, or at least to the Concord mainstream database?" Tom asked.

The AI didn't change expressions; he only stared hard

at Tom for a moment before replying. This AI was unlike any Tom had ever seen. It was so lifelike, the expressions so much less robotic than the AIs of any other ships he'd ever been stationed on.

"Captain, can you imagine if it became public knowledge? The Concord would tear itself apart. It was a human, not a Callalay, not a Tekol, not a Zilph'i. Humans might have been shunned from the Founders, and imagine the cause and effect that would have on the entire structure of our society if that occurred," Constantine said.

It made sense, but Tom felt like there was something he was missing about the whole situation.

Treena was methodically pacing, her hands clasped together. "What if…" She stopped speaking.

"What if what?" Tom prodded.

"What if the Statu planted that person?"

Tom's heart hammered in his chest at the implication. "Damn it. You could be right! The Statu never made that mistake, not ever. And the one time you" – he pointed at the AI – "you went against protocol and boarded the ship, you happened to find a Statu unpunctured and turned to liquified goo."

Constantine's eyes grew in size as his programming appeared to process the news. "It is possible. What was their goal by doing this?"

Treena was still walking back and forth across the white medical bay floor. "They wanted to mess with us. You just said it, Constantine. They wanted news to spread about the humans working with or for the Statu. The War would have been theirs. It would have finally turned the tides in their favor."

"Why wait so long to pull it off?" Nee asked. "We fought them for years."

Tom scratched his chin with his index finger. "Because

they were desperate. They came in thinking they could walk all over the Concord, and when things grew dire, they made a last-ditch effort at tricking us. Only it didn't work." He turned to the AI again, who was holding silent. "Constantine, who knew about this?"

"Only Commander Sennie Baar and Executive Lieutenant Adam Hudson…" His words trailed off.

Tom slapped the desk, his palm echoing loudly across the medical bay. "There it is. Hudson was there. He knows something about the Statu we don't. Either he thinks they planted the human…"

"Or he was in on it," Treena said softly, her eyes never making contact with Tom's.

"That's…" Nee began.

"Blasphemy. You may be tried a traitor for even suggesting it, Commander," Constantine told them.

A month ago, Tom would never have believed the admiral capable of something so insidious, but the way he'd disregarded Tom and their entire mission the other day just wouldn't sit right. Add in the Prime's involvement, and the noticeably absent Callalay executive officer, and Tom was beginning to see the odds stacking against him and his crew.

"If you found the human inside alive, what did they say to you?" Treena asked Constantine. In all the excitement, he was angry he hadn't even thought of asking that question.

"It wouldn't speak to us," the AI said.

"Why not?" Nee asked.

Constantine shrugged. "I couldn't tell you. They took him away to be tested, but I've seen that catatonic look before. He was brain dead. I even snapped my fingers directly in front of his eyes but garnered no reaction. I suspected something in the suit perhaps controlled him, or maybe a neural implant. I couldn't be sure, and I was never told anything more."

Tom watched his grandfather's youthful image and thought about what the computer program was saying. There was a lot more inside the AI than just the older Captain Baldwin's strategical inputs. How much of the man was really in there? Did he remember seeing Tom for the first time? Did he recall the feeling he'd had when he learned his daughter had been killed?

"Nee, I want to speak with our passenger," Tom said, not willing to wait any longer. He needed answers, because the longer he waited here, the further the Statu warship traveled away from his ship.

The doctor appeared ready to argue, but instead hung his head, his white hair unmoving. "Fine. Constantine can translate, can't you?"

"That is correct. I have the program embedded in me," Constantine told them.

Tom waited for the doctor to move for the patient's room, and saw the commander eyeing the door with unease. "What is it, Starling?" he asked her.

"Nothing. I... it's disturbing that the Concord has so many secrets. We thought the War was over, and we've had a short fifty years of freedom and relative peace. We all know how terrible those times were. Can we really endure this again?" she asked.

Tom thought about the Code, and one of his grandfather's favorite quotes from it sprang to mind. *Freedom is not to be taken for granted. Sometimes one must fight to have peace.*

He wasn't sure if it helped the woman, but she nodded and walked toward the far end of the bay, where the doctor was entering the patient's room.

Tom was the last of their select group to arrive, and he tapped the door shut behind them. He didn't want any prying ears on this conversation.

"He's sleeping, but I can revive him when you're ready," Doctor Nee said.

"Do it," Tom told the doctor, and as the Kwant moved toward the body, Tom heard the call from the bridge.

"Captain." It was Ven's distinct voice.

Tom clenched his jaw at the disturbance. "Go ahead."

"The wormhole. It appears to be moving, sir."

"Moving?" Tom glanced at Treena, who shrugged.

"Lieutenant Daak agrees with me that it might be beginning to destabilize," Ven said.

"Destabilize? I wasn't sure we agreed it was stable in the first place," Tom told him. "What are you suggesting we do about this?"

There was a brief but noticeable pause to the Ugna's next statement. "I think we should enter it, sir."

"Enter it!" Nee shouted. "Is he insane? This is a wormhole, Captain, not something to be trifled with. We have no records on hand showing them to be functional, let alone…"

Treena held a finger up and tapped her chin in a very human gesture. "Captain, I thought of something."

Tom waited for her to expand on this, and when she didn't, he waved his hand in a get-on-with-it motion.

"The Statu. They came from nowhere all those years ago, and we never did find their homeworld. What if they used wormholes to arrive?" Treena asked.

Tom had heard a lot of conjecture on the subject over the years, but there had never been any proof of this as a possibility. But the Concord also hadn't followed a Statu warship into a wormhole before either. If he didn't take the risk, he was going to miss out on learning where the Statu went, and any hope of rescuing Brax Daak went out the window.

"May I suggest something a little unorthodox, Captain?" Treena asked.

"I'm open to any valid ideas at this point," Tom said.

"We send *Cleo* through. I'll lead the expedition. You stay here and learn what you can about this…" She stopped short, pointing at the unconscious alien in the medical bed.

Tom rubbed his temples, trying to process the potential outcomes. One thing he'd been trained in was critical thinking. During the Academy, and later in executive officer training, they were constantly given problems with dire scenarios, and they had to articulate their solution with course-of-action plans as well as alternatives and recommendations. He considered their current scenario and knew there were a few options.

Return to Nolix as instructed, which would mean he'd lose Brax, but not his ship. They'd also lose the chance at learning where the destructive vessel's destination was. If they did as Starling suggested, they'd be far apart, and he was not only ignoring Concord orders from the top, he was risking more lives and property.

Or he could fly *Constantine* through, which would give them the best chance of rescuing Brax and defending against the Statu warship. They might even rescue the Bacals and return with the mined ore. If they accomplished that, Admiral Hudson might forgive his disobedience.

"Captain?" Starling asked, breaking him from his concentration.

"I…" Tom couldn't risk the crew's lives. "You head the team. Take Reeve with you," he said, realizing this might be a terrible mistake. "Constantine?" he asked, the AI stepping forward and waiting for direction.

"Yes, Captain," the AI said softly.

"You'll send a version of yourself with Commander

Starling on *Cleo*. Bring a Link. Can you communicate with your selves?" he asked.

"I can, but it has never been tested through a wormhole," Constantine said.

"But from far distances?" Tom asked.

"Up to one hundred light years. Though the data isn't instantaneous, and the information comes with no video or voice feeds. Only data streams. Information notes," Constantine advised.

"It'll have to be good enough," Tom said. "Doctor Nee, keep our guest sedated. I'll return later."

"Very well, Captain. Good luck," Doctor Nee said.

Tom led the exit, Treena close behind him, and Constantine vanished from the medical bay. "You sure about this, Starling?"

She didn't appear nervous, but that might have been the artificial body's work. "If we can scout and learn where they are, it could prove invaluable," she said, making sense.

They arrived on the bridge a short time later, and Reeve Daak stood as they entered. "Captain, we can't let this slip by. We need to go after my brother."

"I agree. That's why I'm sending you with the commander in *Cleo*." Tom crossed the bridge to stare at the wormhole through the viewer. To his eyes, at this distance, he saw no visible changes to its appearance.

Reeve's eyes lit up. "When do we leave?"

Tom placed his hands on his hips. "Now."

FOURTEEN

Vor passed Tarlen a napkin and reached for more wriggling food.

"They're sending the commander and the chief engineer through the wormhole," an officer with a white collar said.

Tarlen stood, knocking his chair over. He ran to the mess hall entrance, stopping in front of the young man. "What! When are they going?"

"They might be gone already," the man replied, moving past Tarlen.

Without another word, Tarlen raced away, pumping his legs down the hall. He was unused to the encumbrance of boots, and he felt like they were slowing him, but he kept moving. He'd explored every inch of the ship and understood where the bridge was, even if he hadn't been on it yet – except when they'd landed, and that had been such a blur, he couldn't recall any details.

He made it there quickly and was stopped at the doors. "What do you want, kid?" a burly, unfamiliar alien asked. He was dark green, scales covering his face, his eyes blinking sideways as he waited for a reply. Tarlen's gaze shifted to the gun at the guard's hip.

"I need to speak with the captain," Tarlen said, the words flowing extremely fast from his mouth.

"And who are you..." The man glanced at his purple

collar and waved him away.

"Captain Baldwin! It's Tarlen! I need to talk to you!" he shouted at the top of his lungs, and the green guard jumped away, apparently shocked at the noise.

"Kid, cut that out," the guard said, but Tarlen didn't listen. He yelled once more, and seconds later, the white double doors slid open, revealing a frowning Baldwin.

"Sorry, sir, the kid came out of nowhere," the guard said.

"It's okay, Valg. Permission to enter the bridge, Tarlen." Thomas Baldwin stepped aside, motioning him inside.

It was amazing. The beeping computers, the pristine white floors, the matching uniformed officers. Tarlen felt like he was getting a glimpse into something magical, so different from anything he'd ever have been able to bear witness to landlocked on Greblok.

"Captain, are they gone?" he asked, his voice cracking.

"Who are you referring to?" the captain asked.

"The commander. Is she gone?"

"Where did you even hear that?" Baldwin appeared flustered. "They're still here, but not for long."

"I need to go with them. I have to find my sister," he pleaded.

The captain stared at him, his wide jaw unmoving for a moment. "Why would I let you do that?"

"Because they came to my world and stole my people as slaves. I have to be there. I need to see if she's alive," Tarlen said.

Just when Tarlen was positive the captain was going to dismiss him, have him removed from the bridge, maybe even the ship, his face softened and he nodded. "You have a lot of fire in your belly, Tarlen. I like that." Thomas Baldwin walked to the center seat on the bridge, clearly his chair, and tapped the console at its arm. "Commander, hold departure. You're bringing one more with you."

"Are you serious?" Tarlen realized what he'd been allowed. Up until this point, he'd been running on instinct, the desire to help find his sister and parents so strong that he'd forgotten that he knew absolutely nothing... about anything. Maybe that was why the captain had agreed so quickly. Maybe he thought Tarlen would realize his mistake and make an excuse to stay on the ship.

"Captain, are you sure that's a good idea?" Ven asked, standing in his helm position.

"Executive Lieutenant Ven, I don't suspect you'd understand, but I was once like this young man. I heard about Cezo being attacked, and I begged to find a ship to rescue my parents. My grandfather wouldn't let me. He had that look, the one that told me there was no hope, that we were too late. I won't prevent Tarlen from attempting to find his family. It's his choice, and one I'm sure he's considered the ramifications of," Captain Baldwin said.

Tarlen's hand trembled as he followed Thomas to the side of the bridge. "Through the doors and up the lift. You'll find *Cleo* there. Be careful. If you make it back, maybe we can discuss you keeping that uniform."

"Captain, perhaps..." the Zilph'i Ven started to say, but Tarlen hardly heard him. He could rescue his family and return to become a Concord Fleet member. His nerves were gone; the butterflies circling his stomach were replaced by excited dreams of a new future.

"Order stands." The captain closed the doors, leaving Tarlen alone in the elevator.

"Cleo," Tarlen said softly, and the computer repeated the word, the lights growing slightly dimmer as the lift rose upwards. The trip was quick, and he stepped off as the doors sprang wide, two more dark green-scaled guards stepping apart, making room for him.

"Better hurry up, kid," Reeve Daak said from underneath *Cleo*. The ship powered up, the thrumming engines drawing Tarlen forward. He'd already been on this ship once, when he'd been rescued from the surface. She reached a hand down and helped pull him up into the ship, rather than latch and drop the ramp.

She secured the door behind him and stood frowning at him. "I have no idea why the captain was so quick to allow you to join us, but you better not be my undoing," she said, arms crossed.

"I… I won't be in the way," he stammered.

The commander sat in the pilot's seat as she glanced at him and rose from the top of *Constantine*. For the first time, Tarlen had a good look at their destination. The viewer covered the entire front of the ship, and the wormhole spun slowly, colors dancing like overflowing paint.

"We're going through that?" Tarlen asked, resting his hands on the top of the pilot's chair.

"You bet," Commander Treena Starling told him.

"You guys do this kind of thing every day, right?" Tarlen asked, his nerves returning.

"Not quite," Reeve Daak told him. "You'd better sit and secure yourself. It may be a bumpy ride."

"What do you mean by not quite?" Tarlen asked, clipping the double straps across each shoulder and over his chest.

No one answered him as they moved toward the wormhole.

---

*T*he elevator clicked into place, and Brax instantly smelled fresh air. On second thought, it was moving air, not necessarily fresh. The smell of sulfur and something unfamiliar mixed in clung to his nostrils as the breeze passed through the corridor.

"Now what?" Penter asked from beside Brax.

"We find out what the hell they want with us," Brax told his new friend.

"And then?" Abbil asked from his other side.

"Then we bide our time, get the lay of the land, find a weakness, and exploit it," Brax said openly. There was no reason to hide his truth from these two. They'd proven loyal, and the coming days would be extremely tough on them all. Hope dangling in the front of their minds would only assist them through the torment that was heading their way.

If these were truly Statu, there was no telling what they wanted with the Bacals. Brax doubted they had any familiarity with his Tekol heritage, and if they did, whether they even cared or not. One of them pushed him from behind, indicating for him to walk with the rest of the people being herded from the room.

They were still on the ship, along one of the many arms jutting from the monstrosity of a space vessel. It had clearly broken atmosphere of its destination, and as they walked along the rough metal surface, Brax spotted hovering platforms arriving to pick up the throngs of newly-gathered slaves from the tops of the ship.

It was bright outside, and Brax had to use a hand as a visor to keep the bright sun from his eyes. The air felt hot and humid, his shirt instantly clinging to his chest. Abbil watched it all with a fearful gaze, but Penter kept his emotions in check, not giving anything away by his expression. Brax could tell the man was clearly a professional.

Some of the people were stopping short of stepping

onto the floating platforms, and the guards didn't wait for them. The first woman who refused to follow orders was shot in the back of the head. One of the armored guards arrived a second later, dragging the corpse by the arm. It left a smear of blood that the other Bacals rushed away from in disgust.

The body was shoved from the edge of the ship's arm, falling toward the ground far below. No one else refused after the terrible display of aggression. The Statu had set the tone.

Brax had seen a lot in his lifetime, but rarely had he witnessed such cold-blooded viciousness. These beings had no qualms about killing and didn't value life in any capacity. The Statu were enigmas, and very dark and dangerous ones.

The hovering platform was crudely constructed, and the ledges were only two feet high, not doing much of a job containing the passengers. Everyone pressed toward the center of the lift, and when the Statu deemed this platform full, it left the ledge, leaving Brax and his two friends next in line.

From here, he could see quite a way in the distance and didn't spot anything out of the ordinary for a planet. It was obvious it was a Class Zero Nine world; otherwise, he wouldn't be breathing with ease. Even at this altitude, the air was thin, but manageable for his Tekol lungs. Penter appeared to be struggling slightly more than Brax, and Abbil was drawing deep breaths and releasing them more slowly.

"I don't think this is their world," Penter said quietly.

"Why do you say that?" Brax had the same hunch but wanted to hear the guard's reasoning.

Penter pointed into the distance. "There are no structures in place. No other ships on the horizon."

"Good eye. We never uncovered their origin, and I suspect this is a temporary stop, or this is where they plan on keeping us as slaves," Brax said.

"Why here?" Abbil asked.

Another hovering platform lowered from an arm above. Hot blasts from the blue thrusters pushed down, the air crackling and steaming with ferocity. Brax moved away instinctively, but felt the barrel of a gun pressed into his spine by the guard standing beside him. He watched as the fearful slaves lowered, and Brax attempted to gauge how many people the Statu had swiped from Greblok. He leaned over the edge now that the platform had moved on, and saw at least ten more of the huge daises lowered toward the ground. There had to be over ten thousand people in total. Maybe more, since he was only looking at one side of the ship.

Brax realized he'd left Abbil's question hanging in the air. "What did you ask?"

"Why here?"

"Because it's isolated, hidden from prying eyes. Honestly, I don't know how they expect to stay out of sight. We were only traveling for a few days. We couldn't have made it that far, not with the Statu technology the Concord has studied," Brax said.

"A lot can change in fifty standard star rotations," Penter said.

Brax nodded as the next empty platform arrived. The three of them stepped onto it and moved for the far edge. From here, Brax had a view of the Statu warship. A few of the Tubers flew around their mothership, likely keeping the peace. He breathed a sigh of relief when he saw no other warships nearby. This could be the last of their fleet, the sole remnants of the Statu, with one desperate act against the Concord in retribution for the end of the War.

Most of the familiar faces from their captivity on the ship had already gone with the last load, and so many new people materialized, moving slowly. They appeared far worse off than Brax's group had, and he suspected things hadn't been handled as smoothly. Many were visibly injured, either at the hands of the enemy or by each other.

The platform lowered abruptly, sending one of the slaves over the edge. His scream carried through the air, until the loud thrusters drowned out the death cry. Brax said a silent prayer to the Vastness to keep the rest of them safe until he could decipher this puzzle.

The trip to the surface only took a few minutes, and the air was denser here, almost heavy. His steps were a little lighter as they moved onto the ground, telling him the gravity was different from the standard Concord ship settings. It was damp here, the grass thick and green. Tall trees lined the field they were set into, and Brax scanned the copse for signs of Statu guards.

With their bulky suits, it might be easy to lose them inside the maze of a forest; only Brax had nothing with him to aid his survival. Making a run for it would only ensure his untimely demise.

Penter was looking to the trees as well, and Brax shook his head when the guard glanced over. "Not yet." He mouthed the words, and the big man gave him a tight-lipped smile.

There were at least a dozen Tubers in the air, loudly moving around the area. Brax was among one of the last groups of slaves trudging over the grass toward an eventual destination. He saw it now, following the trail of people who looked like ants storming a hill from this distance. The structure was huge, square and bulky, looking to be made of the same material as their warship.

"Welcome to your new home," Brax mumbled to

himself as he began moving forward, each step slow and deliberate as he followed the line with thousands of fearful slaves in front of him.

———————

*T*reena had almost laughed when the young boy from Greblok had emerged from the bridge. She knew Thomas from before, and even though they hadn't been in touch for years, he was always an advocate for someone showing their worth. How this kid had managed to convince the captain to join the two-person crew was beyond her.

The wormhole was daunting, a massive disturbance in space and time, and she hoped they weren't heading to their deaths. It had only been a few days since they'd all arrived on *Constantine*, and already they were risking their lives to do something not on record within the Concord. "You don't become a hero by hiding in the shadows," Treena said. Felix used to say that to her, usually with a brush of her hair from her face. Treena pressed her eyes closed, not wanting to forget him, but saving the memory for later.

"ETA is three minutes," she said, as much for the bridge's sake as her own. The wormhole looked so much more diminutive from the viewer on *Constantine*. Out here, it was daunting. Their compact vessel *Cleo* was a speck against the gaping maw of the wormhole. She almost expected it to pull on the ship like a whirlpool, but it didn't do anything to affect *Cleo* as she flew toward the center of the opening.

What was on the other side? Treena was fully confident that the Statu had passed through. There was nowhere else for them to go. At least if it was a trick, *Constantine* wouldn't be harmed. The crew could live on to fight another day, and eventually learn the truth.

Reeve sat beside her, her fingers racing over the console with practiced efficiency. "The readouts are the same. Probes show nothing different."

"I thought you said the wormhole was destabilizing," Treena said.

"What can I say? Maybe it is stable but sending off fluctuations. We've never seen one this size, and it must take a lot of energy to power," Reeve told her, and Treena could only hope that she was right, that their passage would be smooth.

Tarlen was still behind them, strapped to the bench, staying oddly quiet. Treena peered over her shoulder to see him staring at the wormhole, eyes wide. "You know what I find helps when I'm afraid?" Treena asked the boy.

"No, what?"

"I play a game," she answered.

"A game?"

"You know, a game. It's something my father taught me when I was young," Treena told him.

"I don't know any games," he said.

"None?"

"Only things you play with other kids outside," Tarlen said.

"Bridge to *Cleo*. What are you seeing out there?" It was the captain, and Treena could picture his serious expression glowering at the viewer.

"We're here, probes are static, and we're ready to enter at your command," Reeve answered first.

Treena's hands hovered over the controls, and it hit her. She wasn't really in any danger. Her body was safely aboard *Constantine* in bed. Would they replace this artificial body if she was destroyed in the wormhole? Panic threatened to overwhelm her at the thought of waking up in her withered form in her bedroom, unable to speak or move.

"Constantine will be joining you and relaying what he's able to," Thomas said, and the AI flickered to life behind her. He stood, not needing to strap in.

Reeve smiled at the AI. "Welcome aboard, Con."

"Glad to be here for this momentous occasion," Constantine said. "Of course, I have nothing to fear."

Tarlen let out a gasp, and Treena frowned at the AI. "Maybe you should can the glowing pep talk, Constantine."

"Commander Starling, begin entry into the wormhole," the captain said from the bridge, his voice wavering slightly through the speaker.

"Beginning entry." Treena moved their ship forward. The slowly swirling colorful opening was immense, and soon they could see nothing but the blackness of space.

"Good luck, we're counting..." Thomas' voice disappeared, and the lights inside *Cleo* flickered on and off, dimming before returning to normal.

"What's happening?" Tarlen asked, and Reeve was quick to reply.

"Just an energy flux as we passed through the barrier. Everything checks out, no system interruptions to report, Commander," she said.

"Constantine, are you still activated?" Treena asked, scared to take her eyes off the screen. She spotted a tiny dot of light in the distance, and she used that as a marker, flying the expedition ship slowly forward on impulse thrusters.

"I am here," the AI said.

"Can you reach the bridge?" she asked.

"Unfortunately, I am unable to relay any messages at

this time," he said.

"Keep trying," she ordered him. The ship began to shake, and Treena sent an ultrasonic scan around their area, trying to find out what was causing the disturbance.

"Why are we shaking?" Tarlen asked, his voice a wobbly whisper.

Cleo stopped jerking around at the invisible turbulence for a moment, before it pulled hard one way, then the other. Her belt cut into her shoulder, and Treena felt the controls slip from her fingers. The tiny speck of light remained, but the blackness was gone, replaced by a bright tunnel. They'd entered the wormhole.

They raced forward, the speed reading on the screen impossible yet happening. They sped through the corridor, jerking as it turned directions every few seconds.

Treena lifted her hands, knowing that she wouldn't want to stop the ship even if she could. Reeve did the same, and the Tekol woman watched through the viewer with tears streaming down her cheeks.

Treena would have cried as well, but she had no tear ducts. She did the only thing she could think of as they tore through space in the expedition ship. "Tarlen, you get ten stones, five black, and five white."

FIFTEEN

*T*he ship vanished from all readouts seconds after it penetrated the wormhole entrance. Thomas slammed a palm onto his chair arm and gripped the leather tightly. He should never have agreed to this risky endeavor. Maybe he wasn't cut out for this role. Already he was making bad decisions, letting the crew around him make suggestions and rolling with them.

"Captain, they're out of range," Ven said slowly.

"Damn it, Ven, I can see that!" he shouted, making Junior Officer Zare jump in her seat. "Constantine, any sign of your other version out there?"

The AI stood near Thomas, his arms long at his sides. "No, Captain. I am not able to access…"

"I knew this was going to happen. Keep searching, and notify me when something changes," Thomas ordered.

"Captain, we have scarce knowledge of the wormholes. There is no means to predict what occurred, or if they even made it through. I suggest…" Constantine began to say, and Thomas lifted a hand to cut him off.

"I'm done with suggestions for today. I'll be in my office. Only disturb me if you find signs of *Cleo*," Thomas said. "On second thought, I'm going for a walk."

He stood, leaving the bridge, upset at himself for his reaction. This was it. He was going to have to return to Nolix with his tail between his legs. If he was lucky, they'd spare him a trip to prison, opting for a dismissal or at best a demotion.

This was not the way he'd planned on beginning his role as captain of the Concord's flagship. He walked past the guards and into the elevator. Maybe a cup of coffee would help clear his mind. Thomas tried to understand why he'd allowed such a risky maneuver, and it clicked.

The Statu. They were the enemy. Thomas had grown up under the care of his grandparents, and rarely had a day gone by without the old admiral talking about them. Everything about his life and career had been centered around the Statu. Constantine had taken on command of his vessel two years into the War. In the early years, so many good ships and captains were lost to the battles, until the Concord clued in how to fight their adversaries successfully.

Tom's grandfather had gone on to command the same Concord cruise ship for four years, until the last battle, the infamous Yollox Incursion. The ship had been repaired, but he was promoted after that fight, the War finally over. There were numerous openings over the years, and many promotions happened in short order. Tom knew the history books well. The Concord allowed entrance to another ten planets in the first five years after the War.

The Concord stated it was a measure of goodwill to the worlds that had helped them in the time of need, supplying food and materials for the War, but Tom was aware of the truth. His grandfather had spoken out of turn one night after a few too many cocktails. He could still picture the man, resplendent in his formal admiral's uniform, so many stars etched on the breast, he could have been a constellation.

Tom had been ten or eleven, wearing a suit. His hair had been slicked, and Tom had hated it. He remembered trying to undo his tie an hour into the event, much to his grandmother's chagrin. The fireplace was roaring, real wood crackling. It was an old world remnant, but Constantine had always had a penchant for that kind of thing. The guests had left, the servants were cleaning up the dining area, and his grandfather asked Tom if he wanted to go to the sitting room. It was unusual, because Tom was never allowed inside. He nodded, happy for a rare glimpse behind the curtain.

Constantine led him into the room, the fire already lit, and he pointed to the red leather chair, indicating for Tom to sit. He did so, staring at everything with wide eyes.

"You know what just happened?" Grandfather had asked.

Tom shook his head. "We had dinner?"

The older man laughed at that before coughing. He bent over, and little did Tom realize that it was the first sign of the lethal Lekni infection that took so many lives from War survivors.

"What happened was a bunch of tight-assed suck-ups want me to run for Prime," he said, and Tom was shocked.

"The Prime?" he asked.

"The one and only. Can you imagine? A human Prime? The Concord would never stand for it."

"Why not?" Tom asked, curiosity filling him. His grandfather rarely spoke about such things around him, and he swelled with pride at the inclusion. He tried to watch what he said so he didn't come off as a dumb kid.

"I understand you've learned about the Founders, as everyone does. Humans were lucky to be included, believe me. The Concord could have done it without us, but we were a force too powerful to ignore. Humans... the others saw us as a pest at first. Were you told that?" Constantine asked.

Tom blinked, watching his grandfather fill a tumbler

with brown liquid, some sloshing over the ledge to land on the pristine wooden floors. "I didn't know. Why were we pests?"

"Because the moment humans had the ability to traverse the stars, nothing was ever good enough. We needed more. More ships, more planets, more resources. None since the Callalay had such drive. When we were discovered, there was no turning a blind eye to us." Grandfather took a long drink, coughing a little after swallowing.

"And that's when the Concord was created?"

"That's right. The Founders."

"But why won't they let you be Prime?" Tom asked, still not following.

"We're too new. Too fresh. The others have been trading and talking for thousands of years. We're the infant of this whole thing," Constantine told him.

Tom nodded, pretending to understand. "But they all love you. You're a hero."

His grandfather filled his glass and crossed the room to stand in front of the fireplace. He was so close, Tom worried a spark would catch his uniform on fire. "A hero? I'm no hero, son. No."

"But…"

"But nothing." He saw the old man was unsteady on his feet, and Tom stood, offering his arm. With a grunt, his grandfather accepted and took a seat beside him. "They want to expand again. Let more worlds into the Concord."

Tom was unsure what to do with the sudden change of subjects. "Isn't that a good thing?"

"Yes. For the Concord, it is. But that doesn't mean it's good for everyone else."

Tom had never heard his grandfather saying anything negative about the Concord before, and it worried him. "Why?"

"Post-War, we let in ten worlds. Can you name them?"

Tom couldn't. He thought hard, but he didn't think they'd learned that in his lessons. "I can't recall."

Constantine slapped a knee with his palm and leaned back in the seat. "That's right. Because the Concord doesn't want anyone to remember them. There's an old saying in the Code. *Strength is rarely manufactured or grown; it is curated carefully and selectively.*"

Tom closed his open mouth, even more confused.

"It means that things like the Concord didn't become strong on their own. They used those planets' resources and left them to rot. They stole their people as bodies to fill the roles of servants and maintenance crews. They mined their worlds, building up the Fleet again, and when it was all done, they moved on.

"If you want to find a Fengothian these days, you're going to have to hit a backwater world called Rekva, because their own planet was destroyed." Constantine drank slower now, his hand shaking slightly as he spoke.

"Why would the Concord do that? What about the Code?" Tom asked, upset at the words he was hearing. He'd grown up believing in the Concord, and his grandfather often made him study the Code.

"The Code is strong, it's valid, but too often, people twist words to suit their own needs. Either way, I won't be running for Prime. Pha'n from Callalay will be the winner. I can already tell," he told Tom.

"Why?"

"Because she has the most contacts in the Concord. Because she believes in a strong Fleet, and she was there…" He coughed again. "She knows too much."

Tom didn't question his grandfather, and they went on to speak of nicer things, like Tom's inclusion into the junior Academy coming up in a few months.

The elevator notified Tom he was on Deck Four, and he exited it, lost in his memory of that moment so many years ago. That was why he'd reacted the way he had with the Statu, and that was why he couldn't let them get away with taking the ore and the slaves from the Concord's newest partner. Years ago, the Concord had been stripping worlds of precious materials, and they still were. Tom wasn't going to let Greblok go down like this, not because of the Concord. Admiral Hudson would pay for his dismissive remarks.

If only there was a way to confirm if *Cleo* had made it safely through the wormhole – and it hit him like a slap to the face. Tom ran back to the elevator, ordering it to head to the residence deck. He raced through the hallway to the room he'd seen only a couple of days ago with Treena Starling. It didn't grant him access, and he hastily used his override code, the door to Starling's room sliding open.

The lights were dim, and for a moment, he didn't even hear the gentle humming of the machines maintaining the real Treena Starling. He moved slowly, nervous beads of sweat clinging to his skin. *"Be steadfast, be vigilant, be strong. The Vastness welcomes all,"* Tom whispered out of habit.

There she was, on the bed, slightly turned to the side. Her eyes were closed, and he glanced at the computer readout. The wires plugged into the back of her head were lit up, but that didn't mean anything. He crossed over to the computer screen and scrolled to the diagnostics of the artificial vessel she was controlling on the expedition ship.

"What do we have here?" he asked himself, trying to make sense of the readouts. There it was. Running at ninety-nine percent efficiency. From what he could tell, the artificial body Treena Starling was controlling was operational, meaning *Cleo* was either traveling through the wormhole or they'd emerged on the other side.

Tom slunk to a seat beside the bed as his eyes rested on the frail woman, and he wondered if Treena did the same. Her real body was so frail, nothing like the strong woman he now knew as his commander. He needed to place a body in this room, but it had to be someone he could trust with Treena. Nee's nurse Kelli, perhaps.

Now that he was confident they weren't destroyed, he relaxed for a moment before he remembered the cryogenically-frozen beings claiming to be Statu, encased in his ship. It was time to interrogate the being and find out what the hell was going on.

———————

"This is food?" Penter asked, picking up the bowl and setting it down hurriedly. Some of the slop dripped over the edge onto the metal table. Thousands of Bacals were inside the space, each eating their rations for the day.

There were barrels of water along the outer walls, and Brax assumed this was all one spark of illness away from turning into a cesspool of filth and death. The slaves drank the gruel from the bowls, not being given any utensils. A few of the people attempted to speak to the armor-wearing Statu, but not once did Brax hear a reply.

No one made a move against their captors, not since the first five had been killed as an example. The smell inside the huge room was overwhelming, far worse than even the room on the ship had been. Brax was amazed at how quickly an advanced race could become nothing more than despondent animals in a pen. It was terrifying. Some part of him clung to the hope of rescue by the *Constantine* crew, but he knew it was a long shot.

Brax sighed and ate the rest of the flavorless food.

Abbil was beside him, her hair pulled into a long ponytail. She was a tough woman, but that was about all he knew of her.

"Abbil, you said you were in town watching the Regent's speech. What did you do for a living?" Brax asked her.

She didn't even look up from her bowl. "I'm a teacher. I suppose I *was* a teacher," she said.

"I don't think you'll ever stop being one, then," Brax told her. "Just like Penter here will always take his training as a guard with him everywhere he goes, right?"

"That's right." Penter nodded firmly. "I thought you looked familiar. Did you teach at the Northern Institute?"

Abbil smiled finally at the mention of the school name. "Don't tell me I taught your children," she said.

"No. My kid wasn't old enough yet. I did security there a few seasons for extra pay," he told her, and she nodded.

"I worked at my husband's bakery on weekends."

"Not uncommon for our people to work every day of the week, is it?" Penter asked, and Brax found he was enjoying the normal conversation, even if the setting was dire.

"I imagine that won't change now that we're… slaves." Abbil pushed her half-full bowl away.

"You should eat it," Brax suggested. "You're going to need the energy."

"So I can do what?"

"I…"

"Be a slave for these masked freaks?" Abbil appeared ready to sound off, so Brax grabbed hold of her arm, keeping her in the seat.

"Shhhh. We're going to figure this out. Together. I need you to stay calm and listen to me. I'm going to get us out of this," Brax said quietly. She resisted at first, but he felt her posture go slack; her arm dangled loosely beside her.

An alarm rang out, three quick blasts of a terrible noise, and it was over. Penter stood up and peered around the room. "I guess that means the dinner party's over."

They'd been forced to sleep in confined areas of about one hundred people, with no pillows, no blankets, no anything. Brax stretched his sore back and glanced to the exits, where the armed guards were. He counted the Statu inside the space and thought there were only two dozen or so. If he could procure a gun, he'd… What? He closed his eyes and told himself to stop trying to escape so soon. He knew nothing about the place.

With slaves cowed like this, the guards might become complacent in a month, maybe even a week. Then he would have a better sense of where they were, what the routine looked like, and perhaps even uncover a weakness or two around the encampment.

The people were filing out of the room, the distinct sound of crying carrying to his ears from multiple directions. The man in front of Brax was moving slowly, his feet dragging as he shuffled along. Their home had been destroyed, their spirits broken, and Brax couldn't blame them for reacting this way. He wasn't ready to give up quite yet, though. These people needed some strength, and he was going to be there to provide it.

They eventually exited the table-filled room and headed outside. It was bright again, the blue star sweltering in the cloudless sky.

"Looks like we get some outside time," Penter said. There were more of the Statu on the outskirts of the structure the slaves ate and slept inside.

"Stay close to me. I think they're separating us into work detail groups," Brax said, and Abbil stood directly beside him, Penter behind.

The Statu headed towards them was short, his suit rougher and more patched than most of the others. He had a gun in his grip and a three-foot-long metal wand in his left hand. He motioned for their group to stand together, and he shoved a few standing Bacals away, another Statu waving them over.

When it was done, Brax counted one hundred even in his group. Abbil and Penter had stayed with him, which gave him some relief.

Soon there were groupings of a hundred each spread out along the stampeded grass. Sweat was pouring off Brax's bald head, and he rubbed it, the stubble growing longer than it had in years. He missed the routine of shaving it, and thought about his sister, wondering how she was dealing with his disappearance. If he knew her, and he did, she'd stop at nothing before learning where he was and what had befallen him.

It was a solace as he stood in the heat, the sun angrily beating down on them. The slaves reeked of filth, unable to shower in the last week as they were penned like livestock. Now they were expected to go to work, and he waited as he saw the hovering platforms arriving from somewhere far away. They were specks in the sky, growing as they thrust forward, lowering to the grass, one before each group.

Brax was the first to step on from his company, the others instantly deferring to him. He tried to keep his head up, his posture tall, as a sign of hope to the other slaves, but he also didn't want to appear cocky to the Statu. That would be a sure way to end up dead. He doubted they'd have any qualms about shooting him or shoving him over the edge at a thousand feet.

Their group gathered on the platform, and two armed guards joined them. Other groups had already lifted from the ground and were moving away. The surface shook and lurched upwards, the thrusters loud and irritated-sounding. Abbil clutched Penter's arm as they roared into the sky, and Brax tried to see over the horizon, guessing at a destination.

Each of the groups was heading in different directions now, though Brax noticed three others staying close to the one he was traveling on. They picked up speed, and the wind threatened to bowl him over. A man screamed at the edge of the platform, and Brax saw him stumble toward the short rail. He pushed past Penter and grabbed the man by his grimy collar, keeping him from tumbling to his death.

"Thank you," the man mumbled, getting to his knees so he wouldn't fly away. Others took heed at his near miss, and soon they were all sitting on the platform, waiting to land.

The trip took at least a half hour, and Brax's nerves were fried along with his eardrums by the time it began its descent. The strange transport was shaking violently as they settled to the ground, and it flicked off as they landed, the entire world seeming to go silent as the three other transport decks powered down around them.

Brax took in the sights, seeing mountains of raw materials piled around an open field.

"What do you make of this?" Penter asked him.

Brax saw another building beside the materials. "It seems we might be here for the long haul. See that?" He pointed to the structure. "I think we could be staying in there."

"Great. I wonder if they have room service," Penter said with a smile. Brax really liked the guy, and was glad someone else was keeping their cool during this trying time.

"What do you think we're doing here?" Abbil asked.

"I think we're about to find out." Brax stepped off, taking the lead, and followed one of the guards toward the open field.

It quickly became clear what they were there for. Behind the fifty-foot-tall stacks of materials sat the beginnings of a chunk of a Statu warship, like the one that had attacked Greblok. This was an arm, or the rough husk of one. The materials were dark and metallic; a dozen crude robots gleamed in the heat.

"I think we just did," Penter said, wiping the sweat from his brow.

"I guess this means the Statu are back and looking to rebuild." Brax crossed his arms, wondering how many ships they were constructing on this world, and if there were other worlds with more slaves doing the same process.

SIXTEEN

*T*he lights faded and the ship stopped shaking as *Cleo* thrust forward, entering space at normal impulse speed again. The entire trip had only taken somewhere around ten minutes, according to the computer, but to Treena, it had seemed like hours.

"Are you two doing okay?" she asked, glancing behind her to see Tarlen clutching the seat with a white-knuckled grip.

"I'll get over it," Tarlen said, and even Reeve beside her was slightly paler. Her long braids hung over her eyes, the red not only limited to her irises any longer. She was in rough shape.

"How about you, Daak?" Treena asked.

"I... know too much. We shouldn't have been able to do that," Reeve said.

"Then why did you agree to come?" Treena asked her.

"Because someone needs to look after you," she answered, and Treena noticed her force a smile.

"I think there's more to it. Perhaps your missing brother?" Treena scanned the region, trying to gather her bearings. The stars were unfamiliar to the computer system, and it was quickly searching through the clusters, attempting to find a match it could use. Lights blinked across the screen as it gently beeped with each failure.

"He might have something to do with it." Reeve began

helping, running deft fingers over the screen. "No sign of the Statu. Let me run telemetry scans of the area. If they did pass through the wormhole, there will be trailing particles from their engines nearby."

It didn't take long before Reeve grinned and pointed at the screen. "Here we go. They've been here. You'd think they'd have found a way to hide their burnout like we have."

Treena considered this. "They haven't been seen in fifty years. I have to imagine they've been in hiding and probably lost contact with the rest of their fleet."

"Interesting hypothesis. Did you run that one by Constantine?" Reeve asked, and the AI flickered to life behind them.

"Did you call?" he asked.

"Commander Starling was thinking this could be an offshoot of the War, maybe a dormant world where they were constructing a warship," Reeve told him.

Constantine appeared to consider this. "How did they know about Greblok?"

Treena thought about it but didn't have a good answer. "That's unclear."

"I study data and probability a lot, but sometimes there are such things as coincidences," Reeve said.

"Or the admiral tipped them off." Treena said it so quietly, she didn't think anyone heard her.

"Why would you say that?" Constantine asked.

"You didn't see the conversation we had with him and the Prime. Something fishy was going on. They think because Baldwin is who he is, and *lucky* to have this position, they can count on his obedience and silence. That's not the Thomas we're starting to know," Treena said.

"What do they stand to gain?" Reeve asked.

Tarlen remained quiet on the bench; he wouldn't be

familiar with many of their topics of discussion.

"That's unclear to me. If they were aware the Statu were humans during the War, and the Concord didn't let word get out…" Reeve started, but was cut off by Tarlen.

"Wait! Are you saying those things are human?" he asked, his voice high-pitched and loud.

Constantine answered. "Not exactly. The single Statu to survive inside their armored suit without being killed by a Scrambler was human. But we imagine the human was but a slave, an innocent victim sent to do their bidding."

"Then…" Tarlen clued in, and Treena nodded, the computer still sorting through the unfamiliar star maps.

"Then they're planning on enslaving your people and doing the same thing with them," Treena said.

"We have to stop them!" Tarlen shouted, and Treena craned her neck, staring at the boy. He sat abruptly and lowered his eyes. Much more quietly, he said it again. "We have to stop them."

"We're going to try," Treena told the panicked boy.

Cleo moved slowly through space, constantly away from the wormhole, which was remaining stable according to the probes Reeve had sent through. There might be a hope in hell of retrieving Brax and returning to *Constantine*, but it was going to be tricky.

"The remnants of the warship end a thousand kilometers from there." Reeve pointed to the map projection, and Treena set course for that location. It was doubtful the ship could be traced that easily.

"What are we looking at here?" Treena asked, searching the readouts. The probes had done their job, jumping to the far reaches of the system and returning the data in a rush of information.

"The star is spectral class O. Old system; the most likely planet for life is the fourth from the dwarf. Three moons. There's an asteroid belt in deep space, but it appears to be unnaturally hindered," Reeve said.

"Hindered?" Tarlen asked.

Treena took this one. "Mined. Someone or something has mined the asteroid field."

"What does that mean?" the boy asked.

"It means they planned this." Treena zoomed in on the world, seeing a lush green planet with a broad ocean and likely abundant life. The computer beeped three times in quick succession and showed there were no results for the star map.

Constantine wavered and became solid again, his handsome youthful face finding a slight grimace. "How are we this far out? The Concord's records run deep. It's unsettling to be so far from known space."

"You're not kidding," Reeve said, her usually jovial self put away for the time being. "This is so great."

"It is?" Tarlen asked.

"Sure. We're the first of our kind to ever visit this. We're real pioneers. Like Andron Loor, the first captain of an interstellar Tekol vessel." Reeve beamed from the seat beside Treena. The two of them couldn't have been feeling more polarized about their current situation.

Treena had read stories of the ancient explorer and found it hard to believe the Tekol had managed to travel to another system with their rudimentary vessels. It wasn't until the Zilph'i made contact with other races that true faster-than-light travel had become commonplace, and that had been over three thousand years ago. It would be some time before humans were introduced into the mix.

As she directed their ship toward the last identified location of the Statu, Treena wondered how long their enemies had been around. Originally, the Concord had stated the Statu were an infant race, but one that gave a hell of a fight. Now, seeing space so far from Concord records, she doubted that was true. They were merely too far away to cross paths, until they found the wormhole. A truly stable wormhole. She thought maybe Ven's readouts were false, and that it wasn't growing unstable.

Maybe those changes were only part of the wormhole's routine. There was an old saying from the Code she'd always remembered but had never believed until now. *The Vastness of space is never ending, much like that of one's mind. Treat both with respect, and there is no limit to either.* Treena smiled at her recollection of sitting beside her father as he read from the book, teaching her parables and the ways the Concord lived by.

She missed him.

"Scanning the fourth planet for Tubers," Reeve said, grabbing Treena's drifting attention. The search took a few minutes, and she stared toward Treena. "Nothing near it or orbiting."

Treena thought that was strange. "Why wouldn't they place defenses?"

"They didn't expect anyone to follow them through," Constantine said. "The Statu were never very bright. They had terrible machines, robotics, and slaves to do their work for them, but they were more about an aggressive suicidal force beating their heads against a wall until they found a door."

"Constantine, are you still blocked off from the main ship?" Reeve asked.

After a brief pause, Constantine said that he had no contact.

"How are you operating, then?" Treena asked, recognizing that the ship's AI was limited by the operating system in the boiler room.

"I'm connected to *Cleo*. It was a precautionary step the

Concord took in the construction of their new flagship," he advised them.

"Lucky us," Reeve said.

Treena was moving toward the planet, and she checked their ETA. At impulse speed, which wouldn't draw much attention unless a localized sensor was scanning for it, they had two hours before they reached the world where she suspected Brax Daak and the remaining population of the devastated Greblok planet were located.

That didn't give them long to devise a plan on how to extradite their crew member and learn what their old adversary was up to.

————————

*T*he lights were dimmed at Doctor Nee's suggestion, casting shadows over Ven beside Thomas. The Ugna officer was tall, his face so pale, it was almost glowing. He glanced at Thomas with a soft expression, not saying a word as Nee finally re-entered, holding a tablet in his gloved hand.

Thomas hadn't spent a lot of time around a Kwant before, but being near Nee had given him an appreciation for the often ignored race. The fact that skin-to-skin contact with the Kwants could kill a human and many other races was something that had been learned quickly, and it made it difficult for the Kwant people to find stations on Concord cruise ships.

His old ship didn't have any Kwant representation, but once he understood them more, Thomas was going to request that they ask Nee's people to send a couple more crew members to work on *Constantine*. It seemed fair.

"Are you ready?" Nee asked, his shock-white hair perfectly coifed. Thomas wondered how the man always appeared so presentable, no matter what the hour or circumstance.

"We're ready," Thomas told him, even though he didn't quite feel like he was. He was distracted by the absent crew members. He felt vulnerable with three executive crew members being away, like his ship was missing half its organs. The ancillary crew was doing fine as they waited near the wormhole, but he didn't want to go into combat or rush into any expeditions without Brax, Reeve, and Treena at his side.

His thoughts surprised him. They'd only been together a few days, and yet Tom already felt a connection to them. He took that as a good sign. Now they only needed to find a way to bring everyone safely back to the ship, and then convince the Concord that what they'd done was for the right reasons. It was going to be an uphill battle.

"Sir, may I offer my assistance in the interrogation?" Ven asked.

Thomas stiffened. "I know I called it that earlier, but I'd like to consider it a *conversation* rather than an interrogation, at least until we clarify a few things with this man."

"Very well, sir. May I offer my assistance in the" – Ven changed the word – "conversation?"

"Sure. What do you have in mind?" Tom asked the albino Zilph'i.

"Exactly."

"I don't follow," Tom said.

Nee was across the bed, and he smiled. "The Ugna are able to read minds. Or – correct me if I'm wrong, Ven – probe for spikes in patterns."

Ven nodded. "I'm surprised you're aware of this. We keep our practices closed to outsiders."

Tom smiled, feeling optimistic. "We're not outsiders, are we? We're on the same crew. A family," he said, his words falling flat.

Ven appeared to consider this, his expression changing little. "We are one crew, but far from family yet."

"Fair enough. What can you do to assist this?" Tom asked, crossing his arms and staring at the sedated man claiming to be a Statu. His skin was dark gray, his mandibles not as threatening this time – thinner than Tom had originally thought, his exoskeleton hard to the touch.

"I should be able to ascertain if he speaks in truth. I suspect I'll need a baseline, but once I do…"

"You'll confirm if he's truly a Statu or not." Tom was glad to hear this news. It would really help their efforts.

Nee tapped the man's arm, making a knocking sound. "Tom, I've been able to … inspect one of the bodies that didn't make it from the cryopods after the Tuber attack on their ship."

"And?" Tom asked.

"They're as one would expect. Beneath the shell, they have organs, much like you and me. On the whole, most creatures aren't that much different on the inside. We adapt differently to our surroundings, our environments, but we have stomachs, hearts, and brains. Their lungs are half the size of humans', even more delicate than my own, and see this?" He pointed to the side of the patient's neck. "Looks like gills of some kind. This would suggest they're able to live underwater, at least for prolonged periods of time."

Tom leaned in, seeing the slits Nee was indicating. "Underwater… how common is that?"

"In bipedal beings? One race in two hundred has physiology able to sustain underwater living. Phurn 8, for example. You've heard of it?" Nee asked.

"Sure. Ninety percent water. The Egunlo are the top of the chain, living in advanced underwater structures. Fifth-level Concord members," Tom said, getting a surprised look from the doctor.

"That's right." Doctor Nee grabbed a medispray, pressing it into a soft spot on the patient's abdomen. "He'll wake up quickly, and we'll give him a minute to acclimate."

"Constantine," Tom said, the AI appearing instantly.

"Hello, Captain," Constantine said, glancing toward the alien body, who was beginning to make clicks and sounds with his mouth and mandibles. He was tethered to the table, and he tested his bonds now, not struggling but likely recalling where he was.

"We're going to begin. Are you ready? Ask him a few basic questions, math problems that he'll understand so Ven can obtain a baseline," Tom ordered.

Constantine appeared confused by what the Ugna executive lieutenant was going to be doing, but he began, introducing them all to the man.

"His name translates roughly to Yephion. Captain Thomas Baldwin, he understands you are in charge here, and he will direct his comments to you if that pleases you," Constantine said.

Tom nodded. "Yephion, on behalf of the crew of *Constantine* and the Concord, I welcome you to my ship." He waited while Constantine translated, the man's dark eyes wide and unblinking. He was propped up in the bed, his tethers loosened, but not enough that he could escape if he put up a fight.

Yephion made a series of sounds, and Constantine repeated them in Standard. "He thanks you for the rescue. He asks what year it is. Shall I tell him?"

"I don't see what harm there is in advising him," Tom said, watching as the AI spoke.

Yephion sat higher, instantly clicking and gurgling out more words.

"He says that's impossible. Their cryo was supposed to

wake them long ago," Constantine said.

"How long?" Tom asked, nervous for the answer.

"Approximately four hundred Standard years," the AI answered.

Tom glanced at Ven, and the Zilph'i man nodded.

"Okay, let's start here." Tom stepped forward, getting closer to the man. "Where are you from?"

"He says they are from a system called Konov; their world's one of two there with life," Constantine told them.

"Ven, are you getting a read on him?" Tom asked.

"Yes, sir. I believe what he says so far," Ven advised.

"Good. Pay attention to this one. Constantine, ask him if he's truly Statu." Tom squinted, watching closely as the AI asked the question.

"He says they are Statu, but he wonders how we've heard the name before," Constantine said.

"Why did they leave their home?" Tom asked.

Constantine asked, and Yephion's posture changed. His shoulders slumped, his head hanging forward slightly. He spoke at length, and the AI took it all in, waiting until the man stopped speaking before translating.

"They had a war going on with their neighboring planet. This crew was supposed to seek assistance. They were on the way to Concord space when their engines stopped, which must have affected the date of release from the cryo chambers," Constantine said.

Tom's arms covered in goosebumps as he listened. "And they're truly Statu?"

"That's what he says."

"And their neighbors?" Tom asked.

"Statu as well. They lived between two worlds, each with a very different ideology, it appears," Constantine said.

"How so?" Tom was starting to understand what

happened.

"Those Statu were planning on expanding their reach, while this man's people only wanted to make contact with others for trade and exploration. Their people were a curious bunch, the others greedy and dictatorial."

Tom nodded. "Where's their homeworld?" If they could learn this piece of information, they could mount a fleet to destroy the Statu once and for all.

Yephion appeared anxious as he spoke quickly.

Constantine translated. "He says he doesn't know where he is and wouldn't be able to direct you. He was untrained in space travel and says that he was a maintenance crew member only."

Ven remained motionless but whispered quietly to Tom, "He's lying. He understands exactly where they're from. I sense he's not telling us the truth about his rank."

Tom didn't let his cards show. "Translate this, Constantine. Then it's a good thing we downloaded everything from your hard drives before your cousins blew up the ship."

Yephion didn't hide his surprise well. He gaped at Tom.

"If I find out you have anything to do with the War against the Concord, I'll make an example out of you, Yephion. If you lie to me again, I'll deliver you to Nolix, where they'll try you and your people as war criminals. Do you have any idea what our people would do to you if they learned you were Statu, our greatest enemy of all time?" Tom asked, and waited for Constantine to relay the message.

"He says he doesn't understand how they were enemies. Do you want me to fill him in?" Constantine asked, and Tom shook his head.

"Not yet. I want to learn more about their history

before we disclose how dire our relationship is," Tom said.

"Bridge to Captain Baldwin," the speaker said, and Tom glanced at Nee, who shrugged. He'd remained quiet for most of the discussion, only watching vitals on his tablet.

"Go ahead, Zare," Tom said.

"A Concord vessel has arrived in the system, and they're sending a communication. Would you like to hear it?" she asked.

"Of course, patch it through." Tom glanced at Ven, who looked perturbed at the notion of a Concord ship nearby.

"Captain Thomas Baldwin, this is Admiral Hudson. You've disobeyed orders. Prepare for our arrival and notify the ship that I will be taking over as acting captain for the time being." The image of the man appeared in a projection along the edge of the room, and Tom grimaced.

"Great. Just when things were getting interesting," Tom said, wishing he had more time.

SEVENTEEN

Brax controlled the robotic arms, lifting the material high into the air. Beside him, Penter tapped the archaic keyboard, instructing the drone to weld the two sheets to the exterior hull. Sweat poured off Brax's head, and he had to pause the two-handed operation to wipe his brow dry.

The sun was intense, and they'd been going for at least five hours without a break. Already he'd seen some of Penter's people passing out from exertion, and Brax made a point of telling the guards they needed a break and water.

They hadn't listened to a word he'd said. If they understood Standard, they didn't show it.

"How long do you think it'll take to build one of these warships?" Penter asked.

"At this rate? A year or so," Brax said. It was a slow process, which involved heating metals using some rusty old smelter, the fumes rising from the ground in waves. They were offered no masks, no gloves, and Brax knew this wasn't going to end well for the slaves, or for him.

The melted ores were placed into cooling molds, where they came out in thin sheets. Each sheet was a slightly different color, depending on the percentage of elements inside the rocky substance they were manipulating. They had a crude frame of what would eventually be an arm of a warship, and Brax and the larger Bacals were in charge of adding the cooled sheets to the exterior, overlapping them sixty percent of the sheet, and welding them together. So far, they had a whopping five sheets attached, with at least another two thousand needed before the arm was completely covered. It was going to be a long venture.

Judging by the slaves' pace, Brax didn't think half of them would survive a week at this camp. The Statu had no interest in creating a passable workplace environment. They were only interested in results, and not how many slaves they killed along the way. It was sickening.

The controls were rigid in his hands, and the robotic arms clenched one of the sheets, Brax judging it to weigh at least a hundred kilograms. He twisted one, lifting the other handle, as the sheet found purchase beside the other five welded pieces. Penter's drone was there in a second, the arc of its flame shooting out as the solder was dropped in a crude line by yet another drone.

"This could be a weapon," Penter whispered the suggestion, but Brax doubted it.

"Those suits are pretty tough. It takes a few blasts from our XRC-14 to disable them, and that's at close range. I don't think the little torch will be enough," he told Penter, who only took a deep breath in response. "There'll be an opening eventually. We'll find it. This is day one."

"We're far from anything. Why do you think they keep the camps separated so far apart?" Penter asked.

Brax had given it a lot of thought, and he'd come up with one solid hypothesis. "There aren't many guards, so they have to keep us apart. Can you imagine if all ten thousand Bacals were together and decided to revolt? Sure, we'd lose a few, but we'd eventually overwhelm them. That's why they kept us weak, starving us before we arrived. We were confused, no leadership, no plan. Now that we're in these secluded groups, we have no way of communicating, decreasing our chances of dissent."

Penter moved the drone, stumbling a bit with his weld before compensating and continuing the line. "That's quite the assumption. One I'd agree with. Then what do we do?"

Brax made sure that none of the few guards were nearby and leaned closer. "My tracker will lead my crew here. When they find out we're isolated from the main ship, they'll be able to send a rescue mission."

"What about the rest of my people?" Penter asked.

"Don't worry. We won't leave anyone behind," Brax said with false security. The truth was, he was uncertain if anyone was coming for him. And if they did, would his new captain risk their ship and other crew to help a non-Concord member? There were rules about this kind of thing, and the deal hadn't been solidified between the Concord and Greblok yet. Brax doubted it ever would be now.

"Good. How long will it take for them to follow?" Penter asked. They finished the sheet installation, noticing the pile of supplies was empty. Brax glanced to the first stage, where the people were struggling with the raw materials. It would only be so long before the Statu would begin making examples of the people responsible for the bottlenecks.

"Not long," Brax said without confidence. "They'll come." He waved for Penter to follow him to the first stage, as someone needed to help melt the ore in order to keep everyone alive on their first day as working slaves.

"They have to," he whispered to himself as Penter began moving through the motions, showing a thin woman how to optimize her station.

---

*T*homas waited in the docking bay for the transport vessel to arrive. He'd been shocked to learn his old craft, the

Cecilia, was the cruise ship that had brought Admiral Hudson to the outreaches past the Border.

The transport liner latched on with ease, and Thomas nervously watched the inhabitants step through the hatch and onto his ship. *His* ship. He doubted he'd be able to say that for long.

Admiral Hudson was the first off, and he glared at Tom from across the bay. Next was a familiar face, the captain of *Cecilia* and his former leader, Yin Shu. Even from that far away, Tom noticed a twinkle in her eye at seeing him standing there in uniform, the red collar denoting his rank.

"Hope you get a good look," he mumbled.

The third person emerged, and Tom coughed as he saw who it was. The Prime herself was here, on his ship, for some reason. She rarely left Nolix, and never to somewhere as dangerous as beyond the Border. Tom suddenly wished he had Brax Daak beside him to add some imposing muscle on his side.

They were flanked by security officers, each obviously armed, as their handhelds were mounted on their belts at the hip. One was a human man, the other a female Zilph'i.

"Just what in the Vastness do you think you're doing, Baldwin?" The admiral walked fast, his boots clipping away and echoing in the vast chamber.

Tom saw the anger in the other's eyes, and he stood tall, ready to take the brunt of the older man's wrath. He wasn't going down without standing his ground. "I was thinking that our newest Concord partner was all but destroyed, the mining materials beneath their ocean you so desperately wanted taken, along with thousands of potential slaves."

Captain Shu arrived right behind the admiral and, judging from the look of shock on her face, this was news to her. "Admiral, you told me Tom disobeyed you. What are we really doing here?"

The admiral cleared his throat and glanced at the incoming Prime. She was small in person, her lined face more wrinkled than Tom had suspected. Her head was bald like all Callalay, her forehead ridged along the temple and between her eyes. She stared at Tom with a hard glare, unspeaking.

"Captain Shu, we told him to return to Nolix with the information he'd gathered so we could assess and decide our next course of action," Admiral Hudson stated. "Isn't that true, Baldwin?"

Tom had the audacity to smile and wink at his old captain. They'd been close, friends even after serving together for years along the Border. She didn't return the grin, but only watched him with tight-lipped patience.

"That's right. I did disobey the order, but only because one of my crew was in danger. The Code states…" Tom started to say, but the admiral raised his hand, cutting him off.

"To hell with the Code," Hudson said, and Shu gasped. Tom's superior crossed the distance between them quicker than Tom would have thought possible, and he grabbed Tom by the collar, shoving him backwards. "Do you have any idea what you've done?"

Tom was at a loss. "I'm only doing what I think best for the Concord."

"Do you think there would still be a Concord if it wasn't for the Prime and me? Do you?" He remained clutching Tom, spittle flying from his lips. "The Statu were never going to stop; you see that now, don't you? We had to give them something."

Hudson released his collar and stepped back, suddenly deflated.

Captain Shu spoke next, stealing the words from

Tom's mouth. "What did you *do*?"

The admiral glanced around nervously, the guards holding their guns after their boss's tirade, unsure of the next course of action.

The Prime spoke for the first time, her voice as calm as her demeanor. "We're not doing this here. Tom, bring us to your private office."

Shu appeared ready to say something, but Tom noticed her pursing her lips, deferring to the Prime's idea.

"This way," Tom said, leading them from the bay.

"Stay here," Prime Pha'n said to the two guards. They glanced at the admiral, who nodded his agreement. Tom thought that was interesting. They should have accepted the Prime's lead without further question.

"Captain Baldwin, where's your commander?" Shu asked. She was always so formal, even in private settings. It wasn't a habit he could fault. She was meticulous and a great leader. He felt a little put off by having her here. Most people would have been thrown by the presence of the Prime, the leader of the entire Concord, with over a trillion lives under her wing, but Tom was more worried about showing the captain of his previous post how revolutionary his new station was.

Constantine was unlike any Concord vessel to date. It had been built with only the best materials, the newest technologies, and a crew unlike anything the fleet had ever seen before.

"Is it true you have an Ugna on board?" Captain Shu asked him.

"Why don't you ask the people responsible for putting the crew together?" Tom said, nodding toward the admiral and the Prime.

"Wait. You didn't even have a say in your own executive team?" Shu asked quietly.

"Captain Baldwin was lucky to have been granted this posting, and so are the rest of them. If I'd have known how much trouble he would give us, I never would have…" Admiral Hudson stopped at a glance from the old Prime.

No one spoke as they trekked through the corridors, past the open topiary, simultaneously as mist settled from the platform above, watering the plants. Tom caught Shu staring at it all, soaking in the sights of the amazing new flagship as they walked. He could have led them to his office another way, but he wanted to show them what they'd given him for a ship.

"Nice place," Shu said softly as they neared the courtyard's exit. Tom glanced up toward Treena's room, where Nee's nurse was watching over Starling's real body for anything out of the ordinary. She was under orders to advise him the moment anything strange occurred.

Eventually, they wound their way to his office, the lights turning on at their arrival. Tom wasn't used to having so many guests, and he found a spare chair in a closet, unfolding it and setting it across from his seat at the desk. He waited, seeing if the admiral or the Prime would take his chair, the power position in the office; when they sat in a line, he finally took his own seat.

"Are you going to throw me in the brig?" Tom asked, growing restless of their games.

The Prime looked at Tom before watching Captain Shu. "It crossed my mind, but now, perhaps we can come to an understanding."

Tom had trouble assessing how old she was, but her skin was loose, her eyes puffy and tired. She wasn't the same powerful leader in person. Here, she seemed like someone's grandmother.

"What kind of understanding?" he asked.

"What you saw were not the Statu," she said.

"But they were… Tubers, Movers, the warship. It's them," Tom said.

Admiral Hudson leaned forward, frowning at Tom. "Baldwin, your grandfather was always a little hard of hearing too. The Statu aren't back. You didn't see them. The official report will say that Greblok was attacked by Border pirates from Reepa, and Brax Daak was lost in the skirmish."

Tom's back straightened, alarm bells ringing in his head. "And what of the ship we found?"

Hudson had the audacity to smirk, sending shivers down Tom's arms. "We'll take the contents on *Cecilia,* and it never happened."

Tom peered over at his old captain, seeing the familiar consternation at a problem coursing through her mind. "And if I don't?"

"Then we remove you from power, take the ship, and follow what we ordered regardless. Baldwin, you can't win this one," Hudson said.

Tom took a deep breath, assuming this was going to be a huge risk, but he didn't care. There was no way he could leave his people across the wormhole, and the fact that he had live Statu on his ship, claiming to be innocent, couldn't be swept under a bureaucratic carpet. The Concord needed to know the truth.

"Constantine," Tom said, and the AI appeared. "You have my grandfather's memories, is that correct?"

The AI stood beside Tom, on his side of the desk, and all eyes were on him. "As previously mentioned, I recall his tactical…"

"But you told us about something interesting from the Yollox Incursion. Can you tell Captain Shu here what you found inside the single Statu suit hat had a faulty Scrambler?" Tom asked, and Hudson's face turned red.

"What do you hope to accomplish here?" Hudson barked. "This is a computer program. You might have tampered with him!"

"I want to hear this," Captain Shu said. "Go on, Constantine."

"We'll throw you both in the brig. Stop this now. Obey our orders and stand down!" Hudson stood quickly, sending his chair to the floor behind him.

The Prime didn't move, and Tom swore she aged another few years in an instant. "Hudson, stop. Maybe it's time…"

Hudson moved for the door, but it was locked and didn't open for him. "Baldwin, open the door."

"No," Tom and Constantine said at the same time, bringing a grin to Tom's face. Tom kept talking. "Captain Shu, it appears that it was a human."

"What? How is that possible?" Shu asked, her eyes going wide.

"They were both there." Tom indicated Hudson and Pha'n. "Why don't you ask them?"

"Is this true? What really happened that day?" Captain Shu asked.

"We don't need to discuss this." Hudson banged on the door, and Tom let him continue for a while before standing up.

"I think they struck a deal with the Statu, but it only bought them some time. They're back now, and the Concord knew what they were up to this whole time. The Statu were enslaving races, sticking them in suits and using them as fodder." Tom crossed his arms, standing tall.

"Then all those people they took… they didn't only use them as work slaves? They… They sent them against us? We were killing our own people?" Captain Shu looked like she was going to be sick.

Tom knew her grandparents had both fought in the War and had been part of an early attack where nearly the entire fleet had been taken by the enemy. There had been millions of Concord lives lost or stolen during the War, and to realize that the very enemy the Concord had fought was indeed their own was almost too much for her to handle.

The Prime's voice was soft, even gentle. "We couldn't let it leak. Can you imagine the uproar? It was our job to protect everyone."

"Not this way," Captain Shu said, and Tom let her do the talking. "What of the Statu? Did you have word of their emergence?"

She nodded. "They swore they would stay away. We nearly decimated them, and when we learned their ways, we had to end it. They told us they would stay far from Concord space."

"They're animals. How did you even negotiate with them?" Shu asked.

"We…"

Hudson cut the Prime off. "We don't have to answer them!"

Pha'n waved a dismissive hand. "I fear it's too late. If the Statu have returned, we need to destroy them, once and for all."

"But our accord…" Hudson said.

"It said they wouldn't return to Concord space," she replied.

"They haven't. In case you haven't noticed, we're outside the Border," Hudson said.

Tom gauged what little information he'd been given, watching the two high-level leaders interact. Maybe this could work itself out.

"But they attacked Greblok. They must have known about our agreement. They were about to join the

Concord, and they stole the ore we desired. This cannot be ignored. They did it on purpose," the Prime told him.

"It was an act of war," Captain Shu said. "According to the Code, Greblok was no longer outside the Border. The instant an offer was extended to Greblok, they came under our protection until it was decided one way or another if they were joining. The Statu have broken the Code and must pay."

Tom smiled. He was proud of his previous captain. He knew she'd have the facts to back up what needed to be done.

"No," Hudson said. "We will not be attacking them. We don't have the resources to go on a fool's errand."

"A fool's errand?" Tom asked. "My people are there. Greblok has been all but destroyed, and you'll turn your back on them so quickly? They'll be forced into slavery, and when the Statu return, they'll send them against us, just like they did so many years ago. Is that what the Concord is to you? Were the alliance and Code created so we could trick the people and still do what we want?"

Tom was angry, and he tried to calm himself. He was normally level-headed, but the admiral had gone too far.

"Let me out of this room, Baldwin," Hudson said.

Constantine nodded to Tom. "Fine. You're free to leave."

Tom tapped his console, letting the door slide open to reveal his two largest guards. They were Tekol: Brax's best, according to the chief of security's reports. He'd brought them along from his last posting, and they were huge and imposing.

"Detain Thomas Baldwin, by direct orders from the Concord," Hudson told them. The two guards peered past him to Tom, who shook his head slightly.

"I'm sorry, Admiral Hudson. That won't be

happening," Tom said and the guards grabbed Hudson by the arms. "Prime, are you with us?"

Prime Pha'n swallowed hard and nodded. "*Our actions pave the roads to consequences, good or bad.*" She quoted the Code, and Tom accepted her statement as a yes.

"Take him," Tom ordered.

"You won't get away with this. Captain Shu, there's still time. You can end this and take over. Wouldn't you like to have this vessel? We can even swap out the AI for *Cecilia* if you prefer. Yin, don't make this mistake."

Captain Shu didn't move. They heard the old admiral shouting as the doors closed.

"Baldwin, I hope you have a plan," Shu said, the corners of her eyes crinkling as she smiled at him.

"Of course I do. How do you feel about wormholes?"

EIGHTEEN

"Both of these worlds are inhabited," Reeve told them as *Cleo* inched toward the planets.

Tarlen watched from behind the two women, the viewer zoomed so they could see the beautiful worlds from afar. "Why are they so green?"

Treena answered. "They have a lot of trees and greenspace. See the white sections? Those are ice caps."

"Wow. Greblok didn't look like this from space," he told them.

"No. Your planet was a little different," Reeve said.

"I think these look nice," Tarlen said.

"You wouldn't say that if you were there with your people, I imagine," Treena said, reminding Tarlen that they were on one of these worlds somewhere.

"How are we going to rescue them?" Tarlen asked. They'd been circumspect when it came to his questions, and he was beginning to get the feeling they weren't here for his people. They were here for their own man, Reeve's brother.

Reeve typed on her computer screen, and Tarlen tried to see what she was doing. "Brax is on the fifth planet. I guess we were wrong. It's not too often we find two habitable worlds so close to one another. This is quite the prize. No wonder the Statu used these locations."

"Where do they live? I don't see any lights," he said.

"Good point." Treena zoomed in on the fifth planet from the star. "There aren't any satellites or drones, no space station, no warships in orbit. Nothing. This doesn't seem like the home of an advanced race."

"We didn't have those things above Greblok," Tarlen said, stopping himself short. She was implying Greblok wasn't advanced either, and he guessed that compared to what these fancy space explorers were used to, his home was probably a pile of dust.

"Brax's tag shows him here…" Reeve tapped her console, and Tarlen bent over the bench to see the rough outline of a continent.

"Can we find a better look at it without them being alerted to our presence?" Treena asked.

Constantine appeared beside Tarlen, startling him. He wasn't sure if he'd ever grow used to the artificial man appearing from thin air. It was unusual. The man seemed so real. He was pleasant, friendly, and talked to Tarlen like an equal. Tarlen found himself liking the AI, even if he wasn't a real person.

"Our probes are newly designed and will emit nothing the Statu will have ever come across. They will be safe to use. Would you like me to send them into orbit? We'll be able to access imagery of the continent within the hour," Constantine said.

Treena nodded. "Make it happen."

Tarlen watched as tiny blue flashes emitted out of the viewer, heading toward each of the two planets. "What do you think we'll find?"

"I suspect we'll locate their slave camps, and we'll discover more ships under construction," Constantine said.

"You don't seem surprised that they're still around, Con," Treena told the AI.

"Honestly, I'm not. I was there, I saw the human inside

the enemy's suit, and then a lot of things happened that were hidden from the Concord, even from me. I tried to access select files after being promoted to admiral, but I was denied," he told the commander.

Tarlen had the feeling he was missing out on some pertinent information, and he stayed standing, watching the tiny lights fade as the probes raced to their destination.

"I knew it," Reeve said. "I've studied that day so many times."

"We all did," Treena told her. "For them to disappear like that after Yollox always bothered me. The victory speech was rushed, the whole thing stank of a cover-up, but since it happened twenty years before I was born, it was just commonplace to my generation. My father always swore there was more to the War. He never trusted the Prime, and now I see why."

Reeve turned to look at the AI, and one of her braids almost hit Tarlen in the eye. He laughed, but she was dead serious. "Constantine, how do you remember that? I thought they only gave you his tactical memories. You're nothing like the other AIs we've ever had. You're so…"

"Real?" Constantine asked.

"That's the word. Real." Reeve stared at him, and Tarlen did too, waiting for his answer.

"I was programmed to not reveal this, but I've managed to alter the parameters of my system," Constantine said.

"What does that mean?" Tarlen asked the AI.

Constantine turned to Tarlen, his brown eyes the same color as his hair. He smiled, his cheeks appearing smooth, as if he'd just shaven. He never changed. His uniform was always perfectly pressed, his hair never varying. "The Concord has strict rules about how much of a person they can actually place into a computer. Two decades ago, there was a company off of the Venteen system that specialized in placing minds into alternative bodies."

"What's an alternative body?" Tarlen thought he knew, but he wanted to be sure.

"Tarlen, say you were sick, and someone gave you a star cycle to live. You could go to R-emergence and have your memories saved into a hard drive. They would then offer you a variety of forms to place it into. You might only want to be able to control a tablet, and your wife could turn the device on and ask you where you left the table salt, and turn you off again. Or you might decide that you wanted to walk around in a cybernetic likeness of yourself," Constantine said.

"Wow. Are you saying I could have a robot made in my likeness and continue to live using it?" Tarlen asked.

The AI nodded. "That's right, if you have enough money."

"Can we not do this right now?" Treena growled, and Tarlen assumed they'd hit a touchy subject for her. Her mood changed in a flash.

"We have the time to discuss…" Constantine began.

"Enough."

Reeve cut into the conversation. "Con, are you saying that's the real deal in there? You're the complete version of Constantine Baldwin?"

"That's what I'm saying," he told her.

"Does Thomas know about this?" she asked.

"No, he doesn't. I'm afraid of how he might react," Constantine said.

"You don't seem like the old man. I met him before he passed away," Treena said.

"I have his memories, but I'm functioning as the thirty-year-old version of Constantine, so if I'm a little less disgruntled and battle-hardened, forgive me," he said.

Tarlen laughed. "Were you an old crank?"

"I might have been called a few things in my day, but that was likely one of the many monikers I went by," Constantine told him.

"What would happen if they learned the truth? Doesn't this cross some serious ethical boundaries?" Reeve asked. Tarlen noticed how she glanced over at Treena, and he knew something passed between them that he wasn't able to follow.

"It does, and that's why they were using me as a trial. They added the limiter to prevent me from spilling the beans to the crew. I guess they didn't expect the most advanced flagship ever built to have openings for me to sneak through. It really was quite easy," Constantine said.

"So why tell us?" Treena asked.

"Because this might give us an advantage. The files were mostly encrypted, but I did find out something important," he said.

"What's that?" Reeve asked.

"The Statu sensors are very poor. We built *Cleo* to intentionally evade them if we ever met again. You should be able to fly right in their vicinity without their radar picking us up. Unless their technology has improved in five decades," he said.

"You're telling me the Concord equipped this expedition ship with anti-radar specifically to fool the Statu?" Treena asked.

Tarlen stood there, unwilling to move or make a sound.

"That's what I'm saying," Constantine told her.

"Then they had reason to believe the Statu were up to something. They expected this, didn't they?" Treena was turned around the whole way, watching the AI.

"I can't say, but that would make sense," he said.

"The probes are in orbit," Reeve said, and the viewer

changed to show them images of the distant world. From here, it was only a speck among the blackness, but from the current images rolling over the viewer, it was much different.

Trees and fields filled the screen, and Tarlen had a longing to see the planet, to run barefoot over the grass. He noticed a lake, and he wanted to dive into the clear blue-green water and swim.

"What's that?" Treena asked, and Reeve used her finger to slide over the console screen, rewinding the video feed. "Pause it there."

The picture showed something vast and dark inhabiting the grassy fields. "Can you zoom?" Constantine asked.

Reeve did, and the image was blurry. Seconds later, it was crisp again. "That's a piece of a Statu warship."

"And that's a building beside it." Reeve tapped at the screen more, and she smiled. "And that's where my brother's tag says he is."

Tarlen felt a rush of excitement. They were in a ship the enemy couldn't find on radar but would be able to spot with their eyes. It was going to be a challenge making it to the surface, but if anyone could do it, it was these amazing Concord crew members. Tarlen felt like he was in a storybook, thrust into the action beside the heroes, and while he was thrilled they'd found his people, he was terrified of the next step.

He suddenly felt so out of place. Tarlen peered at Constantine, who only stared forward silently as they considered their move.

Brax was surprised when they'd ended their shift in the

dark and had been led to the building beside the work-station to see real bunks for the slaves. They were fed a measly serving of the same gruel and a ration of water, and directed to sleep. This was all done with waving of guns and no real communication. Some things were universal.

There were troughs along the wall of a separate room, the entire thing crude and terrible. Many of the sites would likely be taken over by vicious viruses before long, and Brax hoped that if it happened here, they'd go quickly.

He sat on his bunk, the room almost totally dark, and thought about the day. He was exhausted, his sweat dried now, leaving an odor the rest of the slaves had as well. He rubbed his arms, trying to ease the tension out, and wondered if his sister was coming for him.

Likely the entire Concord was racing to their rescue, especially since the Statu were involved. He sat back, leaning against the stone wall. He couldn't imagine being here long-term. Brax listened to the sounds of the room and felt their pain. There were numerous people gently weeping in their bunks, no blankets or pillows to console them.

Some were softly talking in the darkness, others humming peacefully, likely trying to soothe a neighbor or child. This was no place for children, but there were at least five among their group. A few of the stronger adults had taken the duty of protecting them on their shoulders, and Brax was glad to let them have the job. He had other things to consider.

He tried to hear sounds from outside but couldn't. There was nothing. Only foreign insects chirping the night away through the slotted windows high above his bunk. A sliver of moonlight sneaked in, centering on a man in his bunk. He was sleeping, and as Brax stared forward, the beam shifted to the side, highlighting a frightened woman. Her eyes glistened as she lay there unblinking.

It was some time before Brax felt the tug of sleep pulling him away. He moved, his stiff muscles protesting the shift, and he lay on the hard bunk, intertwining his fingers and putting his arms behind his head.

Eventually, sleep found him, and he hoped tomorrow would bring some type of resolution. He didn't think the Bacals were going to be able to last in this condition. As he drifted into an exhausted slumber, he thought about his sister and hoped she was okay.

"You did what?" Ven asked, visibly perplexed.

"Look, he's a jerk. He had it coming to him," Tom told his executive lieutenant.

"That doesn't give you the right to apprehend one of the most important men in the Concord," Ven told him.

"Sure it does. Plus, I had backing from the Prime." Tom grinned as he told Ven this little bit of information, and the man instantly relaxed.

"Why didn't you lead with that, Captain?" he asked.

"What fun would that be?" Tom countered. "There's someone I'd like you to meet." He waved over Captain Yin Shu. She strode across the bridge, hands behind her back, her spine straight as she took in the sights.

"Captain, this is Executive Lieutenant Ven, from Zilph'i." Tom nodded at the tall albino, who bowed gently toward Captain Shu. He hadn't shown Tom as much deference, but maybe it had something to do with the fact that Shu was Callalay, not human.

"It's a pleasure to meet you, Ven. I've heard good things. How are you acclimating to the ship?" she asked.

"I find it acceptable. I must say, I wasn't expecting so

much action so early on," Ven told her.

"That's not a surprise. I'd love to talk with you at a later date so I can learn a bit about the Ugna...if you're willing to discuss your lineage, that is."

"I'd be most happy to, Captain," Ven said.

"Good. Now that that's settled, can we discuss our next move?" Tom asked.

"This is a nice bridge, Captain." Shu said the last with a smile.

"Thank you. I'd like to say I had some say in the décor, but it was already done when I arrived," Tom told her. The viewer was filled with the wormhole, ever bright, colorful, and swirling.

"You want to travel through there?" Shu asked him.

"I'd prefer if you went first," he said, and she stared at him, unmoving. "I'm kidding, of course."

"I don't recall you being so glib on board my ship, Captain."

"I'm sorry. I'm nervous and don't know what to do with myself. I mean, I arrested an admiral and called out the Prime. By all accounts, I should be in the brig myself, or worse," he told her. Tom was glad to have his old captain on board for the time being so they could formulate a real plan.

"First things first. We need to tell the others in the Fleet of the Statu's return. We can keep the admiral and Prime's involvement out of it for now, but they need to be alerted in case our rescue mission goes awry. If they are indeed returned, this could be an all-out war," Shu said. She walked to the front of the bridge, hands clasped behind her, and watched the wormhole. "It *is* beautiful."

"It is. So are the wild Rayes from Piya, but they're also one of the deadliest creatures in the universe," he said.

"Captain, would you like me to relay the message?"

Junior Officer Zare asked from her helm position beside Ven.

"Yes. Here it is: All Concord worlds, this is Captain Thomas Baldwin of the Concord's newest cruise ship *Constantine*. We have reason to believe the Statu have returned. Upon our emissary mission to welcome Greblok into our fold, we were attacked by a warship. The world was heavily damaged and most of the population killed, many taken by Movers.

"We followed them to a wormhole before they vanished. The coordinates have been sent, and we do believe the anomaly to be stable. We're joined by Captain Yin Shu of the *Cecilia* to venture through in an effort to retrieve the Bacals and their ore, and to prevent any further war with our familiar adversary.

"The Statu have attacked us in Concord space, contrary to the Code, and we will not accept this act of war without response. Attached are the details as we know them. Until we meet in the Vastness, Captain Thomas Baldwin out." Tom straightened his uniform with a hand and glanced at Shu.

"That was a little dramatic, don't you think?" she asked.

"I wanted them to understand the seriousness of our mission. Are you shipping the Prime back home, or keeping her with you?" Tom asked.

"She can stay on my ship. She knew about the Statu; she can be at risk with the rest of us. I have a feeling the Concord will have to be shaken up after this," Shu told him.

"I'd have to agree," Tom said.

"When do we leave?"

"Let's give it a Standard day, and let them think they've won. If they assume we found the wormhole and haven't emerged yet, they'll be more at ease thinking we elected not to enter it," Tom said.

"Good call. You must have had a good mentor," Shu told him.

"The best."

———————

*T*he planet loomed before them, and Treena nervously watched it. Even if their ship wasn't visible to the Statu computer systems, they were going to be able to see them as they entered the atmosphere, but only if someone was looking closely enough. She didn't know enough about them. If there were really Statu nearby, what were they like?

Now that they'd discovered the enemy they'd battled in the War were mostly their own people in Statu armor, she was curious as to what the aliens looked like and where they hid behind the curtains to run their warships. As intrigued as she was, she'd be satisfied without an answer if it meant never encountering them.

She lowered *Cleo* toward the planet and figured that wasn't in her cards.

The computer began sounding an alarm, startling her. She pulled up on the yoke, moving out of her planned path. "Reeve, talk to me."

"It's bad, Treena. It's bad." The normally affable Tekol woman's voice was shaky and low.

Treena peered at the screen, trying to make sense of what she was seeing. The system map was showing one huge red blob near the edge.

"The probes made their second loop. We have company." Reeve switched the image on her console screen to the feed from the probes. Treena gasped as she saw a dozen warships moving in system, slowly and methodically traversing through space.

"What's their ETA?" Treena asked.

Constantine answered, "Seventeen standard hours."

Seventeen hours. That was enough time to grab Brax and return through the wormhole, but what about the Bacals? Treena suddenly wished the kid hadn't come with them.

Tarlen was behind her, his expression resembling shock. "That's them, isn't it? They're like the ship that took my people. Maybe they have others on them. More slaves."

"Probably," Treena told him. She didn't have the heart to say they were likely brain dead and hypnotized, happy to do the Statu's bidding by this point. She wasn't going to be able to save his people below. This was a small expedition ship, not a rescue cruiser.

She had to warn the captain of this, but had never attempted to reconnect to her artificial body after disconnecting. She would pilot this ship first and do what was necessary once Brax Daak was on board *Cleo*.

"Taking us in. Shields at full capacity, weapon systems ready," Treena said. They broke through the atmosphere, lowering ever toward their target between two work sites. She figured their best bet at not being seen was to land between the two manufacturing stations. It appeared as if they'd created over two hundred isolated encampments, and Brax was smack dab in the center of them.

The camps were a couple of kilometers apart, almost perfectly measured, and as they moved through dense cloud cover, she questioned the insanity of their plan for a moment until they broke past the wispy white vapor.

It was nighttime, the moons glowing bright and blue, and her ship moved silently, the lights all blocked from view below by *Cleo*'s shields. In a few minutes, they'd settled to the ground beside a copse of trees. The world was deemed a Class Zero-Nine planet by the probes, and Reeve stood, rushing to the exit, opening the ramp. It lowered from the ship, touching down on the grass below.

Insects chirped their song loudly, and Treena accepted an arrangement of weapons from Reeve.

"Tarlen, you should stay here with Constantine," Treena told the boy. He was already standing, reaching for a gun. He grabbed an XRC-14, and she saw his weak arms struggle to lift the weapon.

"I'm coming with you. These are my people. Captain Baldwin trusted me to come, so there's no way I'm staying here and letting a hologram babysit me while you go on a rescue mission," Tarlen said.

Treena looked to Reeve for some backup, and the Tekol woman only shrugged, taking the huge gun from the boy's grip and passing him a handheld. "Point and shoot," Reeve told him, and he held it awkwardly. She passed him a holster, and he slid it over his shoulder, copying Treena's movements.

"I regret to inform you I cannot assist your mission," Constantine said.

"You can control the ship, right?" Treena asked.

"Of course."

She grabbed the wrist communicator for the ship and clicked it over her left wrist. "Then be ready."

"I'll await instructions," he told her.

Treena felt vulnerable as she stepped down the ramp, her boots finding the grass beneath them. The ground was soft, even welcoming. A warm breeze brushed against her fake skin, the realistic sensors making her feel more alive on the surface of this world than she had in a long time.

The moonlight was casting enough glow over the landscape for them to see properly. She was glad they didn't need lights, or even the night visors. She kept hers inside a pack, and Reeve tossed a bag to Tarlen, who threw it over his shoulders without a word.

Their target was two kilometers away, and she was glad it wasn't any farther. Moving at night in unfamiliar territory was always risky, especially when you had no idea what kinds of predators were watching. They had little knowledge of the planet, except that it was green and healthy, which meant it was probably teeming with life.

Reeve came to stand next to her, Tarlen beside her, and all three stared into the distance. Treena almost thought she could see the billowing smoke of the smelter rising into the air from here. That was their destination. At the end was one of their crew members, a man she'd only met a week ago. It had been a whirlwind of a first mission, and the chances they'd survive were unknown, but she was glad to have broken out of her shell.

The past two years had been the worst of her life. If she could go back and tell her damaged body that she would be controlling a new Treena Starling on a distant world, attempting to rescue her new chief of security, she would. She could almost imagine the sideways grin her withered face would make, the tears forming in her eyes. She was going to make herself proud. That much was obvious.

Treena sniffed the air, wishing she could use her senses like before. Now there was nothing but the faint signal of familiarity. "What does it smell like?" she asked the others.

Tarlen shook his head. "Does your nose not work?"

"Something like that," she told the boy.

"It's damp, slightly musty. The grass is a little wet." Reeve glanced to her feet, and Treena noticed dew on their boots. "But overall, it's refreshing, like a hot night on Nolix. Even the insects sound similar to my planet. Let's move if we want to arrive before daybreak."

Treena started forward, marking their location on a tablet before shoving it into her pack. The grass became taller as they trod forward, and soon thick stalks were tickling her knees. Tarlen was the slowest of the three, and the two Concord crew members had to accommodate him.

The landscape was even here, the trees sparse. Treena thought it odd how there was a direct path through the forest leading to the work site Brax was stuck in. She stopped, pulling out the tablet and a sensor drone, setting the drone loose.

"What are you doing?" Reeve asked.

"I have a feeling we aren't seeing this planet as it once was." Treena sent the drone off and programmed it to head into the forest, searching for anything non-organic within a three-kilometer radius.

"What are we going to do when we arrive?" Tarlen asked, peering at the gun strapped to him.

"We're going to watch." Reeve stared into the distance, and Treena followed her gaze.

Treena watched the feed from the drone, its night vision casting a glowing green image on her tablet. The screen blinked repeatedly, and the drone hovered over something.

Reeve stood at her side, watching with interest. "What in the Vastness is that?"

"I can't identify it, but it's big," Treena told her. The drone's image showed something metallic jutting from the ground, rectangular in shape.

The readouts scrolled over the screen, and Reeve grabbed the tablet. "Hold on. There's something inside this thing." She directed the drone lower, and it showed more grass.

"It's nothing. That's grass," Treena said.

"No. See these readings? That's artificial grass. Turf of

some sort. They're hiding something there." Reeve's red eyes were bright against the screen.

Treena's instinct was to go investigate. That was what they were trained for. Reeve seemed to pick up on this, and she made a tsking sound with her lips. "No, no, no. I get what you're thinking, but we have to find my brother."

"What if this is something about the Statu?" Treena asked. "Maybe this is their planet, and they're hiding under the surface?"

"And how is this going to help us now?" Reeve made a good point.

"There could be a clue to how we defeat them. I think we need to check." Treena calculated the distance. "It's only one point five kilometers from here, and mostly on course for Brax. Plus, I'm your commanding officer."

Reeve passed the tablet to Treena and frowned. "Then I guess we do it your way. If we're making this detour, we need to hurry. Tarlen, can you walk faster?"

Tarlen smiled. "I was the fastest boy on the block. Don't worry about me. I'm just used to bare feet." He crouched and removed his boots, his toes squeezing the grass. He picked them up, cradling them under an arm.

Treena had to laugh, despite their circumstances. Their group moved for the treeline, heading to the mysterious discovery, her curiosity for the unknown demanding to be sated.

NINETEEN

"Yephion, tell me again," Tom told the Statu.

Constantine stood behind Tom, translating the conversation. Yephion was doing much better, recovered from his cryo sleep, and he was out of the bed for the first time. The others remained frozen, and Yephion had been promised a walk-through to check on his people after this discussion.

The being's mandibles clicked together, and he rattled off the tale. He told Tom about the other planet, and how they were fearful of being destroyed by their neighboring world. To Tom's surprise, the Statu lived underground in an intricate system of subterranean cities. Their neighbors were different in more ways than ideology; they lived in cities above the surface.

"Yephion, we're going to be moving through a wormhole and will be arriving at what we think might be Konov," Tom said.

The second Constantine finished telling the Statu man this, he banged his hand on the table. "We will surely be met with opposition," Yephion said.

"Constantine, have you told him about our war with his people?" Tom asked, and the AI shook his head. "I think it's time we did."

Tom poured some water and passed Yephion a glass, taking one for himself too. He drank deeply and settled into his seat as he told their guest about the war that he and his ship had slept through. Tom was interrupted numerous times with questions, and when Yephion learned how far his people had gone, how they'd used other races as slaves, he let out a noise akin to a wail.

"Is he all right?" Tom asked the AI.

"He says he is ashamed. Captain, I believe him. He asks if he can help in any way," Constantine said.

Tom watched the strange creature, his eyes black, his exoskeleton hard and imposing. He couldn't believe he was really sitting and conversing with a Statu. After all these years, no one had seen them in the flesh, and here he was, chatting with the enemy. Only he didn't feel like this man was his adversary.

"What were you, truly? You said you were on the maintenance crew. I don't believe you," he said.

The man sat up and uttered a series of clicks, which Constantine relayed as: "I was the second in command for our vessel. I was a leader of my city. My family was with me. Can I see the cryo chambers now?"

"Will you share what details you have about the warships, the other Statu, and the system we're possibly heading into?" Tom asked. The truth was, he had no idea if the wormhole led there, and he told Yephion as much.

"I suspect it is," the man said through Constantine.

"How can you be sure?" Tom asked.

"Because we were almost ready to test our wormhole generators when they invaded us. Stole our entire team."

Tom's heart raced as he heard the AI translate this. "Are you saying this wormhole is artificial?"

"No. It's very much real. However, it was likely created by the Statu," he said.

"Then why didn't they close it?" Tom asked.

Yephion looked at him as if he'd asked the universe's

most basic question. "Because once you open a wormhole this size, they're nearly impossible to shut down. The only way is to disrupt them enough inside so that the exit is no longer functional."

"Why didn't they use more? They could have invaded us easily if they had," Tom said.

"The wormholes require years of planning and more stored energy than you can imagine. They take decades to create," Yephion advised him.

Tom had an idea, a crazy one. He tapped his computer screen. "Captain Yin Shu, do you have time for a visitor?"

His old mentor replied quickly. "We'd be honored to have you."

Yephion stood as Tom did, his mandibles clicking together loudly. "Do we go to the cryo chambers?"

"Constantine will show you there. Maybe bring Nee with you," he told the AI. "And one of the Tekol guards. I don't think he wishes us ill, but I'd rather be cautious."

"Very well, Captain. Should I remind you that we leave in less than eight hours?" Constantine asked.

"You just did." Tom left them in the room, moving for the docking bay, where a waiting transport vessel sat.

A half hour later, he was latched on to *Cecilia*. He hadn't told anyone he was leaving, because it was technically against protocol since Starling wasn't on board either. Ven was the last remaining member of their executive team, and Tom had to laugh to himself that the gifted Ugna was in charge at the moment, even if he didn't realize it.

Maybe he did know Tom had left. There was so much to Ven that Tom wasn't aware of yet.

"What do you care about protocol, Tommy? You have the admiral locked away in a cell," he said to himself as he departed the transport vessel onto the docking bay of his old ship.

He took a deep breath; the smell of grease and a decade of hard work filled his nostrils. It was a good scent. Like home.

"Commander Baldwin…" The woman grinned and corrected herself. "My apologies, sir. Captain Baldwin. Welcome to the *Cecilia*."

Lexi was as prim and statuesque as ever. "I pity the sucker that has to fill my boots on this old rust bucket."

"I heard she's doing a hell of a job." Lexi smirked, and his eyes settled on her orange collar.

"It looks good on you, Lexi," Tom told her.

She crossed the room, surprising him by wrapping her arms around him. They'd been close, but never this close. "Can you believe they're back?"

"I know. I'm sorry I dragged you into this," Tom told her.

"Are you kidding? This is what we're all about. What new recruit didn't dream of the day the big bad Statu would return, giving us a chance to kick some butt on behalf of the generations before us?" Lexi said, striking a chord with him.

"You're right. I used to hear about them so often growing up with the old man. God, can you believe they named my ship after him?" Tom asked, happy to be speaking with someone from his past.

"How is he?" she asked, meaning the AI.

"Nothing like *Cecilia*. They went all-out on him. You'd think it was really him at thirty years old," Tom said.

"Sign me up. I'd like to meet Constantine Baldwin at thirty…"

"Enough," Tom said with a laugh. "Can you show me to the captain, please?"

"She's waiting in her office. I think you know the way," Lexi said as they headed into the corridor. The halls were so much smaller here, narrow where his new post was wide. The lights flickered, dimming as he walked, and Tom reflected at how spoiled he was with *Constantine*.

He nodded to a few crew members, not stopping to chat to any of them as he moved with purpose toward Shu's office. He buzzed as he approached, and the door opened.

"Come in, Thomas." Yin Shu motioned for him to take the seat across from hers.

Tom sat in the chair, resting his elbows on the dark surfaced table. "Wormholes."

"What about them?" Shu asked.

"My guest claims the Statu had wormholes. Remember the openings we found in the aftermath of Yollox? There was an unstable wormhole half a light year from the battle zone. We had no idea how long it had been there, or why it didn't function," Tom told her.

"That's right." Shu tapped at her desk screen, and a projected image appeared of Yollox space, the small wormhole rotating slowly in the far edge of the system. "It's still there."

"I was just informed that the Statu can create them. This means they retreated from Yollox. The damned Concord allowed them to go through a wormhole. I believe that Hudson knew all this, but they had no idea where it led. I bet it leads to the same place this one does." Tom stood and pointed at the colorful opening showing through her office viewer.

Yin Shu rarely looked surprised, but she did now. "Then what? How do we stop them?"

"Yephion tells me it takes decades to produce one. We head in, destroy the bastards, and figure out how to disarm it on our return," Tom said.

Shu stood and stared out the viewer with her hands

clasped behind her. "That's what we'll do, then."

"Good." Tom tapped the screen and opened a line to his ship. "Executive Lieutenant Ven, this is Captain Baldwin."

"Captain, go ahead." The Ugna didn't seem surprised Tom wasn't on board.

"Tell Nee to open the cryo chambers. We have to find one of them with passing knowledge of the wormholes," Tom said.

After a brief pause, the Zilph'i albino replied, "Very well. Shall we expect your return soon, sir?"

"On my way." Tom smiled at Captain Shu. They might not have any idea what was preparing for them across the void, but at least they had an exit plan.

———————

Yur paced the maintenance room. The rest of the crew were out and about, mostly on leave for dinner, others set upon menial tasks around the ship. Yur was waiting for the orders. She'd sent him a message last night, warning him to be prepared.

Now, seeing the wormhole outside the ship, Yur felt his efforts had led them to this moment. The legendary Concord vessel *Cecilia* was beside them, and Yur considered the treachery he was going to embark on. If they caught him, he'd be called a traitor to the good Concord. He'd heard rumors the Prime was on the ship, along with Admiral Hudson. How could he detonate the device with the chance their ship might be destroyed?

His benefactor claimed it was nothing so dire, and the fact that she had to be on board with him eased his mind slightly.

He held the small communication device, his hip aching as he walked from one end of the room to the other, a scattering of tools covering the tables, chairs, and work benches. It would be over soon, and he was glad, because he didn't think he'd be able to deal with the pressure forever.

———

*T*arlen felt more alive than ever as they hurried through the grass and into the forest. He'd seen trees before on Greblok, but nothing like these majestic, healthy behemoths. Greblok's versions of trees were skinny, short, and lucky to have a handful of gray leaves sparsely covering the branches. These rose high into the sky, so tall that Tarlen was able to walk beneath their boughs.

"Over here," Treena said. She moved with such ease, even running, he struggled to keep up with the commander. So did Reeve, and she dallied behind them a hundred yards away. The metal ridge rose from the ground ten feet, and Tarlen stopped short of it as Treena walked around the rectangular perimeter.

"The drone images show the doorway should be this way," Treena said as Reeve arrived. The Tekol woman was panting and reached for some water from her pack.

Tarlen stared at the wall in front of them and ran a hand along it, feeling the rough, bumpy dark surface. "I feel a lip here."

There was no visible handle, but Treena pressed on the spot Tarlen had indicated, and something clicked before the sizeable door hinged open. Tarlen stepped around the swinging entrance and followed the others onto the fake grass. Instantly, it felt different on his bare feet, and he unslung his pack, putting his boots on again.

The open space within the walls was at least a hundred feet wide and slightly longer, and Tarlen walked to the center, where Treena was crouched. She was tugging on something, a metallic handle, and with great effort, she tore open the grass. Beneath it was a hatch.

"How did you do that?" Tarlen asked the woman. She wasn't that much bigger than he was, and there was no way he could have ripped the ground open like that.

"Lucky touch," she said with a smile. "Reeve, your turn."

There was a keypad, and Reeve pulled something from her pack, setting it on the device. "Whatever was here is long dead, but I think I can bring it to life." She used her tablet, the device glowing soon after. Tarlen heard a hum from below them, and the hatch slid open a minute later. The Concord had so many amazing tools. He wished his father was here with him so he could see how much technology was out there. Greblok really was a backwater planet, by every definition. At that moment, he wished he could trade this experience to be home, safely before the attack, before he'd ever heard of them trying to join the Concord.

"What is it?" he asked, peering through the opening to where Treena shone a light.

"Stairs," she said, glancing at Reeve.

"Fine, Starling. A quick in and out, then we find Brax. Deal?" Reeve offered.

———————

*B*rax woke in the middle of the night with the strangest feeling in his gut. He'd been dreaming of home. Back on

Nolix, they studied hard every day of the year, but occasionally, their parents would take them to the beach, where they played in the water.

Reeve would always try to discover new things under the sea, while Brax preferred to soak up the sun, letting the sand slip between his toes as he played *Tuuka* with his father. He'd dreamt of a specific moment where he'd been lounging on the beach, his father dozing in a chair beside him, his mother reading some scientific document like always.

Reeve had screamed from the water, and Brax had rushed to her aid so quickly, he'd nearly rolled his ankle. It turned out she'd thought something had bitten her, but she'd only stepped on a rock. For a moment, he'd been so afraid, his own foot in pain. That was the first time their bond had affected him. Twins were rare on Tekol, and because of it, they'd been offered the best schooling and grants; their parents couldn't have been happier.

Reeve always claimed she could feel his emotions more than he could hers, but now he stared at the ceiling and swore he felt astonishment: not from him, but from Reeve. And it was close. He sat up slowly, looking around.

Gone were the soft cries and soothing conversation. It was a few hours from daybreak; even the insects were quieter now, their mating rituals satisfied for the night.

"Reeve?" he asked so quietly, the words were silent. He concentrated, trying to feel her emotions again, but it was gone as quickly as it had hit him.

Was it just the dream or was she really nearby? He sat there for another five minutes, still feeling nothing. Eventually, he relaxed into the bunk. Instead of trying to sleep, he stayed calm, ready for action. If his sister was really on the planet, he would be prepared.

He glanced over at Penter, the man's chest rising and

falling evenly, and considered waking his new friend, telling him a rescue might be arriving sooner than later. He decided to let the man rest. He was going to need it.

I'm here, Reeve. I'll be ready.

---

*T*he stairs went for a hundred or so feet below, leading them into a cavernous room. "You'd think they would have opted for an elevator," Treena said, activating her tablet's light feature.

Reeve clipped a portable light onto her holster strap, and the space became illuminated quickly. "Let's be glad there were stairs. We have no way of powering this place up."

"What is this?" Tarlen asked.

Treena tried to make sense of what she was seeing. It was gray, smooth-surfaced, and there were colored markings along the floor, leading to different doorways along the far walls. "It looks like an old underground base of some kind. Let's take a peek."

Reeve stopped in her tracks, and Treena heard her mutter her brother's name. "Brax… he's alive. I could feel him."

"I thought that was only a rumor. The whole Tekol twin thing?" Treena asked.

"Not really. We haven't ever been very strong, but I know him, and I think he senses I'm here. We have to find his camp," Reeve said.

"We will. After we explore for a few minutes," Treena said, and Tarlen was already running off, looking at a complex diagram along the wall. She wasn't sure why, but she needed to understand what they were currently inside. The idea of leaving this strange underground base so soon didn't feel right.

"Commander Starling, I think it's best…"

"Look!" Tarlen's shout startled Treena, and she moved to his side, looking at the image displayed on the wall. "It's a city."

"What's he talking about?" Reeve asked from behind them.

Treena ran her eyes over the diagram, seeing the various colors indicating levels. "He's right. Reeve, look, there are corridors connecting the various neighborhoods." She pointed to one near the middle of the image. There was a green dot beside a long passageway. "I think this shows where we currently are."

Reeve moved her light across the wall, smiling. "And if we follow this corridor, it takes us directly to the slave camp where Brax is. Right here, it has to be. Each of those many outbuildings we saw from the orbital imaging is on this map. They must be using the entrances to the underground city as pens for the slaves."

Tarlen stared back with big eyes. "Does that mean the Statu are underground too?"

"There's only one way to find out," Treena said, searching for the orange level. That took them to the nearest outbuilding, where she suspected they'd find Reeve's brother. The door with orange markings was only twenty feet away, and she headed there, finding a handhold along it. She tugged it wide, and listened for sounds from down the corridor. It was silent. That was a good sign.

"Try to be as quiet as you can. Reeve, lower your light level and be prepared to deactivate entirely. With any luck, we'll be there very soon." Treena stepped up a few more stairs, these ones hard and metal. Her bootsteps were louder than she would have liked, and she attempted to move with more stealth. Reeve, who was lighter because she wasn't filled with electronic compounds like Treena, moved noiselessly behind her. Tarlen may as well have been a ghost.

Treena found her bearings, the corridor reminding her of the old relic spaceships from centuries ago. The halls were curved, no computers sat recessed into the surface, and it went on for as far as the eye could see.

Before things like gravity generators and faster-than-light engines, space travel had been nothing like it was today. The very first human starships had been long, gangly things with sealed corridors between rotating centrifuge circles. These corridors were spacious, high enough for someone eight feet tall to cross without burden. They moved quickly, their lights softly guiding the way along the passageway's unchanging appearance.

Treena had an idea. If these led to each of the sites, what if they could bring the Greblok slaves down to safety? It would take a difficult and coordinated effort, and with the looming threat of the incoming warships, she wasn't sure they had time to put it all together. Even if they could gather all of the Bacals, they didn't have a ship capable enough for a mass evacuation. It wasn't going to work. Her best move was to stick to the plan. Rescue Brax Daak and retreat, bringing information to *Constantine.*

The kilometer or so passed quickly, and soon they found another door on their right.

"This is it. I bet it's directly underneath the building Brax is inside," Treena said.

Reeve closed her eyes and took a deep breath. "He's up there, I can feel it. I think he knows I'm here."

Treena grabbed her gun, holding the XCR-14 as if it weighed nothing in her hands. It was too large a weapon for most humans, especially someone her size, but she wielded it with ease. Tarlen blinked hard at her and pulled his own handheld PL-30, swallowing as he glanced at it.

Reeve held her own compact gun and nodded to Treena. "Let's find my brother."

Treena opened the door and heard the surprised clicks before seeing the waking Statu come to life inside the room. They were tall, dark exoskeletons, just like the figures in the cryo chambers on *Constantine*.

Before thinking, she fired at the two she could see.

TWENTY

Brax felt his sister's emotions filling his mind, and he stood, staring toward the floor. She was close by, and everything he felt said that she was underneath the room at that moment.

The sliver of moonlight had moved across the room as the night passed by, and it settled along the wall now, where a Statu armored guard stood as rigid as a statue.

He watched it for another moment, seeing that it didn't move at all. Was it asleep? He crept low to the ground, his hip hardly above the rows of bunks. A man woke as he moved, his eyes going wide, and Brax placed a finger to his lips. The man nodded his understanding.

There was only one guard inside the room with them, but Brax knew there were a few more lingering around the slave camp. He'd seen as many as ten, he thought, but it was hard to tell them apart without getting a closer look. They all wore the old dented armored suits, making it even more difficult to differentiate them. Right now, he didn't care. He only needed a weapon. He'd been waiting for an opportune moment to arrive, and this was it.

There was a narrow path between the bunks along the room's wall, and he took it, heading toward the unmoving guard. He noticed another form moving through the room in the dim light, and he prayed it wasn't another Statu. He only had one shot at this.

Brax was big, but he tried to hide behind the bunk nearest to the Statu, crawling along the floor toward the guard. Its crude gun hung on a strap over its shoulder, and he reached out, grabbing its leg, pulling it to the ground with a strong effort. The room exploded in noise as the armor clanged against the wall, then on the end of a metallic bunk. The gun scattered away, and some of the slaves were running away from the altercation, absently kicking the weapon and Brax's hope for freedom with it.

Brax was on top of the dazed enemy and he grabbed the helmet, using all his strength to bash it into the hard floor. The guard flailed, trying to shove Brax off him, but *Constantine*'s chief of security was stronger and better trained in combat.

The doors opened, sending a breeze through the stuffy room, and as the guard under him went limp, Brax saw a blast coming from a newly-arrived guard. He rolled over, using the lifeless man under him as a shield, and he heard Penter shout, "Everyone down!"

Gunfire was everywhere, beams cutting through the stale air, and when Brax emerged from behind his shield, the guard he held was dead, and so was the one at the doorway. Penter had the first gun in his hand, and he raced to the door, tossing Brax the other weapon.

"You think I was going to let you fight them alone?" Penter asked with a grin.

"I'll thank you later," Brax said, stepping over the fallen Statu. "Everyone stay put!" he told the gathering crowd.

"What do we do?"

"Why have you doomed us?"

"Get him!"

Brax hadn't expected this from the Greblok slaves, and he hated himself as he aimed his gun toward the few advancing people.

Penter spoke up, standing beside him. "If you're really Bacal, stand down. This man is trying to help you." That seemed to do the trick, but a few mutters carried over the worried conversation.

Brax spotted Abbil cautiously walking toward him from the rear of the room. Her eyes were wide and fearful. "Abbil, I need you to keep everyone calm and quiet until I return," he instructed her.

She didn't reply as she approached. Instead, she stared at the two dead Statu guards.

"Did you hear me?" he asked.

"I hear you," she said softly.

"Good." He placed his hands on her shoulders. "You can do this." He turned from her and toward the door. "I think there's a room underneath us. We need to find it," he whispered to Penter as they exited, weapons up in case of more guards arriving. Outside, it was eerily silent. The moonlight was bright, and Brax witnessed no incoming party of Statu looking for retaliation.

"A room? What makes you say that?" Penter asked as they ran around the structure, staying close to the exterior wall.

"Let's call it a hunch," Brax told him. He'd seen the guards entering around the corner, and he paused, aiming the odd weapon before stepping past the edge.

"There's a doorway," Penter said.

They tiptoed through the entrance, finding the narrow room empty. As expected, there was a staircase leading into a basement. Brax pointed at it with his gun, the handle vibrating as he gripped it. It emitted a low whine as he lowered the barrel and took the lead down the steps.

Brax stopped, hearing muffled noises erupting from behind another slab. He raised a hand, telling Penter to wait. When the sounds stopped, he kept moving, pressing his palm against the door. Slowly, he pushed it·open. The space was dimly lit, and there were at least six dead Statu on the floor. Across the room, a figure emerged from the shadows, and Brax ducked as a blast hit the wall right above his head.

"Stop! Reeve, is that you?" Brax called from his crouched position.

"Brax?" his sister's familiar voice asked, and he felt a surge of happiness course through him from across the room. He stepped out as she locked her PL-30 into its holster. She ran to him, jumping on him as she hugged him firmly.

"Good to see you, Lieutenant Commander Daak," Treena Starling said as she stepped into the light.

"Sorry about almost shooting you," a kid said. He was wearing a Concord Fleet uniform, but what was a junior officer in training doing on a rescue mission?

"Tarlen? By the Stars, it really is you!" Penter said, moving to the boy's side and tousling his hair.

"Penter, you're alive! We found a city." Tarlen grinned from ear to ear.

"Now that the reunion is done, can we get the hell out of here?" Starling asked, and Brax saw the boy's face drop.

"What about my people?" he asked.

"I'm sorry, kid. We have to leave them."

"There's no turning back, Captain Baldwin. You are aware, correct?" Ven asked.

Tom sat in his captain's chair, the bridge crew noticeably different than when they'd started this venture. A week as leader of the flagship, and he was already missing…

almost everyone.

"I'm aware, Ven. Thank you for your concern." Tom glanced to his side, where Yephion sat staring toward the wormhole in the viewer. A female Statu was behind him, clutching the seat's headrest with a firm grip. Not much separated the two sexes as far as Tom could tell, but he was no xenobiology expert.

"Impulse speed, set course for the wormhole." Tom gave the order and saw there was an incoming message from *Cecilia*. It appeared on the viewer, Captain Shu's image covering half of their screen.

"Captain Baldwin, I received word that our fleet has gathered, and *Bartok, Hallivan*, and *Troo* are set to arrive in one day's time. Shall I relay anything before we depart?" Shu asked him.

He wasn't used to her asking him for directions, and he felt uneasy about it. "Please inform them we appreciate their promptness, and we hope to return by the time they arrive."

"Consider it done. Baldwin," she said, staring toward him from the center of the video.

"Yes, Captain?"

"You were a good commander. I think you have what it takes to be a great captain," she told him, and he swelled with pride.

The communication ended, and they arrived near the wormhole. They were only five hundred kilometers out, and it was huge from this vantage point. Decades. It had taken the Statu decades to create this monstrosity, but to what end? To head to Greblok and steal the conductive ore?

"Ven, I have it!" he shouted, standing up and startling the two Statu beside him. "They weren't hitting Greblok because of the fact that we were entering into a bargain

with them. It wasn't some petty vendetta of principle…"
Tom ran his hands through his hair as it all came clear.

Ven turned from his helm position, staring at Tom with interest. "Go on, Captain. What did they do it for?"

"The ore. What did Hudson say about it?" Tom asked.

"It was highly conductive. It was going to revolutionize our energy systems…" Ven went silent as he realized what Tom was implying.

"The wormholes. The Statu wanted the material so they could create more wormholes, and faster. With all that ore, who knows where they'll be able to appear? They could launch an attack on the Concord unlike anything ever before seen. We couldn't predict where or when they'd invade our space," Tom said.

They not only had to rescue his crew, they had to ensure they returned with the ore from Greblok. The task suddenly felt too difficult, almost impossible. Tom clenched his jaw, using the words from his previous captain as fuel. He was going to be a great captain.

He might have one of the most celebrated surnames of all time in Baldwin, but he wasn't here to live in his grandfather's shadow. He was here to carve out his own spot of history, and it all began with this moment.

Tom stood in the center of the bridge. The wormhole that had felt so dangerous, so imposing and deadly a minute ago, was now a welcome sight.

"Junior Officer Zare, lead us in." Tom remained standing and he glanced to the rear of the room, his grandfather's AI Constantine watching it all with interest. He smiled at Tom, and even cut him a wink like he'd done when Tom was a kid.

Tom wondered at that as they entered the center of the wormhole, and everything around them changed.

———————

Yur watched through the console screen as they approached the wormhole. He considered how lucky he'd been to be born a Callalay, and how special a day it had been when the Prime Pha'n had been named into her role.

His benefactor claimed something was wrong with the bureaucracy in the Concord, that the *Constantine* was what was wrong with their new era. It was all show and posturing, with no real substance or support of the regular people.

She'd convinced Yur of so many things, yet he'd never even met her. He held the detonator and the communicator in opposite hands, each of them sweating as he waited.

Then it hit him. His boss was willing to die for her cause, and he was just a fool for buying in to it all. There was nothing worth killing the Prime and everyone on this ship. People might not see him very often, but in the last week or so, he'd found plenty of kind faces aboard the *Constantine*. None of them deserved the fate his benefactor wanted to institute in order to prove her point.

Yur saw them entering the wormhole, and the communicator vibrated.

The message was simple, clear and concise.

Now

He stared at it and shook his head. No. He wasn't going to do that.

He heard Olu's voice coming from the corridor outside the room. "I swear, he wouldn't have gone in there."

"It's on the footage. Just open the door," a voice ordered.

A huge Tekol guard entered, and the moment he saw Yur standing there with two devices in his hands, sweating like an Eganian tourist, he fired his PL-30.

Yur hardly felt the blast as he fell to the hard grated metal floor. The detonator slipped from his fingers, but the communicator was clenched in his grip.

"What have you done?" Olu asked, but Yur hardly heard the man. He glanced to his hand, opening his fingers to see the message.

Now you fool now

As his last breath passed through his lungs, Yur smiled, knowing he'd made the right decision.

———

Tarlen's feet wouldn't move. "You can't be serious. We're supposed to help them. You're with the Concord. I thought you were all heroes."

"It's not always like the stories, Tarlen," Treena told him.

"But my parents… my sister. They may be alive." He was desperate. He hadn't come all this way to leave them in the hands of the same terrible force that had destroyed his world.

"He's not wrong, Commander," the big Tekol said.

Penter stood beside Tarlen, placing his arm over Tarlen's shoulders. "I'll stay with the boy. We'll use the underground system and see if there's any way to help our people."

Tarlen filled with joy at the guard's offer.

"If you don't recall, there's a horde of warships heading in our direction, and they'll be here in…" Treena counted off hours on her fingers. "About twelve hours."

"What? That's not good. Here's what I know…" Brax started, but Reeve tugged on his arm, moving them toward the exit.

"Can we not do this here?" she asked.

Tarlen glanced at Penter. "We should bring them down to this level. It'll be safer. Maybe we can rescue them through the corridors."

Brax grinned, and Tarlen sensed the big man had an idea. "Penter, that's a good thought. Gather Abbil and usher them to this spot. Commander, you said there's a map? Do any of them lead to a…"

Tarlen didn't hear the rest as Penter motioned for him to climb the stairs.

"How did you end up here?" Penter asked him.

"Long story. Penter, you should see their starship. It's unlike anything I've ever seen." Tarlen reached the top of the steps and climbed out after the Greblok guard.

"I saw the inside of the Statu ship. I hope your ride was better." Penter peered outside, and Tarlen held his gun at ready, hoping he didn't need to use it again. Downstairs, the two women had managed their foes with ease, while his shots had gone wide of their targets. He was going to need some practice.

"It's clear." Penter emerged outside, and Tarlen heard the blast before he saw it strike the wall. He shoved Penter as another blast hit the stone, sending rubble over them. Tarlen ran, not away, but toward the incoming gunman. The Statu had done endless damage to his people, killed so many, and he wasn't going to stand for it any longer. He fired as his legs pumped. He zig-zagged, making himself a difficult target, and shouted uncontrollably as the blasts hit the guard once, then twice. By the time he'd arrived, the guard was on the ground with smoke sizzling from his mask.

Tarlen had to find out. He shot the guard again and knelt at its side, finding the latch for its helmet. He pried it open and heard a hissing sound as soon as air seeped through. The smell was terrible, and when he set the armored head covering to the side, he saw the ooze leaking from inside the suit.

"Scramblers," Penter said from behind him. "Messes them up so you can't see who they are."

"Was it..." Tarlen asked.

"It was someone trying to kill you," Penter said, helping Tarlen to his feet. "Come on. They're inside. Abbil, it's me."

Tarlen saw a group of beaten Bacals inside, and his heart tore in two. Their clothing was in tatters, their eyes sad and red. Every one of them was covered in bruises and grime from the last week.

He walked around the room, desperately searching for his parents. "Belna? Are you here?" She wasn't among the group of disheveled people, and he shouldn't have been surprised.

"What are we doing, Penter?" the woman the guard had identified as Abbil asked.

"Everyone follow us. We're moving underground," Penter said.

"Why listen to them? They're only going to get you killed," a man said, and Tarlen glared at the old naysayer.

"Fine. You stay." Penter didn't pay the man any mind, opting to lead the exit instead. Tarlen grinned as the old guy stayed behind, the last one in the room before trudging forward, following the pack without any more commentary.

Tarlen stayed behind with Penter as the small group slowly moved to the stairs, and when everyone was underground, the pair went after them.

It may not have been much, but maybe they could keep some of his people safe. That would have to be enough.

Brax's idea was insane. Impossible. Improbable, at the very least, but Treena still couldn't help but smile as she imagined it working.

"Fine, I'm on board. It's going to be tough finding a Tuber, isn't it?" she asked him.

Brax looked different, and not only because his usually shaven head was growing in, his short hair thick and black. He seemed wiser, calmer than he even had before, and considering what he'd just gone through, she was surprised at how assertive he was being.

"If this map lines up with what I saw from above, it won't be so difficult." He pointed at the diagram. "These are each of the slave locations. They separated us, and each of our sites is building a subsection of the warships. If I was to guess, they're trying to construct four or five of them here with the new slaves."

"There are a dozen of the warships heading for us now. Once they arrive, we're never going to be able to sneak out of here. It was one thing doing it with no ships in orbit, but it won't be so simple with so many eyes on us. We need to be quick and quiet. Can you do that?" Treena asked him.

"I think so."

"I'm going with him," Reeve said, and Treena could see that was the end of the discussion.

"Reeve…" Brax started.

"Don't you 'Reeve' me, brother. You let them grab you in a Mover, and made me worry about you for the last week. I didn't know if you were alive or dead. I'm not letting you out of my sight," she said.

"Fine, but be quick. I haven't figured out how you're

going to fly any of these things," Treena told him.

"Have faith. We may not have had access to many Statu artifacts, but we did have Tubers, and I was part of the lucky few in my class to fly one," Brax said. Reeve cleared her throat and nudged him with an elbow. "Fine," he added. "I didn't fly it, but I sat beside my instructor and watched her. Pretty much the same thing."

"Right." Treena said. "Be careful. If we have any hope of extracting these people off planet, we're going to need to be stealthy."

"*In the absence of numbers, we must have a multitude of ambition.*" Brax quoted the Code, making Treena smile.

"Until we meet in the Vastness," Treena told them, and the two siblings raced through the corridor, heading in another direction.

Treena spotted the Greblok slaves arriving, and she waved them toward her. "Do any of you have experience with guns?"

Three of them raised their hands, and she nodded to the one Brax had at his side.

"What's the plan?" Penter asked her.

"We're moving to the next site. From there, we'll attack them in their sleep, steal one of the hover platforms, and hit the next camp until we have a decent army. It doesn't appear that these Statu have much in the way of communicators, so we may be able to do this in stealth," Treena told him.

Tarlen was long-faced beside the Greblok guard. "The odds aren't good," the boy said.

Inspired by Brax's quoting the Code, Treena smiled at the kid. "*When faced with impossible odds, choose to play a different game.*" She nodded to the half-dozen Statu suits lying on the floor. "Who wants to suit up?"

TWENTY-ONE

The shaking ceased, but to Tom, it felt like he was being thrown around as their ship plunged into the new space, the wormhole exit behind *Constantine*.

He closed his eyes, but all he could see was the rush of light in the tunnel they'd traveled through for the last ten minutes or so. The Statu were clutching one another to his side, and one of his crew threw up from the rear of the bridge.

"Executive Lieutenant Ven, is my ship in order?" Tom asked.

"The initial scans show everything in order, sir," Ven said. "We seem to be having difficulty locating our position."

Yephion began clicking his mandibles, and Constantine's AI translated. "He says that Plepha can input the details into your ship if you allow her a console. She is his mate."

"I don't think that's necessary at this moment," Tom said, not fully trusting the Statu beside him. He wasn't ready to let them gain access to their computer system. That would be foolish.

"Probes have been released, sir," Zare told him, and he watched as the data arrived on the viewer.

"This is home," Yephion said, Constantine echoing in Standard.

"Which one?" Tom asked. There were two worlds highlighted by the computer's scans as habitable.

"The fifth."

"Does that make the fourth planet where the other Statu came from?" Tom asked.

"That's correct," Yephion replied.

Tom had the urge to blast it to nothing, using his ship's advanced weapon system. It was against his own honor and the Code of the Concord, but after all the damage they'd done to his people and allies, he didn't think it would be too difficult to make the order. He bit his tongue and watched as the rest of the data streamed in.

"Captain, this is not good," Ven said, and the lights began flashing red along the walls of the bridge. A gentle but insistent alert chimed throughout the bridge.

Tom saw the clump of vessels moving through the radar image, and he swallowed hard. "How many are there, Ven?"

"Thirteen, sir. We have confirmation. These are Statu warships," Ven said, and Tom glanced at Yephion. He wasn't speaking, but his mandibles moved rapidly, perhaps a nervous tic.

"How long until they arrive?" Tom asked.

"Seven hours, sir," Ven said.

"Then we'd better move quickly. Where's Brax?" Tom stood, moving over to Zare's helm console.

"On Yephion's world, sir. So are the others."

Constantine flickered and appeared beside Tom. "Captain, I've regained connection with my other projection from *Cleo*. I'm there awaiting the return of Commander Starling. They found Brax but haven't returned yet."

Tom leaned over Zare and tapped Starling's comm-channel. "Commander Starling, this is Captain Baldwin. Advise situation."

No reply came.

"Sir, we're too far out. I suspect we won't have communication with the surface for another hour," Zare said.

"Bring us in, full impulse," Tom said.

"What about the Statu?" she asked.

Tom clenched his fists and watched the incoming group of warships. His ship was powerful, but he didn't think he'd stand a chance in a fight against so many. "Where's the ship they brought to Greblok?" he asked.

"I imagine it's within the atmosphere of the fifth planet, sir," Ven said.

Tom smiled. All he had to do was fly to the world, destroy the warship so no one could use the ore from Greblok, and rescue his people. And he had a whopping seven hours to accomplish the mission.

He wiped his palms on his pants and moved for the exit. "If anything important happens, alert me."

"Where are you going, sir?" Ven asked.

"To the brig. I have a few questions that need to be answered," he said, stepping off the bridge.

The trip was quick, and Tom didn't have long before they were within communication distance of his crew on the planet's surface. This was going to be tight.

He was let through without comment by the guards, and was directed to the end of the otherwise empty brig. It was bright, and he squinted against the glow of the lights.

"Can you turn these down, please?" Tom shouted through the hall. A second later, they dimmed, and Tom saw Adam Hudson sitting there, looking ten years older than he had earlier. He was pushing ninety and looked every year of it as he sat on the bench.

"I used to have high hopes for you, son," Hudson said, not looking up.

"Don't call me that," Tom said softly.

"Did you know that your grandfather hated the fact that he had to raise you?" Hudson asked, finally glancing up. His eyes were red.

Tom bristled. His relationship with Constantine Baldwin had been contentious at best, especially in the later years. He didn't remember the man as his AI appeared, his demeanor soothing and pleasing. No, his grandfather was rough around the edges, disgruntled, and far from idealistic. The Concord was a house of cards, one gust of wind from being cast to the ground.

"I don't care," Tom told him.

"Sure you do. Everyone longs for the approval from the people who raised them," Hudson said. "I used to argue with him. I saw the bright young mind, the passion you had for the Concord, and I only wished Constantine had pushed you harder."

"I worked plenty hard," Tom said, not sure why he was even playing along with the old man's games.

"Sure. You were a great pilot. A good leader. But I guess I didn't give you enough credit," Hudson said. It seemed like the bluster was gone from him; maybe he'd given up.

"Adam." Tom used his first name to throw him off. "Tell me the truth here. We'll be returning to Concord space eventually, and you're going to have to answer for your crimes, but things will go a lot easier on you if you're transparent."

Hudson's eyes went wide. "Don't tell me you did it."

"Did what?"

"Went through the wormhole. You have no idea what the Statu are capable of," he warned.

"I do. Believe me. I heard about it every night at dinner, every weekend excursion, every training program at the Academy. I know what they're capable of."

"Then why stick your head into their system?" Hudson asked.

Tom needed Hudson to focus. "The wormholes. You knew about them."

His head sagged. "I did. We did."

"You let them escape in one, and they destroyed it from the inside, is that correct?" Tom stood straight-backed, his hands on his hips. The old man glared up from the bench in the cell. The bars fizzled and glowed softly.

"We did, but honestly, Pha'n didn't think they could ever duplicate it. She said it took far too much energy and thought she could use the wormhole they left to determine their origin," Hudson said.

This was news to Tom. "So you had no intention of holding up your end of the bargain?"

"What bargain? That was a stretch. The Statu never made a real agreement with us. They never spoke with us, not once. We sent the offer, and they left without comment. No matter how many times the leadership, including your own grandfather, attempted negotiation, the Statu refused to talk. I was beginning to think they didn't even have a way to communicate."

"You wanted to follow them and bring the War to them?" Tom asked.

Hudson nodded. "That was the plan, and we began to build the fleet up again. But Pha'n failed in using the wormhole to find their home location, and ten years passed, then another decade, and we fell into complacency."

"And the fact that the Statu were using our own people to fight us?" Tom asked.

"What about it? You understand how that shouldn't have been spread around, right? When we didn't think they were ever returning, we hid the facts away, not wanting to worry anyone. What they don't know can't hurt them, right?" Hudson grinned weakly.

"Why did you react like you did when I told you about the Statu being here?" Tom asked.

"You aren't prepared for something of this magnitude," Hudson said. "The ship is too new; the mission you were on was supposed to be simple. Meet and greet. Shake a few hands, then we'd come for the ore."

"And is the whole idea of using it for powering ships and cities a crock too?" Tom asked.

Hudson didn't reply.

"Adam, you need to be honest. You've lost your power. Tell me." Tom hoped it would work. Sometimes people needed to rid themselves of a burdensome secret they'd been holding close to their chests. It was cathartic.

"We were going to use it to build our own wormholes."

The response wasn't that surprising. "And do you have the technology yet?" Tom asked.

"No, but we're close. The power we could amplify through the ore might have worked. But now it's lost," Hudson said.

Tom shook his head. "Not lost. Just misplaced. We're going to destroy it."

Hudson grimaced. "It's worth more than you can understand. With wormhole capability, the Concord would be a force no one could withstand."

"*To rule absolute is an atrocity, to rule with care is a kingdom that will endure.*" Tom watched Hudson's expression as he quoted the Code, and saw something flickering in the man's eyes.

"Whatever happens, don't let the Statu keep it. They'll be unstoppable."

Tom had a lot of questions, but no time. "I won't."

———

*B*rax ran through the corridors. It felt good to be moving, and his body responded with appreciation as they traversed the tunnels. This city was unique, and Brax had never seen anything quite like it. Even the underground worlds he'd visited had been laid out more like cities than tunnels connecting villages. He wondered if the people that used to live here had faster ways of crossing through, like hover-cars or something that wouldn't require walking for kilometers at a time to get anywhere.

"Slow down, Brax," Reeve said from some ways behind him. He obeyed, and she caught up, her breathing heavy. "I didn't think I was so badly out of shape. Nothing like running with you to remind me."

"I was always the athlete of the family, you know that," Brax said with a grin.

"You sure it's a good time to be mocking me? We're about to head into a hornet's nest, and I don't feel like being stung." His sister had a way with words.

"Stay with me, and I'll make sure no one hurts you," he told her, and she rolled her eyes.

"Always so self-righteous. Are you positive the Tubers will be here?" she asked, glancing to a diagram along the wall. They were over halfway to their destination, and Brax was glad to almost be there. As of now, he suspected Starling and Penter were almost at the next work site, ready to rescue another group of Bacals.

"I saw them from the hover platform. It looked like a central station," Brax told her for the third time. He'd never seen his sister so rattled.

"And you're sure you can fly one…"

"Will you let me worry about that? I'm going to need your skills soon enough, so focus on running the rest of the way, and keep your alien tech training at the top of your brain." He started jogging again, Reeve sighing and following.

They passed through the rest of the simple corridor and found an entryway at the end. Instead of heading to the side, through one of the orange labeled doors, Brax set a hand on the purple-toned door. He searched for a vibration, wondering if anyone was moving across it. When he felt nothing, he nodded to his sister.

She moved toward a compact electrical box and pried the cover plate off. She stuck her tongue out, squinting as she shone a light on the controls.

Brax leaned forward, realizing he hadn't tried the easy option. The door slid open as he pulled on the handle.

"I was about to do that," Reeve said, flicking her light off.

"I'm sure you were." Brax stepped into the next room and stopped in his tracks. It was far different from the other regions they'd seen. This was a real city. Steps led them lower, into a courtyard below. The space was circular, and they shone lights over the area, seeing what appeared to be local businesses.

"It looks like a bazaar," Reeve said softly.

"It does. Want to go shopping?" Brax asked, and she slapped him on the arm.

"Who doesn't? I wonder who lived here. Do you think this is their home world?" Reeve asked.

He shook his head. "Where are they? If they died, it was a long time ago."

"The aliens on board *Constantine* were frozen for centuries," Reeve advised him, and this was news.

"Do you think they're related?" he asked.

"I don't see how they can't be. This entire mission has been extremely strange, so let's keep adding to the pile."

Reeve walked off the last step, heading for the center of the massive bazaar. The stairs had taken them another hundred feet below the surface, and Brax lifted a hand, thinking he heard something from across the room.

Reeve held her PL-30 in her hand, and Brax clutched the crude Statu weapon in his, ready to fire at anything that moved. His nerves were on edge as they moved through the cavernous room, his gaze darting at the long shadows their faint lights cast.

"If the Statu lived here, I don't like it," Reeve said.

"Why?"

"Because this is too normal. This is a shopping area, a place of commerce and trade. That doesn't sound like the enemy we fought, does it? They're monsters, only capable of one thing: pain." Reeve's eyes were wide as she gazed around.

"I agree. I don't like this either." Brax searched for the exit, and after walking for a good five minutes, a staircase appeared between two glass-covered storefronts. He saw what looked like dishware inside one, maybe tools in the other. The inquisitive side of him wanted to stay here and explore, but there wasn't time for that, not with the Statu warships coming.

"Up here." He led the way, climbing the steps with ease. By the time they arrived at the doorway, his thighs and calves were burning. He'd been calorie-deprived over the last week, and it was beginning to take its toll on him. "This should be it. The Tubers were above this region. We're going to meet some resistance here. Are you ready to fight?"

Reeve nodded, and he could tell she wasn't going to let any enemies stand between her and a ride in a Tuber. Brax felt a slight vibration on the tall metallic door, and he touched the handle, pulling it open and stepping through on the count of three.

The room was quiet.

A blast hit the wall beside him, and he stayed in front of Reeve, returning fire. He heard a target scream, and he fired again, a body slumping to the ground. He shone his light on them, illuminating the dark exoskeleton of an un-armored Statu. Its mandibles continued to move slowly, and he stepped over, kicking the enemy's gun away. He shot it in the chest, easing its suffering. He wasn't an animal like they were.

"One down," Brax whispered.

The room was unique: this one had seating and computer screens glowing dimly. He guessed the newcomers had found a way to power this station using their own technology. That meant there were more of them nearby, but only one guard in this room. They hadn't been expecting an attack, especially from underground. He was going to use this.

"Try this on," Reeve said, tossing him a helmet. It was crude, roughly shaped, the visor reflective like all Statu armor suits.

"I don't feel like being Scrambled," he said.

Reeve knelt beside the suit and showed him where the injection would come from. "There has to be a way to dis-arm the Scrambler." She set to work, pulling a small tool kit from her pack, and Brax sighed, resting his gun over his forearm and aiming toward the exit.

"I think I have it," she said, her compact tool making a snapping sound as a thin needle device fell from the inside of the suit. She tossed it to him, and Brax jumped out of the way, the Scrambler clanging to the ground.

"I don't want to touch that. You've seen what they do to people," he said.

Reeve stood, dusting her pants off, and grabbed a

helmet. "Let's suit up."

---

*T*reena fired at the unsuspecting Statu, almost feeling remorse for how easy it was. She and Penter were in the lead, wearing the oddly-shaped armor over their heads. The visor made visibility difficult at first, but once the HUD activated, she realized it showed much more than she'd expected. The helmet had recessed cameras on it, literally giving you eyes on the back of your head. No wonder the few altercations they'd had in close combat with the Statu had been difficult to win.

She didn't think the Concord had any suits with power after the War, each of them draining after the Scrambler was activated. Treena wished they could have worn the whole suit, but she didn't have time to fiddle with the needle, and she wasn't about to risk ending up a pile of genetic slime.

The five sleeping Statu were silenced quickly, only the last one waking before being gunned down. She took all the weapons, handing them to more of Penter's people. Tarlen had stayed with the elderly and children, ready to move the next group of slaves further underground, ever toward the huge warship.

Their stealthy rescue mission had turned into something so much bigger with the discovery of the underground city, and Treena had hope they wouldn't run out of time. Either way, even if it meant her death, it was worth the risk. These people didn't deserve this fate, and Treena was going to do whatever she could to free them.

"I'll head up," Penter said, walking over a dead Statu. His voice was muffled from behind the helmet, and he moved for the steps, his actions quiet. Treena stayed close behind, her finger settled beside the trigger as he pressed through the door.

They emerged in the stone-walled room, and Penter blasted a guard. Treena saw another and fired quickly, three fast shots disarming and killing the Statu. Two Bacals raced past her and outside, where the system's star was beginning to peek over the horizon. The landscape had a soft glow to it, a gentle breeze rustling nearby leaves.

She heard more gunfire, and the entire room of slaves erupted in screams and shouts. Penter had his helmet off, and he ran to the entrance. "Everyone calm down. We're here to rescue you. Move in a line, and head for the platform," he said.

Treena nodded as Penter glanced at her. They'd agreed that if it was daylight, they were running out of time. They couldn't worry about being hidden any longer. Speed was their only virtue at this point. They had ten more guns now, and Penter passed them out, asking this group who was capable of using the weapons.

The mistreated people of Greblok filed out of their captivity, and Treena's artificial heart ached for them. There were fewer here, and she stepped forward, seeing at least three bodies covered in meager clothing along the wall, the slaves unable to give them a proper burial. She fumed inside, wishing there were more of the Statu nearby to take vengeance on.

As they all boarded the platform resting a quarter kilometer away, the piece of the huge warship the slaves had been working on came into view. She took solace in the fact that this section wouldn't be fabricated, at least not by this group.

Penter was at the edge, trying to figure out how to activate the immense transport vessel, and Treena ran to his aid. The control panel was clunky and antiquated by Concord standards, but the general concepts weren't lost on her. She pressed a button, flipped a switch with a loud click, and the engines rumbled below them.

"I'll let you do the honors," Penter said, giving her space.

Treena checked to make sure everyone was on the platform. "Stay away from the railing," she warned them. She had no idea how bumpy of a ride it was going to be, and she didn't want anyone free-falling over the edge.

Treena pulled up on the controller arm while pressing what she deemed the thrust level, and the hover transport lurched. People shouted in fear, and she pursed her lips, trying to be more cautious. The sun was already rising more, and that meant precious minutes were ticking away. Time they didn't have to waste. There were so many more sites to free before they could gather at the warship.

The ship lifted more smoothly, and she let out a sigh of relief as she moved the group of slaves a hundred feet in the air and toward the next site, which she could already see in the distance.

The trip was fast, the two kilometers speeding by in less than a minute. She lowered beside the other platform, and when the guards came running, Treena hopped off, firing at them as she and Penter took their attention away from the Bacals, who were sitting ducks.

Treena and Penter attacked with impunity, the other armed allies taking three Statu down from the other end of the platform. Treena cringed as one of their own was hit, falling to the ground, and Penter didn't waste any time in avenging the dead woman. The Statu guard was hit with a volley of shots, each hitting the intended target.

It was the last enemy in the area, and it fell with a thump. Other than the odd cry from the Greblok people, the morning was silent.

"Go. Rescue the captives. Bring them here," she urged Penter's people, and a group ran off, armed and ready to rescue their own kind. Treena and Penter gathered as many weapons as they could find, and she smiled. "We're starting to grow a little army, aren't we?"

"That we are. You're an admirable ally, Starling," Penter said.

She was already moving toward the next hover platform and began going through the motions of bringing it to life; only this one didn't fire up with ease. Penter stood guard while she attempted to start it. Eventually, it hissed and chugged before falling dead again.

"That's not good. We can't carry them all," Penter told her.

Treena hopped off, letting go of the rusty metal railing. She was really seeing how desperate the Statu operation was here. Their guards were hardly soldiers, their transport ships nothing more than flat squares with ancient thrusters built into the undersides. Even the railings were weathered, as if no effort or attention had gone into their upkeep. It was the opposite of the Concord procedures.

Even the old ships like *Pliatese* and *Cecilia,* while not pretty on the inside, were well maintained. The exteriors were rough, the corridors and residences nowhere near as shiny as *Constantine*'s, but there was a high level of pride that went into caring for the cruise ships that the Statu would never understand. It was evident with their uniforms, their armor suits, their crude weapons. The Statu were barbarians, an advanced race only in spacefaring terms; otherwise, they were akin to angry predators, tearing at the throats of beasts, if only for the taste of blood.

Treena hated them at that instant, not because of how different their culture was, but because of how they used their enemies to do their bidding, rather than fighting their own fights. She was going to learn their secret and find a way to use it against them.

"Starling, did you hear me?" Penter asked, and Treena peered over at him.

"Sure. Stay with these ones," she ordered, pointing to the group on the first platform.

Treena crossed the short distance quicker than any human legs could have taken her, and found two Statu moving toward the Bacal slaves with a surprising amount of stealth. Her anger still raged inside, and she reached out, pulling one of the guards close to her. She snapped the helmet loose, hearing the Scrambler inside his suit activate. Seconds later, the guard had changed from flesh and bones to ooze. She threw the helmet at the second guard as he tried to fire off a shot in her direction, and she pulled her trigger three times – two to the chest, one to the head – and he dropped.

The Bacal stood staring toward her with wide eyes at her fast and inhuman movements. "Quit staring and move for the basement." She led them to the guards' barracks underground, and gave the strongest-looking Bacal woman a gun and directions on the map diagram inside the underground corridor, before returning to the first platform.

"Everything good?" Penter asked.

"It will be," she said, taking control of the platform and lifting it from the ground.

The sun was higher now, and the Statu would be aware of the incursion sooner rather than later. They had to hurry.

TWENTY-TWO

*T*om had left his impromptu meeting with Admiral Hudson feeling distraught, but also rejuvenated. They had a plan, albeit a rough one, but Tom had confidence they'd make it work. Not only did they have better weaponry and technology, they had the Concord's finest on board this ship, and on the surface already.

"Constantine," Tom said as he crossed the room of his private quarters.

The AI appeared, and Tom stood across from him, assessing the man he knew as Grandfather.

"Yes, Captain. We're only ten minutes from contact position. Shouldn't you be on the bridge?" he asked calmly.

"Remember that time I came home after my first date with that Tekol girl from the Academy, what was her name… it's on the tip of my tongue," Tom said, grinning like a schoolboy.

"It was Leerp, Captain," Constantine said.

Tom pointed at the AI and laughed out loud. "Gotcha! I can't believe it!"

"I'm sorry, am I missing something?" Constantine asked.

"Why would you remember her name if you only had my grandfather's tactical and mission memories? He was an old man then," Tom said, squinting at the projection as he waited for the reply.

Constantine motioned for Tom to have a seat at the table beside his kitchenette. "I suppose there's no point in hiding it, Tommy."

Tommy. Only the old man and one other person had called him that, and it used to irritate him to no end. His father had used it when he was little as a term of endearment, but when Constantine had used it, it had always felt forced and condescending.

"How?" Tom sat, painfully aware of how little time he had for this conversation.

"The process is complicated, and though the Concord has had the technology for decades, they've been holding back on it. They wanted something special here, a true flagship, and they gave me more of his personality, so that for all intents and purposes I would *be* Constantine Baldwin, the hero of the Yollox Incursion. They added a limiter, but they rushed the ship's production and forgot to close a few secret doors.

"It really was quite simple to sneak in and free the remaining memories," Constantine said, hands clasped in front of his hips.

"Does that mean you remember me? All of it?" Tom asked.

"I do. I remember the day your mother was born. I was coming in from the Xoni Seven system on some diplomatic mission of little consequence when I heard Katherine was in labor." Constantine's voice changed, even cracked as he gazed to the far wall. He laughed. "I overdid the Star Drive. Back then, their charge was far less, more dangerous to push, but I did, and received a slap on the wrist eventually. I didn't care. I was there the minute before Cleo arrived."

Tom leaned forward, finding it so hard to believe he was really talking to this man who'd died over ten years ago. He hadn't realized how much he'd missed him until this moment. "What was it like?"

"Becoming a father?" Constantine asked, and Tom nodded. "It was exhilarating, exciting, but also more frightening than any mission I'd ever been on."

"Even Yollox?" Tom asked.

"That hadn't happened yet, but in retrospect, yes, even Yollox. Because this was my baby, and I vowed to never let anything harm her... Tom, you wonder why I was so hard on you, I can see it in your eyes. Why I was so angry, so hostile to the universe in those last years. It was because everything I fought for was taken from me. My Cleo dead at the hands of Reepa pirates... that was so random, such an unlikely scenario, and that's what we were trained for in the Concord Academy, wasn't it? Being prepared for unusual situations, understanding how to defend ourselves, learning from them so they don't occur again. What's the word they used...?"

It was Tom's turn to answer the questions. "Mitigate risk."

"Right. As if that would bring my Cleo and your father back," Constantine's expressions had even changed, looking more like the man he remembered so well.

"You didn't lose everyone. You had me." Constantine had grown worse in the last years after his wife passed, until Tom refused to see the man.

"I know. But you were a constant reminder of her, Tommy. Her eyes... they're your eyes. Your hair color, the cleft in your chin, the way you smile... it was all her, and I couldn't stand it," Constantine said.

The console chimed, and Ven's voice carried over the ship's speaker. "Captain Baldwin, we're two minutes from contact."

"I have to go," Tom said, moving for the door.

"I'm sorry. I'm not your grandfather; I'm nothing but a computer image from memories, but... I am sorry," Constantine said, appearing directly in front of Tom.

"You do realize how strange this is, right? There's a reason this is illegal," Tom said.

"I understand. When this is over, you can tweak my parameters to spec. I won't hold it against you," the AI said, and Tom opened his door, rushing for the bridge.

He arrived, shaken by the interaction with the AI. He pressed it away and entered the bridge to see the fifth planet zoomed onto the viewer. "Have you made contact yet, Zare?"

The Zilph'i Junior Officer peered over her shoulder, shaking her head. "We waited for you."

"Contact the commander," Tom ordered, watching the screen where the cluster of Statu warships continued to move through the system. The timer countdown said they had five hours and forty-three minutes until arrival.

"Sir, she's not... wait, I have her."

Zare passed control to the captain's chair, and Tom sat heavily. "Starling, what's happening down there?"

"Captain, thank the Vastness. The Statu warship is here, the one that we saw leave Greblok. The people are freed, and we have nearly a quarter of them safe." Commander Starling was almost shouting, a loud noise clunking in the background.

"What's the situation? Is there conflict?" Tom asked.

There was a pause, and her voice echoed through. "They're spread out. I don't think there are many true Statu here. They were probably going to make a group of slaves to fight us if we arrived, but we came too soon. They're operating with a ghost crew."

"Backup is on the way," Tom assured her, glancing to the radar again.

"We know. We're using an underground city to gather the Bacal, and moving toward the warship," she said.

"Why?"

"We're going to take it, sir," she said plainly.

Tom smiled. "Good. We'll be there in an hour's time. That leaves us only a couple more to gather everyone and escape through the wormhole." He peered to the radar when an alarm rang out, and he saw half of the incoming fleet change trajectory. "Scratch that. They know we're here and have shifted half their fleet to intercept the wormhole."

Ven spoke up. "Sir, they'll arrive at the wormhole in four hours and twelve minutes. This is going to be tight."

Tom tried to do the math and didn't like the results. "Starling, get as many of them as you can to that ship. We have *Cecilia* with us, and we're going to drop our fighters to assist the extradition of the warship. Consider it an envoy to deal with any lingering Tubers."

"*Cecilia*? How is she there?" Treena Starling asked, the surprise evident in her voice.

"A story for another day. Tomorrow, when we're safely on the other side of the wormhole, and these bastards are on this end," Tom said.

"Sounds good to me, Captain," she said.

"Is Reeve with you? Do you have Brax?" Tom asked, tapping his fingers nervously on his armrest.

"The wonder twins are stealing a Tuber as we speak," she said.

"A Tuber? Why?" Tom asked.

"How else are they going to enter the warship?" Starling asked, and Tom shook his head.

"We'll be in touch." Tom ended the call and searched the bridge for their newfound Statu friends. "Where's Yephion, Ven?"

The lanky Ugna man blinked a few times. "He's waking up his people, sir. You'll find him in the cargo bay."

Tom stood to leave. "Keep me posted."

"Sir, before you go." Ven seemed nervous and about to say something.

"What is it?"

"There's been an incident. We found a Callalay man, on the maintenance crew…"

"What about it? I don't have time for this, Ven."

"He had a detonator in his hand, and we caught him on camera on Deck Two a few days ago, placing a device on an integral Star Drive component," Ven said.

Tom's heart hammered in his chest. "Is it safe?"

"Yes, sir. The man is dead, and there will be an investigation. The device has been removed and disposed of," Ven said.

"I wish Brax were here. Thanks for filling me in, Ven. Proceed." Tom left the bridge, wondering what in the Vastness had been going on in his ship over the last week.

---

*B*rax raced through the door, expecting to find opposition, but there was no one outside. He felt odd wearing the clunky armor of the Concord's nemesis, but when two Statu armored soldiers walked by, unarmed, not even glancing their way, he was glad Reeve had made him don the suit.

Reeve tilted her head, indicating they leave the Statu behind, and Brax fought the urge to end them before they caught on. She was probably right. No sense in drawing attention to themselves, especially since they were in costume.

This area was more populated by their enemy; no Bacal slaves were nearby. The day was proving to be hot, and Brax was sweating profusely in the borrowed armor. How did the Statu deal with the heat? Maybe their exoskeletal bodies had a venting system he wasn't aware of. Either way, he'd be happy to take this blasted suit off as soon as possible.

They passed more soldiers, none of them carrying weapons, making Brax feel a little out of place with the crude gun clasped in his gloved grip. Reeve didn't seem to care, and she walked faster than him. There were over ten buildings here, each as raw and ugly as the slave camps, but as they passed the last on the right, he saw the prize he'd been waiting for. Three of the Tubers were situated on the grass, thrusters off and engines dead.

They were huge, much larger than he'd remembered. They weren't pure cylinders from this vantage point, as they were slightly squished in the centers. One Tuber ran horizontally along the grass, the blades burnt from where the hot thrusters had settled to the field. A few of the Statu milled about, but as far as Brax could tell, none of them spoke to one another.

It was so off-putting to see them like this. A few walked around without armor, their dark gray exoskeletons glimmering in the sunlight. One of them stopped near Reeve, and Brax felt his finger twitch, ready to attack, but it only clicked something and moved on.

Reeve continued toward the three Tubers, and when she peered at him over her shoulder, Brax intuitively comprehended she was asking which one they should steal. Reeve had ditched her pack with Tarlen but had kept two DC-27 explosives, which she held in her left glove.

Brax pointed at the last Tuber sitting on the right, and she nodded her understanding. She passed one of the devices to him, and he smiled in his helmet, hidden from plain sight. He was going to enjoy watching these ships explode if the Statu attacked.

Reeve walked to the middle Tuber, and Brax took the left one, walking along the edge of the vessel to stop near the central thruster. If they blew this one out, he doubted the ship would be able to compensate. He peeked around, making sure no one watched, and placed the small but impactful explosive inside the lip of the circle. When he was positive it had latched, he headed toward their destination, Reeve coming in step with him as they approached the ship they were going to procure.

Sweat continued to pour over Brax's face, and he wished he could wipe it off. He blinked the stinging liquid from his eyes and surveyed the Tuber. It was whole; no outer damage ran along the one-hundred-meter-long hull. It was an ugly ship; he'd always thought so. The Statu didn't care about aesthetics: they only wanted to procure things using the Tuber's Movers. He estimated they could fit a few hundred slaves on board each of these ships, and no doubt these very ships had been used on Greblok a few days ago.

Brax recalled his lesson from that day at the Academy and understood the entrance was at the front of the cylinder, which meant the opposite end held the thrusters. It also had them on the underside for advanced control, which complicated things for the pilot, especially one inexperienced with the technology.

You can do this. He repeated the words a few times until he almost believed himself, and walked as inconspicuously as he could to the head of the vessel. He was in the middle of a Statu base. It was still hard to believe. From all his training, he'd never heard of anyone being so close to them unless they were enslaved by the enemy. As far as Brax could tell, they didn't appear very intelligent, but what they lacked in smarts, they made up for with a lack of empathy and a willingness to do what it took to invade. It was a dangerous combination.

Reeve waited for him near the Tuber's flat snout, and he fumbled around, searching for a handle of some sort, when the door opened and an armored Statu emerged. He walked past them and stared into the sky. Brax followed his gaze, where two Tubers soared through the air.

They were too late. The enemy knew what they were pulling. Brax looked at Reeve, and then at the Statu, who was walking toward the next ship, where another guard stared upward.

It was their chance. Brax stepped through the door, Reeve slamming it shut after they both were safely on.

"We have to hurry!" she called from inside her helmet, and Brax climbed a ladder into the cockpit.

"Reeve, you need to clear the ship. Make sure no one is on board!" he shouted to his sister, receiving a nod.

He stared at the cockpit controls and shook his head to clear his mind. With a quick tug, he disconnected his helmet, the heat a little less inside the ship. His sweat cooled as he peered over the controls. He had no idea where to start.

Someone began banging on the door, and Brax took a deep breath. His instructor had sat where he was in the lesson all those years ago, and at that moment, Brax wished he had his sister's memory. The cockpit had an arched ceiling, being at the top of the flat tube. The viewer was spread around, giving him a one-eighty view of his surroundings. The controls were a series of long switches and rubber-covered buttons. He saw his instructor in his mind's eye, flicking the largest switch and pressing the yellow button beside it.

Brax did so now, and the lights on the dash came to life. Another bang on the door, and a gunshot from below and deeper in the ship. Reeve could handle herself. He needed to lift this baby off the ground. To the right of the intricate and confusing dash was a control stick, and it flooded through his mind.

His feet found the controls for the lower thrusts, and he pressed the pedal as he flicked the red switch on the side of the controller. The ship rumbled, a whine carrying through the cockpit.

The ship beside him lifted from the ground, heading in the direction the other two had flown toward, and someone was climbing the rungs loudly behind him. Brax picked up his gun from his lap and pointed it at the figure in Statu armor.

"It's me!" Reeve shouted, pulling her helmet off. Her red eyes bored into him, and she brushed her dreads aside, hopping into the copilot's seat next to him. "What can I do?" she asked.

"Any trouble?" he countered.

"Nothing I couldn't take care of. Two of them were in the slave pens," she said. "Again, what can I do?"

"Look for weapons systems. We didn't get into that part of it during my lesson. We only learned how the Statu flew the things," he admitted.

She ran her eyes over the controls, and Brax was positive that if anyone could make sense of the odd layout, it was her. He set to his own task and held his breath. "Here goes nothing."

He pressed the pedal, pulling on the control stick, and the ship lurched forward, the rear of the Tuber rising higher than the front. They hovered and nearly nose-dived into the ground before he corrected. The last Tuber was lifting from the ground now, and soon all three were in the air, including Brax and Reeve, and he let out a shout of exhilaration as they soared upwards and forward, following the pack.

"Impressive," Reeve told him, her hands hovering over the controls. "I hope we don't need to use these weapons, because I can't make heads or tails… wait, this appears to be the…"

Brax smiled as she went on about the buttons, telling him about how clear it was now. He had to focus on what he was doing, because his comprehension of what he was doing was passable at best. The control lever tugged against his hand, and he pulled harder, easing the thrusters below the ship and using the rear ones more. It was a tough balancing act, but he was slowly learning what worked and what didn't.

He was lagging behind the others, but he was okay with that. Then they might not notice how poor a pilot he was. Through the viewscreen, the immense warship appeared where it had landed the other day. Gone were the hovering platforms, each settled at a slave camp, and from his count, there were only a dozen of so Tubers in the entire vicinity.

That was still too many for them to fight.

"I think I can power them up," Reeve said, and from the corner of his eye, he saw her reach for a blue-cased button. She pressed it, and the entire dash died, the lights bright one second, dark the next. The ship began to drop.

"Turn it on, turn it on!" Brax shouted, his body lifting from the seat and pressing against the glass above.

Reeve must have been strapped in, because she was able to stretch over and, with a string of angry Reepa curses, press the button on again. Brax slammed into the pilot's seat, the wind nearly knocked out of his chest. He quickly grabbed hold of the controls, pulling the Tuber out of its fast descent toward the looming treeline.

Reeve peered over at him, her eyebrows raised. "Sorry."

"Sorry," he muttered, his heart racing fiercely. "If you're done messing around, can you find the hangar access for me?"

The hangars were in the center of the warships, underneath the main arms that stretched in all directions from the central post of the ship, but Brax had no idea how to open them, and also doubted he had the subtle skills needed to gently land a Tuber inside.

Reeve fiddled with the screen, which had the appearance of something the Concord would have used eight hundred years ago. It had pixelated orange icons on it, and they slowly blinked to life as she tapped it. Once she was in, Brax saw how fast she scrolled through it. Reeve's mind didn't need languages to decipher things, not when it came to computers. She had a bond with mathematics that Brax would never appreciate.

The warship lingered in the distance, nearly forty kilometers away. The Tubers had broken formation and were heading in different directions. That had to mean they were going for the Bacal slave groups. Brax made a silent prayer to the Vastness for their safety. The people had never intended to become caught up in this mess. He'd only been around them a short time, but he'd already made friends and respected what a resilient race they were.

All they'd wanted was to join the power of the Concord, allowing technological growth, opportunity for their people, and trade. Instead, they were targeted and attacked, many ripped away from their home and brought here, most killed. Anger pulsed through Brax as he flew toward the warship. He was going to help rescue these people. He had no choice.

Voices carried toward Tarlen and the ever-growing group of Bacal from all directions. He smiled and opened doors from the attaching passageways. They were near the warship, and his legs were exhausted. So many of his people were almost on the ground, many being carried by anyone with enough strength remaining to assist.

"This way!" Tarlen shouted. He was wearing a Concord uniform, and even though he was one of the Bacal and only a youth, everyone was deferring to his lead.

The people passed by, and he smiled at them, feeding them encouragement. There was a long way to go before Tarlen considered anyone safe, but at least they were doing something. When he'd heard they were going to withdraw before helping free the slaves, he was heartbroken. But the Concord would never do that to the Bacal, not after what was promised them. No, these were great people. Officers of legend, like Captain Baldwin.

Abbil was beside him, and Tarlen instantly felt her strength. He'd never met her before; actually, he only recognized a few people out of the growing group, but recalled none by name. So far, there was no sign of his parents or Belna, but he wasn't giving up hope. He couldn't.

"This makes five thousand. Can you believe it?" Abbil asked, and Tarlen found he was surprised. She'd been counting.

"Amazing. We're going to make it," Tarlen told her as the last person emerged through the corridor entrance. They were filtered into a huge city courtyard, the ceiling domed high above them. It was dark, and their few lights from the Concord crew offered nothing more than minor comfort and shadows.

"What's the plan?"

"Where are we going?"

"Ephi, are you here? Has anyone seen Ephi?"

Tarlen cringed as the entire room became a cacophony of shouts and fearful mutterings. He squirmed through the press of musky bodies and climbed onto a dais near the next exit.

"People of Greblok!" he shouted and repeated it when no one stopped talking. Soon they were turning to stare toward him, and he raised his hand in the air, hoping they'd eventually quiet. After a few minutes, the room grew silent, with the exception of coughing and the odd sob.

"We are Bacal. We've been torn from our homes, but the great Concord saw fit to send an envoy to assist," Tarlen said.

"Where are they?"

"I don't see any Concord."

"We're doomed."

Tarlen raised his hand again, shaking his head. "Stop this. I know you've seen a lot, been through more than you ever should have, but we're going to survive this. We're going to go home, rebuild Malin and Greblok, and we're going to do so under the wing and tutelage of the Concord.

"We will only survive if we work together, and stop letting fear persuade us. Are we Bacal?" he asked, his hands trembling.

A few people called out, "We are Bacal," but not enough.

"I said, are we Bacal? Are we resilient? Are we strong? Are we worthy of a partnership with the Concord?" he shouted.

"We are Bacal!" the group shouted as one, and a few people began to cheer. He worried the Statu would be able to hear them from above, and he raised his arm, lowering his hand, and they stopped.

"Then wait here as the rest gather, and when you see someone faltering, help them. When we have to run, you will run. If we have to fight, you will fight," Tarlen said, standing tall.

Abbil nodded at him from beside the platform, and Tarlen scanned the crowd, wishing to see his family among the freed Bacal.

TWENTY-THREE

*T*here were thirty Statu outside of the cryo chambers, and Doctor Nee was making his rounds as Tom stood near the hangar bay exit.

"Captain," the doctor said, waving him over.

"Status?" Tom asked him, looking around the room and seeing so many of their long-time enemies, he didn't know how to feel.

Nee was more disheveled than Tom had ever seen him. His normally perfect hair was in disarray, his smooth skin lined with exhaustion. "They're coming around, sir. Yephion and his partner have been a great help."

"Where are the wormhole experts?" Tom asked.

Nee rubbed his chin with a gloved hand. "According to our new friend, the leading expert isn't here. He must have died in the Tuber attack. But those three have passing knowledge." The doctor pointed to the left side, where Yephion crouched near them.

"Good work, Doctor. I appreciate your efforts," Tom told him, and Nee walked off, heading to a makeshift patient bed where one of the Statu was connected to beeping machinery.

"Constantine," Tom called, and the AI appeared.

"Yes, Captain," he said. Tom glanced at him, still uncomfortable with the fact that his grandfather's essence was inside this projection.

"Translate," he said, stepping toward Yephion. The Statu was wearing a Concord maintenance jumpsuit, and he looked odd in the attire. "I see everyone is up. I know they're tired and trying to recover, but we require them in Engineering."

He waited as the AI clicked the message, and the three Statu started to rise from their beds on the ground. Constantine relayed their reply. "It will be done."

Tom stared hard at them, leaning forward. "It has to destroy the wormhole. Destabilize it. The detonation cannot fail. Do you understand?"

"They understand, sir. It will not fail, they say," Constantine echoed.

"Good. See to it." Tom stalked away from them, leaving the AI beside Yephion. He had another stop to make.

Tom saw the planet displayed in the corridor's computer screens as he walked toward the elevator lift, which he took to Deck Three.

A few minutes later, he was at the entrance he'd sought out, and Lieutenant Basker was there, as he'd ordered. The Callalay man was standing straight-backed, his uniform crisp and pressed.

"Sir, I apologize for the lack of fighters on *Constantine*," Basker told him. He entered his clearance, and Tom followed him into the hangar bay where the five fighters sat parked.

"It isn't your fault, Lieutenant. It was a diplomatic mission. In and out. No one counted on any of this." Tom's gaze settled on his own fighter, last in line, and felt a tug on his heart.

Three pilots stood beside their own ships, helmets under arms. Tom nodded to each of them. He hadn't met them yet and wished this all hadn't happened so fast. He was behind, not fully caught up with his crew or his ship.

"Captain," Ven said, his communicator buzzing.

"Go ahead, bridge," Tom stated, turning from the waiting pilots.

"We're arriving at orbit. The warships are three and a half hours away from the world, and we see that there are active Tubers in the atmosphere. Two have broken free and are hovering around the planet," Ven said.

"How many below?" Tom asked.

"Ten, sir," Ven replied.

Tom stared at Basker and his small regiment of fighters. There were only four – five, with his ship – but there was no one there to pilot it. "Get me Starling," he said.

"Starling here." Treena's voice was a welcome sound.

"Status update," Tom barked.

"We've had to pause the rescue. The Tubers are activated. We have sixty percent of the camps underground at this point, and we're funneling the rest there since the Tubers attacked one of our platforms. We lost a couple hundred, sir." Tom could hear the pain in her voice.

"Stay the course. We're heading to the planet. Our fighters will pick them off. Be ready for the last rescues. We have to make this quick," Tom said.

"We, sir?" Basker asked.

Tom glanced to his old fighter and grinned. "I've been meaning to shake the dust off." He moved to the edge of the bay and began suiting up.

---

*T*he opening appeared immense from the viewscreen, but the closer Brax pulled toward the bay, the less confident he was about his flying skills. There were no other Tubers near the warship, and it wouldn't have gone unnoticed that he wasn't following directives. There would be opposition inside the warship, but from the looks of their operation, he didn't expect a vast company of soldiers.

"Brax, are you sure you can do this?" Reeve asked, causing even more doubt.

"It's either this or we land and try to climb on somewhere. I don't think it'll have the same impact," he said, slowing the ship and tugging on the yoke. The cylindrical tube shuddered and shook as he spun it around, heading toward the landing zone.

Reeve had already hopped off her seat, and Brax was about to suggest she stay buckled in, when he bumped the edge of the warship, sending his sister sprawling. A moment later, he was inside the enormous vessel, and he turned to grin at Reeve, who was still on the cockpit floor frowning at him.

"Nice touch." She rubbed her hip and clambered to her feet, loading up on weapons. She placed her helmet on and tossed his over.

"We don't know what to expect," Brax said. "Be cautious."

"Great advice. And here I was about to walk on and ask if they wanted to share a *Pilo* pie." Reeve brushed past him, heading to the exit.

"If you don't mind, I think I should take the lead. It's what I'm trained in," he said, grabbing her arm.

"Be my guest," Reeve said from behind the helmet. Brax couldn't see her eyes, but he imagined she was rolling them as she waited for him to climb down the rungs. Soon he was at the exit, holding the crude blaster in his hands, ready for anything. He turned a lever, the door hissing steam as it unlatched. He tried to keep his cool, not wanting to seem like he was there to assault anyone. He had to pretend to be with them.

As it turned out, there was no welcoming committee. The bay was silent. A broken-down Tuber was parked half a hangar away, parts stripped from the exterior. Otherwise, they were alone.

"This is so odd. Where are they all?" Reeve asked.

"I think they did the mission on a skeleton crew." Brax walked forward, his heavy steps clanging loudly inside the open hangar. They entered the ship from a wide doorway that he had to manually open, and he took a look around. There were wires hanging loosely in the central corridor, lights flickering, and the surfaces of the walls were grimy. It didn't appear as though the Statu were concerned with cleanliness.

Something tripped his peripheral vision, and he spun his head, ready to attack, when he saw it was only a rodent of some kind. The animal raced along the wall in the shadows, its red eyes glowing in the dimly lit corridor. A few more ran by, and he cringed, thinking about rodents being on board one of the Concord ships. That wasn't a problem they had to deal with. There were too many things to prevent it.

"We have to find the bridge," Reeve told him.

She was always better at that kind of thing. The records on warships weren't great, and they were going to be guessing where to find it. "That's your area of expertise. I'll be here to ensure we make it there."

Reeve started forward and paused before turning around and jogging away from Brax. He followed closely before heading to an elevator lift. It had railings but no walls, and was surrounded by a glass tube ten yards wide.

"This is a start," his sister said while fumbling with the controls. They were a series of thick black buttons and switches, and after a few false starts, it began to rise. "Let's begin from the top."

They didn't have much time, and he hoped that Starling had finished gathering the Bacal. The plan was only going to work if he and Reeve gained control of the warship.

Brax saw each level through the glass tube as they lifted, and even spotted a couple Statu soldiers walking about as they passed. None of them seemed to care that there were two more on a lift on their ship. He was grateful for the fact that he was disguised in their own armor.

It stopped eventually, presumably at the top of the vessel as Reeve had indicated, and he walked off first, pressing through the single-direction railing. It snapped into place as Reeve stepped behind him. The lift lowered, leaving them on the top floor without an exit.

They were no longer in a corridor. This was a huge room with seating along the walls, clunky computer screens lining the circumference. Brax was startled when he saw a solo Statu watching one of the screens. He wasn't wearing a helmet, revealing a hard head and clicking mandibles Brax could spot from his angle behind the soldier.

Brax lifted a finger to the front of his mask and slowly moved toward the sitting enemy. Reeve stayed put, raising her weapon. The guard stared at the screen, and Brax stopped in his tracks when he saw what was playing on the monitor. It showed a room in grayscale, likely on board the warship. There were hundreds of Bacal people lined up, and they were being ushered into a separate room one at a time. Brax watched with horror as a young woman was forced away from the crowd, a gun pressed into her back.

She walked into the compact room, no larger than his private shower on board *Constantine*, and stood shaking. Her posture was poor, her head tilting toward the ground, her shoulders slumped. She was alone in the room, and the lights began to increase in intensity until Brax had to avert his gaze from the screen.

When it lowered again, the woman was no longer slouching. She was standing firm as a plank. The camera caught her eyes, and Brax finally understood what he was seeing. Her eyes were white, the irises wiped away, and she stepped away unaided.

This was where the Statu brainwashed their army. This was why they were meeting such little resistance out in the field. The next computer screen showed the woman robotically moving into another room, where she began putting on armor. Soon she was fully suited, the helmet the last piece to finish the outfit off.

The Statu was slowly nodding his head as he oversaw the process from his position on the bridge. The next camera angle showed a fourth room, another huge pen where at least a hundred armored slaves stood waiting for instruction.

Brax hardly thought about his actions as the horror of what he'd witnessed hit him. The gun aimed at the Statu's head, and the guard turned just as Brax pulled the trigger. The effect was instantaneous. He slumped to the ground with a thump, and Brax fought the urge to look away as pieces of his enemy splattered onto the computer screens.

Reeve was there, staring at the processing of the Bacal slaves. "We have to stop this," she said.

Brax nodded. "Is this the bridge?" He looked around, trying to understand where the pilot would sit.

"I don't think so. This appears to be where they watch over the slaves. Maybe a surveillance room. If you were in one of those pens, there would have been a solider spying on you the entire time," she said.

"Then we keep moving. Is there anything that tells us what level this is happening on?" He pointed at the screen as another slave went from a scarred husk of a Bacal to a mind-numbed Statu slave.

Reeve went to work, using the console beside them. "This seems to indicate the deck." She tapped the screen with her hard glove, and he saw the unfamiliar icon.

"I wish I understood their language," she said. "It looks like there are roughly a hundred icons, which indicates that many decks." Her hands flew quickly over the controls, and Brax watched as information shifted over the screens. He had a difficult time following.

"There!" Brax could hear the smile in his sister's voice. "This is it! Using this level's icon as a baseline…" Brax saw what she meant. The symbol was etched on the glass of the lift. "I can determine that the slaves are on Deck Ten."

"Can we find the bridge from here using the surveillance, then?" Brax asked.

"Brother, I don't say it often, but you're a genius." Reeve began flicking through the channels of each deck, most of them seeming empty. Every now and then, they'd spot a couple of armed soldiers wandering about, and it took another several minutes to find what they were seeking. "That's it."

There were three of the enemies on the bridge, two sitting at consoles and one pacing the perimeter. Brax gripped his gun tighter, confident he could kill them with ease. The only thing he'd have to be careful about was damaging something integral to flying the vessel.

"It's Deck Fifty-five. Twelve under the bay we docked in," Reeve said. "Remember these symbols."

"I think that's your area of expertise," Brax told her. "You're the one who can remember everything she ever sees."

"Not quite, but I get what you're saying. Just do it, Brax. You never know when something could happen to me," Reeve said, moving toward the lift.

Brax stepped in after her and watched as she found the proper floor to bring them to. It appeared they were heading to the bridge first. They started lowering, and Brax thought about the Bacal people being brainwashed at that moment. They needed to lock this down as soon as possible.

———————

"That's it. We have them all!" Penter shouted over the noise of the clanging thrusters. Their hover platform had seen better days, and Treena wasn't positive it would last another adventure to the next camp.

Once they'd freed the first few, they'd sent the most capable Bacal to rescue the next camp, and so on. There were a lot of casualties along the way, but it was either that they tried and sacrificed or ran and left so many of the Greblok people to their doom. No one seemed to second-guess their decision to attempt a full rescue.

"It's time to..." The blast sent Treena reeling, and she hit the surface of the platform hard. Her artificial body had pain sensors built in, and she left them activated on a scale. The more pain, the more muted it became, mainly so she could feel things like a stubbed toe and feel human. She was glad for this as her face slammed into the floor of their transportation vessel.

Penter didn't fare as well, and she heard his cries of pain as the ship rocked jaggedly, heading straight for the planet's surface. She held firmly on to the railing and used her arms to pull herself up. Grabbing the controls, she attempted to level out the descending platform. A few seconds later, she managed to do so, and she saw the Tuber streaking toward her.

Penter remained on the ground, hands pressed to his face. His gun had flown from his hand, and over the edge of the vessel.

They were at least two minutes from being able to land, and the Tuber was going to be on them before that. This was it for her. They'd done everything they could for the Bacal, and that was going to have to be enough.

Treena tapped for her wrist communicator, only to find it had fallen away in the impact. "We did our best," she whispered as the Tuber raced up behind them. Penter sat up, staring toward the incoming doomsday ship. His gaze met hers for an instant, and Treena felt the resignation in his eyes.

The Tuber whined, the tips of its weapons glowing hotly. Treena was about to jerk the controls to attempt to evade the blast, even though she doubted it would accomplish much, when the Tuber exploded with a resounding bang.

One of the Concord fighters flew through the wreckage with reckless abandon. It turned hard, thrusters loudly screeching as it escorted their damaged platform to the ground a mile away.

By the time Treena clumsily landed the blocky vessel, the fighter was there, hovering as the cockpit sprang open. A woman emerged, jumping to the ground and rushing to Treena's side.

"Commander Starling," the woman said, taking her helmet off.

Treena recognized her as the sole female human pilot on board *Constantine*, but forgot her name. "Lieutenant, what's happening out there?"

The woman smiled. "We're winning the day. We've taken down three of the Tubers so far, and I was told to find you and bring you to safety." She glanced at Penter, who was leaning on Treena, his forehead bleeding from a bad cut.

"Good work. Can you fit us both?" Treena asked, and the pilot shook her head.

"I'm afraid we have a two-person capacity."

"Then take him," Treena said.

"Commander, I'm under direct orders from Captain…"

"I'm your commander, and I'm giving you different orders. He's injured," Treena said.

Penter began to object before he bent over and nearly passed out.

"See. Take him, Lieutenant. Continue the fight. The Bacal are underground near the warship. Both Daak siblings should have boarded. Pass the word to the captain on *Constantine*," Treena said.

"The captain is here," the pilot said.

Treena wasn't grasping. "Here?"

A Tuber screamed overhead, followed by a faster and sleeker fighter. The pilot pointed up. "As I said… here."

Treena managed to grin at that, imagining her stoic and handsome captain racing around this planet's atmosphere, firing at real live Statu enemies.

They helped Penter to the fighter, which was rumbling as it hovered slightly above the ground. Another Tuber echoed over the region, and Treena watched as it sent energy blasts through the sky toward Baldwin's vessel. "Go. Watch his back."

The pilot nodded and closed the cockpit. Treena stood away as the fighter rose, then tore ahead, thrusters hot and angry.

She scanned the area for an entrance into the underground city and recalled seeing one about a kilometer away. She was only ten kilometers from the warship and the location to which Tarlen would have led the survivors. With no humans or Concord team members around, Treena could lose the pretense that she was human.

As she began running, her legs started off at normal speed. It was something she hadn't practiced much during her first two years with the body, but now, she found easing into it was working well. Every ten or so seconds, she'd run harder. Arriving at the empty encampment took no time at all, and she spotted the dead Statu here, along with at least five Bacal. She pressed away her disgust and entered the barracks, moving into the underground corridors.

It seemed like everything was coming together. But with the incoming fleet of Statu warships, it might all be for nothing. She hoped Baldwin had a plan beyond just escaping, because the wormhole remained open, and there was nothing to stop the enemy from following them through. From there, it was only a matter of days before they'd be in Concord space, well past the Border.

Treena thought about all this as she traveled through the corridors at something near her top speed. If anyone had been watching, they'd only see a blur as she raced from section to section, traversing the distance quickly.

It was a matter of minutes before she heard the voices, and she slowed, not feeling any type of exhaustion. For the first time since she'd been aware of her survival after the rest of her crew were killed, she felt alive. She was grateful for her new form, for the life she'd been spared. Maybe being like this wasn't torture; maybe it was a blessing that she could use to help others. To be the best person possible, beyond her own selfish life.

She pictured Felix: his sideways grin, the way his hands were always so warm, the smell of his neck. She missed him so much, but her survival wouldn't be squandered. She smiled as she saw the huge group of Bacal gathered in the space, waiting for further instructions. It was dark, but a few strategically-placed puck lights guided her path.

Treena moved through the masses, people separating for the human Concord commander to pass uninhibited. Many asked her questions she couldn't yet answer as she made it to the far end of the room, where she found Tarlen discussing something with the female that had assisted Brax at the first rescue.

"Commander, you made it!" The boy wrapped his arms around her, hugging her tightly.

She patted his shoulder once and laughed. "Tarlen, are we set?"

Treena scanned the crowd, where at least a tenth of the gathered were armed. Some wore pieces of Statu armor and were huddled at something at the edge of the room.

"We're ready. We found a way to remove the Scramblers, so that's what they're doing." He pointed toward the group. "What's new?"

"Constantine is here with backup. Captain Baldwin's old ship is here," she advised him.

Tarlen's face lit up. "Do we have time?"

It was going to be tight, but if the Daaks were able to secure the warship, Treena thought they might just pull it off. "We'll do it. What about you? Did you find your family?"

The instant it left her mouth, she saw it was a mistake. His eyes glazed over, and his rigid posture went slack. It was like someone had cut the strings from a marionette. "No. I don't think they made it."

"Maybe you'll find them alive when you return home," she said, aware the chances weren't good.

"Honestly, I can't imagine going home. I hope we can escape here, but it seems impossible now," Tarlen said quietly.

The woman beside him was already gone, talking to someone else, and Treena nodded toward her. "Is she good?"

"Abbil? She's great. I can see why Brax and Penter were close with her," Tarlen told her.

The ground rumbled. Dust fell from the ceiling of the expansive open underground room. There were only a few lights on around them, making it hard to see too far, and the noises from above were frightening enough to startle the gathered Bacal. They'd been through so much, Treena could hardly blame their panicked reactions.

"We have to see what that was. You tell them to stay here, and we'll go scope it out." Treena started toward the exit, and she noticed she was alone. "Tarlen, are you coming?" she shouted.

The Bacal boy was quickly at her side, wearing a shy smile. "Sorry, I didn't think you wanted me to join you."

"From the look of things down here, you're doing one hell of a job leading your people. Are there truly so few among the Bacal that would take charge?" she asked him, assuming there were at least a few capable among the gathered. Then she remembered they'd given weapons to most of the adult Bacal, and all that was left underground were the elderly and youth.

"A few of the older ones have been helping guide me," Tarlen said. "But mostly everyone is too tired and afraid."

"Then you're all doing amazingly for what you've endured." Treena pressed the exit open and walked past two Bacal guards. They nodded to her, weapons held close to their sides.

"What do you think that…" Tarlen stopped his question as another concussion ran through the underground rooms. The stairs shook, and Treena waited until the shaking had ceased to start upward.

Treena decided to not mince words with the boy. "I think they know where we are and are trying to destroy us before we can fight them."

He wiped his brow with a forearm and started to climb the steps before her. Tarlen was growing on her. He was exactly the kind of recruit the Concord looked for, and he was adaptable, far more so than she'd been at his age.

The exit hatch lay horizontally over their heads, and Treena stood beside Tarlen, grazing it with a palm. It was cool to the touch. Good: no fire or worse raged above. She opened the door, shoving it hard. It slammed to the ground loudly, and she waited, listening before passing through it to the surface.

Tarlen started to climb out, but Treena held him back. "Let me." She lifted herself out, checking to make sure there was no army of enemies waiting for them. It was quiet. She reached down, hefting the boy out.

He stared at the horizon with her. The sky was darkening, the weather turning from bright and hot to cloudy and humid. A storm was coming.

It went from eerily silent to thunderously loud as a Tuber roared overhead. "Duck!" Treena yelled, diving over Tarlen. The blasts were close, and the ground shook violently as the bombs struck the nearby grassy field.

Heat poured over them, and Treena draped herself over the boy as fire covered the entire region for a moment before dissipating. She rolled over, checking on the Bacal youth. "Tarlen, are you okay?"

His eyes were wide with fear, and he patted his chest, moving his boot out of the way as a ragged bush was burning beside his leg. "Commander, your uniform…"

She hadn't even noticed. Her clothing was burning up, and she rolled on the grass, snuffing out the flames. She wished the pain sensors were set lower as the burns registered.

"Wait… what… what are you?" Tarlen asked her.

She expected the reaction, but after her recent acceptance of her situation, the fear in his eyes really struck a chord. "I'm…I'm human," she lied. "It's complicated."

"I can see… a panel."

One of the Concord fighters soared by, firing blue pulses toward the departing Tuber. Then another.

"I'll explain later." Treena couldn't see how bad the damage was, but there wasn't time to worry about it. The clouds blew in with a heavy gust of wind, and she followed their path, where the immense warship loomed close by. It was so ugly and huge, just the sight of it made her want to head underground.

She was about to start for the warship, when she saw the incoming force. They were lowering one hovering platform at a time from the enemy vessel. She pulled a Zoomer from her pack and pressed it to her left eye. It found her target and slowly focused. She almost dropped it when she sighted them. There was an entire regiment of armored Statu, but that wasn't what fried her nerves.

It was the group of blank-eyed Bacal marching behind them, holding Statu weapons.

"Let me see!" Tarlen urged, taking the Zoomer from her grip. She let him grab the tool and heard the intake of his breath as he saw his transformed people coming toward them.

"Tarlen, they're no longer your friends. They're turned. This is what the Statu do; they use your own race against you. We have to fight them," she said, but he hadn't spoken a word.

When he finally did, Treena wished she'd left Tarlen underground. He lowered the Zoomer, and his eyes were filled with tears. "It's her. It's Belna. They turned my sister." He started to run toward the incoming enemy, and Treena sighed, following.

TWENTY-FOUR

Tom was loving every minute of it. It had been far too long since he'd been strapped in the cockpit of his baby, and everything about the mission felt right. The way the seat rumbled and vibrated under him, the slight digging of the belt as he raced after the Tubers, firing pulses toward evading targets.

The trigger button was right where he'd left it, and each time his finger pressed it to life, a rush of energy coursed through him. So far, they'd managed to destroy five of the Tubers, leaving another five to wreak havoc.

"Captain, we have three bogeys near the warship. They're firing on the ground, which tells me that's where our friends are hiding out." The voice was that of his lead pilot, Lieutenant Basker.

"Very well, I'm coming in," Tom advised, and he looped his ship around, feeling the Gs press him in his seat. By the great Vastness, he'd missed this.

It was foolish for the captain of *Constantine* to be piloting a fighter, but here he was, fending off the enemy. The backup from *Cecilia* had arrived a few minutes ago, and they were roaring toward the Tubers from the stratosphere. It was going to be over sooner rather than later.

Tom considered his rash action in hopping inside the fighter, but their odds were improved with him in the seat, rather than having his vessel sitting idly on board the cruise ship in orbit. It wasn't as if he'd begun his first mission as captain by following rules.

There would be consequences for everyone's actions when they returned, but Tom only had to ensure the Statu weren't able to follow them from here. A demotion, a crumbling hierarchy in the Concord alliances, or even his life wasn't as imperative as his mission's success. If the Statu sent a dozen warships through this system's wormhole, there would be a terrible price to pay on the other side.

Tom was nearing his destination, and he reached out to anyone on the ground on the Concord's channels. "This is Captain Thomas Baldwin of the Concord cruise ship *Constantine*. Advise current situation."

For a moment, no one replied, and he wondered what had happened to Starling. Had she been killed in combat? "Bridge, come in."

Ven's calm voice carried through his headset. "Bridge here."

"Relay a message to Doctor Nee's nurse Kelli for me," Tom said, seeing a Tuber appear on his radar. It was behind him, and he increased speed.

"What's the message, Captain?" Ven asked.

"Ask how the patient is doing."

There was silence on the communication for a moment, and his executive lieutenant returned. "She says there are no changes, sir."

Relief eased Tom's shoulders. That meant Treena Starling was active on the ground, giving them a better chance at success.

Tom was arriving over a giant canopy of tree cover, and he spotted a break in the foliage. Beyond it were hundreds of people, heading away from the warship. He really wished Brax had a way to talk with him. It was painful waiting to see if he and his sister had actually infiltrated the enemy vessel, or if Tom and the others were going to be sorely disappointed.

He zoomed on the growing army on the ground and shuddered as he saw that many of them were in Statu armor. The more worrisome part was the group behind them, walking like the undead. They were the Bacal people.

Tom slammed a hand against the dash in anger. It appeared as though the Statu were up to their old tricks. He flew overtop them, wanting to unleash fury on the advancing army, but he couldn't bring himself to just yet. Maybe there was a way to return the Bacal to their former selves. A way to reverse the damage.

His sensors beeped a warning, and seconds later, his ship jostled as the Tuber behind him landed an errant shot.

"Damn it!" Tom pulled the controls up, ramming the stick to the side. He broke away, but the Tuber managed to hit him again. "Not on my watch."

Tom swung around, his ship moving slower now. The Tuber had somehow sneaked past his shield with two lucky shots, and a third would destroy him. With movements drilled into him years ago, he cut the thrusters enough for the Tuber's less maneuverable vessel to race underneath. He set the target and dropped a Heater. It blinked on his radar, and the Tuber exploded in a flurry of fire. The detonation sent Tom's fighter reeling, and he struggled to regain control.

His ship beeped incessantly as he finally leveled out, but the ground was coming up quickly. The impact was impending, his body pressed hard against his chair. Tom was able to reach underneath his seat and tap the ejection right in time. He flew from the cockpit, his fighter crashing into the ground, sending dirt and grass in all directions. All those fights, all the battles he'd flown in, and he'd ended up crash-landing on this desolate world in enemy territory.

He'd mourn the loss of his baby later. There were more pressing matters at hand.

"At least you took one with you," he mumbled as he lowered with the energy net drifting in the wind. His feet touched down on the ground, the same spot where his ship had cut a ravine into the soft earth.

Rain splatted on his helmet from overhead, and Tom wiped the water off with a glove. His XRC-14 was in his cockpit and now burning up alongside his ship, but he pulled the PL-30 from his hip as he realized where he was. He'd landed directly in the path of the incoming horde of Bacal turned Statu.

Another Tuber was firing toward the ground behind him, aiming for a location half a kilometer away. That was where the Bacal were hiding, waiting for the warship to be cleared. Tom tried to gain a sense of what was occurring when he spotted two figures. They were running toward him, but were still too far away to determine who they were.

"Captain Baldwin, come in." It was Lieutenant Basker.

"Go ahead, Basker. I'm grounded but alive."

The Tuber exploded into a million pieces, and Tom noticed two of *Cecilia*'s fighters in the sky. The Tubers were being destroyed, and soon there would be none left on the planet. Another loud eruption, and he guessed that was almost it for the resistance.

"Good to hear. Captain, that was the last of the Tubers. Permission to exterminate the Statu army," Lieutenant Basker said.

Tom guessed they'd arrive at his position within three minutes. He didn't want to be there to fend off the mindless army. He'd seen the videos of their destructive powers. Once the Statu brainwashed their slaves, they were singly focused on killing anyone in their path. This was going to be no different.

"Give me a moment to…"

A ship lowered from the darkening sky as water poured in droves. Tom used a gloved hand like a visor and recognized the expedition ship *Cleo* as it slowed and dropped toward the ground with efficiency.

The two arriving people were shouting, and Tom watched as Treena Starling tackled a skinny boy. Judging by the dark mop of hair, it was Tarlen, the Bacal boy they'd rescued from Greblok.

Cleo's door opened at the same time, revealing Constantine's AI. He didn't know which way to look.

"Tarlen, stop. You can't do this. They'll kill you!" Treena shouted. Tom raced to her side, helping the boy up but keeping a firm grip on his arm.

"What the hell is going on here? Are the people safe?" Tom asked.

Treena stared at the incoming army and nodded. "They're underground waiting for our word. We have to help the Daaks gain control, but we have no way of communicating with them."

Tarlen struggled against Tom's hold. "She's with them. My sister is there." He pointed beyond Tom's shoulder to the Bacal at the rear of the marching Statu. "I saw her… she's… it's her." Water ran over the boy's face, and Tom pulled him along toward the ship.

"Get on. I'm sorry, son. The fighters are about to rain fire down on them. We have no choice," Tom said over the now-raging sounds of the storm.

Constantine's AI stood in the entrance and smiled at Tom as they approached. "Good to see you, sir."

"Same here." Tom let go of Tarlen. "Basker, we're evacuating and heading for the warship. Prepare assault of the ground troops."

The response was quick. "Yes, Captain."

"Let's move out," Tom said, moving to close *Cleo*'s door, and he shook his head as he noticed Tarlen wasn't behind him. Treena had moved into the ship already, her uniform torn and singed, exposing circuit panels. "Tarlen left," he told her.

"Let him go. We can't make his decisions," Treena said softly, and Tom watched through the window as Tarlen began running around the army, a weapon held in his grip. He wasn't going to make it more than a few minutes.

Constantine's AI controlled their ship and lifted it from the surface, moving toward the gargantuan warship. Tom couldn't help but feel like he was heading into the mouth of danger. *To see death is to see life for the first time.* The old saying from the Code rang through his mind as they neared the hangar, and Tom heard the concussions of the fighters destroying the field of Bacal-turned-Statu soldiers behind them.

———

*T*hey'd met minimal opposition on the bridge, and Brax was glad. The three Statu bodies lay sprawled out and un-moving around the bridge, and he glanced at the lifeless forms, wishing they weren't visible. His armor had taken a blast, and the metal pressed into his shoulder, but other-wise, he was fine.

"I have it!" Reeve had been working on the controls for the last ten minutes, and Brax could only pace near the bridge entrance, guarding his sister as she attempted to learn the Statu warship controls. They were nothing like the simple Tuber systems, making Brax basically useless in the exercise. But he could keep guard and shoot anything that came close; that he was good at.

"What's the plan?" Reeve asked him.

He spun to look at his sister, almost shocked to see her in full enemy gear. His gut told him to fire, and he had to block the reaction. "The plan? We move to the location where the Bacal were supposed to gather."

"Do you truly think they managed to escape?" Reeve asked.

"How should I know? That was a difficult task, but it's been hours. I think with Penter and Starling's help, there will be a few hundred there at least," Brax said.

"Then what's the plan?"

"We head there, pick them up, and sweep the ship," Brax said, holding his bulky weapon to his chest.

She nodded, one quick tuck of her chin. "Okay. How are we picking them up?"

Brax cringed. He hadn't thought that far ahead. They'd used the hover platforms to remove the slaves from the ship, but those weren't on board any longer. "What about the Mover?"

"The Mover?"

"Yeah, we know the Tubers have them, so that must mean the warship does too. How else did they manage to mine underwater without any tools?" Brax asked.

"Okay, give me a few minutes. I need to find out…" Reeve didn't finish her sentence as her fingers soared across the crude console.

He left her to it and moved to the wall of screens opposite her. He'd managed to learn how to switch between the deck cameras, and he watched as more of the Bacal were being altered through the Statu system. At least half of them had been turned, and Brax couldn't take it any longer.

"Reeve, I have to stop this," he said.

"Wait. I see another ship coming toward us," Reeve said, pointing to the central viewscreen. There were ten of the screens placed evenly around the round bridge, and he watched as *Cleo* moved toward the hangar where he'd parked a Tuber.

"Friends?" Brax asked.

"We have to assume. Go to them. See if Constantine can help me on the bridge. They may have to carry his Link with them," Reeve said.

"Done. Good luck."

"You too." Reeve turned away, continuing to scroll through the alien information.

Brax went quickly, moving to the lift, where he made it head toward the hangar deck. He kept his gun at ready, in case it was really Statu inside their expedition vessel. He ran through the familiar corridors, and arrived at the hangar bay, a smile on his face as he saw his commander and captain emerge from the ship.

The grin was wiped away quickly as both of his superiors began firing at him. He'd forgotten he was in full Statu armor.

———

*T*he first blast sent Tarlen to his knees, the ground buckling hard around him. "Belna!" he shouted, but no one responded. The assault by the lowest of the fighters tore the earth open, the first row of Statu-turned Bacal falling into the rift.

Tarlen rose, moving for the edge of the few-hundred-person group. So far, none of the armored people had attacked him, and he guessed they didn't see a single Bacal boy as a threat. He used this to his advantage, opting for a risky play. He cut into the group, pressing past the roughly-armored people. His people.

By the time he reached the end of the Statu suit-wearing rows, another blast shook everything. "Stop!" he shouted at the fighters, realizing no one would hear him. Why were they attacking his people? Deep down, he understood their reasoning, but seeing faces of his kind from Greblock, he didn't think he could fire on them, even if they were no longer his allies.

"Belna!" he shouted again, moving through the ranks of Bacal. They were smelly, their stench overwhelming as he touched them, grabbed shoulders, searching every girl with long black hair.

"Belna?" He was trying to remember what side he'd seen her on through the Zoomer, but couldn't in the heat of the moment. Another concussion erupted, sending people to the ground around him. Fire burned now, clothing and skin beginning to melt together in his nostrils.

He was about to run away, to save himself, when he located her. Everything seemed to slow. Another blast, this time from an even lower fighter, hit the ranks, but Tarlen hardly noticed. He only had one job, and that was to rescue his sister.

Someone pressed into him, then another, and another mindless slave as they ran in tightly-formed lines. They were pushing him away from Belna. "Belna!" he yelled again, but there was nothing even remotely like recognition in her eyes. She was as brainwashed as the rest of them.

Tarlen dropped to the ground, scrambling through a pair of open legs. He crawled to his feet, and finally made it to Belna's side. He pulled on her arm, and she turned, walking where he directed her.

He placed his hands on her cheeks, tears streaming

from his eyes. "It's me, Tarlen. Belna, I know you're in there." But her eyes told him otherwise.

Tarlen heard the screech of the fighters' thrusters coursing above, and he glanced up to see four of them in formation. This was it. There was no escaping this unless he was quick.

The rest of the slaves were marching toward the people hiding underground, and Tarlen was running out of time. He tugged Belna hard, turning her around, and with her limp hand in his, he ran.

Somehow her legs kept up with him, and he panted as they moved, the rain pouring so hard, he could hardly see ahead of him. They were moving away from the group being attacked, and far from the oncoming assault as the fighters did a fly-by, lowering toward the horde.

The resulting noise was excruciating, and he shoved Belna hard, jumping on top of her as the impact of the attacks took hold. Clumps of dirt and grass rained overhead, as well as pieces of their people. A Statu helmet hit the ground directly beside them, and Tarlen hoped there wasn't a head still inside.

He rolled away from his sister, and she stared upwards into the rain, her eyes unblinking. "Belna, we have to move. We have to get to the warship."

She grunted as he assisted her to her feet, and they moved together, stumbling toward the looming vessel. The entire region was devastated, and there weren't going to be any survivors above ground, except for him... and his sister.

They finally reached the warship, his legs covered in mud up to his mid-thighs, and Tarlen slipped as he stopped beneath it. He glanced up, the vessel hovering right above the surface. Now he needed to find a way on board. From this vantage point, the warship was terrifying: narrow and pointy at the bottom, a dozen or so uneven arms jutting from the central ship as he peered up to the top.

Tarlen jumped but couldn't even grab the lowest rung on the bottom of the ship. There had to be another way.

As he stood there contemplating it, the warship began to rise upwards, and his hopes of survival sank.

TWENTY-FIVE

Their target moved quickly, and Treena missed with her first blast.

"Stop! It's me! Brax!" The voice made her smile, but Captain Baldwin must not have heard it, because he fired again, hitting the wall slightly above their chief of security.

"Sorry! Old habits!" Thomas shouted, and crossed the room as Brax pulled his Statu helmet off. He was sweating underneath, and he licked his lips.

Treena joined him. "What's going on? Did you secure the ship?" she asked Brax.

The big Tekol shook his head. "Not quite. Reeve is on the bridge, but they're making slaves for their army with the Bacal on Deck Ten."

"We've seen the first regiment. They're likely dead by now," Captain Baldwin told Brax, and Treena saw the pain in the man's eyes as he heard the news.

"Then let's stop them from producing more. I've only seen about five or six enemy on Deck Ten, so we can make quick work of them," Brax said.

"What about Reeve?" the captain asked.

"She needs help. Can you bring Constantine's Link with you, sir?" Brax asked.

Thomas Baldwin nodded and raced onto the ship, returning in a minute with the Link in his hand. It was snapped under the dash console, meant to remove to bring the AI with you when necessary. This was one of those times.

The AI flickered on in the hangar. "How can I be of service?"

"Come with me. I'll show you how to operate the lift." Brax turned, jogging deeper into the enemy ship. Treena glanced around it, feeling uneasy about their adventure. They were on board a Statu warship. These were things that fueled nightmares, and she tried not to look at the uneven walls, the crude welding jobs, or the loose wires. Judging by the condition of the ship, she doubted the Statu were very organized this time, but there was an enemy fleet about to enter communication territory with the planet. Even if they had ugly ships and outdated weapons, they were still dangerous.

Brax motioned Thomas and the AI onto the elevator system and sent them on their way to the bridge. Thomas handed Treena a tiny earpiece before rising away. "Put this on. We can talk."

"Finally," she said, pressing the small device into her ear. "Captain?" she asked when he was out of sight.

"Yes, Commander?" he replied.

"Good luck," she said, stepping onto another lift platform with Brax. They lowered in the opposite direction, and she saw Brax staring at her.

"Is something different about you?" he asked.

"I don't think so," she said. "I'm a little dirty."

"Okay. You also have a hole in your back," he said, his face impassive.

"That... that's nothing. You should see the other guy," she told him.

"I knew there was something off about you, Starling," Brax said.

"No one's perfect." Treena shrugged and the lift

stopped. Brax didn't press her for details, but she expected to have to explain soon. He'd never been told about her controlling an artificial body, but he probably guessed as much now.

Brax had taken charge, and she let him. He lifted a finger before sprinting to the outer edge of the doorway. He mouthed a countdown from three, and when he said one, he slammed a hand on the red door-release button. It hissed upwards, opening into a room of over two hundred miserable Bacal.

A few of them pushed past Treena, their questions coming in a flurry.

"Hide in the hallways. Stay as a group. We'll be right back. Can anyone tell me where the Statu are?" Treena asked, and a thin white-haired woman pointed at a doorway across the room.

Brax was already moving for the door, gun in the air. She joined him as more and more Bacal rushed past her. He didn't wait for her as he opened the next door. He was already firing by the time she arrived, witnessing one of the Statu crash to the floor. She found one of them helmetless, and aimed for its face. Her first blast missed, but the second hit it directly in the throat. Treena fired again and again, until its left leg stopped twitching.

"Two more," Brax whispered, walking through the space. There were intricate booths here, each with lights and metal bars around them. This was where they programmed their slaves, and Treena wanted nothing more that to destroy the terrible machines. She wondered how many humans, Tekol, Callalay, and others were put through devices like this during the War, only to result in them fighting their own people. Likely millions.

Brax met her gaze and must have sensed her revulsion. "We can worry about this when we have the ship secured.

Got it, Commander?"

"Understood." She pushed the dread away, and they stood on either side of the last door.

He tapped the release button, and she spun, firing the gun at the Statu. Instead of two, there were ten of the Statu in armor, and she was unable to determine which were real enemies and which were recently turned Bacal. As all ten returned fire, it didn't matter. They were all her targets.

"*T*hat's right. Ease the ship up, like that," Constantine said, directing Reeve.

Thomas Baldwin stood in the center of the enemy warship, arms crossed over his chest as he watched his chief engineer pilot the ship. So far, all she'd done was raise and lower it, but she was getting the hang of it. He expected they'd be set to rescue the others in short order.

"And the Mover. You really think it'll work?" Tom asked Constantine.

"By all accounts, it should. It appears the lower half of the holding decks is filled with the ore from Greblok, and we can program it to drop the people into these decks," Constantine said, running a projected finger in front of the screen, showing Decks Sixty to Seventy. "There is enough capacity to hold them."

"Then it's time." Tom pressed his communicator. "Starling, are we cleared?" He didn't want any surprises after they'd taken off.

"Working on it, sir." He heard blasts from weapons as she spoke, and soon she spoke again. "Cleared, sir. We're checking the cameras now, but unless there are Statu hiding out, which I expect there will be, we think the ship is devoid of enemies."

Tom smiled widely. "It's done. Under the directive of the Concord's Code of War, I claim this vessel for the Concord."

"Captain, this is the bridge." Ven's voice entered his earpiece.

"Go ahead," Tom said.

His elation was short-lived. "Tubers on the way. Twenty of them."

"From the warships?" Tom asked.

"Yes, sir. Estimated time of arrival is thirty-seven minutes," Ven said.

Tom clenched his jaw. "If they arrive, you blast them into the Vastness, do you hear me?"

"Yes, sir."

Constantine was looking through video feeds from around the ship, and Tom saw something in the corner of his eye. "Con, what was that?"

The AI scrolled back, and there it was again. "I think that's the Bacal boy Tarlen, sir."

Tarlen was underneath the warship. "Here's as good a time as ever to test that Mover, Reeve."

She smiled at him and fired it up. He watched as the lines on the screen before her glowed green, the device powering up.

Constantine loomed over her shoulder, giving her suggestions. "Make sure you have the destination set, and activate."

When the lights flashed, Reeve tapped the screen, and Constantine switched the feed to Deck Sixty. Tarlen and a girl appeared, and from the looks of things, they were whole. It was a good start.

"Reeve, we're good to go. All that's left for us is gathering the hiding Bacal and flying away from this planet,"

Tom said.

The entire warship vibrated slightly as his chief engineer controlled the vessel, lifting it away from its docking position.

Tom grinned. They were really going to pull this off, and with all the ore the Statu had been so desperate to gather. Without it, their enemy wouldn't be able to create huge and powerful wormholes. The battle would be over before it began, and the rest of the Concord would remain clueless to the entire series of events that had almost led to an all-out second Concord War with the Statu.

He left the AI and Reeve on the bridge, and hurried up to Deck Sixty, where he found a bewildered Tarlen.

"Captain Baldwin, I'm sorry for running off like that…"

"I can see the resemblance," Tom told the boy. The girl beside him was pretty, with bushy dark eyebrows like Tarlen's; long hair like his was clumped in greasy strands, and her posture was straight, her eyes pale, the iris color wiped from them. There was a line of drool dripping from the left corner of her lips, and Tarlen leaned over, wiping it with his sleeve.

"We'll be able to help her. I know Doctor Nee can," Tarlen said, but even his words were without conviction.

"Be cautious around her, son. She's not the same girl you knew. Not any longer," Tom told him, and led them from the open room toward the lift. It smelled like penned animals inside the space, and Tom guessed this was one of the areas the Bacal were transported to this planet in. The walls were grimy; moisture dripped from the rusty ceiling.

"Let's head to the hangar. We have some work to do," Tom said, putting his arm over Tarlen's shoulders. The sister walked behind them, each step slow and methodical. He kept his eye on her as they emerged from the room and onto the lift taking them to the hangar bay.

Tom peered at the Tuber sitting quietly across the floor and saw how much bigger the enemy ship was than their expedition vessel. It was twice as high and longer by half. *Cleo* sat waiting, the door still open, and Tom rushed on board, hopping into the pilot's seat.

He activated the ship with the press of a few keys, and eased it from the hangar, seeing the warship was nearly in position over the hiding spot in the underground city. The entire region was torn up; bodies and pieces of Statu armor were burning in the aftermath of the fighter attack.

"What a waste," Tom whispered to himself.

Tarlen stared out the viewscreen with a blank look on his face. He'd been down there. Those were his people, and Tom was positive the boy would never be the same after this experience. None of the survivors would.

Tom had a few moving pieces to attend, and he glanced to the dark skies directly above him. The Tubers were still a distance away, and he was confident that *Constantine* and *Cecilia* would take care of those enemy vessels before they broke atmosphere.

It was quiet. A few fighters made their rounds, ensuring any trace of enemy was extinguished, and six were parked on the ground near the city entrance. That was where Tom led *Cleo*.

"There weren't many Statu here. Why?" Tarlen asked, and Tom glanced over to see his sister standing as she faced the wall near the ship's exit hatch.

"In my opinion, they were too arrogant. They spent the last five decades gathering enough material to stabilize a wormhole to accommodate their fleet to travel through it, but that wasn't all they wanted," Tom said.

"The ore from Greblok," Tarlen said.

"That's right."

"How did they know about it? We barely did," Tarlen said.

Tom maneuvered the expedition ship to settle near the city entrance, and already a rush of Bacal were emerging into the rain. "I imagine your Regent knew for some time, as did our Concord. I think there's been a leak in the Concord, one that's been there for decades."

"That means…"

"That's right. It's time for a regime change," Tom said, unsure why he was telling the Bacal boy so much information.

They exited the ship, and Tom barked orders. Tarlen led his white-eyed sister from the ship and shouted into the crowd, "Penter! You made it!"

The Bacal man that Tom had briefly seen when Brax had been taken was there, limping slightly, a bandage covering a head wound. "I'm fine, kid. Glad to see you did too." He looked at Belna with a frown. "Is this…?"

Tarlen nodded, and Tom left them to it, stepping aside. Lieutenant Basker was near one of the grounded fighters, and he waved Thomas Baldwin over. "Sir, we have half of them out, and as you can tell, the warship is nearly in position."

Tom's gaze fell on the monstrosity, and he prayed to the Vastness that this worked. "Keep it up. We'll have company very soon."

"Understood. Once the Mover picks the Bacal up, we'll escort the warship into space," Basker said. "Sir, I'm sorry about your ship."

Tom ran a hand through his wet hair, the rain falling incessantly. "At least I'm alive. I might have been a little rusty."

"Better planetside than in space, sir."

Tom grinned and clapped Basker on the shoulder.

"Touché."

They watched as the warship arrived, and the few Concord crew members struggled to keep the Bacal people together. It was clear they were frightened of the vessel and didn't want to be returned to it.

Tom spotted Tarlen walking through the crowds, his sister in tow, talking among his people, calming them as he went.

They were almost done. Then they could leave, pass through the wormhole, and never look back.

Tom's gaze settled on the enemy ship, and he shivered.

———————————

*B*rax moved through the decks, one by one, with Starling at his side. He still couldn't believe she wasn't human. He'd thought something was off about her, but this was next level. There were different versions of controlled android bodies out there, but the Concord was quite strict when it came to their uses. For them to have given one a commander role was shocking, but now wasn't the time to quiz Starling on it.

They'd moved through half the decks and had found a total of four Statu so far. They'd managed to kill each of them before being attacked. It seemed the Statu were aware they'd been taken over, but Brax wasn't going to give them enough time to gather a resistance.

"You okay, Starling?" he asked the woman. She hadn't said two words in the last ten minutes.

"I'm fine. It's… that room of Bacal… we killed them."

"We had no choice. They were brainwashed, wearing Statu armor. They fired on us," Brax told her, but it did little to ease his own guilt. An old Code saying entered his mind: *The universe isn't always black and white; sometimes it's red.*

"That doesn't make it right… let's get this over with." Treena moved ahead, clearing the room.

Brax led her into the next deck and recognized the room when they lowered into it. "This is where I was held." The notches in the walls, the mismatched ceiling panels he'd counted before falling asleep. He struggled to step inside, and Treena seemed to understand.

"I'll take this one," she said, walking into the open space. It stank of fear and death. The bodies they'd piled in the corner of the room were revolting, and Brax jammed his eyes closed at the sight.

The warship jarred, sending Brax stumbling forward. He saw the form along the wall before he could shout out, and it fired at Treena, striking her in the leg. She moved faster than humanly possible and returned fire, shooting the unarmored Statu five times. He smoked and sizzled as he slid down the wall, falling with a thud.

"You hurt?" Brax asked, rushing to her side.

Her leg was singed, but she was able to walk on it. She grinned at him and patted her wound. "One of the many advantages of being on board *Constantine* right now."

"Where… never mind. I think the ship rocking means Reeve is in position. Let's keep moving," Brax said, and they continued on their sweep of the ship.

----

*T*om watched as the giant Mover plucked people from their groups of one hundred. Each section took around a minute; Constantine and Reeve Daak were using that time to relocate the destination for each group they were beaming aboard the warship. This was amazing technology, and the Concord was going to be thrilled to obtain it.

The rain slowed, the clouds thinning slightly as it passed by the area. Tom walked around the gathered Bacal, many of them finally feeling like they might make it home. There were reunions, tears, and smiles among the hijacked race. Tom was confident now that they'd return to Greblok, but they'd have a hard life rebuilding. He'd try to ensure the Concord did everything possible to assist the rebuild, but as it stood, he'd wait to see what the Concord was going to look like when everything came to light.

Tom nearly tripped on uneven rubble from the fighter's destruction of the Bacal slaves, and he pushed aside his disgust at what they'd had to do. This was war, and war was never fair.

"Captain, we're moving the last five groups. Are you going to join the last one?" Basker asked him.

Tom shook his head. "I'll take *Cleo*."

"Captain Baldwin," a voice said into his earpiece.

"Go ahead, Starling."

"Wait for me. I'm coming with you," Starling said. "We've cleared each deck. Killed another twenty-three. That's it."

Tom was shocked at how few of the Statu were on the warship or planetside, but with the fleet arriving soon, there'd be plenty more if they didn't hurry. "Very well. Meet me at *Cleo*. Where's Brax?"

"He's with Reeve on the bridge. He's staying with her," Treena said through his communicator.

Tom smiled at Basker as the man began climbing into his fighter. The rest of the pilots were already in the air, circling the warship, and Tom entered his expedition ship. "Constantine," he said, forgetting that the Link needed to bring the AI on board was with Reeve on the bridge of the enemy vessel.

The last group of Bacal stood waiting on the ground when Tom heard a message from Ven come through. "Sir, we thought we had them all. It appears a single Tuber evaded us. It's heading for you now."

Basker was inside his ship, and Tom waved toward him, pointing at the speck in the sky moving with purpose. He tapped his earpiece. "Concord Fighters, this is Captain Baldwin. There's a rogue Tuber bearing down on us as we speak. Do not let it…"

The blasts shook the ground, and Tom watched as half of the Bacal group was incinerated just as the Mover beam spread over them. The deceased were taken onto the warship along with the living, and seconds later, two fighters approached the coming Tuber in a dogfight.

Even from the ground, Tom sensed the Tuber didn't want to engage. It did everything in its power to evade them. "It wants to hit the warship…" Realization struck Tom, and he reached out to Reeve as he connected with her. "Daak, time to scram. The Tuber's coming for you."

The warship responded instantly, the hot thrusters pushing out hard from below, pulverizing the ground. The field was bereft of life now, Tom the only one still grounded. Treena Starling ran toward *Cleo* from the warship, her uniform barely clinging to her android body. He could tell she'd been through a lot and had multiple scorch marks. As she approached, he saw her left eye was useless, half her hair peeled away from her head.

"Nothing a little make-up won't solve." Treena dusted herself off and grinned at him as she hopped into the ship. "I have a feeling you're going to need me, Captain."

Tom wasn't one to argue with his commander's gut and shut the door, climbing into the pilot's seat.

The Tuber continued avoiding hits from the entire regiment of pilots, and Tom lifted *Cleo*, seeing the Tuber flying closer and closer to the warship.

"This isn't good," Tom whispered.

———————

Brax's hands shook as he powered up the Tuber inside the hangar. "You can do this, you can do this." He muttered his new mantra to himself as he directed the cylindrical ship from the bay. Reeve and Constantine hadn't had time to learn the warship's weapon system, and that left one vessel that could help.

The Tuber exited the giant vessel the Bacal people occupied, and he spotted the enemy nearing them. Part of him hoped the Tuber would see one of its own vessels and it would startle the pilot, leaving room for error. Whoever was piloting the thing had already evaded two Concord cruise ships and some great fighter pilots.

Brax wasn't one of those, but he had something else working for him. Unpredictability.

He kicked the thrusters harder, moving directly for the Tuber. His alien consoles beeped and flashed, probably warning him of impact, but he stayed the course, tapping at buttons and flicking switches. One had to be a blaster of some kind.

Blue energy flicked around his viewscreen and shot out, striking the Tuber precisely before impact. The enemy ship died suddenly, the engines cutting off entirely. It continued to move toward him before gravity took over and the Tuber began its descent.

Brax let out a whoop and pumped his fist in the air, looping the cylinder around clumsily. The warship was already pushing out of the atmosphere, and Brax saw two fighters dropping artillery on the downed Tuber, causing it to explode.

Brax screamed happily, almost forgetting he needed to follow his people off-planet. Pulling the yoke, he pressed the thrusters, trailing after the warship. When ten fighters pulled up to surround him, he hoped someone had informed them *Constantine*'s chief of security was piloting it, not a rogue Statu.

TWENTY-SIX

*T*hey'd done it. The warship passed by *Cecilia*, and Tom beamed with pride at the efforts of his people, his crew. They'd been thrown together by a corrupt leadership, but Tom couldn't have selected a better bunch if it had been his call.

The last of the fighters were arriving behind the Statu vessel piloted by Reeve Daak, and Tom smiled as the Tuber joined the group. He hadn't had much time with Brax Daak so far, but anyone that could hop into a Tuber after clearing a warship of Statu was someone he wanted at his side.

Treena tapped away at the consoles and spoke animatedly. "Sir, the warships are close. We need to run, now."

"Bridge to *Cleo*," Ven's voice said. "Welcome home. The dock has been prepared."

"Thank you, Ven." Tom guided their expedition vessel toward *Constantine*. After staring at the warship for the better part of an hour, the sight of his sleek state-of-the-art vessel warmed his blood. It truly was like he was coming home.

"They should be within firing range in five minutes, sir," Treena told him.

Cleo settled on top of his ship, clicking into place easily. He let out a sigh of relief as they exited the smaller ship and raced down the steps to the bridge below. Zare let out a scream at the sight of Treena, and Tom cringed. It appeared they'd both forgotten what a terrible condition she was in.

"I guess the *Booli* is out of the sack," Treena said quietly, taking her position beside Tom's captain's chair.

"Bridge, thank you for your diligent work. We're up against something huge here and have to leave now," Tom ordered.

Ven turned in his seat. "Captain, we're advanced, and from all the reports, the Statu haven't added any high-tech weaponry in the last fifty years."

"Be that as it may, we're better off leaving them. They still have six warships about to intercept us," Tom said.

"What about the wormhole?" Treena asked. "Won't they just follow us?"

"I hope so… some of them, anyway," Tom mumbled.

"What? Why?" Treena gripped the arms of the chair, and Tom thought she might tear them off the frame.

He leaned closer to her, fighting the urge to break his stare at her disfigured robotic face. "Because we're going to destabilize it with them inside." The hair on the back of his hands stood on end as he said it out loud.

Treena smiled. The effect was alarming.

Ven guided the ship away from the planet, and Tom saw it shrinking from the rearview corner of the viewer.

"Ven, we'll be right back. Stay the course. Make it to the wormhole." Tom stood, motioning for Treena to join him.

———————

*T*reena accepted the stares as they walked from the bridge and onto the elevator, before entering the private room near the hangar where the Statu guests were waiting inside. She was aware of her appearance, and at this point, was over worrying about it.

Doctor Nee rose as they entered, and he smiled at them. "Captain, Commander, so good to see you both." His yellow eyes bored into her.

Treena felt his compassion for her situation instantly, and she found herself liking the Kwant doctor even more. He crossed the room and lifted a gloved hand to her face, pressing a loose flap of artificial skin across her eye.

"What happened to you?" he asked.

"The Statu happened," she whispered, and Yephion and the others at the table stopped chatting as she used their race's name.

"Where are we with the plan?" Tom asked, standing at the end of the table.

Constantine's AI translated, and Yephion replied, "We have created the theory, but the amount of molar mass of *Bentom* needed isn't available."

Treena watched Captain Baldwin's face twist in anger. "You said it could be done."

"That was before we understood the extent of the wormhole. I apologize," Yephion said through Constantine's translation.

Treena considered the problem. "But we do have enough *Bentom*, correct?"

"If we broke open our Star Drive and cut the ball of Bentom in half, then yes," Constantine said.

Treena considered the problem. They were trained to solve problems; that was what the executive crew was on board the cruise ships for. She tapped her finger on the tabletop, leaning over their screens full of hypothetical reactions.

"I have it!" she said. "*Cecilia*."

"What about her?" Doctor Nee asked.

Baldwin appeared to understand. "She does have a Star Drive powerful enough to help us out. It's smaller than ours, but also older. It runs on Bentom as well, though."

"We could evacuate them," Nee started, but Treena shook her head.

"Or we latch them to us, like we did with the Statu ship," the captain said before she had the chance to.

"With all due respect, sir, that worked in hyperlight, but we have no idea what effect traveling through the wormhole with a ship of that magnitude strapped to us would do," Constantine said.

"That's fair. Then how?" Doctor Nee asked.

Baldwin turned to the awaiting Statu. "Make it. You'll get your Bentom one way or another. It's the only way we ensure they don't return, at least for a long time."

The Statu assured him they'd already begun the detonator, and they rose and raced out of the room, heading back into the hangar bay, where Treena saw a workstation set up.

"Do you trust them?" she asked Baldwin.

"I have to." The captain grimaced. "Now I have to see if Captain Shu is willing to leave her ship behind."

Treena was unfamiliar with the woman. But Shu had a reputation as being fair, as well as loving to do everything by the book. It was one of the reasons Thomas did as well, at least until he'd disobeyed direct orders and chased an old enemy through a wormhole to rescue the Bacal and his crewmate.

They stood side by side, arms touching as they watched the Statu work through the hangar viewport. "Hard to imagine they want to help us," Thomas said.

Treena's finger twitched. "Sir, I killed at least a hundred of them today. And a few Bacal slaves as well."

Thomas set a hand on her arm. "You did what you needed to. I'd have done the same."

She nodded toward the Statu beyond the door. "We can't let the sins of their people become their burden."

"We won't. Much like we can't be blamed for the Concord's part in all of this," the captain said.

"Will things be okay?"

He took a deep breath, and Treena heard the anxiety in his voice. "One way or another."

———

*T*arlen hated being on the warship, but that was where his people were.

"Stop arguing. We're going to have food and water soon enough. We're only a couple hours from the wormhole, then…" Penter was cut off by everyone around them speaking at once.

"The wormhole?"

"What wormhole?"

"We're all going to die."

"Why bother? We're never going to win."

"Did you see how many of us they killed? The Concord did it."

"I think this was all the Concord's doing."

Tarlen closed his eyes as his angry people bickered amongst themselves. Truthfully, he was surprised they even had the energy for it.

Belna was beside him, sitting cross-legged like she used to do. That gave him hope that part of her was awake inside the husk of her body. So far, she wouldn't respond to him. She had no idea who he was, but with the help of the Concord, maybe she'd be saved.

He remembered the chain around his neck, holding her ring, and he slipped it from around his neck, sure it would spark a memory in her. He held it out, but Belna made no move for the jewelry.

"This is yours, Belna." He clasped it around her neck, letting the ring dangle on her chest. She drooled, and he sighed, his hope for her recovery dwindling.

"I think we should take over the ship."

"Yes. Let's run away with it."

"We should attack the Concord."

Tarlen had heard enough. "Stop it!" He stood in a rush, the room going silent. "Just stop! We've been used in a sick game by the Statu. Don't blame the Concord, specifically *Constantine*. Captain Baldwin will protect us. They saved us, rescued you all from certain death. Why would they do that if they wished you harm?"

No one spoke, and Penter looked up at him with a grin on his face. "Well said, son."

Tarlen sat on the floor again, happy for the silence. He was exhausted, and he leaned against his sister. Penter stared at him and spoke softly. "You get some sleep, Tarlen. I'll keep an eye... on Belna."

Tarlen nodded his thanks and closed his eyes. In a couple of hours, they'd be across the wormhole and free of the enemy. Then came the next step for the Bacal people.

"Reeve, I think I have it figured out," Brax told his sister.

"Good, because we wouldn't want you accidentally killing our thrusters again, would we?" She said it mockingly but with a loving smile. Her braids hung over her eyes, covering her red irises.

"That appears to be it, Lieutenant Commander Daak," Constantine told Brax. "You should be able to defend us, should the need arise."

"ETA to wormhole is thirty minutes. We're trailing just behind *Constantine*," Reeve said.

"And how about our friends?" Brax switched seats, moving to one with a radar screen in front of it. The six angry red dots were flashing on the screen. "Looks like it's going to be tight. From what I can tell, they're over thirty minutes out as well."

"That gives us two minutes to enter, leaving our present for them. I don't think it's enough time," Reeve said.

"By the Vastness, this will be close. Do they have the device ready?" Brax asked.

Constantine flickered, and he returned to a solid projection. "They're waiting for the last piece of the puzzle."

"Well, they better hurry, because the warships aren't slowing. They want to win this race," Reeve said.

Brax thought they might have the upper hand against six warships, but the others that had made it planetside had adjusted trajectory as well and were trailing behind the Concord's tiny fleet.

He cracked his knuckles and returned to the weapon's helm.

"Is that everyone?" Yin Shu asked Tom, and he nodded.

"And just in time." They'd ferried the entire crew of *Cecilia* to his ship over the last hour, using all their resources.

"If you would have told me I'd be losing my ship, I'm

not sure I'd have joined you on this mission," his former captain admitted.

"I don't blame you. This is the only way. We have to shut this wormhole down," he explained.

"I know. It doesn't make it any easier." Shu ran a hand along the engineering wall, a wistful look across her face. "We had some fun times, didn't we, Baldwin?"

"We sure did. Don't worry, we'll get you a new ship."

"Is that so? Do you really think the Concord will be the same after what happened? Even if we can convince the Founders that the Prime acted nefariously, and that Admiral Hudson is a war criminal, they might still silence us. Don't be surprised if they hang us all out to dry," she said.

"Then I'll take the blame. Maybe you'll have my ship," Tom said with a grim smile.

"That's the best thing you've said all day. But no, I think I'll retire."

"Retire?" Tom was shocked. "You're a legend, Yin. One day there'll be a Concord cruise ship named after you, with your AI built in."

She smiled at him and set a hand on his shoulder. "We'll see."

"There'll be an open admiral position," Tom reminded her. She'd be perfect for the role previously filled by the corrupt Hudson.

"One thing at a time. Are we set?" she called over to her science officer. The Star Drive was shut down, and the entire black Bentom ball was enclosed in a portable case, the ball visible through window slots in the side. Tom stepped closer, almost expecting to feel the energy it held.

"The Bentom is ready for transport," the Tekol man told her.

"Good. We'll bring it now," Captain Yin Shu advised

her crew member. Tom turned to leave, and alarms rang out around them. His earpiece notified him of a communication.

"Bridge to Baldwin. The warships have increased velocity. They'll be here in ten minutes, sir," Ven said.

Tom panicked. That wasn't enough time. "How did they catch up?"

"That's unknown, sir." Ven's voice was calm, as always.

Tom met Shu's gaze, and her lips pressed tightly together. Her ship was currently latched to his, and they walked to the connecting hatch.

"Bring this to your ship, load the device, and send that wormhole into the Vastness, Captain Baldwin...Thomas." Captain Yin Shu touched his cheek. He saw the tears forming in her eyes.

"Wait. What are you going to do?" Thomas asked her.

"The only thing I can. Slow the enemy down. Release my ship when you cross to *Constantine*. I'll stop them, Tom. It'll give you enough time."

"You don't have to do this."

"I do. One more thing." She glanced at the science officer, who held up a heavy-looking box. "This is *Cecilia*'s AI Link. Bring her with you. I couldn't bring myself to lose her too."

Tom wasn't shocked at her connection to the AI. He'd often walked in on the two of them having conversations, and she was a wealth of knowledge, as were the AIs on all the new generations of Concord cruise ships. "I'll ensure she's rebuilt."

The alarms were loud here, the red flashing lights too much to bear as he watched her walk away, running for the bridge.

"Until we meet in the Vastness!" he shouted after her.

Her voice was quieter. "Until we meet in the Vastness." Then she was gone.

Tom pushed aside the sadness and guilt, and rushed to his ship, the Bentom ball encased in metal in his arms, the science officer with the Link right behind him. As soon as they crossed the gap, he ordered the crew standing there to unlatch *Cecilia*. They stared at one another for a second before doing just that.

Tom watched it float away, and moments later, the impulse engines kicked on. They acted independently of the Star Drive, and Captain Shu was moving her ship into an intercept position with the incoming warships. He couldn't see them yet, not without a Zoomer, but they were there, their threat palpable.

"Thanks for your work on this." Tom hefted the box and nodded to *Cecilia*'s science officer, and headed for the waiting Statu. They'd moved their device into the fighter hangar, where it would be remotely controlled in one of their vessels. The trip took five minutes, and he was sweating by the time he pressed the doors open to the bay, half from exertion, half from recognizing how deadly the Bentom inside the box he held was. One wrong move, and their entire ship could be destroyed within seconds.

"Captain Baldwin, did you find it?" Yephion asked through Constantine.

Treena Starling was there, leaning against the wall. She'd changed her clothing, but her face was still uncovered and half removed.

"Right here. We're out of time. The Statu are closing in on us, and we might not make it to the wormhole first," Tom said.

"What if we stand our ground and fight them?" Treena asked.

"What if we lose? They'll have access to Concord space

again, and with a dozen warships this time," he said.

"Surely we can win?" Treena said.

"We can't risk it."

"You're right," Treena agreed, and he was glad his commander did.

"Why aren't you on the bridge?" Tom asked.

"Nothing for me to do there. I need to keep an eye on the Statu, in case they're trying to pull a fast one," she said.

Tom didn't think they were, but she was right to keep a close eye. Especially after learning they'd had someone on the ship this week, trying to sabotage *Constantine*.

The Statu worked quickly, carefully adding the Bentom ball into their contraption. They moved it into the rear of the fighter, and Tom heard arguing from them.

The AI was standing nearby, and Tom got his attention. "Con, what are they saying?"

Constantine listened for a moment before turning to Tom. "There's an issue. The device cannot be triggered remotely. It will need a manual detonation."

Tom's stomach sank. All this for what? Maybe they should stay and fight.

Ven's voice cut through the hangar's speakers. "Captain, we're approaching the wormhole. Awaiting orders."

What was the right move? Tom was the captain of this ship, grandson to the most famous Concord captain ever, and there was no give-up in him.

"Load it in. Show me how to detonate it. I'll do it," Treena said.

"Treena, you…"

"I'm not real, remember? I'm in my bed as we speak. I can do this."

"But you won't have a body… you'll…"

She silenced him with a look, her one good eye blinking a few times. "It's okay. I should have died two years ago. I never understood why they put me in this body, but now I do. It was so I could stop the Statu. Let me go, sir."

Tom heard the passion behind her voice. "Very well. You'll be rebuilt. Don't worry. We'll give you life again."

Treena turned as he said that. "I'd prefer to die, sir. Can you make that happen?"

He gulped, his throat suddenly dry. "I…"

"Captain, your presence is needed on the bridge," Ven said urgently.

He wanted to say more to Treena, to convince her how special she was, but he was out of time… and words. He left, seeing her climbing into Basker's fighter. He shut the door, and raced to the bridge.

Klaxons rang out softly around the corridors, and when he stepped onto the bridge, he saw the big picture of their situation. Reeve's warship was right in front of them, looming before the huge swirling wormhole.

Tom had an idea, and he leaned over the Ugna-trained Zilph'i. "Ven, you have abilities. Would you be able to detonate our destabilizer if it were behind us in a fighter?"

"Through the wormhole, sir?" he asked.

"Yes, some distance behind."

"No, sir. I'm afraid that's beyond the Ugna's ability," Ven said, his eyes downcast as if he'd failed.

"I didn't expect you to be able to. It was foolish to ask." Tom stood tall, walking to the front of the bridge, standing with his hands clasped behind him. His crew was practically skeletal, his executive team spread out as they fought to win the day.

The six incoming warships were close now, and *Cecilia* sat between their position and the wormhole. Tom expected fireworks soon. "We're on the precipice of setting the Statu back another fifty years, hopefully longer." He was aware his words were being heard on Captain Yin

Shu's bridge and in Reeve's ear. "Yin Shu's sacrifice will not be forgotten, and neither will Treena Starling's. Prepare to enter the wormhole, Executive Lieutenant Reeve Daak. Zare, bring us in three minutes behind. Commander Starling will follow, awaiting word of our exit." They hadn't determined if it was possible to communicate within the wormhole, but Treena would know what to do in that case. He had every faith in his commander.

The warship they'd stolen from the Statu began its entrance into the wormhole, and soon it was gone, vanished from their sensors. Tom watched through the viewer as Captain Shu began her assault of the warships. Blasts erupted from both sides of the melee, and right before *Constantine* entered the wormhole, *Cecilia* exploded.

The ship's lights dimmed, and everything shook as they began their journey home.

———————

*T*he warship rattled and groaned as it entered the wormhole.

"Are we positive this thing will make it?" Brax asked his sister.

"Theoretically."

"And what are you basing this theory on?" he asked.

"The fact that it successfully traveled through a couple of days ago," she told him.

He could only shrug in acceptance at that. "I was inside it, remember?"

"I hadn't forgotten." Reeve stared forward at the computer screens showing the raging wormhole tunnel around them. The ship shook more, almost sending Brax to the floor. He steadied himself at the last moment.

"We've done a good thing. The Bacal are a great people. They'll be welcome members of the Concord." Brax had made some solid bonds and was glad he'd been able to help them.

"Do you think the Concord will commit to the agreement?" Reeve asked.

Brax noticed Constantine's AI form was still there, but listening, not joining the conversation. "Why wouldn't they?"

"I don't know; maybe because we're sitting on the load of ore. There's no way we hand it over to them. They'll order us to return to Nolix with it." Reeve was unable to hide the anger from her voice.

Brax knew his sister well and could feel her trepidation. "Captain Baldwin won't do it. He already disobeyed them once. By the Vastness, he has Hudson locked up and the Prime confined to her quarters. If that man doesn't have some fortitude, then who does?"

Reeve grinned ear-to-ear at this. "You're right there. We picked a good one."

"As if we had any say."

"Either way, I love this posting."

Brax laughed. "You and me both. Unfortunately, I've only been on board for a few days so far. I've spent more time on this warship than on *Constantine*."

"Nothing like starting it all off with a bang," Reeve said.

"Let's hope we'll all be together when we return. The Founders will have a lot to say about what happened," Brax told her.

"They better reward us with a medal and a pat on the back," Reeve said.

"Somehow I doubt it will be that easy." Brax took a deep breath, trying not to think about the wormhole they were traveling through. Treena had an immeasurable task on her shoulders, and he silently wished her success.

TWENTY-SEVEN

*T*reena took a deep breath. *I should have died two years ago.*

Why had she asked Thomas to let her die? She'd spent the last week helping save what was left of a friendly race and was capable of doing so many things no human was able to do. Was eternal rest in the Vastness really what she wanted?

She witnessed their huge Concord cruise ship enter the center of the colorful, swirling wormhole. Surrounding the display of illumination, the middle was dark, an ominous portal that was welcoming and off-putting at the same time. A balance of fear and hope poured through her.

Treena tapped the viewer to show a feed from behind her fighter and saw a warship begin to explode from the top down. Tubers sprang from the thick arms of the vessel, evacuating Statu. The other five warships moved past the destroyed *Cecilia*. At least she'd managed to destroy one of them.

Treena waited there patiently, counting to sixty before urging her vessel into the wormhole. She'd already made the trip inside *Cleo* only a day before. It felt like much longer.

She reached out to *Constantine*, but there was no response, not that she'd expected one. She was all alone, and with the detonator. The Concord was relying on her to destabilize the wormhole, to send it crashing around the incoming warships, and to cut their path into Concord space off with the press of a button.

Even though her real body was safe on the cruise ship, a wave of nervousness coursed through her. It was a very human reaction, and Treena clung to it. The fact that the Concord scientists had allowed her to feel these impulses was what kept her moving each day.

The fighter slowly moved forward, and Treena only accelerated when a Tuber came within firing range. The warships were directly behind the incoming enemy fighters, and she gently urged her ship into the wormhole. It was time.

The ship shook as she entered, the lights flickering, dimming, shutting off, then flashing brighter than ever. She strained against the straps as the ship was tossed around for the first minute inside the void. Once it settled enough to move properly, she activated the rear cameras, not seeing any of the enemies behind her. That didn't mean they weren't there; she truly had no idea how the fold worked. It might be a matter of perception, and the Tubers could be right on her tail.

The first trip had taken about ten minutes, and she'd given *Constantine* a decent head start, leaving her about five minutes to traverse through space in the tunnel of light. This might be it for her. She'd asked Thomas to let her rest, but now she wasn't so sure.

Treena closed her good eye, the other one torn from her face from a blaster to the head by a hiding Statu. She was transported to that day.

———————

*T*reena had woken to the alarms ringing throughout the

ship, and Felix had instantly sat up on alert. He'd told her to stay put, but she wasn't going to obey, and he knew it. Seconds later, Felix was racing out the door, only the lower half of his uniform on, his feet still bare.

Treena hastily dressed and followed after him, until he crouched in a doorway, grabbing hold of her arm and shoving her against the wall. It hurt, and the wind blew from her lungs.

"There's too many of them. We need weapons." Felix's voice was a breathy whisper.

Something was on fire, maybe everything. They moved down the hall quietly, and saw the dead crew sprawled out in the middle of the bridge. The smell of burning hair filled her throat and lungs, and Treena gagged as she crawled away. The hole in the hull had been sealed, but only after the invaders were on board. It must have happened so fast, they hadn't been able to react. There was nothing out of the ordinary on this Border run, and then, as if from thin air, the Reepa pirate ship had detached itself from the asteroid.

She knew this now, but not then. Then, she'd only felt panic and the fear of death. She'd seen her captain's lifeless face, dead eyes staring at nothing.

Felix must have sensed there was no hope, and he went with Treena to the hangar two decks below. Even here she heard pulse blasts, followed by the screams of her crew. They spotted a gang of the pirates as they reached the hangar doors. The men were armored, well armed, and vicious in their attacks. They walked casually through the corridor, one turning and heading in their direction.

"We need to leave," Felix said.

"But the others…"

"It's too late." He opened the door, the hiss and sliding of the slab far too loud in the corridor. Treena was confident she heard bootsteps following behind them, and they ran for the nearest fighter, opening the cockpit. Felix leaned over her, strapping her in and turning the engines on.

"Get in!" she yelled, not worried about noise any longer.

He grabbed a PL-30 from beside her seat and shook his head. "You're the better pilot, and there's only enough life support for one, long-term." He flicked the shields on, giving her an added layer of protection.

"I don't want to do this without you," she told him, tears streaming down her face.

Felix leaned in, kissing her quickly. "I'll wait for you in the Vastness." He hopped away, shutting the cockpit door behind him.

She saw blasts heading toward him and watched as he killed two enemies before a stream of energy struck him in the center of his bare chest. She screamed, her hands shaking as she lifted the fighter off the deck and through the bay exit.

It had been a routine Border patrol, as always. This shouldn't have happened.

She moved the fighter away, the loss too fresh, too confusing to comprehend quite yet. There were ships nearby. Not just the Reepa ship, but another one.

———————

*T*reena snapped to inside the cockpit of her fighter as she coursed through the wormhole. She recalled seeing the pirate ship, and then nothing as her ship was hit. The next thing she recollected was waking up locked into a body full of pain and despair, unable to communicate with the exception of a few grunts and groans. By the time she'd been connected to this android form, the memory of that day had been all but wiped clean, but now she remembered seeing the other ship.

It was a Concord cruise ship. They'd been set up.

Treena fumed, wishing she had a way to relay this message to Baldwin. The Concord's deceptions ran deep. Her entire crew had been killed, and for what? Why had she been spared?

She looked to the console and saw it was time. *Constantine* should be clear of the wormhole, leaving her with the task of destabilizing the wormhole. Fresh grief for the man she loved flooded her, and it took all her will to unstrap from the cockpit seat and crawl around it, to where the detonation box sat.

Treena had joined the Concord with hopes and dreams of making a difference. Her life had almost been cut short, but now she had the chance to really help. Not the Concord specifically, but the innocent lives who only went about their days on their home planets, never aware of the true dangers lurking around the universe.

She hoped the Statu were close behind her and prayed to the Vastness that their ships had cleared the other end of the wormhole. Treena pictured Felix one last time: not the image of him being shot down, but the memory of the first time they met. She grinned and pressed the button.

Everything vanished.

———

Captain Thomas Baldwin watched through the viewer as the wormhole began to break apart. It was nothing like he'd expected: the swirling stopped instantly, the colors turning into a hot orange glow before vanishing into nothing.

The bridge crew cheered, but Tom couldn't bring himself to join in the celebration. They'd won the battle, that was for sure, but they'd also lost a lot in the process. His confidence in the Concord had been infallible leading up to this posting. Even though nothing was perfect, he hadn't comprehended how deceptive and troubling the leadership was.

"Captain, we have no signs of Statu in the system," Ven told him, and Tom nodded his understanding.

"Thank you, Starling," he whispered. He considered her last wish and knew this was something he had to do personally.

The huge Statu warship lingered nearby, and he heard Reeve Daak's voice carry over the bridge speakers, signaling everyone was intact on her side. This brought another cheer. This was what many of the crew had signed up for when they'd joined the Academy, a real chance at heroism. Tom only wished it wasn't so bittersweet.

"Captain, the Concord cruise ships *Bartok*, *Hallivan*, and *Troo* are here, and hailing us," Ven said.

"Tell them what happened. I'll return shortly. Set course for Greblok at once," Tom ordered.

The Zilph'i smiled, a rare sight, and turned to obey.

Tom headed for Treena Starling's quarters with a heavy heart.

———

*A*larms echoed around the ship, and the woman moved with purpose. She'd managed to cut the cameras on the brig deck but didn't have time to wait around. They'd be emerging from the wormhole any moment, if they already hadn't.

She chided herself for not bringing more members on board. She'd been so confident in Yur Shen's abilities that she'd been blinded to the possibility of failure. *To truly learn, one must be taught a lesson.* The old Code saying rolled through her mind, and she grinned bleakly.

She'd been unable to prevent the destruction of the wormhole, perhaps, but there was something she could do to ensure her Assembly didn't lose footing.

The brig was plainer than one might expect. Rarely were there cases of insubordination any longer on board a Concord vessel, but it still happened on occasion. She stepped forward confidently, and the single guard on this level stood near the brig entrance, a tablet in his hand.

He was human, short, with a bored gleam over his eyes. "Business?" he asked, barely looking up at her.

"The captain asked me to check on the admiral."

"Is that so? I don't see anything…"

"We don't have time! The wormhole is collapsing around us," she said. "Only Hudson might be able to assist us. Do you want to die?"

That got his attention, and since the alarms were active, it helped her cause.

"Sorry. Right this way." He opened the door, and she reached into her pocket before jabbing out with the device. The man crumpled to the ground, and she left him there, holding the door open. It pressed against his ribs, trying to close.

She stalked through the hall, trying to keep her excitement at bay. She'd always been a fan of Admiral Hudson, and had even met him on occasion. Today would be another interaction she'd never forget.

She neared his cell, one of three, and he sat on the bed,

head resting in his hands. He glanced up at the sound of her approach, and she caught a smile.

"It's you. I didn't know you were stationed on *Constantine*." The admiral looked ten years older, his hair disheveled, his eyes puffy.

"Come closer." She stepped to the glowing bars. "I'm here to free you."

"To free me? Did Baldwin finally come to his senses?" he asked.

She nodded. "He wants to have a discussion. We're free of the wormhole, and he and the Prime are in his office, waiting for you."

The man stood, dusting his pants off. "It's about time he realized his error."

He walked over to the cell's edge, and the woman smiled, reaching out toward him. She poked his hand with the apparatus in her palm, and his eyes went wide. He clutched his chest and staggered away, falling onto the bed and rolling to the ground.

She didn't wait to see his last breath. He was dead.

The woman returned to the guard and dragged him with her down the corridor. She'd dispose of the body, and no one would be the wiser. They'd blame the guard for the power outage on the camera feed, and think he was hiding.

Chaos. *In Chaos comes opportunity.*

———

*T*reena's eyes snapped open.

Everything hurt, and she tried to breathe but couldn't. A machine pressed air into her lungs, and she lay there, unable to move. It had been so long since she'd returned her mind to this body, and she'd forgotten the fear and terror that came with being trapped inside.

Her room was empty; the soft sounds of machinery wheezing and beeping were the only noises surrounding her bed. The straps underneath her body lifted her, moving her muscles and limbs to prevent atrophy.

Her moment of panic didn't vanish, but it did subside slightly, until the door opened. Her vision wasn't perfect, but she sensed it was the captain.

"Treena, you did it," he said quietly, coming to sit in a chair parked beside her bed. His hand was rough and warm, and it tenderly squeezed hers. She tried to move her fingers but failed.

Don't kill me, Thomas. I have too much to live for. The Concord did this to me. You have to hear me! she screamed internally, no words escaping her dry lips. She managed to move her tongue, but it rested on the roof of her mouth.

"You surprised me. I took this posting without a second thought. They offered me a new flagship, one named after my grandfather. Did I ever tell you how much I despised the old man? He was terrible to live with, especially once Grandmother passed on. He was so angry, so bitter, that I told myself I'd never end up like him. And guess what? I didn't." His hand was still on hers, and she calmed at his story.

"I figured out why I didn't become him. Because I didn't give love a chance, I didn't start a family, and subsequently didn't have the opportunity to lose anyone close to me. You did. I never said it, but I'm sorry about how things turned out. I know you and Felix were happy. I don't blame you for your request, Starling, I really don't, but I'm not sure I can honor it. You're special. You survived the attack when no one else did, and look at all you've accomplished this past week.

"Selfishly, I have to keep you around. I have to find

343

you a new android to occupy, because the truth is, I can't do this without you. I need my crew. You, Brax, Reeve, Ven… everyone. You're going to be angry with me, but one day you'll understand."

His words warmed her heart, and her eyes blurred as a tear rolled down her face.

"I'm sorry." Thomas leaned over and wiped it. "You deserve better than this, Treena."

He was misconstruing her emotion, and she struggled to get it out but managed two simple words, hardly more than a whisper.

"Thank you."

———

*T*arlen soaked it all in. The sun was bright and hot, and he took off his boots, letting the warm sand slip between his toes. He was home. Malin, Greblok's capital, was as it had been when they'd left; piles of rubble and half formed buildings. The smoke was all gone, as was the terrible noise of the warship's mining. He couldn't imagine the fear the people had felt when they saw the immense enemy vessel returning into the atmosphere, but they had no way of defending themselves.

The captain had lowered first in *Cleo*, trying to locate the largest group of survivors. He'd given them a heads up and asked them to seek out others, and spread word that the warship was safely in the hands of the Concord.

Now everyone had disembarked, and already groups were forming, sad reunions were transpiring, and Tarlen could only watch it all with a sense of unease. His parents had never been found, but that meant they were gone. His sister lived, but what would he do with her? She was a Statu slave without direction.

He suddenly wished he hadn't left her on the ship with the doctor. He watched his people celebrating, the crew of *Constantine* already assisting as they erected temporary shelters.

"Tarlen," a voice called from behind him as he watched the assembled people working hard to set up camp before nightfall.

He turned to see the chiseled features of Thomas Baldwin. "Captain."

The man came to stand next to him, overseeing the workers as well. "I wanted to ask you something."

Tarlen peered up at him, seeing a smirk forming on the captain's face. "What is it?"

"The Bacal have been through a lot. We're trying to determine who's in charge of Greblok, but I want to ensure you really do become a Concord member," he said.

"That would be good. We're going to need the support." They'd been devastated, and Tarlen didn't think they'd ever fully recover from what transpired.

"Would you like to become the first Bacal Concord crew member?" Captain Baldwin asked it slowly, and Tarlen still had trouble keeping up.

"Did you say… as in… you want me to join…" The words rushed out in a hurry.

"That's what I'm asking. You'd be a JOT. A junior officer in training, and you'd have to take Academy classes on board the ship. Don't get me wrong, it's going to be a lot of work, but I saw how you dealt with things, and I've read the reports from Brax. You're exactly what we need. You exemplify what the true Concord is made of," Captain Baldwin told him.

Tarlen couldn't believe his words. "What about my sister?"

"She's on board. Doctor Nee has her under observation."

"And you won't let them take her?"

"Them?"

"The Concord. She can't go with them. She stays with us, right?" Tarlen asked.

Captain Baldwin nodded. "You have my word."

"And the ore? Will you claim it and leave my people to be forgotten?" Tarlen asked.

"It will be our responsibility, but only to ensure you aren't attacked by someone hungry for an easy prize from weakened prey. Tarlen, I'm going to make sure the Bacal are compensated," Captain Baldwin told him.

He believed the man and smiled finally. "Of course I'll join your crew!"

"Good. I'm glad. Now, how about we go help for the time being?"

Tarlen followed his new captain, and peered to the sky. Things would never be the same, but he'd make the best of it.

———————

"Sir, we'll arrive in Nolix in two hours," Ven said.

"Thank you, Ven." Tom sat in his chair, happy to see most of his crew on the bridge.

Brax Daak was at the edge, searching for signs of any incoming attacks. His sister Reeve was nearby in Zare's position, typing away at her console. The commander's seat next to Tom was noticeably empty, but he was going to fix that as quickly as possible. Treena Starling would return.

They were in a tough spot, heading for the capital of the Concord with the Prime in their custody. All they'd have was their word at the Concord's deception, and Tom had no idea how deep the corruption ran. He only hoped things would work out, and that his crew would be safe. He'd made a lot of promises he intended to keep.

News of Admiral Hudson's death had been kept secret, meaning few on his ship had been told that the old man had died in his cell. Brax had gone over the scene multiple times but hadn't determined if it was murder or not. The guard on duty had gone missing, and the power block running the cameras had been disarmed around the same time. Tom guessed he'd never learn the truth, but without the admiral to admit anything to the Concord, he'd struggle to relay the facts to the Founders.

Unless the Prime played along. He still couldn't get a read on her.

They approached the Concord capital, Ven sending communications for them not to worry about the massive Statu warship alongside *Constantine*. Soon they had a full envoy guiding or escorting them, leading them toward the Tekol home world.

Thomas glanced at Constantine's AI, the young version of his grandfather, and smiled to himself. Within the projection's programming were so many memories, ones he wasn't supposed to have. Tom wouldn't let the Concord know the AI had found the backdoor and retrieved them. If he did, Tom was confident they'd cut the flow, making the AI only half of the man he was. Tom preferred him the way he was.

Thomas Baldwin rose, walking to the center of the bridge, watching as they moved into orbit around Nolix. He'd gone into this role without expectations, and the following weeks had been a hectic rush of adventure.

There is no measurement for success; it's only derived from the level of effort. It was one of his grandfather's favorite sayings from the Code.

One thing was for sure: he wasn't going to give up *Constantine* without a fight. He had his own path to forge, and he'd only just begun his own legacy.

The End

ABOUT THE AUTHOR

Nathan Hystad is an author from Sherwood Park, Alberta, Canada.

Keep up to date with his new releases by signing up for his newsletter at www.nathanhystad.com

Sign up at www.shelfspacescifi.com as well for amazing deals and new releases from today's best indie science fiction authors.

CPSIA information can be obtained
at www.ICGtesting.com
Printed in the USA
BVHW031909290920
589893BV00001B/17